"Wow! Intriguing, racy, sexy page-turner."

~**Shelley Olsen,**
Owner of Paperbacks and Pieces bookstore

"A high-speed, high-octane third thriller in Gary Evans' '*Death By*' series. If you haven't been smitten by his murder mysteries, you'll say 'wow' with this hit. *Death by Payback* follows the frustrations of Wisconsin detectives chasing an 83-year-old female killer of 14 young men, leading them across the globe in hot pursuit. This page-turner is filled with mob intrigue, a captivating love story, and a surprising conclusion.

"Readers are left breathing heavily, wondering if Evans can top this one."

~**Rollie Wussow,**
Avid Evans Reader, New Mexico

GARY W. EVANS

DEATH
BY PAYBACK

Death by Payback

Printed in the United States of America
Author Source, 2018

Paperback ISBN: 978-1-947939-79-0
Hardcover ISBN: 978-1-947939-84-4
Library of Congress: 2018963485

www.AuthorSource.com

1

The April sun scratched its way up the back side of Mount Cleveland, in the Bitterroot Chain of western Montana, its promised glow casting the proud peak as an angelic being. At least that's how it appeared from the rustic cabin in the woods inhabited by Genevieve Wangen, now known as Samantha Walters. This Thursday promised to be a busy day for the eighty-three-year-old, who looked not a day over fifty-five. She'd risen before dawn and now was bathing in the still-icy waters of the lake that she fondly referred to as "My Lake."

Of course, no one had seen the body of water since she had moved there, and therefore no one knew of the name she had given it. She hoped that wouldn't change for a while, although once again she longed for company. While talking to either men or women fascinated her, it was the company of men she missed most. She had now been without male companionship for more than sixteen months, since arriving here from New Orleans two and a half years earlier.

In her wake she had left a trail of bodies—many more attributed to her than were due—that had resulted in the posting of an old picture of her on post office walls from Bangor, Maine to San Ysidro, California, and from Baudette, Minnesota, to Brownsville, Texas.

Few were the people in the United States who had not seen a picture of the woman known in various places and at various times as the Wisconsin Whacker, the Black Widow of the Woods, and the Murderess of the Mountains. Few also were the people who, happening along on this cloudless day, would suspect a relationship between that woman and the darkly tanned woman in the lake, softly singing to herself in the early morning light.

In fact, although no one in the Bitterroot Valley knew where she lived, many knew her by sight. She was a person who, in times of financial hardship, reached into her purse and found money for the unfortunate, although anonymously.

People in these parts, if they knew her at all, knew her simply as "Sam." She had appeared on the scene without introduction but, before the first winter was out, had established herself as someone who belonged. And if people in these parts felt you belonged, then damned be those who would seek to take you away. Sam was known by a few business associates from Polson to Finley Point, Bear Dance, Woods Bay, and Bigfork on the east side of Flathead Lake to Kings Point, Elmo, Dayton, and Somers on the west. But though those few people called her by name, bought her a drink whenever she was in town, and even took her to lunch, none knew where she lived. The best anyone would say, if pressed, was, "Somewhere in the hills, I guess."

On this day, she hoped to end her temporary celibacy; the idea of having a man in her bed excited her as she soaked herself in the lake waters and dreamt about the pleasure of wrapping her legs around a real human being.

She planned to drive some forty miles, the first twelve of it on a rutted, private dirt road, to Kalispell, Montana, a community of twenty-two thousand about thirty miles north of Flathead Lake that served as the "capitol" of the Flathead Valley. The community served as the retail, professional, medical, and governmental center for the more than one hundred forty thousand people who inhabited the area.

In previous trips to Kalispell, Sam had cultivated a friendship with Molly O'Leary, general manager of the Golden Lion Hotel. On her last trip to the community, the two women had talked candidly about their likes and dislikes and the things they missed in their adopted Montana homeland.

As one drink became two, and two became a half dozen or more, and Sam decided to rent a room and stay the night, she told Molly that her biggest need was male companionship.

"I'm sure that stuns you. There are some things you never get over, and I have always needed and wanted sex." Taking another sip of her drink, she swallowed. "When I was married, my husband was a great lover. He developed my appetite for assignations and I've never lost it."

Molly tapped a finger against her chin. "Sam, I'm not sure why you've brought up this subject with me. Perhaps you think you know something? If you do, all I can say is you shouldn't." Glancing around the empty room, she tugged her chair closer to Sam and leaned in. "As a bit of a side business to build my retirement nest egg, I do a little matchmaking. I have always chosen my customers carefully, mostly to make sure they have tightly controlled lips." Her eyes narrowed as she leaned back and studied Sam. "Now I have to wonder, which one of those people has the kind of lips that they say sink ships? I am very bothered by this."

Sam blinked. "Oh, my goodness, Molly, there is no reason for you to be worried. I haven't talked to anyone. I had no idea that you might be doing a little, how should I say this, moonlighting? I was simply commenting on my situation, and I felt I knew you well enough to tell you about the thing I miss most."

Molly contemplated her a few seconds more before her face broke into a wide smile. Grabbing a cocktail napkin from the table, she wiped sweat beads from her forehead. "Then have I got a deal for you. Come on, let's take the bottle to my apartment where no one will overhear us."

She led Sam to a door directly over the check-in desk on the second floor of the Golden Lion. The spacious and comfortable apartment surprised Sam, both for its size and for how tastefully it was decorated. *There's more to Molly than a hotel manager. A lot more.*

"This is lovely." Sam waved a hand around the room. "If this was mine, I'd love to manage this hotel, no matter the pay. It's big and it's comfortable. If you did the decorating, I must commend you for a great touch."

"For better or worse, I did it all. I was pleased to get the job and even happier when the owners told me to furnish the apartment to my liking, using their money. I spent it carefully, but this is what emerged. To me it's home. And Sam, the best part is they pay me very well for the work I do. I think I may be one of the highest-paid residents of Kalispell—better than almost anyone but the docs."

Sam grinned. "That's impressive."

"Yes, I do very well. And my side business has begun to produce a handsome profit. I'm very careful to recruit quality clientele and to match them with people who are talented and committed to pleasing their customers in every way. You wouldn't think that would be an easy thing out here in the middle of nowhere, but the rugged individuals who come here to live seem to be skilled in the bedroom arts. You just never know, do you?"

"I guess not, but I sure would like to have a night with one of your most skilled gentlemen. If you could set me up, I think you'll have earned repeat business from a very needy customer."

"I believe I have just the guy. A real stallion. And equipped like one, too. Sound good?"

"Perfect. What's his name?"

"Pete Pernaska. He came here to join a timbering crew. He did that for a few years, but he'd wander in here now and again looking for women. I fixed him up a couple of times and it wasn't long before the girls started asking for him. I wondered what made him so special, and decided to try him for myself. Wow! That's the only description I have for it. I offered him a job. He took it, he's busy, and he loves it. He quit his timbering job. If you're not happy, I'll be stunned."

"I'm sure I will be. My life is close to perfect right now, and Mr. Pete Pernaska sounds like he just might be the last piece of puzzle I've been missing."

2

As Genevieve Wangen, aka Samantha Walters, seemed to be solving her problem, that wasn't the case fourteen hundred miles to the east, where Detective Al Rouse of the La Crosse Police Department was beginning his day the same way he had for two and a half years. Gripped by frustration, he sat at his desk, a stack of newspapers at his right hand and a full cup of coffee at his left. As he grabbed *The New Orleans Times Picayune*, he murmured the same short prayer that had become part of his daily routine: *Please, God, let this be the day.*

Although the message was pretty open-ended, Al knew God could figure it out. The detective just hoped He was paying attention. Twice they'd had Genevieve in their grasp and both times she had gotten away. *Damn, how can one woman be that lucky? Or was she? Charlie and I aren't dummies, so it must be more than luck. Although it's hard to argue that she has a rabbit's foot in her pocket.*

The Times was a great publication, well edited and with a stable of excellent reporters. But to date they'd had little to share that interested him.

As he read through the paper, he stopped at an article headlined, "City Patron Ensures Cemetery Clean-up Succeeds."

The story talked about the effort, funded by Angelo Carbone, that was resulting in the clean-up and repair of New Orleans cemeteries. The reporter pointed out that Carbone had undertaken the effort as a tribute to his niece from France, then went on to

5

say that Savannah Harlowe, whom Carbone had found out about when talking to a reporter a year earlier, had apparently vanished after being introduced to New Orleans's society in a soiree at the Carbone home.

"Although the reports are unconfirmed," stated the report, "Miss Harlowe is believed to have returned to her native France to care for her aging and ill mother, Honey." The report went on to say that Savannah had been the result of a romance between Honey and Rayford Carbone, Angelo's late brother.

Al was intrigued by the report, but very disappointed that it shed no new light on the whereabouts of Savannah Harlowe, who he knew was really Genevieve Wangen. After a raid of Harlowe's house on Audubon Place in New Orleans, items seized in the search provided DNA matches to Wangen.

We've lost you twice, Ms. Wangen, but just remember, the third time's the charm.

Al set down the paper, rocked back in his chair, and propped his feet on his desk. Hands behind his head, he began to think about the trials he and his close friend, Sheriff's deputy Charlie Berzinski, had been through together as they searched for Wangen.

Beware, old lady, because we're after you and neither of us is giving up until we have you where you belong—behind bars.

"Is it so bad you have to talk to yourself about it?"

Al opened his eyes to find Chief Brent Whigg lounging in his doorway, hat in hand. He lowered his legs and straightened quickly. *Didn't even realize I was talking out loud.*

"C'mon in, Chief," he said, a little sheepishly. "Might as well sit and commiserate with me. Help yourself to a cup before you sit down. No doughnuts today, I'm sorry to say."

"Won't hurt me to miss a doughnut or two. Wife says I'm getting fat."

"Aren't we all, Chief, aren't we all."

"So Al, me boy, what's got you lookin' like a thunderstorm today?" The chief sat back in the chair, straightened the holster that housed his pistol, and took a sip of coffee. He smacked his lips and smiled.

Al frowned at him. "It's the damn case. No trace of the old lady. Wouldn't you think something woulda showed up by now?"

"Yeah, I guess you would, but she's a sly one, we know that. Slippery as an eel. More faces than a mime, too."

"But somethin'? Shouldn't there be somethin'?"

The chief sat there for a moment, brow furled. Al could almost see the wheels turning.

He set his cup of coffee on the desk. "You know, Al, maybe you should take a few days off. Grab JoAnne and take off for Milwaukee, or the Dells, or Madison—somewhere you can get your mind off the case."

"Nah, I like travelin', but it has to be for a purpose. Right now I don't have one. If I had a shred of a clue, I'd be off like a shot, that's for sure."

"Just tryin' to help, Al, just trying to help. Well, the day's movin' on and I'm not. Better get at it, I guess." He slapped both knees with his hands before pushing to his feet.

"Okay, Chief, thanks for stopping by."

"In spite of you lookin' like a thunderstorm, the pleasure was all mine. Thanks for the coffee."

The chief vanished around the door and Al got back to his newspapers. But just as for more than eight hundred days now, there was nothing, not a shred that could be connected to Genevieve Wangen.

Slippery is right … slippery as an eel. He sighed and tossed the last paper down on the desk. *Wonder what Charlie's up to?"*

Speed dial connected Al to his buddy at the La Crosse County Sheriff's Office; true to form, his friend was happy as a lark. Frankly, his constant upbeat mood, something new and likely related to the woman he'd recently married, irritated Al to no end.

"How's my little detective buddy today?"

"Dammit, Charlie, do you always have to be so happy? Your mood is disgusting."

"Al, you've been in the dumps for almost three years, and don't you dare blame it on me. This is all of your own making. If you wanted to do something about it, you could."

"Just what the hell could I do about it?"

"Well, how about finding something to be happy about? Crap, Al, you got plenty of things: JoAnne, the kids. Hell, don't you have a grandkid on the way? And if you really want to wallow in it—get that … wallow … pretty big word for me—we can go over everything for the five thousandth time."

"Yeah, let's do that."

"God, Al, don't you ever give it a rest?"

The question was rhetorical. They both knew Al would never give it a rest, not until Genevieve Wangen was behind bars. "We could do it over lunch at the La Crosse Club."

"Well now, that's different, way different. What time?"

"How about noon?"

"See you then."

Promptly at noon, Al pushed open the door of the club. His buddy was already seated, enjoying something yellow in a tall glass. His eyes narrowed. "What's this, running up my tab before I even get here?"

"I was a few minutes early, okay? The hostess offered to seat me and the waitress came by so I ordered an orange juice. Anything the matter with that? Kelly's been after me to get in shape, and I've started."

Al stripped off his sport coat and hung it on a spare chair at the table for four. He started to laugh, then caught himself and pulled out his chair, sliding into place across from the deputy.

"So Kelly has you on the straight and narrow, huh? About time you got that big body of yours into shape. When we find the old lady the next time, it's probably gonna be in the mountains some place. You best be prepared to run after her. We're not losing her again."

"Yeah, she's on my case. Went for my annual physical the other day and my cholesterol is high, the doc told me. That's all Kelly needed to get me on a diet. Guess you'll be glad that your pocketbook will be spared today."

"That is a plus. How's your blood pressure?"

"My guess is it's a helluva lot better than yours, you old worrywart."

"All right, all right, let's order and talk."

Charlie went first and, as predicted, his order was unusually restrained, for him. He ordered a BLT "with the bacon fried crisp," another orange juice, and, much to the waitress's surprise, passed on dessert.

"You sick?" She tapped her pad with a pen. "We've got banana cream pie, rhubarb crisp, and a new sour cream raisin dessert today."

"Damn, Barb, you're makin' it tough. But no, I gotta pass. I'm on a diet, don't ya know."

She tapped the pen again, as if waiting for the punch line. Al took pity on his friend. "Kelly's got him on the straight-and-narrow, Barb. Apparently, some of his readings aren't in the normal range. Does that surprise you?"

"Are you kidding? I'd have bet on him being a tickin' timebomb." She stuck the pen back behind her ear and bustled away to get their orders to the kitchen.

Charlie hitched his chair a little closer to the table, careful to move his tie out of the danger zone.

"Pretty snazzy tie." Al grinned. "But I'm not sure that red and black checks go well with that tan uniform of yours."

"That's what Kelly said, but I wanted to spice things up a bit. I'm not gettin' any younger, you know."

"That is very true." Before his friend could fire back, Al took out a notebook and pen. "Why don't we go over what we know while we're waiting."

Charlie leaned back in his seat. "First, we know the Carbone plane flew to Los Angeles, then northward, made a landing near Portland, but was only on the ground for a few minutes. We assume she got off there, but we haven't really gone much further with that. Do you think we should?"

"Sure, but who's gonna do it? Brent or Dwight aren't going to sanction a trip, and asking folks in Oregon to chase a trail that has been cold for two and a half years isn't gonna work very well, is it?"

"Guess not. Maybe we could make a few calls ourselves. How about that?"

"Who are we going to talk to?"

"We can start with the airport."

"Even if they did have records, I'm pretty sure they're on the Carbone payroll. If the airport isn't, the pilot definitely was, so I'm sure nothing he filed would be reliable."

"Still, it's possible someone there remembers something about that day. Savannah Harlowe is a fairly unforgettable woman."

"Even so, pretty sure you'd have more luck getting a dog to talk than anyone there."

Charlie tapped his fingers on the table. "Is that why you invited me here today, so you could shoot down every suggestion I have?"

Al sighed. "You're right, I'm sor—"

The arrival of their food interrupted what had turned into a rather aimless discussion. Twenty minutes later, Al's paper had one word written on it: Airport. When Charlie had food in front of him, it was generally better to wait than try to have a productive discussion. Finally, both plates were empty and Charlie was wiping his greasy fingers on a napkin. "Okay, so airport. You gonna call or d'ya want me to?"

Al took a swipe at his mouth with his own napkin before tossing it on the plate. "I don't think there's much point in it, but I'll call."

"Well, if you're gonna go at it like Sad Sack Sam, prob'ly no reason to pursue it."

Al stared at him for a moment, then picked up the check and signed his name. "If you think you can do it better than I can, have at it, Charlie." He tossed the pen down on the table with as much frustration as he'd tossed the last newspaper earlier.

"Al, you know you're better on the phone than I am. I rarely use the phone except to set up appointments. I'm just worried about your enthusiasm level."

"Charlie, for god's sake, we're talking about something that happened a long, long time ago. Asking someone to remember that is a long shot, don't you think?"

"Sure it is, but it took the Cubs a long, long time to win the Series again, too. They didn't give up. Why should we?"

"Yeah. That's exactly the same thing." Al shook his head. Maybe Charlie had a point about his bad attitude. He straightened in his chair and injected as much enthusiasm into his voice as possible. "I'll call this afternoon."

Back at the office, Al went back to the Genevieve Wangen file. He began digging at the end of the file, looking for the name of the airport the Carbone-owned plane had left from after Carbone's men seized Genevieve from Al's custody in New Orleans. "There it is." His voice echoed in the room and he looked around, relieved to see no one else present. This time. He pulled a slip of paper out of the back of the file. *Aurora State Airport. Whaddya know?*

Before looking for the number so he could call the airport, Al read through the file, looking for any names that might be useful. Airport manager, Patrick Elroy. Assistant, Tommy Nordqvist. No one else was mentioned. *Guess it'll be one of them. Hope one or the other is still there.*

The airport number was in the file he still held in his hand as he put the phone on speaker and began to dial.

The phone rang and rang before a man finally answered. "Aurora State Airport." He sounded out of breath.

"Is either Patrick Elroy or Tommy Nordqvist there?" asked Al.

"This is Nordqvist."

"Mr. Nordqvist, this is Detective Al Rouse of the La Crosse, Wisconsin Police Department."

"How can I help you, Detective?

"Actually, I doubt that you're going to be able to, but I'd like to give it a try."

"Shoot."

"On August 10, 2015, a brand-new Gulfstream G600, painted cream and blue, tail number N769CE, made a quick stop at your facility, presumably refueling before taking off again. It might have dropped a female passenger off during the stop. I don't suppose you'd have that on record anywhere?"

The man let out a short laugh. "I don't have to check my records, Detective; I remember that plane as if it was yesterday."

Al's feet flew off the desk, his chair slammed into an upright position, and he grabbed the phone receiver from its cradle and punched the speaker button off.

"You know that plane?"

"Absolutely. I fueled it and got it on its way. Yes sir, I remember it well."

"This is amazing, Mr. Nordqvist. You must service hundreds of planes and you remember that one?"

"Yes sir, I do. And it's Tommy."

"Okay, Tommy, tell me what you remember."

"The plane you're talking about landed here about four in the afternoon and topped off on JP54, I believe, then took off again."

"Anything else?"

"Yes, there sure is something else. As you suggested, the plane dropped off a passenger. Nicest looking middle-aged lady I ever saw. Got a liberal view down her blouse, too. I'll never forget it."

"Can you describe her?"

"As I see her in my dreams all the time, I certainly can. About fifty years old, I'd say. Extremely well built. Dark auburn hair, beautiful and silky." The man let out a rapturous sigh.

Al rolled his eyes. "That all you remember?"

"One more thing. The lady had a mole on her left cheek, near her mouth."

"Hmmm, our suspect didn't have a mole last time I saw her. Suppose she could have gotten one, though."

The mole bothered Al, but makeup being what it was these days, might she have created one? Or maybe she'd had more work done. He'd worry about that little detail later.

"You've been very helpful. Thank—"

"Wait, there's more. The lady had a cat with her. And it was obvious she didn't know too much about Portland. She said she needed to buy a car and wanted to know where she could get one. I gave her and her cat a ride to Portland Auto-Plex. Not sure if she bought a car there, but I think she probably did. She seemed to badly want her own vehicle."

Yeah, so she could get as far away from me as possible. Al's grip on the receiver tightened. "Tommy, I've gotta get going, but you've been extremely helpful. That woman you drove into the city is a fugitive, so if you think of anything else that might help us track her down, give me a call at this number, okay?"

"A fugitive?" Nordqvist's words came slowly. "What'd she do?"

"Normally, I wouldn't comment, but you've been very helpful. She's wanted for fourteen murders in Wisconsin."

The young man's gulp was audible. "Uh ... uh ... fourteen ... murders?"

"That's right. So keep my number handy, okay?"

With Tommy's promise ringing in his ear, Al disconnected the call. Blood pounded in his ears. *A new lead. Finally.* Fingers trembling, he turned to his computer and plugged *Portland Auto-plex* into his search engine. He found the dealership on Sandy Boulevard, complete with inventory, and dialed the number that popped up.

He got the receptionist on the line and asked for the sales manager.

"Well, sir," she said sweetly, "that would be John Logano. He's been here for more than twenty years. Why don't I let you talk to him?"

When Logano came on, his voice boomed through the line, conjuring up in Al's mind the image of a big man, overweight, with a plaid shirt and suspenders holding up his trousers. And likely a ruddy face, bulbous nose, blue eyes, and a wide mouth perched above a double chin.

Al almost laughed out loud. He'd never know if his mental image was accurate, but he kept it in mind as he explained his quest and asked for information.

"August 10, two and a half years ago, huh?" said Logano. "Hell, Detective, I can't remember yesterday. Damn good thing we keep thorough records. Automated, too. Let's take a look. August 10. Hmm, August 10. Here we are. Oh man, we sold twenty-three cars that day. That's a big one. Only sold two to women, though. Any idea of the time?"

"I'm guessing evening. How late are you open?"

When Logano told him 10:00 p.m., Al said it could have been pretty close to that late.

"Oh, shit, I remember this one." Logano made a clicking noise with his tongue, as though shifting through memories. "Beautiful woman, too. Bought a Range Rover Sentinel—best car on the lot— just before closing time. Cost her a mint but she didn't blink, just handed over the cash. Damn, that vehicle was beautiful, black with hints of Castleton green and built like a bomb shelter. So was she, matter of fact."

"A bomb shelter?"

"Yeah. Bullet-proof glass. Reinforced suspension. Puncture-proof tires. Virtually indestructible."

"Did you get a name? A driver's license?"

"Oh, we did our part to make it a legal transaction, if that's what you mean. But I'd bet the information is phony. In any case, here it is: Honey Harmon. California license. Want the number we have on file?"

Al's eyes widened. She used the name Honey? As in Savannah Harlowe's long-lost mother? That had to be more than a coincidence. He took the information, concluded the call, and sat back in his seat, barely able to draw in a breath.

So the trail isn't quite cold yet. Now all I have to do is figure out where it goes from here.

3

Three interminably long weeks later, Sam, dressed carefully in a black-and-blue-checked blouse that she'd buttoned to a modest point, and an A-line skirt hemmed to below the knee, made her way back to the Golden Lion. Although her date was not until 3:00 p.m., she was ready before noon and on her way to Kalispell. Arriving shortly before one, she lunched in the pub, spent sixty dollars on the slot machines in the casino, then went to the desk to see if her room was ready.

The desk clerk checked his computer. "Your suite is clean, Ms. Walters. Molly told me you would be paying on your way out, so I think we're all set. She left this for you, though."

Inside the envelope was a short note, telling her Molly had primed Pete Pernaska and had intentionally withheld work from him for the past two nights to make sure he was ready.

"All I can say," wrote Molly in closing, "is that come Thursday morning, I think you're going to be one happy woman." She followed that with the words, "Have fun!" and signed it *Molly*, embellishing her signature with a heart, punctured by an erotically shaped arrow.

Giggling to herself, Sam took the elevator to the third floor of the lodge and found her suite at the end of a corridor. When she walked into the room, a spectacular view of the mountains greeted her.

The wet bar was fully stocked and a fire was already burning brightly, but not so hot as to make the room uncomfortable. *Molly's right; she has taken care of everything.* She opened the bar refrigerator, found a platter of oysters on the half shell, and another note from

Molly: Pete has never needed these for stamina, but if I were you, I'd eat some of them yourself. I think you'll need the lift.

That will be the day. Sam settled into a chair to wait.

A few minutes later, a soft knock interrupted her thoughts and she glanced at her watch. Three on the dot. When she opened the door, she was pleasantly surprised to find a tree of a man waiting, hands on his hips.

She gauged him to be somewhere around six foot four or five, with about 250 pounds of pure muscle. If there was an ounce of fat on his body, she'd be surprised.

"I'm Pete." Her visitor's deep bass voice matched his physique. Her cheeks warmed when his dark eyes roamed from her feet to her head and an appreciative smile slowly crossed his face.

"C'mon in." Sam opened the door wide. "Molly has talked a lot about you. I hope you are as talented as she says."

"Well, ma'am, Molly's Irish, y'know. The Irish are given to exaggeration. On the other hand, I've had no complaints."

The words came out in almost melodic strain, each word pronounced perfectly. "Pete ..." She stopped and looked up at it. "Is it okay if I call you Pete?"

"It's my name, ma'am." His words were soft as cotton candy, gentle and soothing. "But since I'm here on your dime, so to speak, I won't be offended by anything you call me—unless you tell me I have no talent."

"I'll probably not tell you that. But I probably won't tell you you're as good as Molly said, either. I've had some great lovers, and if you can beat the likes of them, I'll be speechless."

He lifted his shoulders. "We can either talk about it or do it. I'm not much for words. Maybe you'd like to sample what you're buying?"

"I am more than ready, much more than ready, Pete."

She had barely freed the words from her mouth when he took a step into the room, closed the door, locked it, and drew her into his arms with a hand the size of a baseball glove on her back. For the next hour and forty-five minutes, Sam's mind was a blur.

Pete wasn't gentle, but neither was he rough. He handled her with the touch of someone half his size. But he made his point ... emphatically. Her mind whirled like a kaleidoscope, which is the way he had taken her that first time. There were moments on the couch, on the floor, across the counter in the kitchenette, and in the bed, although the time they spent on the bed was minimal.

When at last her heart had quieted and her breath again came somewhat normally, she raised her head slightly, not certain if she could speak, and whispered, "Where did you learn how to do that? My goodness, the sweetness of it was incredible, but at the same time it was rough-and-tumble, tender and tumultuous. Oh, my god, I've never experienced anything like it."

He smiled down at her wryly. "I aim to please. I'm happy you had a good time. But I hope we aren't finished yet?"

The question was delivered haltingly, his short breaths matching hers.

"I'm not sure I will ever want to be finished," she told him. Wrapping her fingers in the thick mat of hair on his chest, she admitted, "But if you're ready now, all the action will be up to you. I am totally and thoroughly spent. And that, my dear man, is a first."

His smile was warm and, when he spoke, his words were even more warming. "My dear Sam, Molly told me that you have me for the day. Our first round was perhaps more than I intended, but I did want you to be able to judge if I was someone you'd like to keep around for a few more hours."

In spite of her exhaustion, she burst out laughing at the seriousness of his comment. "Oh my dear Pete, if you make one little move that suggests you're about to leave this suite, I swear I will find the strength to tackle you and tie you up."

"You're but a wee thing," he said, a twinkle in his eye. "If I wish to go somewhere, I will go. But I can assure you that it won't be out of this place until you ask me to leave."

They lay there quietly for a time. Then Sam turned onto her side to face him. "I'd like to see you again. How does a week or two sound?"

Pete grinned. "Perfect." He traced a finger down her arm, sending shivers across her skin. "So I passed the test?"

Her forehead wrinkled. "The test?"

"When I came to the door, you said you doubted I would be as a good as the person Molly described. Now that you have had a brief taste, do I get to stay or must we find someone else to please you?"

Summoning up strength she didn't feel, she slapped his hand lightly. "Don't you dare think about leaving. Once I find someone who has more skill than anyone I have experienced, I will not let them go—ever!"

"That good, huh?" He tossed the covers back and climbed out of bed. After grabbing and opening a Coors from the fridge, he moved to one of the chairs near the fireplace.

Sam followed him, stretching out on the furry rug in front of the fire. "Well, not too bad, anyway," she teased, propping her chin on one hand.

He shook his head. "You are quite a woman, Sam. I never thought I'd find anyone like you in Kalispell, Montana."

"Speaking of Kalispell, I was pretty sure finding someone like you here would be impossible. I can tell you that I have experienced no one who is your equal. And I've had my share of great lovers. More than my share, probably."

He lifted his can of beer in her direction. "Well, then, perhaps you'll give me a good reference when Molly asks. I rather enjoy the work, you know."

"Speaking of work, what do you do? Besides this, of course." She rose to her knees then stood, grabbing her silk robe from the stool and tugging it on.

"This is what I do, for money, at least. I came to the area almost twenty years ago, hoping to get a job in the timber industry, since I had done that work in Albania. Until the early 1990s, Albania was the source of much of Europe's lumber. But that dried up when people became concerned about how over-foresting was affecting the environment. Then the mob began to take over the economy, and I knew that if I didn't want to work for them, I had to get out."

"I'm sure they loved your muscles."

"Yeah, but there were four main branches of the underworld, which was the reason I decided to leave. Even if I had decided to work for one of them, the other three would have tried to kill me. I landed in Minneapolis in July of 1996, but I didn't like the heat and humidity. I bought a car and drove west. Western Montana had a great climate, and it had great timbering then." A distant look rose in his eyes, as though he'd been transported back to those days. "I stopped first in Missoula then headed north when I heard that timbering was at its peak near Kalispell."

Sam tied the belt on her robe. "Are you hungry? I think you've stimulated my appetite. And if we are going to continue, I need to have something to eat."

"I'm starved," he admitted. "But I don't think food comes with the deal."

"Not to worry, I can afford to feed you. It's past dinner time. How about steaks, potatoes, and all the trimmings?"

"Sounds great. The sirloin here is amazing. Big as the plate, tender and juicy. The baked potatoes are large and tasty and the chef, Matt Polka, creates some great sides."

Samantha ordered and set the receiver back in the cradle. "About thirty-five minutes. I asked for the steaks rare; hope that's okay."

He nodded. Sam pointed to the bathroom. "How about a shower and a drink? After dinner, we can work off the food and get ready for dessert at the same time."

That slow smile that did something to her insides crossed his face. "Sounds like a plan."

Sam thought about his words as she started for the shower, loosening the belt she'd just tightened. A few weeks ago, Pete Pernaska hadn't been part of her plans for the future. After the day they'd just spent though, she was definitely going to have to revise those plans.

Showered, in robes, and enjoying bourbon on the rocks, Sam and Pete were relaxing when the doorbell rang. Sam answered it and found two waiters pushing carts laden with food.

She pressed a hand to her mouth. "My goodness, did I order that much?"

"Chef wanted to make sure you had enough," said the waiter who had come through the door first. "He mentioned that he added a few things, courtesy of the house."

"Well, bring it in," she said, throwing open the door. The two waiters pushed the carts in, swiftly set the dining room table in the suite, opened a bottle of cabernet sauvignon from the Napa Valley, and soon had things ready for them. The steaks were as large as Pete had predicted, covering the sizzling platters they were served on. The baked potatoes were huge. In addition, there were sautéed mushrooms, creamed spinach, bacon-wrapped asparagus, and a nice selection of breads and rolls.

One of the waiters set two plates of cheesecake covered with mountain berries and topped with whipped cream in the refrigerator for later.

When they had both bowed and left the room, Sam and Pete sat down at the table to enjoy a long, leisurely dinner. Pete was excellent at asking questions that got Sam to open up about her past, although it was far too early for her to share with him what she did for a living, and how many people had been victims of the concoctions she created. They finished the bottle of wine, demolished the steaks, and put handsome dents in the sides before sliding their chairs back to take a break.

Pete poured Bailey's over ice cubes and they relaxed on the sofa, facing the fire.

Sam touched his knee. "Let's get back to you now. I was captivated by your story earlier, and I want to hear the rest of it." She swirled the Bailey's, the ice clinking against the sides of the glass.

He shifted to face her. "You really want to know more about me? You're paying for my time, you know."

"Yes, but I have already decided there will be many meetings; I plan to make you mine. You might want to think about that to see what sort of an arrangement I can make with Molly to make you a kept man."

"Hmmm, interesting thought. Yes, I will think about it."

She took a sip of her drink, the smooth liquid sliding down her throat. "So tell me all about yourself."

His coal-black eyes seemed to probe her soul. "First, Sam, it's hard to be seated on this couch with you, knowing you are naked beneath the robe, and to think about what to tell you about my life, but I'll do my best. Let me start with when I arrived in America. I have a brother in New York. He left six years before me, and when it was time for me to come, he arranged for me to visit him there. I hated that city, so too big, so too populated; I was uncomfortable the whole time I was there. Horns honking at every turn, lights flashing, people hurrying; it was much too much for me. In the end, though, it was worth it. Before I returned home, my brother helped me start the process to get the credentials that allowed me to stay. We met with the Albanian ambassador to the U.N. and he agreed that when I found work he would help me get my green card. I knew, though, that I did not want to work in New York."

He reached over and brushed back a strand of hair from Sam's face. "After I was with my brother for two weeks, when I thought about what I wanted to do, I realized it was more about what I *could* do. I love to cut trees. I have the skill. I can lay a tree down on a one-inch X any time I want. So when I got back to Albania, I searched on-line for jobs. I talked to many companies, and finally found one in the Northwest, Big Sky Timber. They were working near Glacier Park in Montana, and assured me they would have a job for me if I traveled west."

He stretched his arm across the back of the couch, lightly touching her shoulders. "When I got to Minneapolis, I took the train. Rode Amtrak through your country. It was beautiful. Like Albania. I jumped off in northern Montana, rode the bus to Kalispell, and here I am. For two years I worked for Big Sky. They loved my work. I got several promotions and made big money. When I had saved enough to buy a place, I located a home I loved in the mountains, took a contract on one hundred acres that was conditional on my obtaining citizenship, then concentrated on becoming an American. It took me four years, but it was a proud day when I was sworn a citizen in Kalispell."

Sam clinked her glass to his lightly and he smiled. "I am now a full-fledged American. I live on the place I bought, keep a few steers and horses, and work for Molly. I am not rich in money, but rich in pleasure. The work I do—especially today—is very satisfying. Pleasing women is great work."

"And you do it well." Sam lifted her glass. "How about you freshen our drinks and then tell me more."

He did as she asked. When he was seated next to her again, he leaned back against the couch cushions. "As I told you, I love the work. It is satisfying—very. And today was more satisfying than ever before."

"I'll bet you tell all the women that."

"Not so. I am honest; I always tell the truth. This is the first time I have met someone like you, so I am interested in what you have to say about me being a kept man."

Sam studied his serious face for a moment. "Pete, you are very good at your work, if that's what you want to call it. You have satisfied me greatly, better than anyone has before. Having someone around who is just mine would be a wonderful thing, especially someone with your, umm, talents."

"What would I do? How would it work?"

"I haven't quite thought that far yet. We each apparently love where we live, so asking you to give up your home wouldn't be a good idea, I suppose. But I have needs that are not easily satisfied. That means I would like you near. And often."

"How often?"

"Some weeks, every day. Other weeks, maybe not at all. It won't always equal out, but at least two weeks a month, I should think. I really need to consider this more, though."

"Very interesting idea." He tapped his finger on the side of his glass. "But I would have time at home each week to take care of my property and animals?"

"How far from Kalispell are you?"

"I am southeast of here, about fifteen miles as the crow flies, but thirty miles by road."

"I live in the mountains southeast of here, too. Maybe a little farther away than you, but not too much."

"That would make it easy. If close, I could be home often enough to keep up with the work. I produce hay in the summer and I have a garden, too."

"I think it would work. But I'll have to discuss it with Molly."

"For sure. She is a good woman. Very good in the sack, too. She likes time with Pete." Now he was smiling, the grin lighting up his dark features and making him seem like a little boy.

"That doesn't surprise me; you are quite a man."

They sat nursing their drinks for a time without speaking. When the fire burned low, Sam moved closer to nestle in his arms. He tightened his hold. "Break time is over?"

She took his drink from his hand and set both of their glasses on the coffee table. "I believe it is time to go to work, yes."

And work, he did. For the next three hours, Sam lost all track of everything, time, place, position. The only thing she knew was that she had never been more satisfied.

With the clock ticking toward 11:00 p.m., she gently pushed him off, breathed deeply, and told him, "Pete, you are incredible. I think you need to thank God and whoever made you for how they did it. You are some specimen of a man."

"You have no complaints?" He smiled widely.

She shook her head. "No complaints. In fact, I think it's time for me to talk to Molly."

"Yes, that's a good idea. I can wait in the bar to see what she says."

"Why don't you stay right here? You never know when I might need more attention. Maybe I will after talking to Molly."

"I will wait."

Sam dragged herself from the bed and went in search of Molly. She found her in the pub. On this Thursday night, the place was quiet. There were only two people at the bar, and one of the eight booths was filled by four people. Molly was chatting with the bartender.

The fire blazed, the snapping and crackling echoing throughout the room. The smell of wood smoke was pleasant, sleep-inducing, even. To Sam, the elk, deer, and bear mounts on the wall above the huge fireplace appeared to be dozing.

Molly looked up when she approached. "Hey, Sam. How was he, er, I mean it, your evening, that is?" In the firelight, the gleam in her eyes was mischievous.

Before Sam could answer, Molly gestured toward the bartender. "Sam, this is Rolf. Rolf is my right-hand man. Rolf, meet Sam."

The two shook hands as Molly said, "Sam just spent a few hours with Pete."

"Oh, my." Rolf tugged a towel off his shoulder and polished a brandy snifter. "I must say you look amazingly put together. Most of the women who meet with Pete don't return looking half as good as you."

Molly rolled her eyes. "Rolf is an incorrigible flirt. Watch out for him, he's a mover."

The three of them laughed and then Sam looked at Molly and said, "I wonder if I might have a word with you in private?" She turned to the bartender and smiled. "No offense, Rolf, but I have a business proposition that I want to talk to your boss about."

"No offense taken." He smiled at her as he turned back to the chore of polishing glasses and placing them in the racks above the bar.

"Let's go to my office," said Molly, stepping down from the bar stool and gesturing for Sam to go ahead of her.

Sam started for the door. Her hands, when she clasped them together, were damp with sweat. *Molly has to agree to this.* The two of them had to be able to work out an agreement for Sam to spend a lot of time with Pete from now on. After the day she'd just had, Sam had never wanted anything more in her life.

5

Seated in Molly's comfortably furnished office, the furniture heavy oak and the decor dark, Sam hunched closer to the large desk that separated them. She propped her elbows on the desk and folded her hands together. "Molly, I'd like to talk business."

"What do you have in mind?"

"Let me put it this way. While I don't sense that you're a person given to modesty—and that's a compliment, by the way—I think your description of Pete as a lover was vastly understated. He is the most extraordinary man I have experienced, and believe me, the field I compare him to is anything but small."

"I thought you might like him." A chuckle punctuated Molly's statement. "So the subject is to be Pete? If so, I think we should have a drink to go with it, don't you?"

Molly phoned the order to the bar—a Jack on the rocks for herself and a vodka tonic for Sam. When the drinks had been delivered, Molly settled back in her swivel chair, drink in hand, and said, "So what's on your mind?"

"First, a bit of background. I'm a lusty lady, Molly. And while I'm considerably older than I look, I have never lost my appetite for men."

"I sorta sensed that. It's why you got Pete. I only share his talents with people I think will fully appreciate them."

"He's incredible. And you know what they say about a taste from a well filled with sweet water - the thirst never goes away."

Molly laughed heartily. "I haven't heard that one for years. But it is true, isn't it?"

"It is, especially in this case. To be blunt, I don't want to share him with others. If anyone is going to sap his energy, I want it to be me."

"What about me?"

"Maybe we can work out a deal." Sam leaned forward in her chair. "I'm hoping you might consider letting me have Pete all to myself."

Storm clouds gathered in Molly's eyes. She opened her mouth, but Sam held up her hand. "Before you protest, I know he must be a good revenue-producer for you, right?"

"Absolutely, the best."

"I figured that, and I would never want to cost you business." Sam slid to the front of her chair. "I'm hoping you might be willing to make Pete mine three weeks a month, if he's agreeable to that."

Molly didn't respond. Sam took a deep breath. "I think it could be great for both of us. I'm offering to pay you the average revenue that Pete generates for you in a month. Since I would only have him for three weeks, you stand to make money on this deal, by booking him the fourth week as you do now. Of course, if you want him for yourself, he could be yours on that fourth week."

Molly contemplated her in silence. Trying desperately not to look as nervous as she felt, Sam leaned back in her chair and took a sip of her drink. Molly arose, walked to the fire, grabbed a poker and stirred it, then fed it another log before returning to her chair.

"Hmmm, it's a good first offer, but I'm going to decline." She sat down and gracefully crossed her legs.

"What? When will you ever get another offer like that?" Heat crept up Sam's neck. "A guaranteed income based on your current take? Each year he gets older, you know. This won't go on forever."

"No, it won't, but when Pete begins to fade as a business draw, my idea was to make him mine. He's a great handyman, something that's always useful. And he will be with me each night."

"So are you just saying no, or do you have a counter?"

Molly gazed into the fire for several minutes then turned back to her. "You have sort of caught me off guard, but maybe if you were willing to let me have Pete one day a week during the weeks that he is yours, I'd be more agreeable."

"C'mon, Molly, how naïve do you think I am? My guess is he'll be with you on his day off."

Molly smiled. "And what's wrong with that? Here's the truth, and Toby Keith puts it better than I do when he says, 'I ain't as good as I once was ... but I'm as good once as I ever was.'"

Sam giggled at the comment. Molly joined her. When the room quieted, Sam leaned forward again. "I'm willing to agree to that, *if* you allow me to choose the day."

Molly sighed. "Fine. One day a week, your choice. And Pete works for me every fourth week. Sounds fair. Deal."

Sam leaned across the desk and extended her hand. "Let's shake on it."

They shook hands. A thrill of victory shivered up and down Sam's spine. Pete was completely hers. Almost.

Molly reached for the liquor bottle, but Sam rose to her feet. "Sorry, Molly, but my day isn't quite up yet, and I plan to spend more time with Pete. Do you trust me to fill him in, see if he's okay with our agreement?"

"Sure, be my guest."

Sam excused herself, returned to her suite, and found Pete having a drink, his feet up on the hearth.

He jumped to his feet when she walked in. "How'd it go?"

"Molly and I have a deal, but it's not a deal until you agree."

Over the next five minutes, she detailed her conversation with the innkeeper. When she finished, he looked at her. "So let me see if I have this straight. You have made a business deal with Molly that puts me in your control three weeks a month."

Sam frowned. When he put it like that ...

Pete grinned. "I'm not protesting, just making sure I have all the facts." He sat back down on the couch and patted the cushion beside him. Sam sank down on it and he slid an arm around her shoulders. "And during those three weeks, Molly gets me one day each week, but you decide on the day, is that right?"

"Yes. But if I could have my way, I'd really like it if you confined your attention to Molly on that day. Can you do that?"

Pete's brow furrowed. "Why?"

"Because I don't want her booking you with all kinds of women. I want you fresh when the day is done."

He started to laugh, spilling a bit of his drink onto the hearth.

"Why is that so funny?"

"Sam, I have never been with any two people as good as you and Molly. If you want me fresh, I'd be better off with someone else."

Her grin was sheepish. "I didn't think of that. It's your decision anyway. In fact, all of this is. Molly and I only have a deal if you don't say no to it."

"Why would I do that? I get to divide my time between two women I adore, and get paid to do it. That's a helluva deal. How do you say it … I'm all in?"

For the next two hours, they celebrated. Sam was certain she knew every move there was. Pete demonstrated that she was wrong. When it was over, Sam fell back on the bed. Rolling onto her stomach, she let out a satisfied moan. "Tell Molly I need the room for another day. I'm happy to pay. I'm just too darn tired to dress and drive home."

Pete laughed. "I'll tell her." His voice was soft, almost as soft as the kiss he placed on her cheek, then her back, then her butt. "And I will put up the 'Do Not Disturb!' sign on my way out."

●——•

Sam was snoring gently before he could tiptoe to the door.

"Sleep well, m'lady," he whispered, closing the bedroom door behind him. He tidied up the suite, washed the dirty glasses, dried them and put them away, then attached the sign to the door of the suite and locked the door behind him as he left.

A few minutes later, he found Molly in the bar and they had a drink as he told her about his discussion with Sam.

"So we have a deal acceptable to all three of us?"

"Yup," he said, sipping his drink.

"Pete? How old do you think she is? She keeps telling me she's old, but she looks about fifty."

"She has body of a twenty-year-old, but she's definitely not a twenty-year-old. No way a twenty-something could have learned all the things she knows. Ya know, Molly, I thought there was no one to compare to you. But now I gotta tell ya that there is. Sam is unbelievable."

"So you enjoyed yourself?"

"Yes, ma'am. That's what I'm telling you. And now, before you get any ideas, I'm headin' home. I need to feed the animals. I've got about that much energy left before hitting the hay. God, I'm tired, but I feel great."

"You go on. I think you've earned the sleep."

"Yes." Pete tipped back his head and drained the last few drops of his drink before setting the glass down on the bar with a thud. "I believe that I have."

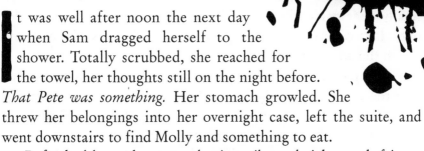

6

It was well after noon the next day when Sam dragged herself to the shower. Totally scrubbed, she reached for the towel, her thoughts still on the night before. *That Pete was something.* Her stomach growled. She threw her belongings into her overnight case, left the suite, and went downstairs to find Molly and something to eat.

Refreshed by a phenomenal prime rib sandwich, ranch fries, a salad, and a couple of Rusty Nails from Fremont Brewing, one of the up-and-coming northwestern U.S. breweries, she was ready for the day. Molly ate with her, and the two women agreed the chef had outdone himself.

As Sam stood at the front desk, about to pay her bill and leave the Golden Lion, Molly stopped her. "Monday is the twentieth of April; what say we start our deal on Monday, May 4, since weekends are time off for Pete?"

Sam thought for a moment. "Gee, that's fourteen days. I'm not sure I can wait that long. It's been a while for me, Molly, and now that I have a renewed taste of what I was missing, it's gonna be a long fourteen days, that's for sure. How about we make it the twenty-ninth—right in the middle? I'll come to Kalispell and pick up Pete, if he agrees."

Molly nodded. "That should work."

"Good. I'll see you on the twenty-ninth." Sam waved as she exited the lodge and headed for her Land Rover. Back at the lake, everything needed attention. The bird feeders were empty, the larger feeders that fed the land-based critters were barren as well, and the grass needed cutting. She had left in such a rush, she hadn't taken time to do the chores as she should have.

As she surveyed the situation, her mind raced. *It'll be great to have a man around the house to help out.* She sighed. As Pete wasn't there yet, she'd better get on with it.

For the next several hours, until the sun slid out of sight, she filled the bird feeders, carried corn and hay to the large bins she had built for the elk and moose, and took scraps of meat cuttings she had frozen and saved for the grizzlies down to the lake. When she finally went inside, she felt good. The special music from the hordes of birds that were again visiting accompanied her as she went in and closed the door behind her.

The big animals would be by, too, but not before night had settled over the area. She feared none of those she befriended, something her neighbors would have warned her against. But even though she regularly passed near grizzlies, moose, and elk during her walk to the lake in the morning, they seemed content to enjoy her handouts enough to allow her to encroach on their territory.

When Sam slid off her coat and hung it up, she went straight to the kitchen. She was both hungry and tired, her chores having worked up an appetite. As she searched for something simple to fix, the male cat, Julie, reminded her that he needed attention, too, constantly rubbing her legs until she opened a can of *Fancy Feast* to augment his dry food. For herself, she ultimately settled on pancakes and bacon. As she fixed her meal, she realized the inside of the house needed a good cleaning as well. That could wait for until morning, though.

When the clock chimed ten, she was ready for bed, leaving the pile of letters she had collected on her way to and from Kalispell unopened on the table. That too would be a task for the next day.

The sun had not yet thought about making an appearance the next morning when Sam padded barefoot to the kitchen, made a cup of coffee, and settled down to open the mail. She was astounded. The pile of letters yielded twenty-two orders for poisons and potions from mobsters the width and breadth of the country. *Damn. Help would be great. Wish Dino were here.* The thought of her former lover sent warmth coursing through her. He had learned his way about the lab and was nearly as good at filling the orders as she was. There was no getting around it; another pair of hands would be helpful.

Well, the dust and dirt are going to have to wait another day. Her first priority today was filling the orders and getting them ready to ship. Tomorrow she'd make a run up the east side of the lake and down the west to mail and retrieve orders. *But first—ugh—at least a fifteen-hour day in the lab.*

All day Sam worked, stopping only now and again to pet Julie and grab a cup of coffee and a quickly slapped together peanut butter sandwich at noon. By 5:00 p.m., the kitchen table was littered with packages to be mailed to New York, Boston, Hartford, Newark, Charlotte, Atlanta, Chicago, Denver, Dallas, Los Angeles, Seattle, and Vegas. And there were more orders to fill. She finished the last one, a sizeable amount of "milk of amnesia," properly known as Propofol, for the don of the San Francisco Italian mob at 10:00 p.m. Too tired to eat, she made herself a stiff vodka-tonic, showered, finished her drink, and tumbled into bed, asleep nearly before hitting the pillow.

Up early again the next day, she loaded her car in the order the packages would be mailed and headed for her first stop at Finley Point. Before her day was over, she would log nearly two hundred miles on roads that were far from super highways. She would make ten stops. On her way to Kalispell, she would check to see if she'd gotten any more deliveries, but the main purpose of that leg of her trip was to spread out the mailing of the packages she had prepared the day before.

Sam headed down the highway, window down to allow the fresh breeze to ruffle her long, auburn hair. *What would a Montana state trooper say if he—or she—saw the cargo she was carrying?* It was a funny thought, but she would need to be the picture of a law-abiding citizen this sunny morning. She scanned the horizon. There was one thing she could say for western Montana, no one could get sick of the scenery. Big Sky Country was, at the very least, beautiful beyond description.

Sam pulled into Polson at the foot of Flathead Lake and glanced at her watch. Her timing was perfect. It was four fifteen and the post office would close in another fifteen minutes. She had two packages to send off and there might be mail to pick up. Four envelopes waited for her.

Hungry again, she checked her GPS. Who would have thought that there would be an excellent sushi restaurant in northwestern Montana? But there was. Vinny's was known for its creations and Sam had a hankering for a Flathead Lake Monster. Lake Monster specialty rolls were to die for: ahi tuna, barbecued eel, and avocado, drizzled with sriracha.

A Monster and a couple of beers were just what she needed to end a long day. And tomorrow would be just as long, judging from the number of letters she had picked up.

After her stop at Vinny's, she headed home refreshed. There was still light in the sky when she drove into her rugged homestead in the mountains. She debated a swim, but opted to feed a loudly meowing Julie and open the stack of letters she had collected.

Oh, god, tomorrow will be another busy day. A quick shower and she was in bed.

The next week passed quickly. She was up early, worked through most of the days and, spent, retired early. The work was pouring in to the extent that she struggled some days to keep up. But it also meant that more and more money was flowing into the trust account of her niece and her greatnephew, and that pleased her greatly.

And then there was Pete. The warm memories of their time together brightened the moments during her morning swim and before falling asleep at night, but to be honest, work was so demanding that there was less time than she liked for fantasy.

The twenty-seventh came and went; she arrived home tired and aching for more of Pete's special kind of love. She'd had many great lovers, but never had she met anyone as talented as Pete. He was a big man in every way. She liked that, but she liked even better that the fact that he was a man among men didn't make him the least bit egotistical. He still worked very hard to deliver pleasure - and he hadn't once failed that first day they were together.

Mmmm, will three weeks a month be enough with him?

The twenty-ninth finally rolled around, one of those early spring days that one could never get enough of. Although it was still very chilly at night, Sam braved the temperatures to head for the lake and a morning dip. The ice had just left "My Lake" and she was sure her dip would be only seconds long. She was right, the moment she submerged herself, she froze; in fact, the temperature was so paralyzing she was glad she had stayed near enough to shore to touch bottom. After wading in up to her neck, she turned around and made her way back to land, hopped out, grabbed her towel, and ran to the cabin.

Once inside she headed for a steaming shower, opening her pores, as her phys-ed. teacher had once described it, and washing out everything bad.

At last she was ready. Pete was to meet her at Finley Point, and she would lead him to her cabin. He was there when she arrived, and the short drive into the mountains to the unnamed lake she had claimed as her own took far longer than she wanted. Once at the cabin, she leapt from the car and into his arms.

"Oh, my god, this has been the longest two weeks of my life. How are you, Pete? I am so pleased you're here. Welcome to my humble abode!"

"Humble?" He chuckled as he set her on her feet. His sweeping gaze took in all the features of the property. "I don't think there is anything humble about this place. It's big, it's beautiful, and if I'm not mistaken, that's a lake peeking at me through the woods. Am I right?"

"You are. I'll be happy to show you around, just not right now. C'mon in. I have other things in mind."

Taking his hand, she led him into the log home. Once inside, they didn't make it to the big bed before she fell into his arms. They embraced warmly, or hotly was probably a better description, each working to disrobe the other as they kissed. Laughing, they tumbled to the floor when trying to get four legs out of two pairs of jeans proved too big an obstacle to overcome.

"That's much better." Her comment was more an intake of breath as she worked one of his legs free of the jeans. At the same time, his hands seemed everywhere—tugging on her jeans, working themselves into private places, trying to undo her bra. Suddenly they both were gasping in laughter as their efforts to free their partners seemed only to increase the discomfort.

"Time out," she wheezed as she struggled into a sitting position. "Let's do this right. I'll take care of undressing me, you do the same for you. And I'll meet you right in there." She pointed at the doorway through which a large bed was partially visible.

She beat him to it, but not by more than a second, and their reunion was frantic but fulfilling.

When he fell from her, she enjoyed watching his hairy chest rise and fall as he sought to get his breathing under control.

"Oh, my god, two weeks of this? Can I stand it? If not, what a way to go."

Her hand fondled the hair on his belly before she worked her way down farther. "Seems like he's out for the count," she mumbled into his chest.

From deep in his chest, she felt the growl start to build. "There'll be no ten-count," he said, comparing himself to a boxer on the ropes.

She began to count, slowly.

Before she got to five, Pete had flipped her over and climbed on top of her.

"See?"

"I am sorry, young man." Sam grasped the railings of the head board with both hands. "I should have known better. And now, Mr. Pete, if you please, let's quit talkin.'"

For the better part of two hours there was no discussion. Finally, she was forced to plead with him. "Stop. Stop. Pete, please. I can't take anymore. Please."

He gently lifted her, setting her down softly beside him, then rolled toward her. "Just remember, Sam, you never want to insult him—never! He's very proud of what he can do."

"And he should be. He … you … you're incredible."

"So I take it you might be up for other things?"

"Other things? Like what?" Sam contemplated him, her chin resting on her right hand.

He grinned. "Don't worry. No more of this right now. I thought maybe you would show me around."

"That would be a real pleasure. Just give me a couple of minutes to recover."

Soon she was showing him around the cabin. When he saw the huge walk-in refrigerator-freezer at the rear of the facility, his mouth dropped open. She told him about buying meat in quantity, butchering it herself, and freezing it. She then showed him the garden and her homemade feeders, before leading him to "My Lake."

She explained that she'd had the contractors create a water source for the cabin from the lake. "Whenever the temperatures are bearable, the lake is my bathtub."

His eyebrows rose at that. "Hmm, that presents some interesting possibilities."

Before they could go too far down that road, Sam showed him the small rustic cabinet that contained soap and shampoo and the large flat rock she used to feed the grizzlies.

"I'm not sure why, but none of the animals have bothered me. It's kind of like we understand each other. We get along quite well."

Afterwards, when they were settled inside, sitting at the table and eating sandwiches and drinking coffee, Pete studied his cup before looking up. "Sam, what am I going to do when I'm here? I can't spend the entire time in the bedroom or I'll go crazy."

"For starters, if you really want to do something, you can take care of the outdoor chores. Keeping the feeders filled is becoming nearly a full-time job with those hungry little critters. And the grass seems to grow a foot a day. I have trouble keeping it like I want it."

"Those things for sure. But what will you do?"

Her laughter appeared to please him, but his look turned serious when she replied, "Pete, I have lots of work to do, more than I can handle. I'm going to tell you about it, but today isn't the right time. Let's get to know each other a little better, see how it goes, and we'll get around to it, okay?"

"I guess. I just want to earn my keep."

"I think you've paid in advance," she said, and they both laughed.

For the next several days, they played for hours, sometimes at the lake in the morning. Following their morning swim, Pete would work outdoors until lunchtime. Sam took some of that time to work in the lab. Lunch was quiet and relaxed then both would return to their work.

Dinner was their most enjoyable time. A drink or two marked the late afternoon, a time when they talked and talked. They shared the cooking, and Sam was quick to conclude that Pete was the far better cook. He created some of the most delightful dishes, often bringing things with him from his house for them to share after he'd gone home to take care of his livestock. He brought elk and moose and bear, too. She loved all of it, but made him promise that he would never make her look at a freshly killed animal, nor would he ever hunt near or on her property.

He assured her that was not a problem, and life went on, better than ever, in the mind of Sam. And Pete seemed content, too.

When the three weeks had passed, Sam was sorry to see him go, and she told him so before proving her words with actions. He assured her he would be back for more in another week.

"Yes, just a week." Sam turned the page from April to May, something she'd been reluctant to do as it was a reminder he would soon be gone. Now it was a promise he would soon return. "But I'm going to miss you, Pete. Maybe next week we can talk about what I do for a living."

"When you're ready." His words were gentle and unassuming. "I don't want to push. When the time is right, I figure you'll tell me."

As his pickup disappeared down the rutted road, she bit her lip. She was going to miss him. It would be a long, long week. And it wasn't as if she could rest, either. The next day, she would have to make a mail run, and if it was anything like it had been, there would be lots of work to keep her busy.

But more than that, she was tormented by her past. *How much can I tell him? I like him; I want him around. If I tell him about my past, will he run?* That thought scared Sam so much that she pushed the questions out of her mind and went to the lab, knowing the hours before she saw Pete again would go a little faster if she lost herself in her work.

7

Al Rouse was tormented by ghosts of his own as he sat in his office on Monday morning and thought about what he'd learned the week before. So the old girl had, indeed, gotten off that airplane when it stopped in Portland. And she'd bought a car—a rugged, luxury car. *What does that mean?*

Lost in thought, he didn't look up until a shadow fell across his desk.

"Ahem. Am I disturbing you?"

Al blinked at the sight of a smiling Chief Brent Whigg standing in his doorway, as he often did at the start of a day.

"Chief, hi, c'mon in."

"Let me guess. You were thinking about where to find a certain Genevieve Wangen, and wondering how to convince me to let you take a trip to try and find her?"

Al shook his head. "Not quite, but darn close. Chief, you know me too well—too damn well."

"So maybe you'd like to fill me in?"

Al spun his chair around and grabbed an atlas off the bookshelf behind him. Flipping through it, he found the page with the state of Oregon and pointed to Portland.

"This is where she went." As he spoke, he tapped the large dot with his index finger, then flipped back a few pages to the one showing the northwest region. "Look at how large the northwest portion of our country is: Oregon, Idaho, Washington, Montana.

39

Huge ... absolutely huge. And not very heavily populated, either. I think she's somewhere inside this area." He outlined the entire northwest with his index finger.

"I had lunch with Charlie on Friday, like you suggested, and he chided me for being so depressed. In fact, he went further than that, suggesting I had no right to be down if I was unwilling to do something about it. He pointed out we had done little to find Wangen since she got away from us again in New Orleans."

The chief's smile was understanding. "Al, I think Charlie is right. I know you made a few phone calls, didn't turn up anything, and you've been moping ever since—way too long, if you ask me."

"No question, you're right. And when I got back from lunch, I made a couple more calls and, as luck or providence would have it, I got the right person in each place. So now I know a few more things than I did, but not enough ... not nearly enough."

"You found out some things. Good. Care to share?"

"I don't have anything conclusive, that's for sure, but I do know that she got off that plane when it landed in Portland. If you can believe it, when I called, the guy who helped her after she left the plane answered the phone. He actually remembers giving her a ride into Portland. How crazy is that?"

"Does he remember anything else?" The chief leaned forward, tilting his coffee cup until a splash of coffee landed on Al's desk and he straightened it quickly.

"He took her to a Portland auto dealer that sells luxury cars. When I called there, I lucked out again and got to speak to the salesperson who sold her a vehicle. She bought a used Range Rover that had been outfitted as if it was going to be a mob car."

The chief's forehead wrinkled. "What do you mean?"

"The windows were bullet-proof glass. The suspension was reinforced and the tires the best there is, the kind of tires that remain inflated even if punctured."

"*She* had this car refitted like that?"

"No, it had either been built that way or overhauled by a previous owner, but when she saw it, she apparently wanted it. Badly. She paid top dollar for it. Cash, of course."

"Does the dealer have her information?"

"Yes and no. The sales manager and salesperson told me she was skittish about providing identifying information. They wanted a sale, so they looked the other way, even though they figured the information she gave them wasn't legit. I don't think it was either, although she may have made a mistake when she gave it to them. She called herself Honey Harmon."

"Honey? As in …"

"Exactly. Savannah Harlowe's mother."

"Gotta be her." The chief lifted a hand, palm up. "Let me guess, they have no idea where she went."

"You got it; none at all."

The chief had grabbed a pencil and was doodling on a sheet of paper on Al's desk. Without looking up, he rubbed his chin contemplatively. "Have you run the car?"

"Not yet; I planned on doing that at some point today though. Too early to have anyone answer the phone out west."

"I guess. Call as soon as you can though, it feels like a good lead."

"Maybe not so good. No license plate makes it difficult."

"Pretty specialized vehicle though, that should help you track it down."

"I'm certainly going to try."

The chief's bushy eyebrows drew together. "That Berzinski actually got through to you, didn't he? Happy to see you're done your moping."

"I'm not moping, but I do have to be realistic too. It's only three hundred miles from Portland to the Canadian border. She could be in Canada. Then what?"

"Tell you what, how about I check out what's available to you north of the border." The chief reached into his pocket, extracted a pocket-sized notebook, and used the pencil to jot something in it. "Damn, at my age, I have to write everything down."

"I know what you're talking about, believe me." Al studied the map in front of him. "How many states do you figure we should cover?"

The chief leaned over the atlas. "Hmm, good question. I guess, if it was me, I'd start with Oregon, Washington, and Idaho."

"That was my first thought, too, but now I'm wondering about adding Montana and Wyoming. Seems to me it might be easier to get lost in either of those states."

The chief glanced at his watch. "Damn, news huddle coming up with the media. I gotta get going. Tell you what, start with Oregon, Washington, and Idaho. See what you find. If you don't come across anything promising, add Montana and Wyoming. I'd stay away from California, though, unless you've eliminated the other five. We've never gotten much cooperation from those beach bums out there."

He stood, finished his coffee, and set the cup next to the Keurig on the credenza. "Thanks for the brew, Al. And the talk. Glad to have you back with us."

Al grinned wryly. It did feel as though he'd been lost somewhere for a while. And it was good to be back. He studied the map for a few minutes then began to list questions that he wanted answers to. When he'd written down every one he could think of, he reached for another book propped up on the shelf behind him between State of Wisconsin bookends.

Al worked for an hour, using every tool available to him to try and find the Range Rover the woman had purchased in Portland. His first call was back to Portland Autoplex, but when the phone rang and rang, he looked at his watch and realized it was only six thirty in the morning in Portland. *Better find something else to do for a while.*

For the next two hours, Al concentrated on completing two investigation reports. After he'd he filed the last one, he dialed the number for the luxury used car dealership in Portland and pushed the button to put the call on speaker.

The receptionist recognized his voice and immediately turned him over to the sales manager.

"Hi Detective, interested in a car?"

"No, but if you have a VIN for that Sentinel, I'd love it."

"I suspect I do. Hang on a minute."

Al listened to some maddening kind of new music as he twiddled his thumbs for what seemed like an hour.

"Got it right here; have a pen and pencil handy?"

A minute or so later, Al had written the number, repeated it back to the sales manager, and escaped from the phone, his ear tingling from the music and the guy's booming voice.

He searched the National Insurance Crime Bureau database, often the most effective way to track a vehicle. This time he was stymied. Nothing.

Damn, who would drive a car without insurance? Seems like a person would be crazy to do that.

But although he repeated the process, nothing.

Walking down the hall, he knocked on the chief's door and got an immediate, "C'mon in."

Al turned the knob and pushed into the room. "Hi, Chief. Need some help."

"Help? What kind of help?" The chief grimaced. "This has been one helluva day already, Al. Hope to hell you're not going to hit me with somethin' problematic."

"Nah, nothing like that. Just need some ideas." Al paused, but when the chief seemed disinclined to prompt him, he went on. "I got the VIN from the Seattle dealership that I told you about. Went on the National Insurance Crime Bureau database and did two searches. Didn't get any sort of hit. Any thoughts about next steps?"

"No hits? Damn, that's unusual. Hmmm, let me think. Have you done a state's APB? Guess that might be a next step for me."

"Makes sense."

"Start with the states we discussed and see what you get."

"I just wonder if the cops in those states will be observant enough. Heck, they don't even have speed limits in some of those places, right?"

"I know Montana didn't at one time, but I suspect that's long gone now. I'd make the notice pretty specific. Make sure you suggest the vehicle will probably be kept out of sight most of the time. Might want the patrol group in those states to ask their local cops, especially sheriffs' deputies, if they've seen any cars matching the description."

"Thanks, Chief, I'll do that."

Al had only gone a few steps down the hall, when the chief hollered, "Al, no Sentinels in any of those states?"

Al turned, went back to the chief's office, and lounged in the doorway. "There are Sentinels, all right, a few of 'em, but not a whole lot. And I didn't have one black one turn up."

"Well, it was worth a shot. Keep me informed on how the investigation goes, okay?"

"Will do."

Ten minutes later, Al had written and sent the APB to Oregon, grabbed his coat, and headed out the door.

Please, God, just one little break. He'd come back to the land of the living, but if he couldn't find a single lead that took him anywhere but straight into a dead end in his hunt for Genevieve Wangen, he wasn't sure just how long he'd be able to stay there.

s Sam left the mountain at dawn the next day, she was already lonesome for Pete. But she sang along with the radio as she traveled, and soon was in a brighter mood and anxious to see what the mail would bring. Alternating her route, she stopped first at Polson, then proceeded up the west side of Flathead to Kalispell and down the east to Finley Point and home. She picked up twenty-four envelopes addressed to Samantha Walters. None of the envelopes included a return address and all the addresses were typed.

Best that way. It meant that no one had a real idea of who they were from. And there likely were no fingerprints, either, since the senders would be careful.

Back at home in the late afternoon, she mixed herself the customary vodka-tonic and sat sipping it while she opened the mail. All the envelopes contained orders. Most were for customary sedatives, but two had special requests. The Gambino Family in New York had heard about the death-dealing spray she had made for Angelo Carbone, how she didn't know. The Trabia Family, doing business in San Francisco after leaving Italy two decades before, wanted something "exotic ... something that kills on contact ... something that can be administered from a distance."

She pondered that request for a time. Would the spray meet their demand? For it to work for the Trabias, she'd have to figure out how to make two adjustments. First, she had to increase the killing distance, and second, she would need to contain the flow to

45

a tiny stream, rather than letting the mixture disperse into the air as it did now.

She thought about that for a time, made a note to call a supplier the next day, and then decided it was time to find something for dinner.

A TV dinner—turkey, mashed potatoes, dressing, and gravy—satisfied her hunger. She finished the cleanup at eight thirty, showered, and went to bed.

The next day she drove south of Flathead Lake, turned off at a rest stop, and made a call to a firm in Los Angeles that distributed aerosol containers manufactured in China. She explained thoroughly, or so she thought, what she needed. The person on the other end of the line spoke broken English. Finally, her frustration growing, Sam asked to speak to a supervisor. A man with a pleasant-sounding voice who spoke unaccented English took the phone.

She carefully explained that she was looking for a personal-sized dispenser, but one that was extremely powerful and ejected its contents over a long distance.

"How do you define *long*, Madame?"

"Fifty feet, at a minimum."

He was silent a few seconds, as if considering her request. "Yes, perhaps we can do that. I will have to contact people in China. How can I get in touch with you?"

"When will you know?"

"Hmmm, let's see, it is now ten thirty in L.A. That means it is one thirty tomorrow afternoon in Beijing, so I should be able to get in touch with someone. I will likely have a response for you within twenty-four hours."

"Great." She gave him the number that he could use to text her. "I don't have signal where I live, but at ten thirty Pacific time tomorrow, I will drive to a place where there is signal to get the text."

"Excellent. Tell me exactly what information you are looking for."

"First, can the effective length of the spray be adjusted upward to between fifty and a hundred feet; second, can the stream be condensed so it doesn't disperse like it normally would; third, if those things can be done, how quickly could I obtain an order for fifty of the devices; and, fourth, how much will the per device cost be? Does all of that make sense to you?" A scratching sound, as though he was taking notes, reassured her.

"It does," he answered. "I will have a text waiting for you before noon tomorrow, hopefully."

Sam disconnected the call. A thrill of excitement rippled through her. This time tomorrow, she just might have what she needed to ensure all of her customers were very, very happy.

●━━ ·

Up early the next day, Sam went for a swim in the lake. Her friendly grizzly showed up a few feet down the beach but, as was customary, he came no closer, other than to acknowledge her with a deep-throated growl that she took as his good-morning greeting.

Breakfast finished, she went to work in the lab and stayed there until, checking her watch, she saw that it was already twelve fifteen Pacific time. She finished the order she was preparing, wiped her hands on her apron, and headed for the used Jeep she had acquired so she could keep the Sentinel for special occasions. She needed to get to Finley Point, where she could pick up a cell signal.

When she did, she discovered a text waiting. The Beijing firm had agreed that it could produce a high-powered aerosol container that provided a fifty-foot spray. The big problem was making certain the spray did not disperse in flight. That would require testing, which would delay the order up to a week, and the price would be triple her usual cost.

None of those things troubled her, with the exception of the idea that the spray might not hold together. She prepared and sent a text advising her importer that the tests should be conducted and, if the sprayer was perfected, she would increase her order to 150 canisters at the higher price.

That done, she returned home and continued working.

On Sunday morning, she woke with a smile on her face. Pete would be back tomorrow. Her heart felt as though it might leap from her chest at the thought of seeing him. And of having him almost completely to herself for the next three weeks. She used Sunday to tidy up, cut the grass, and fill the feeders.

The next morning, Pete's pickup drove into the yard promptly at 9:00 a.m. Sam ran across the yard and flung herself into his arms. When she stepped back, she reached for both his hands. "Are you up for a drive?"

"Hmm." He squeezed her hands. "I rather thought you might like a little morning sugar before we do anything else."

"As tempting as that thought is, I do need to ship some orders this morning," she told him, "and I should pick up mail, too. If you'd rather not go, I guess you can stay here." The latter sentence was accompanied by a pouting look that made him laugh.

"Okay, okay, I'll go," he said, chuckling. "I just thought you might be ready for some honey."

"Who says I'm not?" She let go of his hands and started for the Jeep. "Sex in a vehicle can be fun, too, you know?"

"No, I don't know," he replied. "I have never tried that."

She spun back around to stare at him in disbelief. "Really?"

"Really. When women pay good money for loving, they generally want to end up in a comfy bed, not in the back seat of a car like a couple of teenagers."

"Well, you have been missing out. It's fun to act like teenagers sometimes. Tell you what, help me load the Jeep and by sundown you will no longer be able to say that."

"I look forward to it, m'lady. Lead on." He swept an arm in the direction of the Jeep.

As they made their way up the east side of the Lake to Kalispell, Pete shifted in the passenger seat to face her. "Sam, you amaze me."

"Why's that?"

"You're a very mysterious woman." He ran a finger down the sleeve of her jacket. "It seems as if you make this drive a lot. You mail and pick up at each stop. Do you run some sort of mail-order business out of your house?"

She stared out the front window at the road ahead. *Am I ready to have this conversation with him?* "I do."

"How does that work?"

She shifted her gaze from the road to him. "What do you mean?"

"I've just never seen any evidence of that kind of business at your place. Where do you keep the product you sell, or the shipping supplies?"

Sam pursed her lips. "I'd rather show you than tell you. And I can't do that until I'm sure I can fully trust you. Can we talk about this more at dinner tonight?"

The rest of the trip passed quickly, and by the time they arrived home at four thirty, after a thirty-minute stop down an abandoned lane in a forest where she kept her promise to give him a new experience, the sun had drifted halfway down the sky beyond the lake. Over drinks, Sam sorted and opened the sixteen envelopes, then prioritized the orders and set them aside.

Supper was grilled Angus ribeyes, fried potatoes, canned green beans from her garden, and for dessert Sam had taken a cheesecake from the freezer.

When they'd finished, she took his hand and led him to the living room. She poured them glasses of Bailey's on the rocks as Pete got a fire going in the woodstove.

"Great dinner," said Pete, applauding as he walked over to join her on the couch. "Those steaks were as good as I have eaten, and I've been to some of the great steakhouses in this country."

Sam smiled. "I had incentive. I wanted to stoke up your energy as I'm expecting a great night."

"You'll get it," he promised as he took the glass she held out for him and sat down beside her. "Just give me a little time to recuperate from our adventures in the backseat this afternoon." He crossed his legs, resting an ankle on one knee. "So have you decided yet?"

She blinked. "Decided what?"

"Whether or not you trust me enough to tell me about yourself and what you do."

Sam bit her lip. Did she? She studied his face. The dark eyes that met hers were open and honest, appearing to hide nothing. She let out a breath. If she was going to share this much of her life with him, she would have to take a chance. "I'm less worried about whether I can trust you, and more worried that what I tell you will change the way you feel about me."

He set his glass on the coffee table, reached for her hand, and pressed the back of it to his lips. "Nothing could change the way I feel about you, love. Nothing."

We'll see. For the next hour and a half, Sam told him most of what there was to know about her life, her illegitimate birth, how she was raised by an aunt and uncle, had been married twice, and her background in pharmaceuticals."

"Drugs?" He played with the fingers of the hand he still held in his. "Why drugs?

"I moved to Wisconsin—to La Crosse on the Mississippi—to be near a niece, although she didn't know about me until much later," she told him. "I had to make some money, so I began working in a drugstore. I was lucky. The owner did a lot of compounding, making his own drugs from herbs, spices, and potions he kept on hand. I loved helping him. Finally, I got good enough at it that I could work on my own, which he fully supported. I worked there until meeting my second husband.

"Henry had a lot of money, and he adored me. He worked in an auto business near Chicago and he owned a huge house in the suburb of Arlington Heights. As a special surprise to me, he built me a lab. That started it. People heard about what I did and started to ask me to make things for them." She reached for her glass with her free hand and sipped her Bailey's. "Word spread, and I was busy as could be."

He crinkled his forehead. "So you worked for clinics and hospitals?"

"Some," she admitted, "but the majority of my customers were tiny operations, single-vet clinics, small-town docs, places like that."

"So you still make drugs for those types of businesses now?"

"Ummm, not so much." She gently tugged her hand from his and stood up to walk over to the woodstove. She pulled open the door and poked at the logs to get the fire going again. *Here we go.* When she was ready to face him, she shut the door with a clang and turned around. "I had a little trouble in Illinois and wound up living in Alabama. I got friendly with some folks who worked, how should I put it, either outside the law or on the wrong side of it."

The furrow in his forehead deepened. "You mean crooks?"

"I suppose. And underworld figures. In fact, I was about to marry into a mob family in the south when some lawmen I knew in Illinois came looking for me. My friends were kind enough to drop me off near Portland. I had purchased this place a few years earlier for just such a time."

"So you work for the mob?"

"I prefer to think of myself as an independent contractor, and I don't just do work for the mob, I have lots of customers. Although none, I'm afraid, has a very good reputation." She walked back to the couch. "But they pay me well and that allows me to live as I want."

"So where the hell do you make the stuff?" He glanced around the room as though he might find a work space tucked away in the corner. "You'd need a pretty big lab, wouldn't you?"

Sam held out her hand. "Come with me."

She took him into the cooler, then through the freezer. At the back of the spacious walk-in appliance, she pressed a hidden button and waited as a part of the back slid aside to reveal the sparkling, stainless-steel laboratory.

"My god!" Pete's eyes grew huge. "I don't believe it! There's no hint of it from either inside or outside the house. This is unbelievable. Sam, you are a woman of many surprises."

She tried to gauge his reaction to her revelations in his voice. It sounded like genuine surprise, even admiration, not condemnation. The muscles that had tightened up across her shoulders as she laid her life bare before him loosened up a little.

Pete wandered around the lab, touching everything he passed from the large, well-lit work table, to the shelves filled with bottles and jars, many of which he picked up and studied before replacing, to the machines and mixers that helped put together the creations.

He looked more and more dazed as he wandered. Finally he'd made his way around the room and stopped back in front of her. Reaching for her hands again, he looked into her eyes. "How many orders a year do you fill here?"

"I average seventeen a week right now," she told him, "so about nine hundred a year, right?"

"884."

Hmm. Impressive mind. That could be useful. "The numbers are growing," she said. "Next year might be more than one thousand."

He let out a low whistle. "That's a ton. What's the most you think you could handle?"

"That would be max - if I continued to work alone. Of course, if I had a good partner, who knows. Fifteen hundred? Eighteen hundred? Two thousand? Many more than I can produce now, that's for sure."

He tightened his grip on her hands and met her gaze steadily. "Could I be that partner?" he asked softly.

"I don't know." She lifted her shoulders. "Maybe. I'd have to see you work before knowing for sure."

"Then, if you will allow me, I would love to work with you, show you what I can do."

"We can give it a try. Tomorrow, though. Tonight we will just enjoy each other's company."

The tour finished, she walked him back to the house. "Mix me a gin-and-tonic, will you, please?" She waved a hand toward the kitchen. "Make whatever you want for yourself."

A few minutes later he had returned with her drink and a Jack and ice for himself. He chose the rocking chair and sat there rocking silently while he swirled the ice in his glass. When the drink was about two thirds gone, he looked at her. "You know, back home there are a lot of organized crime families who would love the stuff you make. We could probably double your production just by opening up Albania."

"Pete, I told you that ramping up production means that I will need a hard-working partner. That may be you; it may not be. I'm willing to consider it, but let's take things slowly, okay? Tomorrow we will begin to fill the orders that came in today. You can watch me work. Once you think you have the hang of it, I'll let you do a couple of things. This work isn't easy, and it has to be exact. Not everyone can do it."

"I understand. I was just thinking that your talent would be in great demand across the pond. The organizations in Europe are always fighting. I believe there is a lot of money to be made."

"I suspect you're right." She took another sip of her drink before setting the glass down on the table. "But until we find out that you can both do the job and want to do it, we're stuck with the customer base I have."

"Makes sense." He stopped rocking and got up. "No more talk about that tonight. Need another?"

She handed him her glass. He went to the kitchen and soon returned with freshly made cocktails for the two of them.

"You know, Pete, you make a great house-husband," joked Sam, trying to lighten the mood. "And you have other great talents, too, you know. My appetite for those is very high. How about we finish these drinks and head off to bed. I have plans for you."

"Ah, I too have plans. Missy, you're about to be tussled until you scream for relief."

She giggled. "That'd be the day. You're good, but I'm not sure even you can keep up with me. We'll soon find out."

The teasing went on as they lingered over their drinks. He came to the couch, edged in beside her, nuzzled her neck with his lips, cold from his drink, and mumbled sweet things to her as he worked down her neck. Meanwhile, his left hand crept up the gap between her legs. His touch was infuriatingly sexy, but the fact that she was wearing slacks was a real turn-off. She wanted his hand on her flesh.

"Mmm, Pete, gimme a minute, huh? I want to get into something more comfortable," she whispered.

"But I don't want to let you go," he gasped. "I'm getting comfortable."

"You'll be more comfortable in a couple of minutes, I promise."

Extricating herself from his embrace, she fled to the bedroom, rifled through her drawer, and found her powder-blue negligee, made of a material so flimsy and transparent that it was like gossamer. Quickly she changed, dabbed a few drops of perfume here and there, and was back to him in under three minutes.

"Mmm." His gaze was appreciative. "Much, much better. Now let's see, where was I?"

Moving her to his lap, he kissed her deeply, his right hand moving down from her shoulder to her breast, while his left hand began again to widen the slight valley made by her legs. Steadily, his hand explored her legs, moving ever upward. Soon he was exploring her recently shaven mound. And then his fingers found their way to her most sensitive spot, stopped there, and the sensation was, well, incredible.

"Pete, Pete, easy; I'll be finished before we start," she moaned.

"That's the idea." He smiled. "You can finish as many times as you want; I'll just keep going."

Apparently, that was true, because soon she abandoned her efforts to stop the sensations before they overcame her and gave her body over to his ministrations. And that led to a wild night. In fact, it was well after 3:00 a.m. when he finally carried her to bed.

Fully sated, Sam curled up under the blankets and let sleep overtake her.

●━━━•

The sun was high in the sky when Sam awake. Her eyes still closed, she listened to the birds, which were creating a cacophony of sound so loud it seemed as if a feathered train was storming through the bedroom.

Beside her, Pete propped his head on his hand and tickled her nose with his tongue, teasing her more fully awake. When his hand began roaming over her body, she attempted to slap it away, then relaxed under his touch.

"If we're going to do this again," she said, yawning, "you're going to have to be slow and gentle. I hurt."

"My, my, is that a message of surrender?" he asked tenderly. "Last night you went to sleep gasping for more. As I recall, you were unhappy when I called a halt; you nearly threw me out."

"That was then. I didn't know what I was doing; I was drunk with passion. This is now, and I hurt."

And so the morning lovemaking was tender, light, and effortless. She arched up to meet his touches, and when he entered her, he did so smoothly.

"Hmm," she mumbled. "You really are something; you might be able to keep up with me after all."

"*You* are something." He rolled onto his back and laughed. "Actually, you are insane. Last night it was as if you couldn't get enough. I shifted gears several times and you were still pleading for more. That's when I said, 'Enough!'"

"I remember," she said into the hair of his chest. "I didn't want to stop; l wanted it to go on forever. You are a marvelous lover. I just have to learn not to use you all up in one go."

"I don't mind you trying." He grinned and lifted her fingers to his lips.

Sam's stomach growled. "I don't know about you, but I'm hungry. And a light breakfast isn't going to do it today."

"Not for me, either." He let go of her hand and tossed back the covers. "But let me cook for you. You rest; I'll deliver."

He did, returning a half hour later with a tray laden with eggs, ham, hash browns, juice, and coffee for two. It might have been the best breakfast Sam had ever had, and she told him so.

"Then maybe I've earned my keep today?" His eyes gleamed.

"Not a chance. Today you learn to become a lab rat, remember?"

"Of course." He swung his legs over the side of the bed and reached for his robe. "We must get at those orders."

She grasped his arm. "Remember, this is serious business," she cautioned. "We will take our time, and no fooling around. There will be plenty of time for that later, when the work is done, do you hear me?"

He patted her hand. "Kjo eshte ajo qe ju mendoni se."

"What?" she asked, screwing her face into a frown that made him laugh.

"I just spoke to you in Albanian," he said. "You better learn the language if we're going to do business there."

With his prediction of business expansion hanging in the air, Sam let go of him and climbed out of bed. In the bathroom, she grabbed her bikini bottoms from the shower rod. "I'm going to the lake for a dip. Want to come along?"

"Not if I have to wear clothes."

"Go as you want, and at your peril." Laughing, she fled the room, pushed through the front door of the cabin, and headed down the path.

Stripping off his boxers, Pete followed her out and chased her down the path. If anyone or anything saw them frolicking, it was the moose or the grizzlies, because the lake was devoid of human traffic, as it always was.

Al glanced at his watch, thumbed through his calendar, shook his head, and sat back in his chair to think. His suit pants were freshly pressed, a nice lightweight material in midnight blue. His red-striped tie was carefully tied. All in all, he looked the picture of a put-together man of success. The problem? That wasn't the case.

Two days had passed since he had sent his inquiry to Oregon, asking for information on any black Land Rover Sentinels. No one had responded. He had just finished sending the same message to law enforcement offices in Washington and Idaho.

When he had messaged agencies in Oregon, he had been hopeful. Now that feeling had been robbed by the silence and Al was worried that nothing he did would produce any hint of Genevieve Wangen's whereabouts.

He looked at his watch again. Nine-thirty. The day had barely begun and he was as frustrated as he usually was at day's end. Now what? Charlie. That's what I need, a taste of Berzinski realism.

He picked up the phone. "Hey, man, what're ya up to?"

He held the phone away from his ear as his boisterous colleague let him have it with both barrels.

"The day sucks, and it ain't even started yet." The voice was so loud that Al moved from behind his desk to shut his office door.

"I feel the same way; what's making your day such a problem?"

"The old man—Sheriff Hooper—thinks I oughta go over to Barre Mills and see what I can find out about some house break-ins

57

in that area. That's a duty for rookies, ain't it? Hell, man, I'm a veteran."

"Well, ya know, big guy, every once in a while us veterans have to take a turn in the tank. Want some company?"

"Really? You wanna go along? Hell, yes, I want company. Hallelujah, the day is looking up."

Al was waiting at the curb when Charlie pulled his SUV up close to allow his friend to hop in. Three hours later they had delivered the suspected burglar—who'd started confessing as soon as they shown up in uniform at his front door—to the La Crosse County Law Enforcement Center and Al was feeling better about the day.

He and Charlie had a chance to talk on the way to Barre Mills, and the big man had urged him to let things rest for a while.

"Who knows what's goin' on out there," he told Al. "Just let it simmer. You'll hear when there's something to be told." He pulled to the curb outside the police department and gave Al one more dose of Berzinski prophecy. "Ya know, Al, I got a good feeling about this West Coast thing. I think we're gonna get her this time. So I think what you oughta do is go back into your office and work on some other things until you get word from the folks out west, then we'll figure out what we're going to do after that."

"Guess you're right, Charlie, but this waiting business is for the birds. I want action."

"Let it simmer, Al. Just let it simmer."

Al walked into his office a few minutes after one, hung up his coat, and moved to the desk. He found several files and a stack of messages waiting for him.

As he sorted the messages, one stopped him short and he leaned back in his chair and stared at it. "Well, I'll be damned."

10

Sam reached the lawn and stopped short. Her bird feeders had been torn down and strewn about the lawn, and the hay she used to feed moose, elk, and deer littered the lawn. Just disappearing into the bushes was a grizzly bear, a big grizzly, too, bigger than the one she thought of as her friend. She yelled to Pete, waited for him to join her, then showed him the mess.

"Bear?"

"I saw one leaving, which is why I screamed. Damn, is this going to be a problem?"

"Doesn't have to be." He was struggling into the jeans and boots he had left on a stump. "You go on in. I'll pick up the mess, fill the feeders, and join you in the lab."

Sam nodded and headed into the house. She grabbed a stack of mail off the kitchen counter then made her way to the back of the walk-in freezer and activated the hidden switch. Once in the lab, she set down the mail—the sixteen orders they'd picked up the day before—on the gleaming, stainless steel counter.

In a few minutes, Pete came in and rolled up his sleeves. Busy sorting the orders, Sam talked as she worked, explaining to him what she was doing.

"So Pete, I've laid out the orders the way we will fill them. We work from bottom to top, right to left, okay? The next step is to get out the materials we will need to fill the orders. Those, too, I have set out in priority order so I can do my work quickly."

The selection of the drugs and potions was done with meticulous care - select, check, check again. Once, when Pete picked up a container to read the label, she slapped his hand. "Leave those alone! We do things carefully here. I'll tell you what I'm using when I'm using it. You can see the containers before I put 'em away, okay?"

Suitably contrite, Pete retreated to a stool and sat down to watch. When she glanced over at him, he appeared entranced as he watched her careful process in getting things ready.

When the selection was complete, Sam moved the first letter to a bench across from the one holding the orders and containers before checking the labels again and moving the ones she would use to the table where she worked.

"Compounding is an art. That's what I do. And that's why my work is in demand."

"What's compounding?"

"It's creating drugs from raw materials. Depending on the order, I crush, mix, and/or liquefy. That's basically what compounding is. Using raw materials to create a useful tablet, powder, or liquid. This first order is for Propofol, a liquid mostly used by vets to anesthetize animals. I doubt this order is for animals, though."

Picking up the containers one by one, she said, "Propofol is made of isobutylene, a liquid, triphenylantimony crystals, and isopropyl ether, another liquid. This one is very dangerous. It's highly explosive, so I handle it with great care."

Gingerly, she used a mortar and pestle to crush the carefully measured crystals into a fine powder. Working with great precision, she slowly added the liquids, carefully measured, to a container, then tapped the mortar to free the crushed crystals into the liquid. When that was done, she poured the now yellowish liquid into a small bottle, tightened the cap, and returned the order to another section of the preparation table and placed the filled bottle on top of it.

"I had no clue it was so sensitive. Is this how all medicines are made?"

"Yes and no. The steps are the same, but the big pharmaceutical houses mix large batches of these drugs so they have them on hand when orders come in. They would separate manufacturing, packaging, and dispatch functions. Here I do it all, one step at a time. It's a touchy business, potentially fatal. I work very carefully. There is no room for sloppiness."

"I can see that." He watched as she began the second order. By the time noon rolled around, ten orders were ready to package for mailing.

As she prepared to work on the eleventh order, she turned to him. "Pete, how about making some sandwiches? I don't eat back here for obvious reasons, but when they're ready, call me and we'll eat inside."

Twenty minutes later he called her to come to the kitchen. Sam took a big bite of the BLT he'd put together. It was delicious. "I may want you to cook for me all the time."

"I did most of the cooking in Albania, whenever I was home."

"Well, you certainly have the knack. You must think my cooking pretty boring."

When they had finished, Pete cleaned up the dishes while Sam returned to the lab, instructing him to join her as soon as he finished. Twenty minutes later, he was back on his stool, watching her.

As the clock turned to three, she began the fifteenth order of the day. She handed him the letter. "Your turn."

Although he snatched the paper from her hand, it shook as he handled it.

He's nervous. Good. That will make him more careful. Sam almost smiled, remembering how nervous she'd been too, when Mr. Thompson, the druggist, had first started allowing her to help him.

Pete studied the paper carefully then selected the containers he needed from the few left on the preparation table. Responding to her directions, he mixed the order under her supervision and stood back to allow her a closer look.

"Perfect. Bottle it and put it over there. Then you can get to work on the last one."

The last order called for a complicated product that contained seven ingredients. Pete had to crush two ingredients and do a double mix in the final prep. He worked with extreme focus, precisely measuring each ingredient. She was extremely pleased. He had picked things up quickly and he was meticulous in everything he did.

They cleaned up the lab together, restoring every container to its proper place. They each took one container, boxed it, prepared the invoice, then wrapped the package and attached the printed label. By the second round, Pete had picked up the process well enough to become a real help. He took care of the first three processes, leaving the wrapping and addressing for Sam. Soon the job was done.

"Great work. Pete, I'm proud of you. You did very well."

His face lit up. "So will I make a good assistant … do you think?"

"Too early to tell, but I'm very encouraged." She set the last package down on the counter with the others. "How about we forget work for a while. Let's go swimming."

"Great idea."

They left the cabin and walked to the lake in their work clothes. Soon they were swimming nude and reveling in the icy coolness of the water.

"You know," he told her, blowing water out his mouth, "I could get pretty used to this life."

"I hope you do. If you keep learning like you did today, I'll have to consider making you a full partner. And that would mean I would have to renegotiate with Molly."

"Sam, I am owned by nobody. You must remember that. I enjoy my role with the two of you, but I alone decide what is good for Pete."

"You're right, I'm sorry."

He smiled. "Don't be sorry, just understand. I love this life. Who could be upset with two women like you and Molly? I just don't want everyone to think I'm a kept man. Can you understand that?"

"Of course."

For the next hour, they teased each other as they swam. Neither was ready to go inside. They'd had a hard night and a hard work day, too, and the cool lake water was a great rejuvenator.

Swimming close to her, Pete splashed her cheek with a spray of water. "You're not so mysterious as you think, you know, out here in your secret hideaway. Already I can read you like a book."

"Oh you can, can you? Then tell me what this means." With a quick movement of her arm, she splashed water in his direction. The spray fell short. "Damn. How the hell could anyone miss something that big?"

"I presume you're referring to my manhood?"

"No, dammit! Your head."

He grabbed her and dunked her, lifting her quickly out of the water and laughing as she tried to wiggle from his grasp. At last, he pulled her close.

"You'd better be good the rest of the day or I'll bring you back out here and the next time you won't get off so easy."

"Yes, sir." She gasped for breath while trying hard to salute. "I suppose you think you're going to discipline me, don't you?"

"That will depend entirely on you." He made his way to the edge of the lake and splashed onto the shore. Stooping down, he scooped up his clothes then straightened and headed for the cabin.

Laughing, Sam ran from the lake, water dripping off her body, bent swiftly to retrieve her clothes, and followed him up the path.

Once inside, she chased him into the bedroom, tackled him, and drove him to the bed. For the next two hours their antics were wild but tender. At last, spent, they fell back on the pillows.

"My oh my, a great helper, cook, and this, too. I am going to have to keep you around. I knew what I was missing, but had no idea the cure would be this good."

"Hmmm," he murmured into her ear. "This is just the beginning."

Sam snuggled closer and closed her eyes. Just as she was about to drift off, the most outrageous noises she had ever heard Julie make jolted her upright. Not only was he caterwauling, he was flying around the cabin, leaping from window to window.

Sam tensed. "What in the world?"

11

They've found me again. She knew
that working for the mafia was an
incredibly lucrative venture, but it also
had its distinct disadvantages, chief among
them being that she drew the ire of other mob families
when they figured out who had supplied their enemies with deadly
chemical weapons. As well-hidden as she sought to be, she had been
tracked down and her home had been ambushed twice before. No
one had ever found this place though. Was she about to be driven
from another home she loved?

Sam rolled from the bed and went to the window, where Julie
had finally settled and stood, front paws on the sill, peering through
the glass. At first, she saw nothing, then something at the edge of
her vision moved, and she refocused just in time to see what she was
sure was a cougar move into the forest.

"So that's what had you upset? That was one big pussycat." The
muscles that had tightened up all over her body relaxed. She'd take a
four-legged intruder over a two-legged one any day. She smiled and
petted Julie's head. What a watch cat he had become since she moved
to the mountains. Nothing got past the male cat with a female name.
If there was any sort of visitor to the house in the woods, Julie knew
it immediately and wailed for his mistress.

Sam wrapped herself in a robe and headed for the kitchen,
pausing in the bedroom doorway to look back. Somehow Pete had
managed to stay asleep through all that noise, so she lowered her

voice and spoke to Julie. "Want some food, you living alarm clock? Oh, you do. Well, then, follow me."

An hour later, she was busy in the kitchen when Pete walked into the room. Sam glanced at the clock on the wall. Almost six thirty. Early for him, but she was happy to see him. He came to greet her with a kiss, but backed away quickly.

Sam frowned. "What's wrong?"

He laughed, reached for her hands, and held them up. They were covered in flour. Sam looked down at herself. Dabs of the white powder dotted her sleeves and apron, too.

"You know," he nodded at the flour canister on the counter, "if that wasn't there, I might think you are into something illegal."

Sam put on her most innocent look. "Who, me?" She soaked her hands in the sink, dried them, shook the flour off her apron, and gave him a proper kiss.

"Pete, you were an amazing student yesterday. You picked up on what I was doing faster than anyone I have known."

"My goal is to make more progress today, and the rest of the week. Then maybe you will make me a partner."

"I think you can safely assume that offer will come, but it takes more than the two of us to approve it, you know. What will Molly say?"

His brow furrowed. "I think Molly will be most upset about losing me from her bed. I suppose the money is nice for her, but I've worked for her for a while. She's good at business. I'm guessing she has salted plenty away. If we tell her our plans and she rebels, maybe we can provide her with a personal day every now and then."

"But maybe not too often."

"We'll discuss it with her." He wrapped his arms around her waist and drew her close. "But don't give that away until you have to. Your business is really exciting. Not sure when I've enjoyed a day more. I want to learn all there is to know."

"And I'm happy to teach you. But right now, I'm thinking about later. If I tell you the only thing you have to do this evening is mix drinks, will you be okay with that?"

"Shume e drejte."

She stamped her slippered foot against the wooden floor. "Doggone it, Pete, cut it out. My grandma used to do that to me all the time. She spoke in German because she knew I didn't understand. I want to understand every word you say, so speak English, okay?"

"I'm not gonna promise. What I said was 'damn right' in Albanian." He let go of her and backed up until he was leaning against the island. "Speaking of Albania, there is a lot of money to be made there. I say it again because I want to be certain you are hearing what I'm saying. A few of my old friends got involved with the mob. I don't know what they are doing now, but I'll bet they're still working for them, if they're alive. If we get to the point where we want to extend our reach over there, maybe I should head home on a business development trip?"

"First things first. For now, you need to concentrate on learning the business. But it is a good idea. If we do get to that point, then yes, a trip would be great."

"Will you come along?"

"Nope, I'm a USA gal. I've had my share of international travel and I'm home to stay. But a visit for you might make sense."

They worked diligently through the day. Pete handled four orders on his own with no trouble. To demonstrate that he was earning her trust, when afternoon came, she told him to finish the last two orders and she would see about dinner. She was busy cooking when he came into the kitchen.

Tilting back his head, he inhaled deeply. "Mmm. Something smells amazing." He set a vodka-tonic on the counter beside her. "The orders are done, how about dinner?"

He reached for the lid on a pan on the stove, but she gently pushed his hand away. "Dinner is a surprise. Just enjoy your drink. In fact, why don't you take it out on the porch? I'll join you in a couple of minutes."

"Don't forget to check the orders I prepared." Pete picked up her drink and carried both of the glasses out onto the porch.

She checked the orders before joining him. Her feet ached from standing all day, and she sank onto a chair with a groan. Pete handed her the drink he'd brought out for her and she lifted it in his direction. "To you, and the great progress you are making."

He clinked his glass to hers before they both took a sip. Sam leaned back, enjoying the view of the back of the property and, from the corner of her eye, of Pete. "I saw a cougar on the property early this morning."

His hand jerked and a few drops of drink splashed onto his jeans. "What? When? I was with you all night."

"You were sleeping. Julie woke me and I went to the window and caught a glimpse of it." She set her glass down on the arm of the chair. "I have to admit I was a little nervous when she first started yowling. I've had two different hideouts discovered and invaded by men working for the mob, so now I'm pretty alert to any sign of trouble."

A look of chagrin crossed his face. "Then I should be as well. I'm sorry I slept through that."

She lifted her shoulders. "It's not your fault. When you live on the edge of danger, as I do, you develop the instinct to smell it out. That will come for you the longer you work for me."

He set his glass down too and leaned forward, elbows on his knees. "I was found out in the night one time as well."

"Really?" Her eyebrows rose. "Do tell."

"I made the mistake of falling in love with the wife of a powerful politician. He was in local government then got a powerful national position when the Republic of Albania was created in 1991. He was gone almost all the time and his wife—nearly as beautiful as you—was left with three children and no social life. Someone recommended me to her when she needed some handyman chores done. One thing led to another and soon we were in bed. I believe she liked it. And I liked being the favorite of a beautiful and powerful woman."

"How did it end?"

"The way it always ends. Her husband found out. In fact, one of my former friends told him. He came looking for me with a gun. Fortunately, she sent a message with another friend and when he arrived at my mother's house, I was gone and my mother had no idea where I was. At least he was decent enough not to take it out on her. I fled north to Paris, then to London. No matter where I went he found out. So I borrowed money from my uncle, sailed to the States, and worked my way across the country to Kalispell. When I arrived, I gave myself a new name to reflect that fact that I had a new life now. In Albania, I was Agim. When I got here, I became Peter."

"I've had a few names, too," she admitted. "I've been Genevieve, Rosalie, Savannah, and now I'm Samantha, Sam. I like Sam."

"I do, too."

Sam leaned forward and grasped his hands. "Thank you for sharing that story with me. I find myself wanting to know everything there is to know about you. And wanting to share with you about myself which, believe me, is not usual."

"Then I appreciate it all the more." He leaned in and kissed her.

When he lifted his head, she took a deep breath. "If you'll excuse me, I'm going to check on dinner."

Peter nodded and picked up his drink.

When she was satisfied everything was ready, Sam slid open the patio door. "All set. Come on in."

Peter pushed to his feet and followed her inside. "Smells wonderful, like home!"

"It better. I'm serving what I hope is traditional Albanian fare."

"Let me guess." He wrinkled his nose as he sniffed, making her laugh. "My bet is tave-kosi and tave-elbasani."

"What the heck is tave-kosi and tave-elbisi?"

"It's tav-e-kOsi and tav-e-L-be-see, which is roasted lamb and yogurt. Is that it?"

"Close. The main course is a lamb stew prepared with yogurt. The stew will be served with rice cooked in vegetable broth, as well as eggplant. I even managed to find a couple bottles of Rakia, which I hear is a favorite drink in Albania. And for dessert, sweet cakes with honey." She held her breath. Would it please him?

"I can't believe you did all this for me." His voice was husky, as though he had a lump in his throat.

Warmth rushed through her chest. "You've done so much for me; I wanted to find a way to thank you. We will start with the Rakia, and then with dinner I found a couple of what I am told are excellent Albanian wines."

His eyes widened. "Where the hell did you find those?"

"A liquor store in Missoula ordered them for me. I go there about once a month, and I wanted something special to go with this dinner."

He took her face in his hands and kissed her, then whispered in her ear, "Thank you, dritë e syrit."

Sam swallowed hard. Maybe she didn't need to know what every word he said meant. This time she could read the translation in his eyes.

They enjoyed their Rakia, or grape brandy, as the manager of the liquor store had explained to her. Dinner was very tasty, the wine was great, and the dessert rounded things out nicely.

"My god." Pete rubbed his stomach as he pushed himself away from the table. "I am stuffed. That was wonderful, Sam, as good as my mother makes. You are a woman of surprises."

"Don't expect Albanian food for every meal, or even that I'm going to cook all the time. You do pretty well yourself. I love the way you cook, so you're not off the hook."

"Yeah, yeah, I know. I'm number two in this house."

"And don't you forget it. Now, since I cooked, I believe you are on to do the dishes."

●——— •

Over the next three weeks, Pete proved to be an exceptional intern, to the point that on the final Friday he was with her, he handled all of the preparation. Sam concentrated on the packaging, although she checked each order carefully to make sure everything had been done correctly.

Following dinner on his last night with her, while they were sitting on the porch talking, Pete reached for her hand. "Sam, I really don't want to leave. What if I were to stay? I mean, I'd have to go home and take care of some things, but I could do that early tomorrow and be back before noon. I just love it here; it's home."

She sighed. "I'll miss you, but I think you have to go. Perhaps Sunday I should go in and have a talk with Molly. Might as well cross that bridge now. You're a tremendous help. Suddenly this is all fun again."

"I could go with you to talk to her."

Sam shook her head. "That's one I have to handle myself. I have to make this my idea. I don't want her anger reflecting back on you."

"I appreciate that, Sam, but Molly is a good friend. I'd like her to know that I'm not running out on her. It's just that, with you, there's no need to have any other women. I do want her to know how much I appreciate all she has done for me though."

Sam contemplated him for a moment before nodding. "I'll make sure she understands that."

"Good." He squeezed her hand before letting her go and leaning back in his chair.

Sam crossed one leg over the other and reached for her glass of wine. "So you think the European mobs would be interested in our products?"

"I'd bet on it. I don't think any of them have access to this kind of ..." he paused, as though searching for the right words, "... business persuasion tools. I think they'd pay a lot to get their hands on some of these drugs. The big issue will be trying to restrict the interest to one mob in each of the areas."

"And how would you define these *areas*?"

"Well, Europe is essentially divided into four of them, north, south, east, and west. Russia has a lot of organized crime. Then there's China and Japan, maybe even New Zealand and Australia."

Sam's mind was spinning. "I never even thought about all of those possibilities. Of course, if we tried to expand into all of those countries, we wouldn't be able to handle the business. There's some danger in growing too quickly. But I would hate to turn down any opportunities."

They sat there, silently rocking as the sun slipped behind the mountains. The birds quieted as darkness closed in, but it was so peaceful the two of them stayed where they were, content in their own thoughts.

Finally, Sam broke the silence. "Pete, when I was in New Orleans, I became very friendly with the Carbone family. They control Louisiana, although they have done a lot to legitimize their dealings. I wonder if either Don Angelo, or his son and heir apparent, Dino, would be interested in joining us in an expanded venture. I've done lots of things for Angelo, and he has done lots for me, too. What do you think?"

A thoughtful look crossed Pete's face. "You know, it's easy to get carried away when you've just had a great dinner and a few drinks. I think one step at a time might be a better approach. As I see it, it starts with our talk with Molly. If that goes well, we can make plans for me to go to Albania. We can put out feelers there and, if we get some business, see how it goes. If we do well and the feedback is good, we can consider ways to build up our client base, and figure out who is going to help us in the business. Make sense?"

"It does. We should both be very cautious of moving too fast. Absolutely, first Molly. Then we can think about next steps."

She sat quietly for a while, sipping on her wine, before setting down the glass. "If you move in, what will happen with your place? You've got animals, don't you?"

"Yes, twenty-three head of beef and four horses, a couple of pigs, too. And I grow a little hay and corn, just enough to feed the animals. The beef makes me some money and keeps my belly full. I love to ride the horses. The pigs are messy, but their pork sure tastes good." He reached for the bottle of wine on the table and refilled both their glasses. "To be honest, I've been thinking about that. I have a good friend in Kalispell who thinks I have the greatest deal in the world. He wants to own a place like mine. Maybe he and his wife could move into the house and run the place. He works construction in summers, but has winters off. That might be one solution."

"Sounds like it could work. I might go see Molly tomorrow, after you leave, instead of waiting until Sunday." She rocked forward in the chair and rested her hands on his knees. Now that they had a plan in place, she couldn't wait to get started on it. All they had to do now was get Molly to agree to let him go. "Pete, pray that Molly will be understanding. Pray long … and hard."

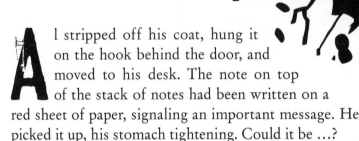

A l stripped off his coat, hung it on the hook behind the door, and moved to his desk. The note on top of the stack of notes had been written on a red sheet of paper, signaling an important message. He picked it up, his stomach tightening. Could it be …?

The memo was from the office receptionist. *A Lieutenant Munson with the Missoula, Montana, Police Department, called. He thinks he may have seen a Land Rover like the one you inquired about. You are to call him at 406-593-2200.*

Yes. YES. Al snatched up the phone so fast he almost sent the receiver flying. He dialed the number and asked for Lieutenant Munson, drumming his fingers on the desk as he waited. After a few minutes, a soft-spoken man came on the line. "Tad Munson."

"Hi, Lieutenant. It's Al Rouse from the La Crosse Police Department in Wisconsin. I received your message and I'm anxious to talk with you."

"Hi, Detective. Let's dispense with the formalities, okay? I'm still not used to being called Lieutenant. Tad fits me much better."

"I feel the same way, Tad, so call me Al. The note I got says you may have seen a vehicle like the one I'm interested in?"

"Yes, sir, I did. Beautiful vehicle, looked like it was floating on a cloud. Must have some suspension system, which would be very useful out here."

Blood pounded in Al's ears. "The vehicle I'm looking for, according to the dealer, has been completely refitted. It's more like a luxury tank, I'm told. The suspension system was among the items redone, so it sounds like you might have seen the one I'm looking for."

"Sure could be. Vehicle I saw drifted right over the potholes that plague us out here twelve months of the year."

"Any chance you noticed if the driver was male or female?"

"Definitely a female. No question about that."

Al clutched the receiver tightly. "That's excellent news. If it's the one we're looking for, she's a suspect in fourteen murders in our community."

Tad let out a low whistle. "Fourteen murders? How has she not been brought in yet?"

"We had her in custody—twice, actually—and she escaped both times. The first time she drugged me, the second time the mob sent their men, dressed as cops, to sign her out of prison under the guise of transporting her to the airport in New Orleans for extradition to Wisconsin. They did take her to the airport, but she did not end up in Wisconsin. We know she landed somewhere in the Northwest, but we lost her in Portland."

"Wish I'd known all that when I saw her. Although, based on what you said, maybe I'm glad I didn't."

"She's slippery, that's for sure. I'm anxious to hear anything you can tell me about her."

A squeaking sound came through the phone, as though the lieutenant had leaned back in his chair. "About two weeks ago, I was down in Missoula—we're headquartered in Kalispell—and I stopped at the post office to mail some thank you cards, as my wife and I have just had our first baby."

He paused as if waiting for a response to that news.

"Congratulations," Al duly offered. *Come on, come on.*

"Thank you. Anyway, as I was walking out, a very attractive woman came in carrying a number of packages. I remember that well, because I offered to help her carry them and she rather brusquely dismissed my offer, not nastily but curtly. She was stunning. Auburn hair, about five foot five, well built with an angelic face. I walked back to the car, made some radio calls to headquarters, and while

I was communicating, she came out and got into a Sentinel—black with traces of green. I took special note because there were no plates. I was about to go talk to her about that when I noticed the Montana 'applied for' tag in the back window. I didn't think another thing about it until your message made the rounds."

"From your description, I think she's our gal. Sure sounds like it, at least. Was there anything else about her that you remember?"

"She had a mole."

"Like a beauty mark, you mean?"

"Yeah, a black mark on her left cheek, near her mouth."

"Like Marilyn Monroe?"

Tad paused. "Marilyn Monroe?"

Al repressed a sigh. "I'm guessing you're too young to have known Marilyn Monroe."

There was a soft laugh on the line, then Tad said, "Yes sir, just graduated from the University of Montana and qualified for lieutenant's bars when I tested out of the police academy."

"Too bad, you're missing out. In any case, it sure sounds like this could be the one. You only saw her the once?"

"That's right. Just once. Believe me, I would have known if I'd seen her again."

"So how do we go about finding that Sentinel in Montana?"

"Well, given what you've told me, I should be able to use the license-applied-for status to see what I can find. Of course I'll also keep my eyes open in case she drives by me again."

"I'd appreciate that. But look as quietly as you can. I'd hate for her to get an early warning that we're on to her."

"I will. And I'll check with the Missoula Post Office, too. Maybe she's a regular customer there."

"Good idea. Just make it clear to the person you talk to that, as this is an ongoing investigation, they need to stay quiet about it."

"Count on it. I should be able to get back to you within a few days. I might just drive down to Helena, the state capitol, and visit the license bureau myself."

"That'd be great. Thanks a million for your help. If you do see her again, remember this is one dangerous woman. Be careful."

"Yes sir, I will."

Al replaced the receiver, rose from his chair, did a bit of a dance step, then stopped and looked around. *Hope no one saw that.* Content that he was alone, he straightened his chair, and walked out of his office whistling.

Chief Brent Whigg looked up, eyes wide, when Al strode into his office, pulled up a chair, and sat. "You're whistling? What's up, new grandkid?"

"Nope, not a grandkid. But something big." He paused. "We just might have her."

The chief stared at him. "Who, the old lady? You got a lead on the old lady?"

"I believe I do, Chief. She might have been spotted in western Montana."

"Well, I'll be damned. Tell me everything."

Al related his conversation with Tad Munson. When he finished, the chief wiped his brow with his hanky, sat back, and folded his hands behind his head. "I'll be a son-of-a-bitch. Al, this is great news. Have you told Charlie and Rick?

"No, I just got off the phone and came straight here. Thought we should talk about it before I call anyone else."

"So this Tad Munson. Savvy guy?"

"I think so. Very young, but seemed to know what he's doing. I'd say he's already moving forward with steps to try and track her down."

"I hope she doesn't get wind of the chase. He'll be careful, right?"

"We talked about it. He said he'd be very careful. I think he will."

The chief rubbed his forehead again, blew his nose, and stuffed his hanky in his back pocket.

"Hate to say it, Al, 'cause I suspect you won't be happy, but it seems to me there's nothing for us to do here until we find out more."

"No argument, Chief. Heck, maybe she was just passing through. Maybe she's in Wyoming, or the Dakotas. Question is, what do I tell Charlie and Rick?"

"I think you gotta tell them what you have. They deserve to

know. Just make sure they keep it to themselves. We don't even want 'em talking to their wives, do we?"

"No, we don't. Their wives are close to Julie Sonoma, Genevieve's niece. I don't think she'd try to find her aunt and tell her, but you never know. Best to be cautious."

Al left the Chief's office and was almost back to his office, when it hit him. *Damn, what a dunce I am. I know exactly what I'm going to do while I'm waiting to hear back from Tad.*

When Sam woke, she had a vague recollection of Pete kissing her goodbye and leaving the bedroom, although she hadn't been fully conscious at the time. She had slept dreamlessly and was feeling very comfortable in her bed. After Pete's kiss, she had snuggled into his pillow, still bearing the scent of him, and settled in. It was after nine when she woke up again. *Time to get the day underway.*

After her swim, she ate a slice of toast, made the bed, did the little cleaning, and gathered up the packages they had filled the day before, anxious to get to Kalispell and talk to Molly. Along the way she would mail the packages. After loading up her vehicle, she headed up the east side of the lake. The day was another beautiful one, cloudless and crisp, and to her left Flathead Lake looked like a giant mirror, reflecting images that assured her the mountains were in wonderful form.

In Kalispell an hour and a half later, she headed for the Golden Lion. As she approached the desk, the young male clerk waved, then began to look in his reservations file.

"No, no, Mark, I'm here to see Molly. It's not a scheduled visit, so I don't even know if she's around."

"She's around. I think I just saw her heading into the restaurant. Might be having breakfast."

"I'll take a look," she replied, thanking him with a sweet smile.

Molly was just pouring syrup on a stack of pancakes when Sam entered the dining room.

"Hey, Sam," she called, waving. "Had breakfast?" When Sam shook her head, Molly pointed to the chair across from her. "Join me. I could use the company."

Sam sat down and the waiter immediately set a steaming cup of coffee at her place then took her order for eggs over easy, bacon, and toast.

Molly stabbed her fork into a piece of sausage. "Damn, I'm hungry. Had a strenuous night; need to replace some calories."

Sam handed the waiter her menu and leaned back in her chair. "Hmmm, and just what were you doing?"

"Yup, that's it." Molly punctuated her statement with laughter. "Let your mind wander to your most carnal thoughts. We acted them out and then some."

Sam laughed, too, at the rapturous look on Molly's face. "Do tell."

Molly set down her fork. "Oh, m'god, Sam, I met the best-ever cowboy. He just happened to wander in to play the slots about ten last night. It was pretty slow around here and I stopped to say hi as I walked through the casino. Well, one thing led to another, and then another, and then, oh my ..."

"Must have been special. Not sure I've ever seen you this wound up."

"Oh, it was special, all right. I don't think this dude had been off the range for a couple of years, the way he acted. He rode me up one side, down the other, and didn't turn me loose until after I'd lost my voice."

"I sensed the hoarseness. He's just passing through?"

"Nah, that's the best part. Says he's sick of herding cattle and sleeping on the ground. He took a job as manager of the UPS center in Polson. I think he's headed for a job here, although he doesn't yet know it. I'll make him an offer—complete with unusual fringes— that he can't refuse."

"I bet you will." Sam smiled. Could this be her lucky day?

Molly picked up her fork again. "What brings you to town? A little early for a next trip, isn't it? Sick of Pete already?" She took a bite of the sausage and chewed.

"No way. In fact, that's why I'm here."

Molly swallowed. "Uh oh, here it comes. I can just hear it: Pete is so great, I just can't get along without him. We're gonna have to renegotiate. Am I warm?"

"Yes, hot even. But it's not exactly what you think."

"So it's not about sex?"

"I didn't say that, but it's not all about sex. I haven't told you this, Molly, but I operate a small manufacturing and mail order business out of my house. It's what I have done for most of my life. I've never had aspirations of expanding because I was anxious to keep it a one-person business. That's changed now."

"Because of Pete."

"That's right. I had some orders to fill this week, and when Pete arrived on Monday, he was intrigued by the business. He spent some time in the lab with me and was the quickest study I've seen. He has some ideas about business development that I'd like to take advantage of. Long story short, I can't expand unless I have him full-time."

"So you came hoping to make a different deal."

"Exactly. I'd like to take him on as an employee, with the idea of him becoming a full partner. I think it would be a great situation for him."

"I'm sure it would," agreed Molly, scowling. "And in the meantime, my bed is empty and cold."

"C'mon, Molly, you just told me this new cowboy of yours is the greatest thing since sliced bread. You said you were going to offer him a job. How does a cold, empty bed figure into that equation?"

Molly lifted her mug of coffee to her mouth and took a sip, slowly and deliberately, as if contemplating Sam's words. When she set the mug down, she nodded. "I guess you have a point. And the cowboy's name is Sarge; at least, that's what I know him by." She studied Sam across her empty plate. "So whadda ya have in mind?"

"For starters, I was hoping you might be happy for Pete, the fact that he has a great opportunity and all."

"And my business goes to hell so yours can do better? Doesn't seem fair, somehow."

"Well, if this Sarge is half as good as you say he is, then an enterprising businesswoman like yourself ought to be able to figure out a way to replace the income ... and keep your bed full and warm at the same time."

Molly frowned. "The two men aren't the same. Each has his own special strengths. Life would be better with both of them."

"I'm sure it would, but how many can you entertain at the same time? Trying to juggle both might be a recipe for disaster. If you piss 'em both off, you could wind up with neither - and so could I. Would you like that?"

"Hell no, I wouldn't like that."

Sam reached for her mug and lifted it in Molly's direction. "Then let's talk business."

Molly uncrossed her arms. "Go ahead, I'm listening."

"I had planned to offer Pete to you for your personal pleasure one day every few weeks," began Sam, "but I don't think, by the sounds of it, you need a boy toy. So what could I offer you instead?"

Molly tapped manicured nails on the table top. "One big worry I have is being able to offer Sarge enough money to entice him to leave his job. Do you think the 'fringes' will be enough?"

"I'm not sure, but maybe I can help."

"How?"

Sam pursed her lips. "What if I offered to temporarily top up Sarge's salary by a thousand a week?"

Molly's eyes widened. "That's generous. Pete's that good a businessman, huh?"

"He's good, yes. So if you agree, I'll top up Sarge's salary, but only for four months. Then I'd want to renegotiate."

"So I wouldn't get Pete at all?"

"Absolutely not; if I'm paying you to employ Sarge, Pete's all mine."

Molly played with her fork, spinning it in her fingers. Finally she stopped, looked at Sam, and said, "Okay, four months. But the deal doesn't end at that point, we just re-negotiate. If everything is going well, you keep the subsidy in place for two more months and then Pete's yours free and clear."

Sam's shoulders slumped. "God, Molly, it sounds like we're buying and selling meat."

"In a way, we are. But we've earned the right, haven't we?"

"I don't really think anyone has the right to treat another person that way, but since we care about these guys, and only want the best for them, I guess it's okay. I still wouldn't put it to Pete or Sarge that way, though."

"Good idea."

"In any event, I'll take your deal. I'll subsidize the pay for four months then we'll talk. If we decide it's going well, for both of us, the subsidy continues for two more months. Then Pete's all mine."

"That's what I said. I'll stand by my word." Molly held out her hand.

Sam shook it. "Good, then we have a deal. Assuming, of course, that Pete agrees. In spite of this conversation, I am very aware that I don't own him, and that he makes the decisions about his own life."

"Of course."

Sam let go of Molly and drained the last of her coffee. "I'd better be on my way. I have to head down the west side of the lake and mail some packages on the way. It'll be late afternoon when I get home."

She started to pull her wallet from her purse, but Molly waved a hand through the air. "It's on me. You travel safely. And give Pete a kiss for me."

Sam shot her a look, but Molly just laughed. "Make it a good one."

When Sam drove onto her lot in the woods, Pete's pick-up was already in the garage. He was sitting on the porch, drinking a Jack and, she guessed, cola, because it was in a tall glass.

"You beat me," she called, as she got out of the Jeep. "Good day?"

"Very good." He smiled widely. "How about yours?"

She scowled. "Terrible. Nothing went right."

His smile disappeared. "I take it Molly didn't go for it. I assumed when you were gone when I got back that you went to talk to her." He patted the chair beside him. "C'mon, plant yourself. Let me get you a vodka-tonic and you can tell me about it."

The two drank as they talked. Sam kept the ruse going for a few minutes, as Pete got more and more worked up. Finally, she couldn't take it anymore and burst out laughing.

He set his glass down on the table between them with a thud. "Damn you, Sam. Are you kidding?"

"I am," she admitted, laughing so hard she could barely get out the words.

They settled back and she told him about her stroke of good fortune with Molly having met the cowboy, Sarge, and the deal they had struck. "I do realize that you aren't property to buy and sell. That's not what this is. I'm taking you on as a partner, if you're willing."

He reached for her hand. "Sounds good to me. So I'm free to join you?"

"You are, if you're able to figure out how to deal with your place and animals. Were you able to talk to your friend about moving onto the property?"

"I was." His tone was grave. "Let me refill the drinks and I'll tell you about it."

He got up, picked up her glass, and disappeared inside. Sam watched him go, her stomach twisting. Were their perfect plans about to be derailed?

Back a minute later, he handed her the drink, then sat in the rocker and sipped his—this time a Jack on the rocks—before cradling the glass in both hands and looking at her.

Her stomach tightened. "Needed something stronger in order to tell me?"

"Yep." Pete grimaced. "So after I did the chores and cleaned up, I drove by the trailer park to see Jim and Anne. I was lucky; Jim had taken the day off to get some things done around the trailer park, so they were both there. I told them what I was thinking. I offered them the house, free of charge, in exchange for caring for the animals and doing the chores, and told them I'd split any beef and pork sales with them fifty-fifty."

"Pete, that's a great deal—for them, that is. Don't you think you're giving away too much?"

He shrugged. "I was hoping to make the deal, but it doesn't

make much difference now. Anne told me that if that was the best I could do, I might as well take off. I was shattered." He stared into his drink, a sad look on his face.

Sam swallowed hard. "So they rejected the offer? Just like that?" *So much for the two of us going into partnership together.*

He swirled his drink, his chair creaking as he rocked. When he looked up, his smile was mischievous. "Got you! We're even. They jumped at the offer. They gave their notice to the trailer owner today and will move in at the end of the month. For the next couple of weeks, Jim and I will split the chores, so I'll have to go over every other day or so, but that won't be so bad."

Sam got up, walked over to Pete. She knocked his hat off his head and wound up to sock him, but before she could finish the punch, he jumped to his feet. "I think I'd better cool you off." He bent down and scooped her up, throwing her over his shoulder as he walked to the lake. When he reached the shore, he tossed her in, clothes and all.

She clambered to her feet, spluttering, and smacked the surface with her hand to splash water all over him.

An hour later, they stumbled from the water, laughing. Sam grabbed her clothes and started up the path, Pete right behind her. Once inside, they took turns drying each other, then he told her to sit and relax while he made dinner.

He made her what he called his hamburger special: two patties of prime beef, sandwiched around a fried egg and topped with sautéed onions, peppers, and mushrooms. He loaded potato wedges on the plate, along with fresh tomato slices. Sam stuck the last potato wedge into her mouth and leaned back in her chair, pressing one hand to her stomach. "I'm pretty sure that was the best burger I've ever had."

Pete looked pleased with himself as he reached for her empty plate and set it on top of his.

Sam lifted a hand. "You cooked, I'll do the dishes."

He didn't argue, just handed her the plates and she carried them into the kitchen to wash.

By nightfall they were settled in their rockers on the porch, enjoying the quiet as the chirping of birds was replaced by the gentle whirring of the bugs. *Funny, none of these bugs seem to sting. That's a lot nicer than Wisconsin, Illinois, or Louisiana.*

Sam rested her head on the back of the chair and sighed. "I hate to discuss work on a beautiful night like this, but now that you're here to stay, we should talk about the future. We need to talk about the business, how to build it, and if and when you should go to Albania."

"If I go, I wish you would come with me."

"No, that would be too risky. Now that I've found what I want, I'm not about to lose it to carelessness. I haven't told you the whole story, but there are people trying to find me who would like nothing better than to capture me and put me behind bars."

He contemplated her for a moment before reaching for her hand. "Maybe some day, honey, you'll share it all with me. Until then, I'll do as you say."

She squeezed his hand. "That's how it has to be, for now. If anyone tracks me down here, not only our work, but our lives could end up on the line."

14

The days that followed were a whirlwind. Each week there were two batches of new orders to fill. Pete's education progressed steadily. Sam now trusted him with each step of the process, and being able to divide the chores among them cut down considerably on the amount of time she had to spend working. To collect orders and mail packages, they each took half the route, alternating trips between east and west, but always stopping in Kalispell to see Molly.

One day Pete took Sam to his place, and she was amazed to see how picturesque it was. The homestead was nestled in a narrow valley between two mountains, and as they drove up the long, winding driveway, they passed a small lake that he said provided his animals with their water year round.

As they entered the farmstead, he proudly pointed out the house. "The only thing special about that is that I made it. I cut the logs from the property and shaved and shaped them. Rented a small lifter to get things in place, but it's pretty much all mine."

She studied the building. "That's pretty darn special."

"It was a labor of love. I cut more than two hundred trees to make the house and barn. The worst part was pulling the stumps. That's work, I'll tell you, hot and sweaty. But when I'd finished I had clear fields for hay, corn, and one I use for grazing. I switch things around each year. Better yields that way."

He took her by the arm, walked her up the log steps, and opened the door of the house. When she came through the door, her jaw dropped open. "Pete, it's beautiful." She ran her fingers along the glistening countertops made of half logs that were polished to a mirror sheen. "You did all this?"

"Yes, every bit of it. It's just simple, but it works for me fine."

"It's wonderful. I love it. If you had asked, I'd have moved here."

"No, you wouldn't. You couldn't have. There's no place here to run the business. Any expansion would be clearly visible, and it's way too close to the highway and Kalispell."

"Still, it's lovely."

"I like it, but it's just a plain old cabin. One big room and a bathroom downstairs and one big room and a bathroom upstairs."

"But you made it with your own hands. If nothing else, I would love it for that. But it is wonderful, truly. It's spacious, airy, light, and neat and clean, too. It's perfect."

"If we ever want to, it will be here for us to move into. But that won't be for a while."

"I guess not." Sam continued to run her fingers across the counters. As she looked around, she imagined him, bare to the waist and sweating, as he labored to make it his creation. The mental picture turned her on.

"Pete, I have this incredible urge to make love to you. Please take me upstairs."

They walked up the stairs hand-in-hand, and she got her wish. He treated her with more gentleness than she had experienced with him. It was a wonderful diversion.

"That was sensational." She reached up and trailed a finger down the side of his face. "Do you think we could duplicate it at my house?"

A look of hurt flashed across his face.

Sam bit her lip. "I'm sorry. I meant at our house. I really do think of it as our home, not just mine anymore."

"Sam, people make a home. This is the first time that this has felt like a home to me. That's because you are here. And you are the very first woman I have brought here. So if we achieved something special, it was because of us. And that, yes, can be recreated at our new home."

"Which we should go back to now, or I'll get so comfortable here I might not want to leave."

●—— •

A short time later, Pete pulled the truck into the driveway of the cabin and turned off the engine. "Want to have a quick swim before we go in?"

"Absolutely." Sam climbed out of the vehicle. They shed their clothes, joined hands again, and walked into the water. While they were floating on their backs, a roar suddenly erased the silence. Pete scrambled to his feet and looked south. The grizzly stood on the shore, as close as he had ever been to them.

Sam clutched his arm. "Should we be worried?"

Pete rested a hand on the small of her back, trying to reassure her although he was far from certain they had nothing to be concerned about. "I'm not sure. You can't be too careful with grizzlies." They both grew quiet. He focused on the bear, who was close enough now that he could see his eyes.

"Pete! His right eye is all inflamed. Look how red and milky it is."

"You're right. That's got to be really sore. Not sure that a bear with a sore eye is better than a bear with a sore foot, but just to be sure, let's go out a little deeper and see what happens."

They backpedaled to deeper water, stopping when the water reached her chin. The bear ambled down the pathway toward the shore. When he reached their clothes, he picked up Sam's bra, swung it around on his massive paw, and gently put it down. After that, he lay down and watched them.

Sam tightened her grip on Pete's arm. "What are we going to do? We can't stay here all night."

"I'm not sure he wants to fight," Pete told her. "Look at him; he seems to be waiting for us."

He studied the animal. The giant bear, reddish-brown in color, had settled down in the middle of the path, his head on his front legs. From that position, he appeared to be watching them carefully.

Sam let go of him. "Maybe one of us should go closer, see what he does."

He nodded. "I'll go. You stay here. If anything happens, swim to the far shore and get help, okay?"

"But—"

He kissed her. "I'll be fine. Don't worry." Even to him, the words sounded a bit silly. How could either of them not worry as he approached a huge, unpredictable wild animal? Pete made his way slowly to the shore.

The bear lifted its head, shook it slowly from side to side, then lifted a paw, as if in greeting. The giant creature lumbered to its feet and took a few steps up the path before stopping and turning to look back.

Pete's forehead wrinkled. *Does he want me to follow him?*

As if the animal could read his thoughts, the bear grunted. The sound was neither loud nor threatening, more like a message that said, *about time.* He took two more steps up the path, turned again, and made the same sound. Pete looked back at Sam. "Should I follow him?"

Sam lifted her shoulders. "It seems as though that's what he wants. Just be careful."

He nodded and waded the last few feet to the edge of the water. The bear studied Pete carefully. When he stepped onto the sand, the bear walked back up the path, stopping when it opened onto the grass of the yard. *I hope like hell he's not hungry and thinking I'd make a great meal.* Pete drew in a steadying breath and forced himself to keep moving. In just a few steps, he would be beyond the place where he could return to the water before the bear could reach him.

"Mr. Grizzly," he said softly, "I'm coming to you. Just relax now."

He took a step, stopped, and said again, softly, "Relax ... easy." He held up both hands in a gesture of submission before taking another step and stopping to speak to the giant creature again. This went on step by step, until Pete reached the yard. The bear had waited for him, but he turned away now, slowly, as if to reassure Pete he meant him no harm. Pete followed in the footsteps of the animal's enormous clawed feet as the bear padded toward the cabin. Near the steps, the bear stopped and stretched out on the grass. It again made the soft grunt, as if to encourage Pete to come closer.

Pete walked slowly toward the house, scanning the area for possible avenues of escape if the bear decided to charge, but as he drew closer, the animal seemed to relax even more, flopping onto its side while keeping its eyes on Pete.

Footsteps sounded behind him. Pete glanced back as Sam stepped behind a tree. Somehow he'd known she wouldn't stay in the lake like he'd asked. At least she had some protection where she stood.

As Pete drew even with the bear, he stopped. They studied each other, man and bear. The bear made the first move, moving one giant paw to its sore eye as if suggesting the man could help.

Pete talked to him softly. "Okay, old friend. That's a sore eye, a very sore eye. Must hurt like crazy." His soft words appeared to lull the bear into an even more relaxed state. Pete started to breathe a little easier. "I have to go inside to see if we have something that could help. Just going to go inside for a minute. I'll be right back."

Before entering the house, he gestured for Sam to walk to the dwelling. "I think he's okay. C'mon up. You'll be safer here."

Sam carefully crossed the yard, skirted the animal, and made her way onto the porch.

"You watch from here. I'll see what I can find that might help."

The bear offered no opposition as Pete entered the cabin. On the bookshelf in the den, he found a book of Sam's on Native American medicines. He flipped through the pages until he found that one effective sore eye treatment utilized leaves of dandelion plants. The leaves were steeped into a tea. The liquid was then drained and the steeped leaves were used on the inside of a moist compress.

Could he get close enough to place a compress on the bear's eye? Pete chewed on his lower lip. It was worth a try. He returned to the yard, kept up a reassuring litany as he walked past the bear, and picked a handful of dandelion leaves.

"I'm gonna help, big buddy. Yes, I am," he crooned. The animal lay there quietly, not taking its eyes off Pete.

As he moved back to the porch, he gestured to Sam to join him inside, and quickly told her what he wanted to do. She stepped in to make the poultice.

She put the leaves in a small pan of water, brought it to a boil, then turned the heat down and covered the pan, leaving the leaves to rest for about ten minutes. Was the bear still outside? Pete peered out the window. The animal was right where Pete had left him, seemingly asleep.

Sam took some large gauze pads from the medicine cabinet in the bathroom, brought two of them to the kitchen, then drained the water, leaving just enough to moisten the gauze. She packed the leaves between the two pads and used small strips of adhesive tape to bind them together. Handing them to Pete, she said, "Be careful. He might not like this."

He took the compress to the door, walked out to the yard, and showed it to the bear. The grizzly was now wide awake and sitting up, resting on its back legs, not a very reassuring position.

Although he was totally out of his element, Pete was not about to leave the animal in pain. When he was five feet from the bear, he stopped. "This will make that eye feel better, but you have to let me work with you, okay?"

He held out the hand containing the compress. The bear extended its neck to smell his hand, but while it sniffed audibly, it did not raise a paw. Pete took a step forward. "I need to put this bandage over your eye, old friend. If we can keep it on there for a few minutes, it will make things better. Promise."

The last word was uttered with a good deal more confidence than he felt. *Dear God, please let this work. Help my friend here, but also keep me safe.*

Pete extended the hand holding the compress. "Now, old buddy," he almost crooned, "we're gonna put this on your eye." He pointed to the bear's right eye. The large animal studied him intently, growled softly, but did not move.

Pete took another step. The bear studied him. Barely breathing, Pete reached out and gently placed the compress over the bear's right eye. The big animal flinched and emitted another low growl, but settled back as Pete held the compress in place.

"That's a good boy." Ignoring Sam's sudden intake of breath behind him, he reached out with his right hand and softly rested a hand on the bear's head. *Is this actually happening?* For two minutes the twilight tableau remained in place, neither the man nor the bear moving. "Please, God, let this work," Pete whispered. "This big guy came here seeking our help. I don't know what I'm doing, so I could sure use your assistance."

What seemed like hours later but in reality was only about five minutes, Pete scratched the bear's head and said, "Now big guy, I'm gonna take this off. Let's see if it helped."

As he began to remove his hand, the bear growled and raised his left paw.

"Okay guy, I get ya," Pete said. "I'm gonna move my hand, but we'll leave the compress there."

He took his hand away and the bear remained motionless. If the mood hadn't been so deathly serious, it might have been comical. The bear with an eye patch, sitting motionless before a totally nude male. Thankfully, Sam must have relaxed enough to see the humor too, as she chuckled softly behind him. Pete took a cautious step back. "I'm gonna go up on the porch now, okay? Probably oughta get some clothes on. The bugs will soon be out. Don't imagine they bother you much, do they?"

The bear seemed to listen intently, moving its head from one cocked position to the other, but carefully enough that the compress remained in place. Pete went up the stairs, grabbed Sam's arm, and the two of them went into the house. She followed him up to their room. She'd dressed at the lake, so she settled on the edge of the bed and waited for him as he pulled on jeans and a T-shirt. Neither of them spoke. Was she afraid, like he was, that if they talked about what had happened it would turn out to have been some kind of weird dream? As terrifying as the incident had been at times, it was the most incredible thing Pete had experienced, and he didn't want to find out he'd imagined the whole thing.

When he was ready, he led the way back outside. Pete gestured for her to stay at the top of the stairs while he went down. "Old friend, we gotta get that thing off your eye. I'm afraid if we leave it there too long, it's going to make your eye worse."

He reached the animal and held out his hand, but stopped before touching him. "I'm gonna take that off now, fella. Easy now, easy." His hand slowly moved to the compress and he peeled it gently off. He could swear the eye looked better. The bear shook its head vigorously, then relaxed on its haunches. Pete took a couple of steps backward. "Tell ya what, if you wait there for a minute, I'll see if I can find something for you to eat. Then you can be on your way, okay?"

The bear appeared to understand. He didn't move as Pete turned to head back up the stairs. He stopped at the sight of Sam, standing on the porch holding a large platter filled with fatty cuts of meat.

"I think he'll like these." She handed him the platter. "Carry it out to the yard, though; I'd rather he not come up on the porch."

"What about me? I'd rather not be dinner, thank you very much."

She waved a hand through the air as though the idea was ridiculous. "He clearly likes you. You'll be fine."

Pete shook his head, but clutched the platter and went down the stairs, crossed the yard, and stopped at the top of the path. Setting down the platter, he called for the bear to come and get the food.

As if he knew exactly what Pete had said, the bear clambered to its feet and ambled toward the path. When it got there, it sniffed the meat, then looked up at Pete, let out another soft, snuffling grunt, lowered its head, and began to eat.

"That's a good fella. Finish up and have a good evening. I'll get the platter later."

Pete walked back to the cottage and closed the door behind him. He and Sam stood shoulder to shoulder at the window overlooking the lake and watched the bear devour the meat.

"That," said Sam, "is one for the books. Where the hell did you get the idea to use dandelion leaves?"

He pointed to the book of Native American medicines. "You can thank them."

"Damn good book," she agreed. "I've adapted quite a few of the remedies for my uses."

"Yeah, but I was on a friendly mission."

She elbowed him in the ribs. "You have no idea how happy I am that you're safe."

"You? How do you think I feel?"

Pete gestured to the lawn. The bear had finished the last of the meat and was licking its chops aggressively. Then it ambled down the path, turned south, and disappeared.

On the twelfth of September, a cool, clear Saturday, Sam drove Pete to Missoula. She'd taken the Sentinel out of the garage for the occasion, although he had suggested that the situation didn't warrant risking the car being seen. Still, Sam had insisted. They'd passed a couple of police cars along the way, one parked on a side street. Pete watched both cops carefully, but neither appeared to notice the green-black vehicle as he and Sam drove by.

Pete boarded the Sky West flight at 6:30 a.m., just as the sun was peeking over the mountains. Although he had argued vociferously with Sam, she had prevailed, spending nearly thirteen hundred for a first-class, round-trip ticket rather than the thirty-six hundred for economy, which would have suited him fine. He reached the Tirana International Airport in Albania at eleven twenty Sunday night, enduring three layovers and crossing seven time zones en route. He checked in at the Hotel Millennium Tirana just before 1:00 a.m.

As exhausted as he was, sleep wouldn't come. Tomorrow he would be meeting with some of the most dangerous men in Europe. Either he would come out of those meetings with contracts that would rocket their business to international status, or no one would ever hear from him again.

15

Finally giving up, Pete tossed back the covers and swung his legs over the side of the bed. The sky outside his window has just begun to lighten. He had six hours until his noon meeting with Saimir Krasniqi, who, along with his brother Bruno, was one of the leaders in organized crime in Europe. After lunch, he would rent a car and drive southwest into the hills near Elbasan, capitol of the province by the same name. There he would meet Semion Moglevich, one of the toughest crime bosses to come out of the Ukraine, and now the leader of the mob in Moscow.

These meetings were extremely risky, and he patted his breast pocket, reassuring himself that the letter of introduction supplied him by Angelo Carbone, head of the New Orleans family, was still in his possession. The letter was part of an outreach effort from Sam to the don. In it, Carbone urged that Pete be treated with the "utmost respect and kindness—as I would be treated if visiting."

Ready early and fighting nerves, he took a cab from the hotel to Delicatezze Di Mare, known far and wide for its fish dishes. He might not have selected the upscale eatery, but the message from Krasniqi informed him that was where they would meet.

As he sat in the entry way, putting in time as he had arrived early, he looked down. His legs were shaking. He re-crossed them, gripping his knee to still it. His stomach was tied in knots. When the appointed hour arrived, he rose and spoke the code words to the attractive hostess, who escorted him to the elevator. As soon as he boarded, she turned and walked away. Two tough-looking thugs waited for him in the elevator. When the doors closed, they roughly turned him around and patted him down thoroughly. Obviously satisfied that he was unarmed, they led him to a table where their boss sat waiting. Although Pete stuttered a bit when introduced, Krasniqi didn't appear to notice, just greeted him warmly. The mob boss nodded and the thugs retreated to a place near the elevator.

While the luncheon was tense, Krasniqi, every bit as tough as his reputation suggested, led the discussion with braggadocio and egotism, but mellowed a bit when Pete showed him the letter from Carbone. After that, he answered every question with straight-forward, accurate answers or, when he didn't know, said so, which Pete appreciated.

Relaxing a bit as the discussion went on, Pete told what he thought was a funny story about brothers from Tirana who tried to outwit the mob and wound up with their heads decorating gateposts outside the city. His host laughed heartily, clapped him on the back, and said, "Ju mendoni se eshte qesharake? Eshte e vertete!"

Pete remembered enough Albanian to know the man had said, "You think that's funny? It's true!" The implication was clear: be careful or you will wind up in the same place.

That set Pete a little on edge, but it seemed to put his host in a good mood, and they laughed and joked throughout lunch. When Krasniqi found out Pete was from Korce, he grimaced. "Pasi krenar Karee, tani shtepi e kultivuesve te grurit dhe krijuesit buke!"

It was not a compliment, Pete knew, but an indictment of the area he'd grown up in. Krasniqi had noted Korce once was proud but was now the home of wheat growers and bread makers. Pete accepted the statement, smiled, and returned the quip. "Por askush nuk me barkun bosh."

Krasniqui laughed at his response, that at least no one there had an empty belly, and the two men drank more wine before getting down to business. Two hours later, Pete left the restaurant with a lucrative order for sedatives and poisons, a promise for much more business if the product worked as promised, and a bit of a buzz from all the wine. He was grateful his nerves had not resulted in anything of major embarrassment.

His nervousness turned to delight when he saw that the concierge had ordered a full-size Mercedes for him. He had hoped for that, because he had been told that while most of the Balkan states drove ancient copies of the boxy Renault 12 made by Dacia, Albanians, though poor, loved their cars and often drove Mercedes. One reason he was grateful for the car was that it was built like a tank and made to handle the appalling condition of the roads. He doubted there had been much improvement in Albanian infrastructure in the two decades since he'd left, and even then the roads had been a collection of potholes and mud.

Although the roads were every bit as bad as he feared, Pete was satisfied with creeping along at fifteen miles an hour on the thirty-mile drive to Elbasan. In the city finally, he pulled up to the Hotel Monarch, the best in Elbasan and located in the center of the city. He checked into a suite—a spacious bedroom, kitchenette, and modern bathroom—evidence that the American dollar was still valued.

He showered, shaved again, then dressed in denim, jeans, and a shirt worn out to conceal the pistol he had holstered to his belt. Although he knew the gun would likely be taken from him, he felt the extra protection during the drive was worth the risk. Back in the car, he drove into the hills, reached the designated spot, and found a car filled with native Albanians waiting for him. Large and muscular, most wore scars that he assumed were from battles fought for their boss. He greeted them cautiously. He again was frisked, the pistol removed.

The largest among them, apparently the leader, ordered him to move his vehicle off the road. When he climbed out from behind the wheel, he was grabbed and shoved into the back seat of the car, the toughs who bracketed him smelling of garlic and sweat.

His welcoming party was all business and talk was at a minimum, limited mostly to nods and grunts. The car slowly made its way deeper into the hills, and when they had driven for most of an hour, the driver pulled over.

One of the men tossed him a black hood. In broken English, the leader said, "Wear it." The rest of the drive passed quickly, but the hood was stifling and when the car groaned to a halt, Pete was ready to be free of it.

Two men pulled him from the car and yanked the hood from his head. Even the smells of well-ripened manure were preferable to the sweaty, smelly hood.

They were in a farmyard. The goats and sheep seemed as hostile as the men who had brought him there. Two milk cows snuffled along the ground, seeking grass. Two men stood leaning on the hood of an ATV painted in camo colors. They waved him over, their faces lined and hard. Pete joined them.

"In." One of them jerked his head in the direction of the truck bed at the rear of the ATV, and Pete climbed in. They drove through the farmyard and into the hills behind the house, moving slowly up the hill until, finally, they crested a rise. Pete peered around the cab to see all of the valley spread out below him. They were on a plateau containing a collection of buildings. Several women appeared to be cooking at an outdoor fireplace on a large patio.

The ATV stopped before the largest building. One of the men took his arm and ushered him inside. Pete's stomach tightened. He recognized the man waiting for him. Seated near a fire on a straight-back chair was Semion Moglevich, the ugliest, toughest-looking person he had seen. Moglevich was not a man to be trifled with. He had earned his stripes the hard way and now headed one of the largest crime organizations in Europe. It was also one of the most successful and one of the most hated. Pete was hoping for a significant business deal. Looking at Semion, he repressed a shudder as he whispered a short prayer for safety and extended his hand.

Although Semion's face was criss-crossed with scars and his nose had obviously been broken several times, a smile lit his countenance as Pete moved to shake his hand.

"Welcome, brother," he said in almost accent-free English. "It is good to have you here. Thank you for your letter of request for a meeting. I was happy to accept. I am certain you will enjoy our mountain hospitality."

One by one, Moglevich introduced the members of his gang, then gestured to the chair at his right, as if Pete were one of the family. *Or is that wishful thinking?* Pete pushed the thought aside as he settled onto the hard wooden chair.

The good humor continued as the women he'd seen cooking outside waited on the men, serving drinks and appetizers.

"They are good at other things, too," said his host, leering. "So if your trip has made you lonesome, there is no need for you to sleep alone tonight."

"Thank you, my friend, it is, indeed, a kind and generous offer. I hope my refusal will not offend you. I have a woman back home, and enjoy my male parts sufficiently not to want to sacrifice them."

Laughter echoed around the room. Moglevich clapped him on the back. "It will be as you wish. But if you change your mind, just say the word."

Over drinks Semion told Pete he had spent more than half his time in the States, concentrating on Kansas City and Chicago.

"But I wanted to meet you here because we are both on home turf, eh? I thought the comfort of the home hills would loosen your lips so I might learn how the Carbone Family secured the drugs that allow them to rule Louisiana without challenge."

"Brother," Pete clapped a hand on his shoulder, "that's what I am here to tell you. If you are having trouble, I think you're going to like what I have to say."

"Great," said Semion, "but first, we eat." He took Pete by the elbow and guided him to a table, set simply for two. "Sit."

Pete studied the man across from him. He'd always thought that Semion was ugly and tough, but when he smiled, the scars seemed to disappear and his face was actually ruggedly handsome.

Once they were settled, Semion poured Rakia. After several glasses, he clapped his hands, and suddenly the room was filled with women bearing plates of food. There was lamb stew with mountain vegetables, the tastiest Pete had ever eaten, and his mother was a great cook. The women also served tender cuts of beef and pork, platters of more vegetables, and a large basket filled with Armenian breads, including Choereg, a traditional Easter bread, and two types of flat bread, matnakash and Lavash. All of the food was exquisite. Pete ate until he was stuffed, but Semion put away twice as much.

As the women cleared the table, Pete said, "I must compliment you, Semion; your colleagues are beautiful, every one of them."

Semion beamed and patted his full belly, obviously enjoying the compliment. He called the women back into the room to be introduced to Pete. There were seven of them, all in their twenties and thirties, all beautiful and full-figured. *Hmm.* Had he been too hasty earlier, in turning down Semion's offer?

Semion told the women to introduce themselves. Pete tried to remember each name as the woman said it: Anayis, Peleni, Keghani, Tapni, Yeraskh, Yerchanguhi, and Zarig.

When they'd finished, Pete inclined his head to the group. "Ti je e bukur dhe te talentuar. Faleminderit per sherbimin tuaj!" He wasn't exaggerating, they really were all beautiful and talented and the gratitude he expressed for their service was sincere.

Laughing, they left the room. Pete watched them go. "Are they all relatives?"

"All are relatives of my men," Semion told him. "Two are wives and five are daughters, but if you have changed your mind about sampling their favors, they would be honored."

"Tomorrow, my friend," Pete grasped his host's arm, "I will wake up and hate myself for declining what is a very generous offer."

"Aah." Semion sat back and crossed his hands over his ample stomach. "You are a man of principle. I like that. Yes, I like that. You and I, I think, will do good business together."

And with that, the meeting began. Semion drove a generous but selfish bargain. "Pete, I must have exclusive rights to your products in the Russia. Will you grant me that?"

How should he respond? He didn't want to give too much away too easily, but had assumed Semion would make the request. Pete decided to shoot straight, as he'd already come to like this well-spoken mountain man. "I never thought it would be any other way, Semion. Yes, exclusivity in Russia shall be yours. But to be clear, the agreement does not extend to other countries in the former USSR."

Semion pursed his lips. "You are excluding some areas I might like to open."

"But that is for the future."

Semion nodded slowly. "We best see how the products work first, eh?"

"Of course."

Back and forth, they debated over Semion's demands, each ultimately giving a bit.

Finally, with the clock passing midnight and nothing more to decide, Semion poured one more for each of them and raised his glass. "Good, good. To good business."

"To good business," echoed Pete, clinking his glass against his host's.

Pete was happy with the negotiations. He hadn't wanted to deal with the area that Semion would control anyway. It was fraught with feuds and political unrest. The players changed constantly and without warning or logic.

Semion appeared quite happy, too, likely because he had already won any of the necessary battles in those areas and controlled crime across that part of Eurasia.

"Now that business is done, my friend," said Semion, placing his glass on the table and stretching, "I wish to have one more discussion, and make one more agreement."

"And that is?"

"I want to know if anyone has yet stepped up and won China?"

His heart rate picked up. Did Semion want to take over that market as well? "No." Pete picked a piece of lint off his shirt sleeve, trying to appear nonchalant. "No one has asked about China yet."

"Then I am asking now," Semion told him. "If you agree to that request, I will triple my order. That, however, assumes exclusivity in that area, too."

"I must think, my friend," Pete told him. "Perhaps you will let me sleep on it and I will deliver my answer in the morning."

"So you will spend the night?"

"I think the Rakia made that decision for me." Pete lifted his glass and they both laughed. "There is no way I could drive these hills in my current state, even if I knew my way, which I don't."

The banter between them continued for another hour. Many bottles of Rakia and other alcoholic drinks were consumed, and when Pete could no longer keep his eyes open, one of the young women,

Tapni, appeared at his elbow and helped him to his feet. Pete leaned on her as she led him to his cottage at the end of the group of buildings.

When they reached the mud and thatch hut, she let go of his arm. "You will wait out here, okay?" Her accent was thick, but her English reasonably good. Pete braced himself with a palm pressed to the side of the cottage as she went in. At last she called for him, and he found his bed made up and a tray of grapes, cheese, and bread set on the small table next to it. Several drinks lined the table as well, not all of them, thankfully, alcoholic.

He thanked her for her hospitality, at which point she asked him, "Do you wish me to stay?"

He very nicely but firmly told her that while he was honored by her offer, he had a woman back home in America to whom he had pledged his loyalty.

She curtsied, smiling, and said, "Aja eshte nje zonje me fat, me te vertete!"

Pete smiled too, thinking of Sam. *Actually, I'm the lucky one.*

Tapni backed out of the building and he was left alone in the soft candlelight.

He sampled the food, as delicious as dinner had been. He carefully removed three Aleve tablets from his case and took them, washing them down with the bottle of water on the tray at the side of his bed.

When he retired, the bed, which was a mattress on the floor, seemed to him the most comfortable he had ever slept in. Layers and layers of furs were covered with a feather duster, plus a large skin atop that to ward off the mountain temperatures. He crawled under the blanket and closed his eyes. If Sam was beside him, the night would be perfect.

●——·

When he awoke the next morning without any trace of a headache, Pete was shocked. Equally surprising were the three bars of service showing on his cell phone.

He texted Sam with the results of his talks the previous day. He carefully explained the deal he and Semion had negotiated for the territory once known as the USSR, as well as Semion's request about China, asking her advice about what to say to him later.

While he used the soap, towel, and water in the pitcher beside the bowl on a table in the corner, his phone pinged, signaling that a text had arrived. He stood in front of the mirror, naked, and had nearly finished running the razor over his face he heard a noise and, glancing behind him, saw Tapni delivering a bowl of fruit, along with a cup of coffee and a pitcher of milk.

Too startled to think of covering himself, he stood stock still as she looked him up and down, then said, "Une bera nje gabim te madh duke lene mbreme!"

He laughed at her assertion that she had made a big error by leaving the night before. "Tapni, ju jeni nje grua e bukur e re. Une jam plak, ika kaluar tim. Ju jeni me te mire me njerezit ketu!" He hoped his words—that she was a beautiful young lady and he was an old man, past his prime—would let her down gently. "You are better with the men here," he added.

Pointing at his flaccid penis, she shook her head vigorously and he laughed again. Wagging a finger at her, he assured her, in Albanian, "You likely have had better, and you will have many more who are better!"

He kissed her on the cheek and guided her to the door.

Still chuckling, Pete read the message on his phone. Sam told him she had checked with Angelo Carbone and been told that Semion was as trustworthy as anyone he knew. Carbone was confident that any deal made with Semion would be beneficial for Sam and Pete.

Do it! was the end of the message.

He acknowledged the text, promised more communication later, told her he missed her, then quickly donned his jeans and shirt and exited the house to greet the day. It was another beautiful morning, cool and clear. The women were already at work at the fire, and Tapni hurried over and urged Pete to head straight to the building in which he and Semion had met the day before.

His host was already eating. When Pete sat down, Tapni brought him food, bread, butter and jam, smoked meat, fish, and fruit.

When Pete sat, Semion looked up and extended his hand. Pete shook it. "Semion, I have checked with my partner at home and she checked with Don Carbone. The don had some very good things to say about you, my friend. And so, China is yours."

Semion arose, clapped him on the back and hugged him. "You are a good man, Pete, a very good man. We will do excellent business together, you and I."

When breakfast was finished, Pete rose and held out his hand. "My word is my bond, Semion. All that we have agreed upon will be the way that it is until you no longer wish it that way."

Semion stood too, and clasped Pete's hand between both of his. "I do not see that happening," his host said.

"Then I will take my leave. You have been a wonderful host. Thank you, my friend."

"You are quite welcome. And when we meet again, it will be as brothers. You understand?"

Pete nodded, smiling.

"Tapni has gathered your belongings and has returned them to the ATV you arrived in. And now, dear friend, I must bid you good-bye. Travel safely."

Semion took him by the arm and helped him to the ATV. When he got back to the farmyard, the car that had brought him there waited for him. This time there was no hood, and the mood among the four men with him the car was jovial as they returned him to his Mercedes.

They moved his belongings to his car, then lined up and saluted him before bowing him on his way.

Pete watched them grow smaller in the rearview mirror, until they faded from view. Then he turned his eyes to the road ahead. "Well," he smacked the steering wheel with the palm of one hand. "That couldn't have gone better. Sam is going to be extremely happy with me when I get back home." Still, he couldn't stop the voice of warning ringing through his head. *Can this continue? Is it possible? These meetings surely won't get easier. If I thought Semion was tough, what's ahead could be a whole lot worse.*

16

Al hunched over his desk, staring at the familiar stack of newspapers. Having finished *The Seattle Times*, he straightened up, ran his hands over his flat-top gray hair, and teetered back in his chair to think.

Just where the hell could she be? Is it that hard to find a gorgeous woman and a conspicuous car? Why can't there be a break in this case, just one little break?

Exhaling loudly, Al pushed to his feet and went to fill his coffee cup. The Keurig sputtered and gurgled as it dispensed his favorite Green Mountain Hazelnut for the third time that morning.

So much for cutting down on the stuff. *God, JoAnne'd have a fit if she knew.* Three cups. Not good for the hypertension, she'd be quick to remind him.

As he stood there, moving the cup from his right hand to his left because of the heat, his phone shrilled.

Damn, who wants me this early? Bending over the desk, he snatched up his phone, barely restraining the urge to curse as a few drops hit the top of his desk. "Rouse here."

"Detective Rouse, this is Tad Munson. I hope I'm not bothering you, but I wanted to let you know right away that we may have seen that Sentinel again."

Al set the cup of coffee far enough out of reach to not be a problem then sat down and rested his elbows on the desktop. "Really? Where?"

"Well, sir, we got the APB a coupla weeks ago, and in addition to the wire, I delivered it personally to all the P.D.'s and sheriff's offices in my territory. Hadn't heard a word until this morning, and I'm not even sure about the reliability of the report I have."

"Trooper, this is one of the few damn leads we've had since the old lady escaped custody in New Orleans. Very little has happened since I spoke with you last, so even if it's a weak lead, it's welcome."

"Gotcha. Well, a coupla minutes ago I heard from a trooper down in Missoula who thinks he may have seen the vehicle. Problem is, he was parked off a freeway entrance, processing reports and I'm guessin' at least half asleep, when this dark-colored Land Rover—he thinks it was a Sentinel but he's not sure it was black, since it was nighttime—drove by headed south on I-90, toward the Missoula airport."

Al gripped the receiver tighter, blood pounding in his ears. "How long ago was this?"

"Two days. Nothing struck him at the time, and he had the next day off. It wasn't until this morning, when he came into work and checked the board, that he remembered there was an APB out on a vehicle like the one he'd seen. He talked to the chief and then called me. He was awfully damn sorry, sir. He apologized over and over, saying it had been a long shift and he was just too sleepy to be very alert."

"What's his name?"

"Clyde Abraham. He's a young cop but he's a good one and he's going to be great, given what I've seen of him. He feels like crap this morning, that's for sure."

"So you talked to this Clyde?"

"Yes sir, I did."

"Can you tell me what he had to say?"

"I can do better than that. When I realized he could be talking about the car I spotted a couple of weeks ago, I recorded his call. Want me to play it for you?"

"I sure do."

"Okay, here it is:" "Saturday morning at about four, I was parked just off Airport Boulevard, out near Trumpeter Court, when this Land Rover Sentinel goes whizzing by me. It didn't dawn on me until later that it might be the vehicle you are looking for."

"Was it black?" asked Tad.

"Hard to tell, it was just before dawn when it went by. I'm sure it was a dark color—but black? Well, that I don't know. And I'm sorry to say, sir, I didn't remember about the APB at the time, so I didn't think to go after it."

"I don't suppose you spotted the driver, either?"

"No, no I didn't. Just the vehicle."

"Which way was it going?"

"It was heading toward the airport on the I-90. Traveling real fast, but not fast enough that I felt the need to chase after it, unfortunately."

"Do you remember anything else at all?"

"Nope. I just kind of glanced at it and went back to my paperwork."

"Okay, thank you. If you think of anything else, let me know immediately."

"Yes, sir."

The recording ended. Al rubbed his temples with his free hand. A weak lead indeed, but it could suggest that Genevieve was still in that area, somewhere. Unless she had been flying out somewhere that day. "Was there anything else, anything at all?"

"Nothing useful. One thing is for sure, though, we're going to be on high alert in this neck of the woods. If we see anything more of the vehicle or the driver, you'll be the first to know."

"But Tad, tell your people to be careful," cautioned Al. "Remember what I told you the last time. This woman might be over eighty, but she's as spry as a fifty-year-old and she's slippery as a fish. Whatever you do, if you see the vehicle and the driver is a woman, be very cautious. If you try to take her, don't do it alone. Make sure you have plenty of back-up."

"Yes sir, I hear you. We'll be plenty careful. And we'll make sure you know everything the second we do."

"Thanks, Tad." Al's grip on the phone relaxed. "I appreciate you calling. This is the first good news I've had on the case a long, long time." He replaced the receiver and reached for his coffee. It wasn't much to go on, but at this point any hint that Genevieve Wangen might be settled in one spot and that spot might be Montana, was more than welcome.

17

The drive from Elbasan to Korce was about eighty miles as the crow flies, but it was more like 120 miles by road and it was going to take several hours across rugged terrain. But it was a new day and Pete was headed to his first home and barely able to sit still in the seat of his car.

It was a trip he was anxious to make. He had not been back to Korce since he had left more than sixteen years ago. In the meantime, his father, Adem, had passed. For lack of funds, Pete had been unable to return for the funeral six years earlier. But now he was back and anxious to see his mother Beshar and all the relatives he had left behind.

He stopped in Elbasan before heading southeast toward the Morava Mountains and home. His mother and father had farmed in the hills outside Korce, but since his father's death, his mother had sold the farm and moved in with his sister Dardana. Dardana was married and the mother of three children. She lived in a small house with her husband Fitim, who was an accountant for one of the Korce industries.

As he drove, Pete thought about his childhood, growing up on the farm. It was a hard life, but a good one, as he and his siblings had roved the hills and played all sorts of children's games. In the summer they swam in a nearby stream and in the winter they attended school, walking two miles from their home to the one-room building where lessons were taught.

Thoughts of those days ran through his mind as he drove, but he thought also of the good fortune that had marked his trip thus far. He had made two major deals, and if nothing else happened the rest of the trip, it would still have been successful. But maybe there would be more stops before he was done.

The China agreement would significantly expand the business beyond the point that he and Sam could handle. An expansion of that magnitude would bring with it many complexities. Overseeing the operation would be a huge task, one he and Sam would have to share. And where would that be done? Kalispell was too small to hide such an operation and the people who would staff it. Somewhere like Portland or Seattle, or Denver, maybe. Although those cities came with problems, too.

Seattle had been the center of a massive amount of drug trade, and government agencies had swarmed to the area to collar the criminals, which probably ruled out that city. Where to locate would be a major discussion topic for him and Sam when he got home.

After four hours of driving on rugged roads and through mountain passes that made him grateful for the Mercedes, he began to see familiar sights. Immediately his enthusiasm to be home grew and his foot pressed down on the accelerator.

He drove into Korce a little before 4:00 p.m. and took a drive around the city. He loved the thought of being home, and although he was anxious to see his mother, he wanted also to fully refamiliarize himself with his hometown.

It was after five when he arrived at his sister's residence. The yard was filled with children who surrounded the car, jumping up and down.

When he opened the door, six or seven children grabbed him. He didn't know which were his nephews and niece, but he hugged each of them. Then, looking up, he saw his mother. Older by far than the woman he remembered, the smile—the wide, wide smile—was the same. There were fewer teeth in her mouth, her tanned face was lined with wrinkles, and the wisps of hair peeking out from the scarf that covered her head, once honey-colored, were now white.

He went to her, finding her arms just as warm and loving as the ones that had bid him farewell sixteen years ago. His sister was there too, still beautiful but about three times larger than the young girl he had hugged when he left.

The celebration in the yard continued for a time before Dardana urged him to come inside. She glanced back over her shoulder and instructed the oldest of the children, Gjergj, the Albanian version of George, to bring in his uncle's luggage, then took Pete's arm and led him up the front steps.

The house, although modest in size, was neat as a pin. In contrast to many Albanian dwellings, the generously sized windows emitted plenty of light. Dardana poured coffee for him, their mother, and herself, and they sat at the table and talked.

After what must have been an hour of nonstop conversation, a man came in.

"Pete, this is Fitim," said Dardana.

"Aha, I finally meet my brother-in-law. Fitim, thank you for allowing me to visit your house and family."

The tall, dark, handsome man with a wide smile and rugged face grasped his hand and shook it vigorously. Pete liked him immediately and soon they were conversing like brothers.

"I am pleased that you can visit, but what is it that brings you to Albania?" Fitim leaned against the fireplace as he spoke, rubbing his hands to warm them.

"I have a business in the United States, Fitim. Since I joined my partner, a lovely woman named Samantha, we can handle more business. I am visiting hoping to find customers."

"And what do you make that would be of interest to Albania?"

"My partner is an expert in making drugs and potions that help people keep their territory or gain new territory."

"The only people here who would be interested in that are with the mob."

"You are very quick, Fitim. That is who we serve and that is who I have been meeting with."

Fitim studied him carefully. "Have you had success?"

"Great success. It has been a very profitable trip."

"This is great interest to me," replied his brother-in-law. "Perhaps we can talk more later."

"Of course. Whenever you want."

Fitim nodded and went to join Dardana to assist her with dinner. Pete asked if he could help, but Fitim's response to that was to open a Hyseni Deutch beer and bring it to him.

"This is a great pilsner." Fitim offered him the bottle. "It's my favorite. Tell me if you like it."

Pete lifted the bottle to his lips and let some of the amber liquid trickle down his throat. "It's excellent," he reported.

Fitim smiled and started back to the kitchen. "Enjoy."

By the time dinner was ready, Pete had already concluded that Fitim might be useful to Sam and him. They would need a distribution and collection man in Europe, and if Pete could determine that the job would be reasonably safe, Fitim might be ideal.

"You know, Fitim," he said as he got up to go to the table, "I'm thinking we could use someone like you in our business here. Do you think you might be interested?"

"Hold that thought," replied Fitim. "We'll talk after dinner."

The idea tucked away, they enjoyed a hearty dinner of roast pork and root vegetables, good, solid Albanian fare of the kind Pete had missed for sixteen years. After dinner, Fitim lit a pipe and sat in a rocker near the fire. He offered Pete the chair opposite him, and the others gathered around as Pete told them about America and answered their questions.

Gjergj's sister Rezarta and his brother Ledion wanted to know all about Sam. As Pete told them about the beautiful woman who lived alone in a cabin in the mountains, they gazed at him as if hypnotized. Pete repressed a smile. Sam would enjoy knowing she had apparently been granted fairytale significance with his niece and nephews. Their dark eyes grew even wider as he told them about Ben the grizzly. When Dardana finally informed them it was bedtime, they protested vociferously, asking him to tell them more about the bear's sore eye.

Fitim granted them fifteen more minutes, and Pete told them about the compress and how Ben returned for a day or two for more treatment of his sore eye.

Gjergj, kneeling on the rug by the fire, bounced up and down on his heels. "Where is Ben now?"

"He lives in the mountains near our house," Pete told them, grinning. "He comes around a couple of times a week to beg for dinner."

Gjergi, Ledion, and Rezarta sat and listened, mouths hanging open, as Pete told them that Sam fed the bear beef cuts, which the big fellow carried off toward the lake to eat.

"This Sam, she is very rich, yes?" asked Ledion.

"Yes, she is rich, but I think even if she wasn't, she would make sure the bear was well fed. He has become quite a pet, although an unusual pet, to say the least."

Later he walked upstairs with Fitim to say good night to the children. Nine-year-old Rezarta reached her small arms up to hug him, saying, "Tomorrow, Uncle Pete, you have to tell me more about Ben. Promise?"

He hugged her back. "Tonight I will think, Rezarta, and tomorrow there will be more Ben stories, okay?"

Her kiss on his cheek conveyed excitement and anticipation, so he said, "But first, you must get a good night's sleep."

"Okay, Uncle Pete." She pulled her teddy bear close and snuggled into the covers. Pete and Fitim rejoined the women on the first floor near the fire to continue their conversation.

When talk swung around to what Pete was doing in Albania, he decided that organized crime was well enough known for him to talk about it.

So he told them about Sam's business and the concoctions she mixed for crime lords in America. His audience appeared rapt as he talked, and although he made sure his comments were straight-forward, he understood that they were attaching a sort of romance to his words, which concerned him.

He held up a hand. "What we do is illegal. If we are caught, we will go to prison for many years. But we are very careful. When I got to know Sam, she eventually told me about her business. I was very interested. She let me watch her as she mixed the potions. Then one day, she let me mix a concoction on my own. I was really pumped up when she told me I had done it perfectly.

"From then on I was anxious to help, and eventually I came to know the business well enough for her to trust me with all aspects of it. It was then that I told her there might be great business opportunities here in Europe. Over time, we decided to see if that was true, so I came over to investigate the possibilities. I have landed two great deals in my first two stops. But those two deals are going to force us to expand the business greatly. That worries me."

Fitim had seemed to hang on every word, his eyes never leaving Pete's face. Now he leaned forward, gripping the arms of his chair. "Could your business move here?"

"It can probably be operated anywhere, but Sam has made it clear that she doesn't want to leave America. I would also worry about the type of workers we would find here. I think they would soon try to take over the business."

Fitim grimaced. "You are likely right about that. You would certainly have to rule the operation with an iron hand and a gun."

"For that reason," said Pete, looking Fitim in the eye, "I think manufacturing has to be done in the USA. But distribution will need to be carried out here. Maybe that is something you would like to head up? Of course, I'd have to get Sam's okay on that before we decided anything for sure."

"Yes, and even though it might be a great thing," said his brother-in-law, "Dardana and I must talk, too. I earn well now, but I am, how do you say it, dead ahead where I am?"

Pete nodded. "At a dead end, yes."

"Yes, dead end," said Fitim. "But I would need guaranteed money, because I have these mouths to feed."

"Yes, you do. And you have done a very good job of caring for Mother. I have done nothing to help you, and that makes me guilty. I need to help with the bills, and I must see that you have an even better job. With guaranteed money. I think Sam and I will be able to offer you both."

For the next week it seemed, life was one big party. Fitim and Dardana opened their home to every relative—and a number of people who weren't related—anxious to see Pete and hear about his adventures in America.

As the week drew to a close, Pete was exhausted. On Friday evening, he asked Dardana and Fitim for a word at the end of dinner.

"You have been wonderful hosts," he began, "but I really need a break. It has been a constant party since I got here. I'm not used to that. I'm sorry, but I must rest."

His sister and her husband chuckled, but they must have understood that he was serious, because it was if his sister had taken down the invisible *welcome* sign outside their home, and the visits and partying stopped.

Fitim told him later that Dardana had sent out the word that Pete was exhausted, didn't feel well, and needed to rest. "Good Albanians, you know, are anxious to please."

"I hope I didn't offend them. But I do need some peace."

"Of course you do. And we are determined that you should get it here. The next few days will, how shall I say it, be filled with quiet for you."

For the next few days, Pete napped and spent time with his mother, even driving her to the old farmstead, which looked much the same. And he entertained the children with more stories of Ben. Each day he communicated with Sam on several occasions, telling her his concerns and worries about the business he had developed.

The Thursday of his third week away dawned rainy. The clouds scudded along, seemingly about to touch the ground. It was the kind of day that reminded Pete that winter was ahead. The damp cold invaded everything it touched, and his sister made sure the fire was burning brightly. He spent the day rocking in front of its warmth and exchanging texts with Sam.

She had heard from Angelo Carbone, and the Louisiana don was thinking about how to accommodate the business. She told him that Angelo had sent along the name and number of Izzy Mulfetti, a friend of the don's and one of the crime family bosses in Italy. Mulfetti had told Don Angelo that he wanted to meet Pete before he left Europe. He wanted to talk business.

Pete called the number and Mulfetti himself answered the phone.

In broken English he thanked Pete for calling. Mulfetti invited him to visit before he left Europe. Eventually they agreed that they would meet in Rome and Izzy would invite "a couple of friends" from northern Europe to join them there on the first Thursday in October. Pete disconnected the call and drew in a deep breath. Was all of this really happening? He drew a trembling hand across his forehead. He wasn't entirely sure what he was getting himself into, only that it was too late to back out now.

●———•

A few days later, after a tearful farewell to his family, Pete drove to the airport. He landed in Rome shortly after noon and checked into the Hotel De Russie. Mulfetti had prepaid for the $700-a-night suite for the next four nights, even though they would only be meeting there the next morning.

At 10:00 a.m. the buzzer rang, and when Pete opened the door, he found four suave-looking businessmen waiting, two of them surly.

The first to greet him was Mulfetti, a man who was as wide as he was tall. His head was shaved, and a prominent scar ran from above his left eye to his right cheek. The man's dark eyes appeared to see everything. Although he wore a smile, it didn't reach the oily pools that were his eyes. Nonetheless, he threw his arms around Pete, kissed him on both cheeks, and thanked him for being willing to meet with him and his friends. Then he introduced Winston Kray from London, Arthur McGraw from Glasgow, and a handsome black gentleman from the Werewolf Legion in Stockholm named Abdi Nur, a Somali who now headed one of the largest crime units in Scandinavia.

Pete held out his hand to the group of chairs arranged in a circle in front of the fireplace. "Please, sit."

Nur didn't waste time on small talk. "We desperately need your help." He leaned forward and clasped his hands between his knees. "We are under tremendous pressure in Northern Europe. A group of start-up gangs began nibbling at our flanks a few months ago, but that has quickly accelerated into much more. Last week, they killed four of Winston's men and three of Arthur's lieutenants. I know I'm next, because they have told me so, in a note pinned to one of Arthur's dead colleagues."

"So they are trying to wrest the territories the three of you control away from you?"

"That's right," replied Nur. "Knowing something about you and your work with the Carbones and others in the States, I appealed to Izzy to make contact with you and arrange the meeting. Thank God you were willing."

"And what is it exactly that you want from me?"

"Everything that has been done for the Carbones. We want to deal a crippling blow to these upstarts and we're willing to pay whatever it takes."

Pete pursed his lips. "Before we can make a deal, I need specifics. By that I mean, where do the fights occur, under what sort of conditions, by how many attackers, etc.? Until I know those things, I'm afraid we can't help."

"Now see here," began Kray, "this is serious and we need help. We came here expecting to get it."

"And unless we know more about what you are combating, the kinds of challenges you are facing, where they are occurring, and by how many assailants, Mr. Kray, you are wasting both your time and mine."

McGraw stood, scowling. "C'mon, let's get out of here; I told you this meeting would yield nothing."

Pete walked to the door and opened it.

Mulfetti hurried to Pete. "Please, Pete, close the door. May I have a moment with you alone?"

Pete exhaled loudly and shut the door. As they stepped into the bedroom, Mulfetti grabbed his arm. "I am terribly sorry. I know these people need your help—and desperately. Kray and McGraw are uncommonly dour this morning, but they are good people. Nur is wonderful. Please, give us another chance."

"Mr. Mulfetti, I mean no disrespect to your colleagues, but it seems obvious two of them came reluctantly and believing there was little help here for them. I'm fine with that. Perhaps we should let it be."

Mulfetti's shoulders sagged, but he nodded and followed Pete out of the room. When the two of them walked back into the suite's main area, Nur rose. "Mr. Pernaska, I'm afraid we have left the impression we do not need the kind of weapon you can supply us with. That is, on our part, a serious mistake. Our organizations are severely threatened and we are desperately in need of help. Could we continue our talks, please?"

Pete sat down on the brown leather armchair closest to the fireplace. While the fire snapped and crackled, Nur told him about the struggles the upstart gangs were creating. Pete listened and searched the eyes of his guests, finding in them continued hostility, but perhaps also a little interest?

When Nur had finished, Pete smiled, placed his hands on the table in front of him, and looked each of his guests in the eyes. His gaze was steady and friendly. "There is no question the products we make can help you."

Nur propped an elbow on the mantel above the fireplace. His face, in contrast to his associates', held no animosity. "Could you tell us what you might offer to help us with our problem?"

"What is it you want to do? We have products that will paralyze but not kill and products that will kill."

"We need to send an unmistakable and emphatic message." Nur smacked the fireplace mantel with an open hand. Pete forced himself not to jump. "I don't think knockout drops will do the job."

Pete stretched his arms across the back of the couch, trying to appear relaxed. His stomach was on fire and he hoped the nervous sweat was not visible to his guests. *What an idiot I was to suggest Europe to Sam. If—and it's a large if—I get out of here alive, I should head home and keep my mouth shut.* Two months ago he'd been quite content working for Molly. Why had he not stayed where he was? *What on earth made me think that I was capable of conducting high-level talks with some of the most powerful crime bosses in the world?*

It all made his head spin a little. He shifted on the couch, trying to still his stomach. "Our products are much more than knockout drops, I assure you, but it sounds as if putting someone or several people down permanently would be preferable."

All three leaders nodded. Pete lowered his arm and straightened on the couch. This might be an opportunity, but he had to appear certain of himself and his words.

Twenty minutes later, he had explained exactly what the product was and what it could do for them. An uneasy harmony had been restored, an order for death-dealing sprayers had been placed, and the meeting was over.

As his guests prepared to leave, Nur and Mulfetti were gracious; Kray and McGraw, however, remained surly.

"This better work," said McGraw, his Scottish brogue a near growl. "Otherwise we'll have a new enemy." He slammed his hat onto his head and he and Kray hurried out.

Nur rested a hand on Pete's shoulder. "Please forgive my colleagues. They are good men but skeptical and stoic, sometimes downright nasty. You have not seen them at their best."

Pete frowned. "They do seem difficult."

"Not difficult," said Nur. "They are desperate."

18

Sam had worked nearly all weekend without sleep to fill the orders she had picked up Friday. The absence of Pete was wearing on her. Orders had piled up, and although she worked hard but carefully, she felt pressured. Without thinking, she had packed the boxes in the Sentinel. By the time she realized her mistake, she was too weary to move them to the Jeep. She didn't like to use the Sentinel for two reasons: the vehicle was too conspicuous and she was trying to save it for special occasions.

Reaching Highway 35, she turned north to go up the east side of the lake. A half hour later, she arrived at the post office in Woods Bay. Carrying an armful of packages so high it partially blocked her view, she started to enter the building and bumped into someone. Embarrassed, she stepped back, ready to apologize, then stopped, her stomach clenching. She was looking into the eyes of a police officer. "I'm so sorry. In too much of a hurry, I guess."

He looked her up and down, smiled, and tipped his Smokey-the-Bear hat at her. "No harm done, ma'am." Then he was gone.

Sam mailed the packages, returned to the car, and headed north on Highway 35 to Kalispell, about five miles away. As she was leaving town, she spotted the trooper's car on the outskirts of town. Her instinct was to push down on the accelerator, but she didn't want to attract his attention so she stayed at the speed limit and kept her face turned slightly away from him. As soon as she was out of sight, she pressed her foot down on the gas pedal and sped toward Kalispell and lunch with Molly. Her friend smiled when Sam strode into the Golden Lion. "Making the run yourself, I see. Where's Pete?"

"He's in Albania on a business development trip and I'm beside myself with loneliness. I am so used to having him around, Molly. I miss him terribly."

"Bet you're looking to rent Sarge."

Heat flooded Sam's cheeks. "Nope, not into that. Pete's got my heart now and I'm gonna be true blue."

"Can't say I'm disappointed," Molly waved her into the seat across from her. "Don't want you messin' with another of my men anyway."

"Now Molly, that's not very nice. After all, we made a business deal and Pete signed off on it, too."

"I know. When's he getting back?"

"Another week. He'll have been gone a whole month. I can't wait to have him back."

The two friends enjoyed a sandwich and a beer together before Sam started back to Polson, where she would mail the last of the orders she had worked on over the weekend. *Home by sundown for sure. God, hope I can sleep tonight. It's just not the same without a man in my bed.*

●━━ •

As the day drew to a close, Al sat at his desk, staring at a map of western Montana. He had blown up the area from fifty miles east of Flathead Lake to the border with Idaho on the west and Canada on the north. He'd been looking at the map for more than an hour and now he scratched behind his ear with a pencil. *How in the hell are we going to find her in this mess? It's deserted, completely desolate.*

He glanced down at his watch. Quitting time had come and gone. Many of the lights in the bullpen area were dark, as was the chief's office.

Al decided to leave the map in place so he could see it first thing in the morning. He grabbed his suit jacket from the back of his door, snapped off the lights, and headed out. He had taken about three steps when his phone rang. He thought about letting it go to voice mail, but something made him turn and go back.

"Rouse," he barked as he picked up the phone.

"Al, it's Tad Munson. I'm pretty damn sure your girl is in this area of Montana."

Al tossed his suit coat on the desk and dropped onto his chair, his heart racing. "What makes you think that?"

"I'm sitting here with Willie Midthun," Munson told him, "and Willie thinks he bumped into her at the post office in Woods Bay about halfway down the east side of Flathead Lake."

Al gripped the receiver tightly. "Willie, what can you tell me?"

"Well, Mr. Rouse, I—"

"It's Detective," interrupted Tad.

"Sorry, Detective, but as Tad said, I think I saw the person you're looking for in Woods Bay today. I'm a state trooper, too, and I had stopped off to mail some cards for my wife. As I was coming out, I almost ran headlong into this attractive redhead. Wow! What a looker."

"She's that, all right," acknowledged Al. "Can you describe her?"

"Not likely to forget that one for a while. She was attractive, stunningly attractive. The whole package was primo. In her fifties. About five foot five, maybe 120 pounds, auburn hair. The only distinguishing mark was a mole on her left cheek. She has a smile that would melt an iceberg."

"I think that's her." Al straightened in his chair and tried to keep his voice steady. "Any idea where she went?"

"I was parked outside Woods Bay when a car passed by me, heading north. I was deep in the middle of reports, but I caught enough of a glimpse to realize the vehicle was a Sentinel, and that the driver looked to be the same woman I'd just bumped into. I took off after her, but she had disappeared, I'm sorry to say. I have a pretty hot car, but that Sentinel must be really hot. I drove around a while, hoping to catch sight of her, but nothing, not a trace."

"Even so, you've made my day. I'd love to know exactly where she is, but it's great to get confirmation that she's still in Montana, or was, at least, earlier today." Al picked up a pen from his desk. "Any idea what she was mailing?"

"No, but she had her arms full of small boxes. Almost covered her face."

"I'm betting those packages held poisons and potions for mobsters." Al tapped the pen against the blotter. "If that's right, then it's likely she is making them nearby."

"Who's the manager at the Woods Bay P.O. now?" Munson asked.

"Herbie Johnson," said Willie. "You know him, Tad. Big guy. About six foot three, 265 pounds, ears that look like Howdy Doody."

Munson laughed. "Hell, yes, I know those ears. We should stop by and see him tomorrow."

"Sounds like a great idea." Al stopped tapping the pen and clutched it between his fingers. Was it possible? Could they be closing in on Genevieve Wangen again? Adrenaline coursed through him, but he forced himself to speak slowly and clearly. "Try not to do anything to tip her off, though. As I've mentioned, she's extremely slippery. If she suspects we might be on to her, she'll disappear and we'll be back to square one."

"Munson!" A man's voice boomed through the phone and Al winced and moved it away from his ear.

"Sorry Al, that's the boss. Gotta go."

"No problem. I appreciate the call. And I know I don't have to ask, but please let me know if there are any new developments, however small."

"I will."

Al hung up the phone and leaned back in his chair. *Don't get too excited.* He'd been down that road before and it had only led to disappointment and humiliation. Twice. Still ... He pressed his fingertips together and allowed himself a minute to visualize catching the old woman and locking her behind bars for good.

A smile crossed his face as he stood up and grabbed his coat. Maybe this time that dream would finally come true.

19

After Mulfetti and his group left, Pete closed the door, slumped against the back of it, and inhaled deeply. *I'm glad that's over.* His forehead wrinkled. That northern European group could cause problems, though. The meeting certainly hadn't gone as smoothly as the other two, but given that this was a whole new world for him, it had likely gone as well as could be expected.

In exchange for a deal to supply the mafia bosses with substances that would give them an upper hand in their dealings with other crime figures, Pete had extended to them exclusivity in their areas, since, as he had told them, he and his partner had no dealings in England, Scotland, or Sweden.

After that, he'd been content to sit back and listen, aware that he was out of his element but not wanting any of them to figure that out. The amounts of money they had initially offered were considerably more modest than those of Saimir Krasniqi and Semion Moglevich, although still not terrible.

Pete figured the best strategy was silence, so he listened, speaking only when spoken to, and otherwise trying to get by with nods and grunts. The strategy appeared to work, as the deals gradually improved.

By the time they'd finished talking, the money offered for services rendered was incredible. *I guess I'm a millionaire now.* He grinned wryly. The stakes were high, though. That kind of money didn't come without a lot of risk. Pete held a hand out in front of him. It was trembling. Hopefully none of the other men in the room had noticed.

He ate in his room that evening before retiring in good time so he would be ready for his flight home. His phone rang early the next morning. Still half asleep, Pete grabbed it and pressed it to his ear. "Hello?"

"Pete, this is Mulfetti. I just received an urgent phone call from Abdi. Can you call him right away at the number I'm going to give you? It's one you don't have."

Pete sat up and rubbed his eyes with his thumb and forefinger. What was going on? Were the deals he'd made about to fall through? The meetings had gone far more smoothly than he'd anticipated. Too smoothly, maybe. Chest tightening, he dropped his hand and opened his eyes. "Yeah, sure. I'll call him." Mulfetti gave him the number and Pete punched it into the phone.

Abdi answered on the first ring. "My dear Peter," he began. "I returned home last night to a critical problem and an urgent need. The Bredang Warriors, a formidable competitor led by Suyar Gurbuz, an ethnic Assyrian-Syriac from Turkey, attacked our warehouse in Stockholm last night and burned our entire inventory. We must not let this action go unchallenged, and an effective counter requires your help."

"What do you need?"

"One hundred of those long sprayers you told us about, the ones that kill at fifty feet."

"That's a huge order; I'm sure we don't have that many in stock. How soon do you need them?"

"No more than three days." Abdi's voice shook a little. Clearly the attack had thrown him.

"Let me see what I can do." Pete winced. What would Sam say about this unexpected and huge order? Would they be able to handle it? "Are you going to be at this number for the next hour or two?"

Assured that Abdi would wait for his call, Pete hung up. Then he had to wait for Sam's call, lamenting the lack of cell phone service at her home in the mountains. When she called an hour later, she sounded sleepy.

Pete pictured her, hair mussed from the pillow and eyes half open. A stab of pain shot through his chest. Man, he missed her. "Napping in the middle of the day?"

"Look, buster, while you've been gallivanting all over Europe and Asia, I've been working my fanny off to keep up with orders here. How about you get home and help?"

He'd like nothing better. "I hate to break it to you, but you're about to get a whole lot busier. One of our new friends over here needs a hundred sprayers—and he needs them in three days."

"One hundred sprayers? Pete, that's almost impossible. I think I have about fifty in stock ... maybe a few more than that."

"Tell you what, I leave this afternoon, so I'll be home around ten tomorrow night and can help you get the order finished. Will we able to do it?"

She sighed. "I don't know, but I'll see what I can do. I'm glad you're coming home. I miss you terribly."

"I miss you too." Pete disconnected the call and held the phone in his hand for a moment, the sound of her voice still echoing in his head. Then he took a deep breath and called Abdi back. He told him that he would have a few more than fifty sprayers on their way as soon as his partner could get them ready - likely Monday. The other forty-some sprayers would be made when he got home and air freighted to Abdi as soon as they were done. "Will that work for you, my friend?"

"I can definitely live with that." Abdi sounded deliriously happy, and the tension in Pete's shoulders eased. "If you can deliver as promised, my friend, there will be a handsome bonus in it for you."

Pete hung up the phone. A bonus sounded good, but he'd settle for being able to complete this order to Abdi's satisfaction. If they failed at this, their first international assignment, it could be catastrophic. Word would spread quickly and not only would they lose all their new business, but several of the most powerful and dangerous men in the world would be upset with them.

Pete's shoulders tightened up again.

He ate a delicious dinner on the plane, thanks to another upgrade to first class. On the ground in Chicago, he walked swiftly to the gate where he departed for Minneapolis. On his way, he purchased a copy of *USA Today*, hoping to catch up with the news of the day.

A headline, "Mob warfare breaks out in Sweden," caught his attention and he stopped walking. The account noted that open hostilities between two organized crime giants—the Werewolf Legion, a mostly Somali group, and the Bredang Warriors, comprised mostly of Turks and Iraquis—had flared in a suburb of Stockholm on Friday night, leaving fourteen gang members dead.

It seemed the Warriors had gotten the better of the Werewolves, since ten of the dead were identified as Somali immigrants.

The final paragraph of the news article contained threatening quotes from the leaders of both gangs, promising vengeance on their opponents.

Hmm. Pete folded the paper and stuck it under his arm. Would it make a difference if the Somalis had the sprayers?

When his plane landed in Missoula, he disembarked quickly and ran into the arms of Sam, who was waiting in the arrivals area for him.

"Oh, m'god, it's good to see you." She clasped her hands behind his neck. "I have been so lonesome for you, Pete. You'll never know."

"I'm here, and I hope it will be a long time before we are separated again. I missed you, too. How about taking me home?" He grabbed his bag in one hand and her fingers in his other and they fled to the parking lot, where her Jeep was waiting. They talked nonstop on the drive back to Polson and then on into the hills. As they neared her home, he said, "Have you seen Ben?"

"Every day. It's like he knew you were gone and was bound and determined to make sure no one took advantage of me."

He frowned. "I sure hope no one tried."

"No one did. And if anyone had, they would have gotten a firm 'not interested' from me."

"I'm glad to hear it. But Ben was good, was he?"

"He'd come to the yard every night, let out a roar, and I'd go out on the porch with a plate of food to greet him. He'd come to the bottom of the stairs to get it, but never once did he put a paw on the step. He was a real good boy."

"It's amazing, isn't it, how he seems grateful for the help we gave him with his eye?"

"It is. Now it's almost as though he's watching over us to make sure nothing happens. I wonder what he'd do if anyone questionable showed up?"

"Let's hope we don't find out. I don't want any bad guys coming by our place. Or any other interruptions, for that matter." He lifted her hand to his mouth and kissed it. Pink spread across her cheeks.

When Sam drove the Jeep into the yard, Pete smiled, happy to be home. He grabbed his luggage and headed up the front stairs. Sam held the door open for him. Once inside, he dropped the suitcase and took her into his arms.

"I have missed this place, but what I really missed was you. I can't wait to get you into bed."

"I can't wait either, not one more second."

In a frantic rush clothes were removed and strewn across the floor. Pete carried her to the bedroom and tossed her onto the bed and neither of them did any talking for quite a while after that. When at last their breathing eased, she looked up at him. "My, you really did miss me."

He used his index finger to draw circles on her stomach. "You know, Sam, when I was in the hills with Semion, he offered me a beautiful and young Albanian girl named Tapni. She was exquisite. But I want you to know, I sent her away untouched. All I could think of was you."

She touched his cheek with one hand. "I believe you. Is that a test passed, do you suppose?"

"I think it is a clear sign that you are the only one for me, the one I want to spend the rest of my life with."

He stroked her arm for a few minutes then grinned. "That sounded like a proposal."

She smiled up at him. "Yes, it did."

"If it was a proposal, what would your answer be?"

"I thought I was far too old to think about marriage, Pete. But you make me feel like a schoolgirl again. I have never been this happy, not even with my Henry. In spite of what I should say, I guess my answer would be, 'Hell, yes!' What do you think of that?"

"I think we should consider it a proposal, and begin to plan a wedding. I suppose we'll have to wait a while. Our new business is going to take all our time for several months, I fear, but once spring comes, I think we should do it; we should get married."

"Sounds great. In my spare time, I'll get to planning."

A thrill of anticipation shot through Pete. He'd never given much thought to marriage, but suddenly he wanted to marry Sam more than anything else in the world. He'd have to push wedding thoughts aside for a while, though. With everything that was on the line with their new venture, any distractions could end up being deadly.

20

After two cups of coffee and fruitless scans of fifteen newspapers, Al logged onto his computer. The first thing in his inbox that caught his eye was a long message from Tad Munson. He pulled his reading glasses down from his forehead.

I imagine this is reaching you in the morning, Al. I hope you had a good night. As disappointed as I was that the old lady got away from Willie, I was grateful that he saw her and confirmed that she is still in the area.

My wife, April, and I had dinner with Willie and his wife, Cheryl, last night. We were enjoying pie and coffee when April asked us what we were working on these days. I don't normally go into the specifics of a case, but as our wives are very active in the community, I figured it wouldn't hurt for them to keep their eyes open for this woman too.

I told them we'd been speaking with you, and you'd asked us to be on the lookout for a black Land Rover Sentinel, that the female driver should be considered armed and dangerous, and that she was wanted in Wisconsin for fourteen murders. That got their attention.

When I described her, Cheryl's face went pale and she told us she thought she'd seen that woman at the Golden Lion, a local motel, casino, and eatery on a hill above Kalispell. Cheryl had been having lunch with a friend when she noticed this attractive, auburn-haired lady having lunch with manager Molly O'Leary. Can you believe it?

So Willie and I are heading to the Golden Lion today to have a little chat with Molly. I'll let you know how that goes.

Oh yeah, Cheryl said it looked as if this woman and Molly were good friends—or at least knew each other before the meeting.

Small world, right?

Tad

Al was staring at his computer with his mouth open when Chief Brent Whigg knocked on the partly open door. "When I was a kid, Al, my mother used to tell me to shut my mouth before I ate a fly."

Al closed his mouth. "Oh, hi, Chief, c'mon in; I have a wild story to share with you."

He provided some background on the situation in Montana, catching the chief up before reading him the email.

"Damn!" The chief smacked a palm down on the desk. "Sure sounds like your old lady has taken up residence in Montana, doesn't it?"

"It sure as heck does. That's one, two, three, four, five sightings in communities near Flathead Lake," said Al, counting them off on his fingers. "Five different people saw her in a span of less than a hundred miles."

"How big is that lake?"

"More than fifty miles long." Al picked up the map from the desk and pointed to the body of water. "It has a shore line of 185 miles, the biggest freshwater lake west of the Mississippi."

"But still, the area where she's been seen is a fairly constrained space."

Al set the map down and picked up a pen to point at it. "Four of the sightings have occurred in the area from Polson to Kalispell and along the east side of the lake. The fifth sighting was in Missoula, down here, but the cop who saw her thought she was likely traveling to the airport. It might not be a large area, even if you include Missoula, but look at how rugged and desolate it is."

"Hmmm," said the chief, rubbing his chin. "I see what you mean. Lots and lots of mountains."

"Countless places to get lost." Al stared at the map, his shoulders sagging. "She might be there, but looking for her will be like trying to find a needle in a haystack."

"How good are the cops?"

He looked up. "Why?"

"Well, based on the territory, if we sent you out there now, you could likely spend a year and never see her, right?"

"Oh, hell, I wasn't thinking of going, at least not yet. We don't even know if she lives there. Maybe she travels through the area from somewhere else. Who knows? I think we have to have a pretty damn good idea of where she lives before we think about going out there. This Munson seems to be on the ball. I'm happy to see what he can find out first."

"Good." The chief pulled a handkerchief from his pocket and wiped his forehead. "That makes my job easier. I thought you were going to try and talk me into financing a trip for you and Charlie and Rick."

"Aww, c'mon, you know me better'n that. I wanna know we can catch her if we're going out there."

"Well, there was that vacation to New Orleans now, wasn't there?"

"And we had 'er, too."

"That's true." The chief shoved the handkerchief back in his pocket. "So I'll trust the Rouse Rash when the time is right and you tell me you're itching to go over there and follow up on these leads yourself."

"Thanks Chief. I'll let you know when I hear from Tad Munson."

"All right. And if there's anything I can do to help, just let me know." Whigg rose from the chair and started for the door. He stopped with one hand on the frame. "You know, Al, that was pretty damn clever. You got me so interested, I didn't even have time to steal a cup of coffee."

"Here, let me get you one."

"Nah, I've got my own. You get on with your work."

Al tried to follow the chief's advice. Problem was, as long as he was waiting for the phone to ring and Tad Munson to give him some news, any news, about the woman he'd been tracking for years, there was no way he was getting anything else done today.

21

Sam pulled the covers up around Pete's shoulders. He was so tired from his travels that he was asleep before she leaned over and switched off the light beside the bed. She brushed her teeth and pulled on a nightgown before creeping in beside him, careful not to disturb him. *Poor man, he really needs some sleep. Probably should have waited until tomorrow to wear him out completely.* She grinned, not at all sorry she hadn't been patient.

My, what a man. I am so lucky to be loved by this rough but gentle Albanian. She studied his face, peaceful in repose. *I love him more each day.*

Content with her thoughts of the wedding to come, she snuggled into him and closed her eyes.

The sun had barely crested the mountain the next morning when a thunderous roar shook the cabin, followed by a determined scratching on the bedroom window.

Sam crawled out of bed and stumbled across the room to the window. Ben sat on the grass, looking up at her.

"What is it?"

Sam turned at the sound of Pete's voice, thick with sleep. "I think your friend came to say good morning to you. Better come over and greet him."

Pete tossed back the covers and swung his legs over the side of the bed. When he came up to stand beside her, he laughed. "Look at you, my old friend. You and I better have breakfast together. What do you think of that?"

The bear snorted, almost as if he understood. When Pete turned and walked to the kitchen, Sam's eyes widened. The bear had gotten up and was ambling toward the front door. She watched until he disappeared around the corner, then got dressed and headed for the kitchen. Pete came through the doorway with a plate in each hand. One held red meat, smoked meat, and sausages. The other was laden with buttered bread covered in jam.

"Sam, could you open the door, please?" Pete inclined his head in the direction he'd just come. "And if you'd be kind enough, bring my coffee out when it's brewed."

She held the door for him before heading back to the kitchen to wait for the pot to stop dripping. After pouring a cup for Pete and one for herself, she carried both out to the porch. Pete sat on the top step. Beside him, his large rump on the third step and his paws on the ground was the grizzly. They were eating and talking.

She handed Pete his coffee and settled back in one of the chairs to observe their interaction. Pete would talk, the bear would turn its head and listen, then would utter a series of snuffling snorts as if in response. This went on for a better part of a half hour, man and beast each lingering over their breakfast in order to talk to each other.

Pete told Ben about his visit to Albania, his meetings with the gangsters, the deals he had made, and how he and Sam were going to have to take on some help to fill all the orders they were going to get. "Sure wish you could assist us, old friend," he said.

The grizzly shook its head from side to side, as if telling him no, he wouldn't be much use in the lab. The he reached out and rested one large paw on Pete's shoulder.

Sam drew in a breath. As incredible as their bond appeared to be, the bear was still a wild animal and therefore unpredictable. She didn't exhale until the animal pulled back his paw. "I think he's telling you he would like to help some other way," said Sam.

"I think so, too," Pete agreed. "We'll think on it, Ben. You be thinking, too. We'll come up with something you can do."

It was almost as if the bear grinned in response, then let out the weirdest noise they had heard him make.

Sam's forehead wrinkled. "Do you suppose that means, 'Great?'"

"I wouldn't be surprised." Pete set his mug of coffee down on the porch beside him. "Ben, there's even bigger news. Sam and I had a talk last night. We decided we are going to get married next spring. How'd you like to be my best man?"

The bear lowered its head before bringing it back up and making the funny roaring noise again.

Sam chuckled. "I think you have a best man."

"I think so, too." Pete grinned. "Better pick a maid of honor who is not afraid of large animals."

The bear nodded its head again before turning and meandering toward the pathway. Sam came over to sit beside Pete on the porch steps.

"So you feel it went well in Europe?"

Pete picked up his mug and wrapped both hands around it. "Almost too well. Were you able to get some of those sprayers out to Abdi Nur?"

"I sent them a day ago, shortly after you called me. He should have them by now, or tomorrow at the latest. We had fifty-seven in inventory, so that's what I sent him. I've started working on the additional forty-seven he needs. If you help me, we can have them done tomorrow and out Monday."

"Good, we'll get going on that now." Pete stood up and followed her to the lab. "Looks like you've been hard at it."

"I have. I set up an assembly line that allowed me to work fairly quickly, but it will go a lot faster now."

As they began to work, Pete told her about the war in Sweden, and that a rival group had set Abdi's warehouse on fire. "I'm pretty sure he wants to use the spray cans to wipe out that opposition."

"If he can get near them, he can do it. The damn things are very lethal. These new sprayers have lots of benefits, too. The spray system is even better than I hoped it would be. The potion stays together until it has traveled exactly fifty feet. At that point, it disperses in about a one-foot circular pattern. And it should kill on contact. One real benefit is that there is no danger to the person operating the canister."

"He'll love it. But if it wipes out the opposition, we can expect the number of orders to increase dramatically - and that's just one product for one customer. How are we going to handle the pressure?"

"I've been talking to Angelo quite a bit. We have ruled out this area for a heavy-duty manufacturing site. The population is just too small. Any influx of people would come under heavy scrutiny. We don't think the Northwest, especially Washington, is good, either. Too much federal pressure there. Angelo thinks we should come to Louisiana. He has an abandoned warehouse in the bayous south of New Orleans that he believes would be ideal.

"The area has a number of businesses, including several casinos that the Carbones operate, so workers for the plant could go in and out without creating any suspicion, since they would blend in with the casino workers. The problem is, one of us is probably going to have to be on site there once the plant starts to operate. I'm guessing you might want it to be you, since you would probably rather not have me spending any more time with Dino than I need to."

His head jerked. "I can trust you, can't I?"

"Of course you can, but I'm not sure we can trust Dino. You'll like him when you meet him, but you will soon come to see that he has a way of getting what he wants."

"And he wants you."

"He did. We've agreed that whatever we had in the past is over, but the two of us had talked about marriage at one point. I'm not sure how he will react when he finds out we are engaged."

Pete pursed his lips. "I think you're right and it better be me who goes."

"It would make me feel better." She rested a hand on his arm. "I think you'd start to have doubts, even if I was a perfect angel."

He grasped her hand. "*Can* you be a perfect angel?" His eyes met hers above their clasped hands, his gaze a challenge.

"I have told you I want to be yours. My word is iron-clad, Pete. If anyone but you tried anything with me, I would fight like a tiger."

"That would be some fight to watch. But let's hope it doesn't come to that." He pressed his lips to the back of her hand before letting her go. "So it's settled then. I will go and get the plant organized and operating in New Orleans. I'll stay until it can run effectively without me."

"I think that's the best plan. But the two of us should work together to get it operating. You go first and hire the workers. I will order the equipment and supplies and join you there after everything is delivered. We can get the plant operating. Then you can supervise things there for a time and I'll come back here." She screwed the lid carefully onto a canister. "I've given this a lot of thought, and while I agree with Angelo that our major operation should be in Louisiana, it makes sense to keep the domestic business here, as we've been able to handle that end of things until now without arousing suspicion. We will use New Orleans to handle Europe and Asia. I'd like to keep the two operations separate so if one draws attention or has to be shut down, we still have the other."

Pete took the canister from her and set it gently into the package he had prepared. "That makes sense. Now we have just one more issue to resolve."

"What's that?"

"You need to figure out how to tell Dino that we are a couple and will be married next spring."

"That's fair. It should be me, and I do need to tell Dino directly. Maybe he won't mind; he's very busy learning. He will be the next don and Angelo is ready to retire as soon as his son is ready to take over."

He tilted his head and looked at her.

"What?"

Pete smiled. "You're crazy if you think Dino will be happy to hear you are going to marry someone else. You're pretty damn special, you know. If he has been with you, you can bet he wants more."

She laughed. "Are all you men that starved for good love? I'm nothing special, you just think I am."

He studied her for a minute, his face screwing into a frown. "Sam, dammit! You forget what I did before you came along. I can assure you I've had more than my share of women. I'm pretty sure, since they were paying, they were putting out the best they had. None of them could hold a candle to you, none even came close."

"You, Mr. Pernaska, are biased. But I am very pleased that you think I am so good. That should mean I don't have to worry about you sampling other candy."

"That's a promise. I have become a one-woman man." She went to him and he took her in his arms and kissed her sweetly. Her tongue explored his mouth until he took her by the shoulders and held her out at arms' length. "Sam, if you don't stop that, we're not going to get our work done. And that might mean that our European business will be over before it starts."

Feigning contriteness, she backed away, bowing. She took her seat on the stool and marveled at his muscles as they rippled while he worked. *Wow! I could be in bed with that guy every minute of the day.* In an effort to stifle her impulses, she excused herself and went to the kitchen. Searching the pantry, she found a German chocolate cake mix and coconut cream frosting to go with it. She busied herself in the kitchen, mixing and baking the cake. While it was in the oven, she made sandwiches, loaded them onto a plate, stacked two empty plates under the one she had filled, grabbed a bag of chips, and headed back to the lab.

Pete had worked up a sweat, but he also had made great progress. The number of finished orders had grown to thirty-four.

Sam set the food on the table in the corner. "Well done, Pete. We shouldn't have any trouble finishing this order today. And I put a cake in the oven that will be ready to frost by the time we finish those next few orders."

An hour later they had finished the fourty-three containers and were sitting on the porch with cake and tea. Pete swallowed a mouthful of warm cake and held up his fork. "As soon as we're done here, we'll box up the canisters for shipping. We'll need to get them to the post office in the morning so they ship out tomorrow." He reached for his cup of tea. "I'm worried that Abdi has a major problem on his hands. He's a really nice guy and he's paying us big money. I'd like to get him what he needs to fight off this threat."

Sam nodded. "We'll drive into Kalispell first thing tomorrow."

"When you sent the last packages, how long did they say it would take for Abdi to receive them?"

"They said three-day delivery guaranteed. But getting that sort of commitment costs a mint. We ought to get in touch with your friend and ask him if he has the first shipment. If not, the post office owes us some money."

Pete mixed them both a drink and brought them out to the porch. Shortly after they'd settled in their rockers to watch the sunset, Ben came waddling up the path.

"Hi, fella," called Pete. "C'mon up here and sit a while. Can I get ya a beer?"

Ben nodded his head as he approached the steps. When he reached the first step, he turned around, then backed up, sat on the third step, just as he had that morning and, looking back over his shoulder, let out one of his funny sounds that they assumed inferred agreement.

"Are you seriously going to get him a beer?" asked Sam as Pete got to his feet.

"Damn right, I am. I asked him if he wanted one. He said yes, so I'm going to get one."

A few minutes later Pete returned, carrying a bowl full of beer. He set it down on the top step. "There you go, big guy!"

The bear got up, turned, and put his snout into the bowl. He finished the liquid in one long, loud snort. Then he reared up and made the funny sound Sam now recognized as approval.

"I think he wants another," said Pete, laughing. "Should I get him one?"

"Well, not more than one more. I don't want a drunk grizzly on my hands. But if he's going to keep coming to cocktail hour, we'll have to teach him how to drink out of the can."

"Now that's a crazy idea." Pete carried the empty bowl into the cabin.

When he returned a couple of minutes later, he was carrying a can of Coors and an opener. He stopped before the bear and said, "Here's how you do it." With that he tipped the can up and feigned drinking the liquid. The bear growled, so Pete opened the can—four holes around the lid—and held it out. The bear sank back on its haunches, took the can in its two front paws, and turned it upside down over his mouth. The beer ran out of the can into his mouth, only a little slipping down the sides of its jowls.

"Well, I'll be damned!" Pete slapped a hand against his thigh. "Will you look at that? This is one damn smart grizzly."

Both Sam and Pete laughed heartily as Ben finished the beer and crushed the can in his right paw.

"Just like a guy." Pete shook his head. "I can't believe it."

"That was quite a show. But no more beer tonight." Sam held up her glass. "Next he will be wanting Scotch or vodka. And that, my sweet Pete, is a no-no. You can do what you want with the Jack, but the Scotch and Vodka are mine."

Ben hung around for a while, and then with a snorting sound that Sam interpreted as "thanks," he walked down the path and disappeared.

Pete stood at the top of the stairs, hands on his hips. "I wonder where he goes. Do you think he has a den around here?"

"It's almost hibernation time, so it seems reasonable that he will winter nearby. Do you think he has a female friend around here somewhere?"

"Hmm. I never thought of that."

"I read somewhere that gestation for grizzlies is between six and nine months, and that mamas deliver while hibernating. So if he does have a girlfriend, he's probably already taken care of that."

Pete stared down the path where the bear had disappeared. "Does that mean we could have a family of grizzlies here next spring?"

"I guess it does. Which would make us, what, parents? Grandparents?"

Pete snorted. "If so, it's past our bedtime. We should head upstairs."

Sam carried her glass into the kitchen and set it down by the sink, heat already coursing through her. "Race you to bed, Grandpa."

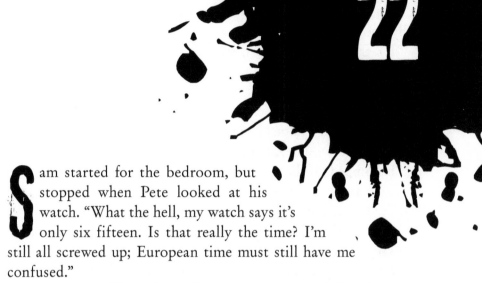

22

Sam started for the bedroom, but stopped when Pete looked at his watch. "What the hell, my watch says it's only six fifteen. Is that really the time? I'm still all screwed up; European time must still have me confused."

"Yes, it's six fifteen, but I thought you were ready for playtime?" *I certainly am.* She reluctantly returned to the island.

"What about dinner? Aren't you hungry? I know I'm hungry." He grabbed an apron from a hook in the kitchen and tied it around his waist. "What would you like for dinner? I'll cook."

"Make me something Albanian." She licked her lips, already anticipating a good meal. "Surprise me."

"Well, let's see, we could have lakor, or pastiche, or how about spinach pie?"

"Yuckkk! I hate spinach. Hate it!"

"Good, then that's what we'll have. It's time you learned how good it is for you and how great it can taste."

Sam hopped onto a stool at the island to watch him. Soon, dressed only in jeans and the apron, he was busy in the kitchen. *Mmm. I'd be quite happy to have him for the main course.* Sam grinned and clasped her hands on the island to keep from reaching out and interrupting his work. He made a trip out to the garden and apparently found what he wanted, because he was back quickly, a bowl filled with greens in his hand. He took eggs, milk, and sausage from the fridge, flour from the cupboard, and soon was hard—and noisily—at work.

It wasn't long before the most tantalizing smells were coming from the oven.

Sam tilted back her head and sniffed. "What's that? It smells really good."

"It's traditional Albanian fare. And you aren't going to eat it, because spinach is yucky, remember? I guess I'll have a quiet dinner by myself."

"Pete Pernaska, I'll decide what I'll eat or not eat." She smacked the island with her palm. "It smells good enough that I think I'd like it. I'll scratch the spinach out of it."

She jumped off the stool, mixed herself a vodka-tonic, grabbed a magazine and a pillow, and headed out to the porch. A few minutes later Pete came out, carrying a tray with their dinner on it.

He set a salad, featuring the last produce of the season, at each of the two place settings, then served some kind of incredible-smelling delicacy in pastry. Sam devoured the food that melted in her mouth like a cloud, cleaned her plate, and held it up. "Could I have some more?"

Pete leaned in and squinted, as if examining her plate. "What happened to the spinach? I don't see any."

"Damn you, Pete, the food was great. And it didn't taste like spinach, so I ate it. I'm not sure what you did, but you covered up the spinach masterfully."

"Hate to tell you this, but there was a definite spinach flavor to the pie. You also ate spinach salad."

"I did not. I know spinach when I see it, and that wasn't spinach."

"Well, you're wrong. I think I know what I put into my own dishes."

She frowned, but before she could argue further Pete chuckled and took the empty plate from her. A minute later he set a second helping in front of her. As she bit into it, she rolled her eyes and said, "Pete, how do you make the crust? It's the best ever. Light and flaky ... it almost floats."

"If there is one thing every Albanian woman learns to make, it's good phyllo dough. My mother made the best. I learned from her the hard way."

"The hard way?"

"Yes. She never cooked with a recipe. She made everything from memory. I had to be in the kitchen with her, slowing her down so I could note every ingredient and the amount of it she used.

"It was funny. She shook everything into her hand and then into the bowl. I had to stop her and tip her hand into a glass and guess at the amount. We didn't own a measuring cup."

"Really? Why not?"

"It's the way all the women cooked. My mother always said it was, 'by guess and by gosh.'" He laughed but he had a faraway look in his eyes, as if he was picturing the scene in the kitchen as he was trying to learn.

She reached across the table to touch his arm. "You must have learned very well. This is delicious. I love it."

"Then you love spinach, because it definitely tastes like spinach. And so did the salad." His brow furrowed. "Have you actually tried spinach before?"

"Of course I ..." She stopped and drummed her fingers on the table, trying to remember. "Well, maybe I never actually tasted it, since it looked so yucky."

He raised his hand, palm up. "It looks like a leaf, and you like plants."

"Well, yes, but ..."

"But nothing. I will teach you to like many things you think you hate but have never even tasted. You must have been a rich, spoiled kid. We would not have dared to say we hated something. We always ate what was on our plate, and it was always good, too."

She lifted her shoulders. "If this is what spinach tastes like, I might have made a mistake."

"Sam, Sam." He shook his head. "You're going to have to tell me the other things you hate. I'm sure I can fix it in a way that will make you love it."

Sam pressed a hand to her stomach. "After that meal, I believe it." With the food gone, Pete opened a bottle of pinot grigio and filled their glasses. They sat there and talked, the candlelight casting a warm glow inside the cozy cabin. Pete told her of his visit to Europe, carefully describing the people he had met and the scenery he had enjoyed. "I'm very worried, though, about Abdi and the challenges in Sweden.

"You know, Somalis were to me like spinach was to you. I disliked them vehemently, thought them arrogant and disrespectful, impatient and demanding. But I had never met one. When I was introduced to Abdi, he was nothing like that. He is a well-educated, well-spoken gentleman. I sure hope he got the sprayers and that they are helping him."

Sam reached for his hand. "Let's get up early in the morning, finish packing the forty-three spray cans we prepared today, and leave in good time. We can call Abdi as soon as we get to the lake. That way you'll at least know what is happening."

"I like that idea. I'll wash the dishes and put things away and then we can head to bed. You just sit there and sip your wine."

She let him do as he suggested, watching him through the glass door as he made short work of the dishes. She sighed. *I could definitely get used to this.* After putting the leftovers in the fridge, Pete rejoined Sam for more wine. When the bottle ran dry, he washed the two glasses, did the final clean-up, and they headed for bed.

Later, as he held her in his arms, Pete whispered in Sam's ear, "I can't get Abdi out of my mind. I'm glad you suggested calling him tomorrow. I need to know what's going on in Sweden."

Her eyes heavy, Sam nodded. She still had concerns about whether or not they were ready to expand into Europe, but they were going to have to go ahead with their plans. Pete's heart was already there, and she couldn't bring herself to disappoint him.

Even if it put them both in a very precarious position.

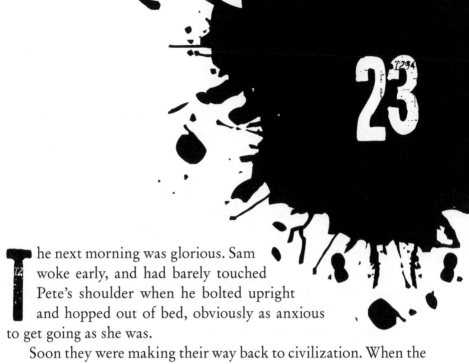

23

The next morning was glorious. Sam woke early, and had barely touched Pete's shoulder when he bolted upright and hopped out of bed, obviously as anxious to get going as she was.

Soon they were making their way back to civilization. When the lake came into sight, Pete turned north toward Kalispell then pulled off at a roadside stop to make the call. Abdi's phone rang and rang, but there was no answer. When the voicemail kicked in, Pete left a message and the two of them continued their drive.

When they reached Kalispell, they drove straight to the UPS depot. They mailed the packages and picked up the handful of envelopes waiting for them before starting back down the west side of Flathead.

"I feel guilty not stopping to say hi to Molly," said Sam.

"I understand that, but I don't want to be at the Golden Lion when Abdi calls. I want to be able to talk freely."

As if Abdi had heard him, the telephone rang at that moment. Pete pulled off to the shoulder of the road and answered the call. "Hi, Abdi, how are things there?" As he listened to the response, his face twisted into a grimace and he shook his head several times. "I'm very sorry to hear that," he told his new friend. "Have you made any gains on them? They were? Great. That pleases me. Well, the other fourty-three are on the way to you. You should get them in two or three days."

The two men continued to talk, Sam monitoring half of the

conversation. As she sensed the conversation winding down, Pete said, "How many? Really? That will take a while. Can we send them in installments? Okay, good!"

A few minutes later, he concluded the conversation. *What was that all about?* Sam studied Pete with interest. He pulled back onto the highway and put the Jeep on cruise control. "Abdi wants four hundreds pray containers."

Her eyes widened. "Four hundred! Do you know how long it will take us to make four hundred?"

"I do, but he will accept them in shipments of fifty, if that's easier for us. I think we can make fifty in a day if we work hard, don't you?"

"Sure, we can make fifty a day, but what about our other orders?" She lifted up the handful of envelopes they had picked up in Kalispell. "There are eight or ten here and we have six more stops to make."

"I know, I know. Let's see what else we get. We'll open them at home and then figure out what we are going to do, okay?"

"I guess so," she said glumly. "I never thought I'd see the day when business was too good. That worries me. Too many chances to get caught, in addition to too much work to do."

"I thought I did well in Europe," he said softly.

"You did great." She squeezed his arm. "I'm very pleased. But we do need to realize that a sudden influx of new contracts comes with other issues."

"Such as?"

"Such as having to set up a new business in New Orleans, and hire the right people to help. We also need to work things out with Dino. And—"

He raised his hand. "Didn't we talk about Dino already? I thought that was settled."

"We did, but I haven't spoken to him yet, so nothing has really been settled. It's easy to talk about but a lot harder to resolve, don't you think?"

"I suppose so, but I'd feel better if we had a strategy."

"If you're dealing with the mob, it must be face-to-face. Anything else is seen either as a sign of weakness or deceit. And if it's your problem, you had better be the one to solve it. Substitutes are greeted with derision." Sam's chest squeezed. Was she ready to talk to Dino face to face? How would he react to the news that she was marrying another man?

"So we go to New Orleans."

"Or I go to New Orleans."

"Over my dead body will you go alone. You're about to be my wife. You're not meeting any former lover without me along."

She frowned. "I guess you don't trust me then?"

"That's not it; I don't trust him."

Sam shifted in her seat to face him. "You know, I think you and Dino would hit it off. You're both nice guys. You're both straight-shooters. You're direct and to the point, and you're good businessmen. In another life you might have been partners."

"That may be," Pete gripped the steering wheel tightly. "But for now all I want is for you to get this talk over with."

Sam studied his profile. From the tight set of his jaw, he was right. As hard as the conversation might be, the sooner she could meet with Dino and let him know that she was with Pete now, the better.

●———•

An hour later they stood in the lab looking over orders. They'd received twenty-six requests for compounds and potions, in addition to the order from Abdi.

I can't leave. Pete's chest tightened. "You know, as much as I hate the thought of it, you are going to have to go see Dino alone. There's too much work here for both of us to be gone, even for a day, and the only way for us to move ahead is for you to go and see Dino and Angelo and pave the way for me. Then I can go to New Orleans and get the business up and running."

"That was my thought to begin with. I want you to know that I do hate the thought of going without you. I'll miss you."

"I know. Just don't miss me so badly that you have to hop into his bed."

"That's a promise." She wrapped her arms around his neck and kissed him.

He tugged her hands loose and held them against his chest. "Tell you what, how about I make supper while you get things into priority order and everything set out for tomorrow?"

Her eyebrows rose. "Two nights in a row? I'm going to get spoiled."

He kissed her forehead. "That's the idea." He let go of her hands. "Go to the lab and I'll call you when the food is ready. Need a drink to take with you?"

"Nah, wine with dinner."

"Okay." His forehead wrinkled. "I wonder what happened to Ben tonight. It's past cocktail time and he hasn't showed up for his beer yet."

"Hot date, maybe." Sam winked at him before heading for the lab.

Pete began preparing what he hoped would be a simple meal. Grilled burgers, sweet corn, a lettuce salad and, if needed, potato chips. He went outside to start the grill. As he nursed the coals into action, Ben walked into the yard looking slightly the worse for wear. He had a cut over his eye and several patches of fur missing from his back and his shaggy head hung low.

"What the hell happened to you?" Pete asked as the animal walked up to him. He gingerly patted the bear's back. "Let me take a look at that eye. It needs attention."

The wound was still oozing blood, although it appeared as though the worst was over. *Some antibiotic ointment should do it.* Five minutes later, Pete had cleaned and treated the wound and Ben was enjoying his second can of beer.

"Guess you needed those, right, big guy?"

With Ben taken care of, Pete got back to dinner. He made sure the coals were ready before going in to check on the corn. He mixed himself a drink then tended to the salad. When Sam joined him, he mixed her a vodka-tonic.

"You know, Pete, I've been thinking. Tomorrow I am going to call Angelo. I want to set up that trip to New Orleans, and I'm hoping Angelo will send a plane for me. I don't want to fly commercial. I'm afraid that would tempt fate."

You going to meet up with an ex-lover is tempting fate. Knowing it would only cause trouble, Pete kept the thought to himself.

They finished their work by eleven thirty the next morning. "We'll go to Polson," Sam announced. "I don't want to send any more out of Kalispell. We've dried up that source for now."

While Pete was busy inside the UPS office in Polson, Sam called Angelo and told him it was urgent they get everything ready in New Orleans for more production. She told him about the latest orders and her idea to retain domestic production in Montana and to use New Orleans for international orders. Then she told him that she had something she had to discuss with him and Dino in person and asked if he would send a plane for her.

He pressed her for details, so she told him about her relationship with Pete and how she wanted to tell Dino that she planned to marry him.

Angelo was silent for a moment then laughed heartily. "Ah, cherie, this is just what the doctor ordered. Dino has been mooning over you ever since you left. He's a good boy and learning quickly, but for the last few months, he's not been worth a damn. I think this is just what's needed to get him back on track. He's going to be heartbroken, of course, but he has something he can immerse himself in to forget you, and that will bring my retirement closer. Yes, yes, this is all going to work out just fine."

He agreed to send a plane for her at the end of the week. "It's cold up there, isn't it?" he asked. When she told him the temperatures were in the forties, she could almost feel him shiver. "Then you must come now; it's the right time."

They agreed that the plane would fly into Missoula midmorning the following Saturday to pick her up. Pete would stay home and keep the local production going, in addition to working on filling the rest of Abdi's orders.

"My dear," the old man told her. "It will be good to see you, good to have you back. We must have a family dinner Saturday night. Yes, yes, a party."

"Angelo," Sam bit her lip. "Let me talk to Dino first. I'll meet with him Saturday afternoon. After we speak, he can decide if we should have a party or not. I will leave it entirely up to him."

24

The bell above the door of Ma's Café jingled merrily as Al walked in. All the early morning diners looked up as he entered. Most of them knew him and several waved. Al and Charlie Berzinski were regulars at the south side café.

Al loved the place for the homey atmosphere. Charlie just loved any place that served food, so Al wasn't surprised that his friend was already in place at their customary table in the corner.

"Mornin.'" Al shrugged out of his coat, hung it on the back of his chair, and rubbed his hands together to warm them. "Feels like fall out there this morning."

"Well, what the hell did you expect? It is fall." Charlie had wrapped his beefy hands around a coffee cup. "It'll warm up here pretty quick if you have some hot news for me."

"What're you havin?'"

"The usual," said Charlie.

"Charlie, you have more usuals than I can count. Which one is it today?"

"Four eggs over easy, two strips of bacon, two sausage links, a slab of harm, hash browns, and a waffle."

While Charlie rubbed his belly in anticipation of the meal to come, Al shook his head. "I can't figure you out. You eat like a horse and you maintain the same weight and most of your body mass is muscle. How do you do that?"

Charlie rocked back on his chair, stuck his thumbs in his

suspenders, and said loud enough for all the patrons and Ma to hear, "I have a job that requires actual work, Detective Rouse. I don't cool my jets behind a desk all day. If you adopted my work ethic, you'd be a slim-trim-fightin'-machine too."

Al looked around to see everyone smiling. "Look here." He pulled out his chair and sat down. "You think you have everyone fooled about how hard you work. What do you think those smiles mean? They look pretty skeptical to me."

Just then Ma arrived, balancing three plates on her arms. She set them all down in front of Charlie before turning to Al. "The same for you, Detective?"

"Well, sure as heck not the same as him. But the usual, yes—two eggs scrambled, two strips of bacon fried crisp …"

"Two pieces of rye toast, no butter, strawberry jam on the side."

"You got it."

With a wink, Ma turned back to the kitchen. Al stuck the menu he hadn't even looked at into the metal holder on the table. "Better get your long johns out of hock, big guy. We're probably going to Montana one of these days."

"You think she's out there?"

"Four sightings in a few days."

"Wow." His friend's eyes widened. "Holdin' out on me, are you?"

"Not intentionally. I know the chief and sheriff have been talking. I thought Dwight might have filled you in."

"Al, we been busier than hell over at our shop. String of burglaries around the county have kept us all occupied. How about the P.D. Busy there, too?"

"Actually no, surprisingly. The students are back. UWL opened last week. No real problems, though, and no drownings either, thankfully."

"That *would* be a problem." Charlie set down his fork. "Might mean that we're chasin' the wrong person."

"No chance of that." Al took a sip of coffee and leaned back as Ma dropped his plate in front of him. He and Charlie focused on their food until Al broke the silence. "Can you stop by on your way to work?"

"I guess so. Whatcha got?"

"I wanna go through all the latest reports with you. I would've done it sooner, but I had a couple of things to catch up on first. When we're done here, let's go over to my office and I'll take you through the reports."

"I'll text Dwight to let him know I'll be late."

Forty minutes later, the two lawmen were seated in Al's office as Charlie was brought up to date on events in Montana.

"So you see," said Al, tapping the map between them, "I'm pretty sure this woman is Genevieve, but we're hoping to get some warrants soon so we can confirm her identity. Once that happens, I think we can talk Brent and Dwight into sending us out there to see if we can get 'er."

Charlie clasped his hands together. "Wouldn't that be—" The shrill ringing of Al's phone cut him off.

Al snatched up the receiver. "Rouse."

"Hey, Al, it's Tad and Willie. We just came from the Woods Bay Post Office and Herbie Johnson was of great help."

"Just one moment, gentlemen." Al walked across the room and closed his door. When he got back to the desk, he put his phone on speaker, grabbed a pad and pen, and said, "Charlie Berzinski is with me, too. So give it to us. What did he have to say?" He covered the receiver and looked at Charlie. "Tad and Willie just had a session with a postmaster out there at an office Genevieve uses."

"She's a regular," burst out Willie, clearly unable to contain himself. "She stops by to ship packages and pick up mail every couple of weeks. She has a box at the post office in the name of Samantha Walters."

"Yeah," Tad chimed in. "Herbie told us she's friendly. He was pretty interested in why we were asking about her. Willie was quick on that one. Said she had just obtained Montana plates and Montana troopers made a practice of visiting and greeting all newcomers. We don't get all that many of them, you know."

Al's eyebrows rose. "Is there such a practice?"

"Sure," said Willie cheerfully. "They give us the names of the newcomers to our area and encourage us to visit them. I haven't seen anything for a Samantha Walters in our area, though. Have you, Tad?"

"Not a thing. Either she slipped under the radar or she hasn't yet registered her vehicle in Montana. We have a sixty-day registration deadline out here, but lots of people ignore it."

"Any chance we can get a look at her mail?"

"Well, as you know, we'd have to get a warrant to open it, likely from both the federal and state folks. I'll have to ask the boss about that," said Tad.

"Any pattern to her visits?"

"Herbie says she comes on different days every two or three weeks. Apparently, there is always mail waiting for her and she usually has packages to send."

Willie broke in to say, "The package mailings have tapered off recently, though. Herbie thinks she might be using UPS or FedEx out of either Kalispell or Missoula."

Al exhaled loudly. "So now what?"

"We're gonna head up to Kalispell and have a little visit with Molly O'Leary," Tad told him. "We're thinking that could be a pretty good contact."

Al ran a hand over his head. "That one worries me, guys. Based on what your wife said, Willie, it looked like Molly and Genevieve—or Samantha—are pretty good friends, right?"

"That's what she thought," agreed Willie.

"If that's the case, we can probably assume that as soon as you guys leave, Molly will contact Genevieve and tell her you were asking about her. The minute that happens, it's likely she will move on. Maybe hold off on that for now. Once we have the warrants to confiscate her mail, we can pull DNA samples from the labels and stamps on her packages and determine if Samantha Walters is our girl. As soon as we know that for sure, we can decide what our next step should be. What do you think?"

"They can do that with DNA now, can't they?" asked Willie.

"Sure can," said Al. "In fact, DNA from letters was a key factor in tracking down a recent serial killer."

Tad cleared his throat. "I'll talk to the boss about getting started on those warrants right away. Then I think we should go back to Woods Bay and impress on Herbie how important it is for him not to mention our visit to anyone, including his two employees. We'll let him know that warrants are pending so he understands the gravity of the situation. Make sense to you, Al?"

"Whatever you can do to make certain Herbie stays quiet would be great. And we need to expedite getting the warrants. If my office can help with that, Tad, just let me know."

"Will do."

Al lowered his feet to the floor and leaned in to prop an elbow on the desk. "You guys have been great. Charlie and I really appreciate your efforts."

"It's our job," Tad said. "And by the way, this is the most exciting our job has been in a while, so really, we owe you."

"Damn right," agreed Willie.

"Okay," said Al. "Let's stay in touch. Let me know about the warrants, and in the meantime, if you see her again, do not—absolutely do not—try to take her down alone. If you do, you'll get burned. She's as good as Houdini … and a helluva lot more dangerous."

25

Sam drove the Jeep to Missoula on Saturday morning, to the airport where Angelo had told her he'd send the Gulfstream to pick her up. Already missing Pete, even though he was in the passenger seat beside her, she reached out and ran her fingers through his hair. "Will you be okay while I'm gone?"

He caught her hand in his and brought it to his lips. "I'll miss you, but I'm sure I'll muddle through."

"I mean it, Pete. I have a sickening feeling that with business booming, the accelerated mailings from this area have put us at risk of being discovered."

He shrugged. "If anybody comes around, Ben'll take care of them, don't worry."

Sam tugged her fingers from his. *I have to get through to him.* "I'm serious. This isn't a game we're playing."

He shifted in the passenger seat to face her. "Do you really think anyone could find us way out in the middle of nowhere?"

"The people who are looking for me are very smart. That adds an element of great danger to what we are doing. I'm just afraid that our recent good business fortune will leave a trail that allows those hunting me to close in. In fact, I believe we should alter our plans. We need to figure out a way to move the business out of Montana— all of it."

Pete leaned against the door of the Jeep and stared at her as if she was crazy. "Really? What brought that on?"

"When you were in the UPS center, a strange feeling came over me, as if someone was watching us, someone who was lurking around, planning to do us harm."

"Sounds to me as if your trip to New Orleans can't come quickly enough. I'm glad you're going today."

"So am I. I just pray it isn't too late." She turned into the airport parking lot and parked the Jeep. Pete grabbed her bag from the back and the two of them walked toward the Gulfstream waiting for them on the tarmac.

The stairs were down and Sam climbed up, Pete right behind her. When she entered the plane, she drew in a quick breath. Dino, as handsome as ever, walked toward her, arms wide and a huge smile on his face. Before she could react, he swept her into his arms and kissed her deeply. When he let her go, she met Pete's gaze. He didn't look happy, but he held out his hand. "I'm Pete. I'm guessing you're Dino."

"That's right." Dino's eyes held a mischievous twinkle as he shook Pete's hand. "I've heard a lot about you. Sounds like we might be working together."

"Yes it does," agreed Pete. He lifted the bag. "Where should I put this?"

"Here, give it to me. I'll take care of it."

Pete pulled it out of his reach. "That's okay. I'll put it away. Just tell me where."

Dino's lips twitched. "Okay, fine." He gestured to an overhead bin. "You can stow it up there."

Pete stalked over and lifted the lid of the bin.

Dino caught Sam's eye and winked. She pressed her lips into a thin line and looked away as Pete walked back over to her. He pulled Sam close and kissed her passionately then let her go and, without a backward glance at Dino, walked to the exit and disappeared down the stairs. Dino sat down and patted the seat next to him, looking at Sam. She instead took the seat across from him. He gazed at her a moment, but didn't speak, just fastened his belt. She did the same. The engines spooled, the plane rolled toward the runway, and soon the beige and cream Gulfstream was skimming down the strip.

Pete watched the Gulfstream until it glided into the air and he lost sight of it in the clouds that covered Missoula.

With a long exhalation of breath, he retraced his steps to the Jeep, got in, buckled up, and prepared for the long, lonely ride back to Polson and points north. Six miles northeast of Polson, a police car approached him, heading in the opposite direction. Pete watched him from the corner of his eye, but the officer didn't appear to look over as he drove past and Pete relaxed. He didn't arrive home until nearly 5:00 p.m., and when he drove into the yard, Ben was waiting for him.

Pete retrieved a beer for each of them from the fridge, secreting a second for Ben in his back pocket. He opened it for the bear when the first one was done.

"Well, Ben, it's been another long day and now we're alone. Sam left today for New Orleans. And she's with Dino. Any idea how much that worries me? They were lovers, you know? Pretty obvious he still loves her, too. Damn, it was hard to let her go."

The big animal snuffed in response.

The nice thing about Ben was that he listened intently, almost as if he understood. And when Pete finished his ramble, the bear hung his head, and turned and walked back into the woods.

Meanwhile, the Gulfstream was on final leg of the journey to New Orleans. It had been a somewhat tense ride, but Sam and Dino had gotten through it with no angry words spoken.

They'd engaged in small talk for a while, but then silence descended, until Dino cocked his head. "So what's up Savannah, I mean Sam? You seem different."

"I suppose that's true." She looked him directly in the eyes. "Much has changed since we last had a real chance to talk."

"So bring me up to speed."

For the next twenty minutes, Sam talked to him about her

arrival in Montana, remodeling the cabin to include a laboratory, and starting her business anew in the West. When she had gone through the business details, she settled back and took a healthy gulp of the vodka-tonic he had mixed for her.

"I'm not exactly sure how to tell you this, Dino, but the man you met, the one who brought me to the airport, is my business partner. He is also about to become my life partner. We plan to be married in the spring."

He stared at her for a minute, but there was no bristling. His eyes became sad but they reflected no anger.

"Ah, Sav … Sam. I knew the moment I saw the two of you that you were in love. I could see it in both of you. Much as I hoped I was wrong, your confession comes as no surprise."

"It was not intended as a confession. Pete Pernaska is a wonderful man and I love him deeply. Please understand, romance between you and me was wonderful also, but it was not something that could last. I am much too old for you. You need someone younger, someone who can be all the things I cannot be."

"Thank you for telling me," Dino said finally. "Does my father know?"

"I told him when I asked him to send a plane for me."

Dino chewed on his bottom lip. "Don't tell me, he was happy for you, right?"

She lifted a shoulder. "I didn't get the idea that he was angry."

"No, I don't suppose so. He keeps carping at me because he says I'm not concentrating on the family business hard enough. Which I'm not." He undid his seatbelt, slid to the front of his seat, and reached for her hand. "To be honest, I've missed you."

"I've missed you, too, but Dino, we both know I'm much too old for you. I'm probably too old for Pete, too, but we have come to make a very good pair - in business, for sure, and in bed, too."

"Is he living with you?"

"Yes, for the past few months. I met him through a friend in Kalispell. He worked for her … doing all sorts of jobs. And, yes, before you ask, that was one of them."

"I'll bet you swept him off his feet." A wry smile crossed his face.

"It was mutual. He's a very nice man, very kind, very good, and a hard, hard worker."

"And good in the sack too, I bet." Dino sighed. "As much as I hate to admit it, I sensed all those things when I met him. Samantha, I want to be furious at you, and I really want to hate him, but I can't. I actually liked the guy. And I love you. I won't go so far as to say that I'm not horribly disappointed, though. I just can't see my life without you in it."

Sam shook her head. "Dino, I'm old enough to be your mother. We were very good together, that's certain. And we'd continue to be good for each other for a year or two - maybe even a few. But then I'd be an old hag, and you'd still be young and vibrant. It's best if you find someone your own age. Think how in awe she'll be at the things you can teach her. You are one very talented lover, as I recall."

The mischievous glint entered his eyes again. "Do you recall our times together, my darling? Because I do, all the time."

Warmth rushed into her cheeks. "All I will say is that you are very hard to forget."

He laughed. "What am I ever going to do without you?"

"You won't be without me. I'll still be in your life, but now as a business partner. That's a much more important role. We can still be very good for each other, better than we could be as lovers. I really believe that."

"I'm not sure I do." He squeezed her hand and let her go. "But I guess I'll have to learn to be content with what you can give me. Tell me about your business and the things we are going to do together."

And so for the next hour, until the plane landed at Lakefront Airport in New Orleans, skimming over the waves on Lake Ponchartrain as it made its approach, she told him about her domestic business and the new international business she and Pete were developing.

"Home sweet home," said Dino, smiling, as the wheels touched the ground. "Well, Samantha, I have strict orders to bring you straight to my father, so as soon as we have deplaned, we'll drive to his house."

When they reached the Carbone Industries hangar, which

contained the three family jets, three black Lincoln town cars waited for them. Sam knew all of the men from their days in the swamp, and she greeted them with hugs, as long-lost friends. Grinning broadly, the men took her luggage and helped her into the car with Dino. Then with one car ahead and another behind, the three-vehicle caravan swept out of Lakefront and headed for Angelo's house.

It was a joyous and tear-filled reunion, and when the hellos and kisses and hugs had ended, Angelo, Dino, and his siblings gathered in Angelo's study. As the meeting got underway, Dino told them he had news to share. When everyone had a drink and the assembly had quieted, he said to them, "Samantha not only has a new name, she also has a new beau, and she's planning to marry him next spring. I met the man this morning and I like him. He's a good guy and soon, I hope, will be a very good business partner. And speaking of which, she has some developments to share with us, so let's hear her out."

With that, the eyes swung to Sam, who quickly broke the silence, talking about her move to the mountains, the continuation of her business there—a business that had aided the Carbones— and her meeting Pete Pernaska, their time together, their business association, his trip to Albania and the opportunities that he had opened up.

After telling them these things, she admitted, "We now have more business than we can handle. Either we have to sacrifice some of the opportunities, or bring others into the business. When that became the case, I told Pete that my choice would be to partner with the Carbone family."

Before anyone else could speak, Angelo, whom Sam had observed quietly watching his children as she spoke, held up his hand. "I'm sure you all have questions, but let's allow Samantha to finish. When she called me, I thought she had a good plan. I told her I was interested. That led her to send Pete to Europe. Now she has a more detailed proposition for us. Please listen to her carefully."

Sam folded her hands in her lap. "Thank you, Angelo. While Pete was in Europe, he established ties with the families in Albanian, Russia, England, Netherlands, and Scandinavia, controlled by the Somalis, who operate principally in Sweden. Many of these introductions were arranged by or aided by Angelo." She nodded in his direction.

"Pete returned with contracts for orders that outstrip our ability to fill them. That is why I proposed a partnership with you. As I see it, I will continue to live in the northwest, in an undisclosed location, for security reasons. I can handle all domestic orders there, for now. I'd like for you to handle all international orders here."

Dino set down his glass of brandy. "Where would we do that?"

"Angelo told me you have a vacant warehouse that he thinks might be ideal for a production line. I'd like to see it and confirm his opinion. That done, I'll order the equipment for the operation here. I will then return to get the operation up and running, after which Pete will come to supervise. It would be nice if the family could appoint someone to eventually take over the business here. That would leave Pete and me free to concentrate on domestic orders, which makes sense, as you would not be competing with any other families in this country."

Angelo pursed his lips. "Dino?"

"Samantha is a shrewd businesswoman, so if she thinks this is a great idea, so do I. I'd love to have Chandler work with Pete to learn the business and maybe get ready to operate it one day. What do you think, Father?"

"Chandler is a very good choice, if he's willing." The patriarch held up his glass to his eldest son. "What do you say?"

Chandler nodded. "Seems like a good fit for me. I'd be happy to take on the challenge."

"Then we are in agreement." Angelo set down his glass with a thud. "Samantha, would you be willing to work with Chandler to teach him the business?"

"Of course." She smiled. *Excellent choice.* Chandler had many skills, including a great way with people. Although his father didn't believe he was as ruthless as he needed to be to run the family, he would be perfect in this role and would handle the diplomatic side of things beautifully. "I think Pete and Chandler will make a very good combination."

Some of the apprehension she'd been feeling left her shoulders and she relaxed against the back of her leather armchair. The operation here would be in good hands, which meant they could take on even more business than they already had. And she and Pete would be able to concentrate on their own affairs at home.

Including making sure no one searching for her ever found out where the two of them were.

The next morning, Sam called Pete to update him on what was going on. "The family is completely onboard with helping us, and Chandler will do an excellent job running the international arm of the business."

"What about Dino?"

"What about him?"

"Did you tell him about our plans?"

"Of course. He seemed a little disappointed, but overall I believe he is happy for us."

After a short pause, he asked, "Are you sure about that?"

"Yes. I think he realized that keeping our relationship professional is best for everyone involved. His father expects much from him, and in order for him to realize his potential, he must stay focused on the family business."

"Okay, good."

Sam frowned. Pete didn't sound completely convinced. When she got home, she'd have to find a way to show him he was the only man for her. The thought sent heat coursing through her. "I'm hoping to order the new equipment in the next day or two so I can get home."

"The sooner the better. Ben misses you."

"Just Ben?" she teased.

"No, both of us. Although we have very different ideas on how to welcome you home."

"I certainly hope so." She giggled, more anxious than ever to finish up business in New Orleans and head back to her cabin. "I want to be careful not to use the same airport too often. Do you think if I fly into Coeur d'Alene it would be too long a drive for you to pick me up?"

"It's about a four-hour drive; that's not too far at all. And Coeur d'Alene is large enough that a private jet landing there shouldn't create a stir. I'm anxious to have you home, Sam. Let me know when you're on your way."

"I will. Goodbye for now. I love you."

"I love you too."

Sam hung up the phone and pressed a hand to her chest, shocked at how much she missed Pete already. She worked steadily through the day and by three-thirty had completed orders for the equipment and the inventory. Then she quietly knocked on the door of the study, where she found Dino and Angelo deep in discussion.

"Come in," the old man urged. "We're at the point where a break will do both of us good. Something to drink?"

"Thank you, no. But I do have something to ask you."

"Anything, my child. What is it?"

"Could I possibly take the jet back tomorrow, to Coeur d-Alene this time? Pete will pick me up there so we're not using the same airport too often."

Angelo nodded. "That makes sense. Of course you will take the jet."

The arrangements made, Sam changed into a bikini and walked outdoors to the pool for a swim.

It was a beautiful late fall afternoon, and she swam laps briskly for forty-five minutes before she looked up and found Dino, drink in hand, smiling down at her.

"You are a beautiful sight," he told her tenderly. "Not sure I have fully given up on experiencing those curves again."

She treaded water as she sent him a mock glare. "We have an agreement, remember?"

"We do, but expect the boy in me to come out every now and again."

"Okay, I'll expect that, but don't expect me to forget our agreement."

He walked to the bar, mixed a vodka-tonic, then helped her out of the water and draped a large towel over her shoulders. She toweled herself off before picking up her drink and joining him poolside.

Dino leaned back in his lounger chair. "This is my favorite time of year. Dad and Mom love it hot and humid, but I sure as hell don't. In the middle of summer, I'd rather be anywhere else."

"I don't think that's going to happen," she told him, smiling.

"You're right." He sighed. "The family business is here and always will be—at least I hope so. That means I'll be here, too."

They chatted until the Carbones' cook, Sam's old friend, Miranda, called them for dinner. After they had changed and joined the family at the table, Sam told them she'd ordered everything for the new production and it would be delivered in two weeks or less. "So …" she lifted both hands, palms up, "While it's been lovely to see you all, I will be returning home tomorrow."

"So soon?" Dino's sister Vonell had been twirling pasta onto her fork, but she paused mid-twirl. "I thought we'd have a few days to spend together, at least."

Dino covered Sam's hand with his. "She needs to get back to Pete. They're busy with work and wedding plans. And I'm sure he misses her terribly."

Sam offered him a grateful smile. "I miss—" Her phone buzzed and she pulled it out of her pocket and glanced at the screen. "My goodness!"

"What is it?" Dino pulled back his hand. "Trouble?"

"Depends how you look at it, I guess. Pete says all hell has broken out among the mobs in northern Europe and we're swamped with orders for sprayers."

"Sprayers?" asked Chandler.

"One of the crime bosses, a Somali in Sweden, asked for an adapted version of our aerosol container, like the one you used." She nodded at Angelo. "When I left, Pete was in the middle of filling an order for four hundred sprayers. Now it looks as if everyone wants them." She sent a quick message confirming her departure the next day to Pete and tucked the phone back into her pocket. "Now I really do need to get home. I'm sorry, Vonell. Hopefully I'll be back in town soon and we can have a longer visit."

The idea was appealing, but even as she spoke, Sam wondered when she would have time to take another trip, or if she even should.

As much as she loved this family, coming here again anytime soon just might not be worth the risk.

Once aboard the Gulfstream the next day, Sam slept all the way to Coeur d'Alene, waking with a start when the wheels hit the ground. She was enormously happy to see Pete's face in the window at the fixed base operation at Coeur d'Alene. She'd only been gone two days, but it had felt like weeks.

When the stairs were dropped, she raced down then and across the tarmac into his arms. "Oh, my, I've missed you!" she cried, kissing him deeply. "Oooh, that feels so good. I can't wait to get you home."

"There are a lot of turnoffs between here and home," Pete whispered in her ear. "We don't have to wait, you know."

She slid her hand through the crook of his elbow as one of the pilots came up behind her and handed Pete her bag.

"Ma'am." He offered her a quick salute before returning to the plane. Sam had forgotten what it was like to be treated with such deference. Now that she was working with the Carbones again, and their business was doing so well, maybe she would be able to enjoy that kind of treatment more often.

Her stomach tightened as they walked toward the Jeep. *Assuming, of course, no one discovers where we are and I find myself back behind bars. This time for good.*

26

When they reached home, Pete showed her the pile of orders that had come in. Europe needed 560 sprayers. The five domestic orders were for simple-to-make products, some of which they even had stockpiled. Those would be quickly filled. The sprayers would not go together so easily.

"We really need that new lab." Sam stood in the middle of the room, as if trying to figure out how they would keep up with orders before the New Orleans operation was ready to go. "We need it now."

Pete came up behind her and massaged her shoulders. "We'll have it soon enough. Until then, we'll just have to do the best we can."

They worked hard all day and finished up a hundred sprayers by eleven that night. Either Ben didn't show up for his evening beer or they didn't hear him. When they finally finished, Sam went to the kitchen and tossed a frozen dinner into the oven. Pete cleaned up in the lab then came in and showered, returning to the kitchen just in time to eat.

"I have missed you so much," he said, taking her into his arms and kissing her. "But I'm not sure I have enough energy in me for more than what you just got."

By the end of the next day, 250 canisters had been completed and packed up, ready to be shipped out. Pete stood back to admire the pile of boxes. "I think we should split up tomorrow. You go to Flathead Lake with twelve boxes and I'll go to Deer Lodge, Anaconda, Butte, and Helena with the remaining thirteen boxes.

Hopefully we won't attract too much attention if we spread out the shipments that way."

The following day Pete drove his route from memory, collecting orders as he went. Because he had been there just a couple days earlier, there were only a few. He was home by the middle of the afternoon, and decided to start on the domestic orders while awaiting Sam's return. He left the envelopes he had picked up that day on the table.

When five thirty rolled around, he left the lab to check for Ben and found the big grizzly waiting outside on the porch. He mixed himself a Jack on the rocks and brought two beers for the bear, setting them on the top step. Ben retrieved the first one and worked at it for a time. He finally got it open and swallowed the contents in a single gulp.

"Better take it easy on the second, old friend," cautioned Pete. "It's your last one for the day."

As if he understood, Ben drank the next can slowly. Pete grinned as he watched. "I'll go get you something to eat." Still drinking, the bear nodded and Pete went inside to rustle up a plate of beef trimmings left in the fridge.

The bear ate hungrily, shook his head as if to say "thank you" and then waddled down the path toward the lake.

Pete returned to the lab. He had just finished the domestic orders when he heard a noise in the cabin. The door to the lab opened and Sam flew into his arms, kissing him wildly as she wrapped her legs around his waist.

"I missed you. Let's screw!"

And they did; there was no other name for it. It was wild, frenzied, fast, and rough. When spent, they lay on the lab floor, exhausted and puffing.

"Wow, that was a fantastic homecoming present." Sam rested her head on his chest. "You're a great lab manager, Pete, but you're even better in the sack."

"Sack?" he asked, looking around at the confined environment they were packed into, between counters covered with drugs and bottles and cans. "This really ain't that romantic, Sam."

She laughed. "As they say, any port in a storm. My, what a landing that was!"

They stayed there for a while, both of their bodies twitching as calm was restored. Then Pete kissed the top of her head. "Tell me about your day."

"Pretty normal, really. Made it to Missoula in record time. Everything went well until I got to Butte and headed to Helena. Then it started to rain like a banshee, so it was a slow drive. I took Highway 12 on the way back. That wasn't any faster, but it cut off quite a few miles. The roads weren't the best, though. They are gonna be horrible, come winter."

"It's always that way," Pete told her. "During summer the logging trucks tear up the roads, winter comes and tears them up some more, and then they don't get fixed 'til spring. Welcome to Montana."

"Well, say what you want, the scenery is spectacular. It's like the roads are there to slow you down so you pay attention to everything you are passing by."

"Yes, it is beautiful. Almost as pretty as Albania. Someday I will show you my country."

"That would be nice, but right now, I'm hungry enough to eat a bear." She clapped a hand over her mouth. "Ooh, did I say that? Sorry! But I brought a large pizza home with me. It just needs to be heated."

"Ben would be devastated by your comment." Pete attempted to scowl but ended up laughing at the horrified look on her face. "As I've just worked up a pretty good appetite, I say we go eat now."

He clambered to his feet and reached for her hand to help her up. Sam followed him out to the kitchen. As he reached for plates, she carried the pizza to the table. Pete set down the plates and went back for cutlery. "Ben was by to see you earlier," he called over his shoulder. "Had a coupla beers and the plate of food you left for him. He'll probably be back tomorrow. I think he misses you."

Before they sat down, she mixed a drink for him and one for herself, then paged through the envelopes on the table.

"There is one here from Stockholm. Should I open it?"

When he nodded, she tore the envelope open, removed the paper inside, and read. "Uh oh." She bit her lip. "It's from Abdi. Now he wants three hundred spray cans that travel fifty feet, but he wants the spray to diffuse at fifty feet to cover a ten-foot area."

"That's pretty simple, isn't it?" asked Pete. "Don't we just have to manipulate the end attachment?"

"I think so, but we'll have to play with it to make sure it works."

"Why don't you go get one? Supper will be ready when you're back. We can test it with water after we eat."

True to his prediction, he'd tossed a salad and brought it to the table to have with the pizza by the time she had returned. They washed dinner down with a glass of wine. Pete cleaned up quickly, and they headed for the garage where Sam filled the spray can with water. They put a piece of cardboard on the garage door, measured off fifty feet, and tried the sprayer. A drop of water appeared on the target. Pete used pliers to fiddle with the end attachment but overcorrected; the water spattered, covering and extending beyond the cardboard. He worked at it some more, tested it again, then again. Finally, he got the combination just right. They tested it five times and each time it worked perfectly.

Pete dropped the sprayer, scooped Sam up into his arms, and spun her around. When he set her back on her feet, he kissed her soundly. "That, my love, is a good day's work."

Pete might have slept later the next morning, but Ben's insistent roar when sunlight peeked into the clearing woke him and he slipped out of bed. Frost crunched beneath his feet when he walked out of the cabin to greet the bear and give him some breakfast.

"You know, old friend," he told the bear, "I don't want to spoil you. You need to keep up your hunting skills, you know. We aren't always going to be here for you."

The bear sniffled and snuffled, as if agreeing. But the grizzly finished the plate of food before walking off into the woods and disappearing amid the aspen and pines. Pete watched him go. Soon it would be time for the bear to take his long winter nap. *I hope he has a place picked out.*

He returned to the kitchen to find Sam making eggs and bacon to go with thick slices of toast slathered with butter and jam. When they'd finished eating, Pete pushed back his plate. "Should we get to work?"

Sam reached for his plate and set it on top of hers. "There's no rush. We'll have to wait a few days before making another mailing run. What would you think about going out? I'm hungry for a restaurant steak."

Pete feigned a hurt look. "You don't like my cooking?"

She pushed back her chair and stood. "I love it, but sometimes a girl longs for a little civilization."

"Okay, why don't we get a room at the Golden Lion and spend the night?"

She tilted her head. "Lonesome for Molly?"

"Now what kind of a question is that? No, I'm not lonesome for Molly, but the Lion has the best food and the best rooms, too."

"You're right," she agreed. "Okay, let's have a night out. That would be fun."

By 6:00 p.m., they were in Kalispell and had checked into a suite. They ate dinner with Molly, catching each other up on what was going on in their lives. "Pete, did you see how bad things are in Europe?" asked Molly.

Pete shook his head, not meeting Sam's eyes. "We've been pretty busy. What's going on?"

"Hold on, I'll show you." Molly left the table, returning a moment later with a copy of that day's *USA Today*.

Emblazoned across the width of the front page was the headline: "Gang Warfare Rocks Europe."

The story, uncommonly long for the publication, described the warfare among organized crime figures that had broken out in Sweden and now had spread across the heart of the continent and south to Albania and Italy.

Molly read the story out loud. Pete reached for Sam's hand under the table, tightening his hold when he heard the names of several people he knew.

When Molly left to speak to another customer, he leaned close to Sam. "They need help," he told her softly. "Things aren't going well for the people we work with. The other gangs have gotten together to try and take over European operations. We have to get those new sprayers to them."

The article ruined the evening and the mood. Molly returned and they both got up. "Sorry Molly, there's an emergency with Sam's business. We're not going to be able to stay tonight after all." Pete reached for his wallet, but Molly held up her hand.

"It's on me." She hugged Sam. "So good to see you both."

"Thanks Molly." Pete held Sam's coat for her as she slid it on. "We appreciate your hospitality."

Sam squeezed her hand. "Yes, we do. And it was good to see you too."

Pete followed her out to the Jeep. Neither of them spoke until they were halfway home, then Pete rested a hand on her knee. "I worry about Abdi and his friends. They are really nice guys trying to do the right thing. They had backed off the heavy-handed tactics. Now they're back in the middle of it, and they are getting their asses whipped."

"We'll get the sprayers done and off to them. Sam slid closer to snuggle under his arm as he drove. "I want to help your friends."

The next day they were up before dawn and working in the lab. By sundown, they had finished three hundred sprayers to fill the order, and an additional seventy six for good measure. They packed them up and loaded them into the Jeep and Pete's pickup in anticipation of mailing runs the next day.

The packages sent, life in the woods settled down. Two days after they returned, the first serious snowstorm covered the Flathead National Forest, cloaking their home in a mantle of white eight-inches thick. The snow stopped mid-afternoon and Ben ambled into the yard, his footprints breaking up the pristine look.

In spite of the cold, the three of them sat outside and enjoyed their drinks and beers. They fed the giant bear a plate of food. After he had eaten, Ben, uncharacteristically, hung around as if hesitant to leave.

With daylight gone, the temperatures slid below freezing. "Old friend," Pete said, finally. "It's time for all of us to get in out of the cold. I think the time has come for your winter nap."

No sooner had the words left his mouth than Ben walked to the path leading down to the lake, turned, and gave the loudest roar they had heard from him. The trees seemed to shake at the sound, and snow fell from the branches. Then Ben was gone.

They walked inside; Pete stoked the fire while Sam added a quilt to the bed. "Think we'll see him before spring?"

"I don't know," he said, an odd sense of loss assailing him. Was it possible he had grown that close to a wild animal? "I don't speak bear. But that last roar kind of seemed to say goodbye, didn't it?" He unbuttoned his shirt.

Possible or not, he was really going to miss that old bear.

A l was tired of waiting. He hadn't heard from Tad Munson in a while, couldn't hurt to check in. He reached for his phone.

"Hey, Al," said Tad. "I was just about to call you. We have that warrant you wanted."

Al blew out a breath. "That's excellent news. So what now?"

"I expect Willie any moment, and then we're going to drive over to Woods Bay to see Herbie Johnson at the post office."

"How do you think that will go?"

"Willie knows him better than I do, but he's a pretty good guy, long as he can keep his mouth shut. You know how small towns are."

"Sure do. Well, you can either put the fear of God into him or beg him to remain quiet. Hopefully one or the other will work."

"Will do. Hey, I see Willie pulling into the parking lot now. I'll go catch him before he comes in and we'll head out."

"All right; let me know what happens."

"Should have a report for you before noon." The line went dead.

Al settled back at his desk. After a moment, he grabbed the phone again and called Charlie. The big guy said he had a couple of calls to make but promised to be in Al's office within the hour in the hope of being there when Tad called back.

He was good as his word. A few minutes before eleven, he walked into Al's office puffing.

"Got any doughnuts?" he asked as he tossed his hat on the desk. Although Charlie had been named chief deputy two years earlier, he still wore the brown uniform of a regular deputy, preferring that over street clothes, he said, "Because it's too damn expensive to buy dress clothes."

Al tossed him the bag of pastries he'd brought in with him that morning.

"I've got a feeling," said Charlie, sitting down and rummaging through the bag. "No bear claws? Well, what the … oops, here's one." He tucked a napkin into the collar of his shirt and sat back. "Could you get me a cup of coffee, Al? I'm sorta settled in here."

"Anything else, your highness?"

"Aww, c'mon, Al, I've had a busy morning. Just tryin' to relax a little, ya know."

"Sure, you just sit back there and relax. If there's anything you need, you just let me know." His sarcasm didn't appear to faze Charlie in the slightest.

Al's phone rang. He abandoned the Keurig and hurried back to his desk. "It's Tad," he said, glancing at the screen. He punched the speaker button. "Hey, Tad. Al and Charlie here. Have you got good news for us?"

Before Tad could respond, the sound of Willie laughing came through the speaker. "You shoulda been with us. Tad was phenomenal … put the fear of God in Herbie."

"I think it was a two-person deal," said Tad. "But Willie's right, Herbie was groveling when we left. He's been postmaster for thirty-eight years and this is the first time he's ever been served with a warrant. He was like a poor kid with his first pair of shoes, no real idea what to do with it."

"So what happened?" Al slid the phone a little closer to Charlie, who was listening so intently he'd actually stopped eating his bear claw.

"When we went in, we got Herbie alone in his office at the back of the place," began Tad.

"And Tad looked so serious, I thought Herbie was going to wet his pants," continued Willie. "Tad brought out the warrant, told him we were seeking a killer, and if he didn't help us, we'd have to bring him in for obstruction of justice and a slew of other things. Scared the hell outta him."

"Willie's right," chimed in Tad. "When we were done, Herbie was shaking, literally, and more than happy to give us anything we wanted. He tore the labels off several packages the woman had brought in yesterday. They were fairly big boxes—not heavy, but an awkward size. About four feet long and two feet deep."

"Hmm." Al pursed his lips. "Interesting."

"Yep. There were seven of them, all with overseas addresses. Three were going to Sweden, two to England, one to Italy, and one to Albania. Is that what you expected?"

"Not necessarily," said Al, "but it's not surprising, either. Don't know if you've been following the action, but there are major gang wars going on over there. My guess is the old lady is supplying one side of the fight with some kind of chemical weapon to use on the other."

"I'll be go'ta hell. So you think she's manufacturing the weapons somewhere around here?" Willie wasn't laughing now.

"That's our guess." Al bent closer to the speaker to make sure the men on the other end heard every word. "That's why it would be a bad idea for you to try and take her down yourselves. Once we know if this is the woman we want and have pinpointed her whereabouts, we'll put together a team to bring her in, okay?"

"Okay." Willie's voice trembled a little, as though he was shaking himself now.

Good. Al nodded at Charlie. Whatever it took to get the message across.

"Tad's gonna drive the labels down to the FBI office in Missoula, like you told us," said Willie. "I'll spend some time on the west side of the lake, hoping to catch sight of her and add some information to the things we know. But don't worry; I'll stay out of sight."

"Sounds good. Just watch your asses, both of you. She's one foxy lady—and I'm not talking about her looks. Just remember, she killed fourteen people in Wisconsin, and based on what we know of her, we can't rule out the fact that there have been more victims since she escaped here. Don't be getting any ideas about being heroes."

Al disconnected the call, confident he'd turned the tables and put a little fear of God into the two men himself.

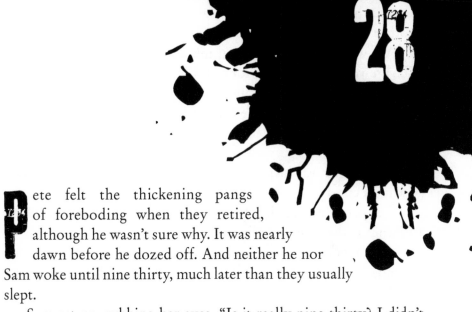

P ete felt the thickening pangs of foreboding when they retired, although he wasn't sure why. It was nearly dawn before he dozed off. And neither he nor Sam woke until nine thirty, much later than they usually slept.

Sam sat up, rubbing her eyes. "Is it really nine thirty? I didn't mean to sleep this late."

Pete tugged her back down beside him. "What do we have to do? The orders are filled and mailed. We won't make another run for three days. My only real task is to attach the plow to my pickup so I can open the road. That will only take an hour or so. I have everything ready to go."

"Then I guess we can stay here a while longer." Sam snuggled up next to him.

It was noon when Pete finished snuggling her, and even though he hated to extricate himself from the comfortably warm bed, he sat up, yelped when his bare feet hit the floor, and padded to the main room to breathe new life into the fire. Soon he was in the shower, where Sam joined him. Afterward they toweled each other off and headed to the kitchen.

They both dove into waffles made from Sam's recipe.

He patted his stomach. "Best damn waffles I ever ate."

"Just remember that when any thoughts of straying enter your mind."

"Small chance of straying. You have that little machine that purrs every now and then. If ever I thought about straying, one thought of that and those thoughts would be gone. I love you, Sam. Just think, another few months and we'll be married."

"We will. Guess we better think about that one of these days. Who are you going to have for a best man?"

He frowned. "I'm not sure; I'm not that close to anyone. Not in this country, anyway. Maybe I'll just have Ben."

She laughed. He planted his hands on his hips. "And just what's wrong with that?"

"Nothing. I was just laughing at the thought of the big grizzly wearing a corsage."

That made him laugh too. "Have you heard anything from New Orleans? Is the equipment in yet?"

"Not a word. Any day now, though, I suppose. Of course, we have to go somewhere to get reception so I can find out."

"I guess I better get that plow on."

Sam followed him to the front door where he pulled on a heavy coat, hat, gloves, and boots. "See you soon." After a quick kiss, he left her. It was mid-afternoon when he came back in, stomped his feet on the mat inside the door, kicked off his boots, and walked to the fire to warm his hands.

"I hate to tell you," he said, "but you're no longer a prisoner. At least you're not if you know how to drive the snowplow."

"I bet I can figure it out. But isn't that what I have you for?"

He adopted a hurt look, slumped into a chair, and said, "And here I thought you loved me."

She jumped into his lap and soon thereafter had convinced him yet again that she did indeed love him.

Afterwards, she hugged him close and he mumbled into her neck, "Ishunkweeshuddiveottmorroanckwiyrfrndsi nnaorluns. Wshudalspkpordsslngswedtht."

She pushed herself away, laughing. "Would you like to tell me what you just said?"

Very slowly, enunciating every syllable, he said, "I said, I think honey, we should drive out tomorrow so you can check with your friends in New Orleans. We should also pick up orders while we're out. Got it?"

Sam slapped his arm lightly. "I understood you this time, you idiot. Before you were talking into my neck."

"Maybe I should have said it a little lower."

"I like your baritone. No need for bass."

"Not a lower voice."

Her cheeks turned pink. "Probably wouldn't have helped, but it would have felt good. Maybe later you can practice."

He smirked. "I don't need any practice. I know what I'm doin.'"

"That's the truth." She wrapped her arms around his neck and kissed him. "You certainly do."

Early the next morning, Sam fried bacon and eggs for them as Pete went out to load the boxes in the back of the pickup.

They drove out of the hills to the glorious sight of the blue-black waters of Flathead Lake, a giant jewel in a pristine setting. When they reached the first overlook, Pete pulled the truck into the wayside and got out to check the load as Sam made the call to Angelo.

To Sam's surprise, it was Dino's voice that came over the line. "Carbone residence."

Her forehead wrinkled. *Why does he sound so tense?* "Dino? It's Sam."

"Samantha! How are you? And when are you coming to see us?"

"That's what I'm calling about. Has the equipment arrived?"

"Yes. Everything is at the warehouse, waiting to be unpacked," he told her. "Not sure about the supplies, but I know all of the equipment is here."

"Then I think it would be a good time for Pete and me to come down there and get things set up."

"The sooner the better; Chandler is anxious to get started."

"Good. Any chance of the plane picking us up on Friday? We'll need tomorrow to finish the orders we pick up today. We'll box those up and bring them with us to ship from New Orleans."

"I'll talk to Dad, but I'm sure that can be arranged."

Sam pressed a hand to the dashboard. She missed that old man who had become like a father to her. "How is Angelo doing?"

"Actually, he's not feeling well today." Dino's voice grew serious. "I've never known him to take a day off, but this morning he said he was going to stay in bed. I'm worried about him, Sam. This isn't like him at all, particularly since he works at home now."

Her chest tightened. All the more reason to get to New Orleans as soon as possible. "Watch him carefully, okay? At his age you can't take chances. Call a doctor if he is running a fever."

"We will. Did you know he turned ninety-four on his last birthday? He's slowed down the last few months, but to have him take a day off to stay in bed is something totally new. Mom is worried sick."

"How old is your mom?"

"She's only sixty-seven, a child bride. But they are the picture of storybook love. If one doesn't feel well, they both feel ill. It's as if they live inside each other's bodies."

"I know they're close. And I'm worried about him too. Promise me that you'll have a doc come by to see Angelo."

"I was thinking of calling him, so if it will make you and Mom feel better, I'll do that right away. And I'm sure it will be fine to send the plane. Expect it at the airport in Helena at 11:00 a.m. on Friday, unless you hear from me. That will get you here about two or three. If Dad's feeling better by then, we'll have dinner here so we all can meet Pete."

"That sounds great. We won't stay late though, as we'll need to get an early start on Saturday."

"How many guys will you need to help you?"

"Two able-bodied men should be enough to help with the unpacking. And an electrician, plumber, and carpenter would be good, too."

"Done. See you Friday."

"See you then. And Dino?"

"Yes?"

"Thank you." She meant for more than just the help with the lab and the plane. Judging from the hesitation before he spoke again, he obviously understood that.

"You're welcome. I only want the best for you, Sam. I hope you know that."

"I do. And I want the same for you. Give my love to your dad." Her throat had thickened and she disconnected the call before she could break down. She sat for a moment, collecting herself, before motioning to Pete that she was finished. She watched as Pete strolled toward the truck. Breaking up with Dino had been the right thing to do. Their eyes met through the glass and he smiled. Definitely the right thing to do. Still, talking to Dino reminded her of how much she had loved him, how much she still cared about him and his parents and siblings. For a long time she had felt very alone in the world, and without her realizing it was happening, the Carbones had become her family.

●—— •

Pete opened the door and slid into the driver's seat. "I should call Abdi before we move on."

Sam nodded and handed him the phone. Since it was nearing dinnertime in Europe, Abdi answered.

"Pete, I am so glad you called," said their Somali friend. "Things here are improving, thanks to your sprayers, but we need more of them, many, many more. They are needed now in England and Scotland, too. And I think Izzy wants some for his arsenal."

"What kind of numbers are we talking about?"

"One thousand would be great to start, but we are burning through them pretty quickly. They have given us a great edge, and we don't want to lose the advantage. So the need will be ongoing."

"I'll see what we can do, my friend. I will contact you soon."

"I'll wait to hear from you."

The call over, Pete pulled away from the wayside. In Kalispell, they stopped at the Golden Lion for lunch but didn't see Molly. On the way to their table, Pete grabbed a copy of *USA Today*, thinking they could catch up on the news as they lunched.

As Pete read the top half of page one at the table, Sam paged through the business section. "Pete, look." She handed him the paper.

A headline in the bottom right hand corner caught his attention. It suggested gang warfare in Europe was threatening to interrupt business on the continent. Pete read the story with interest then handed the section back to her. "Our friends need help, that's obvious. They appear to be holding the advantage, just as Abdi said, but they need more sprayers. The article reported murders in Sweden, England, France, and Italy. Not good, Sam. We have to meet their need for sprayers."

Sam set the paper down on the table. "Are we sure we're backing the right side in all this?"

He contemplated her questions, one he hadn't spent a lot of time considering. "The names came to you from Angelo. I met with them at your suggestion. Seems to me if Angelo recommended them, given what you've told me about him, then we're backing the right side. Either that, or we're wrong to be working with the Carbones, too."

"You're right; Angelo would have kept us on the right path. Sorry I even brought it up. What did Abdi ask for?"

"He needs one thousand sprayers for now, and likely more. And Izzy wants some too. He says they are working, but that they have to keep up the onslaught if they hope to win the war."

"You know, Pete, I didn't tell you, but I included a generous portion of Death Camas in the solution we loaded into the new containers. It's from a deadly wild flower that is hard to detect—impossible, some say, in an autopsy. That will make it difficult for the European authorities to find, and to track to us."

"That's fantastic." Pete smacked a palm against the steering wheel. "I told Abdi I'd call him again soon."

"I heard that. Well, we'll do the best we can to help."

Pete slid an arm around her shoulder and pulled her to his side. His head spun a little as he considered how much his life had changed in the last few months. He pressed a kiss to the top of Sam's head. All for the better, though. Whatever the future brought, moments like this made all the risk and anxiety more than worth it.

29

Pete drove the pickup to the airport on Friday, as it had begun to snow. When they pulled up to the Helena Regional Airport fixed base operation, the sleek beige and cream Gulfstream was already parked on the tarmac. Pete wheeled up to the gate, Sam leapt out to open it, and they drove to the plane to transfer the packages. That done, Pete returned the pickup to the parking lot and climbed the stairs to the plane.

Dino was waiting for him in the cabin.

"Hi." He stuck out his hand. "I thought I'd ride with you, take the opportunity to size up the competition a little better."

"Dino," Sam protested, getting up from her seat and coming to stand beside Pete.

Pete's eyes narrowed. Was the man mocking him? Maybe working with this family wasn't a good idea after all.

Dino lowered his hand and slapped him on the shoulder. "Just kidding, Pete. Sam told me you were the better man, that there was no contest between us. I really do want to get to know you better though, since you're going to be part of the family too."

This gracious admission settled Pete's mind and soon he, Sam, and Dino were visiting like long lost friends.

Dino wanted to know all about Albania and Europe and their business there. The two men hit it off completely and by the time the plane landed in New Orleans, they seemed like brothers.

Two Lincoln Town Cars pulled into the lot as they emerged

from the plane. As they drew closer, Sam drew in a quick breath and hurried toward the lead car. Pete watched as an old man emerged from the back seat and pulled her into his embrace. *Must be Angelo.* The man held Sam out at arms' length before kissing her on both cheeks and letting her go. He turned to Pete and extended his hand. "You must be Pete. Sam has told us so much about you."

Pete grasped his hand. The man might be old, but he still had a grip of steel. *Good.* He'd need all the strength he could muster if he was going to help him and Sam with their expanded enterprise. "Yes, sir. She's told me a lot about you too, and your family. I'm looking forward to meeting everyone."

Angelo nodded and released him. He shoved his hands onto his hips and looked at Sam. "Shame on you, young lady. Dino told me you thought I was ready to cash it in. I can assure you that this old body has more life left in it than it might appear. When I tell you to worry, you worry, hear?"

"Yes, Angelo," she said sweetly, reaching for his hand and holding it between both of hers. "I was just worried. I always worry about the men I love. And you're near the top of the list."

The old man's chest puffed out a little as he smiled at her. "You and Pete ride in back with me. Dino, you sit up front, we have business to discuss."

Pete's chest squeezed. *What is that about?* He shot Sam a quick glance. She lifted both her shoulders before sliding into the backseat after Angelo.

Pete followed. Was something going on they were unaware of? Was there trouble? What could Angelo want from them?

As the cars left the airport, Angelo settled back and drew his coat tight around himself. "There is not just trouble in Europe these days. It's as if the European situation has encouraged the Cabrera Family in Atlanta to once again agitate trouble against us. Two days ago, two of my trusted men were ambushed coming out of a casino in Biloxi. They were killed and left at my gate with notes pinned to their coats promising vengeance on the Carbones."

With the old man's words, silence settled over the car. They drove for a few minutes before Sam said, "What does that mean, Angelo? Does it mean more killings? Open warfare? What?"

"We don't know for sure. We just know that the gauntlet has been tossed down and now we either strike or wait. Dino wants to strike. I favor waiting."

Dino stretched his arm along the back of the seat. "The last time we waited I nearly lost my life, and so did Sam. I say we go after them in Atlanta, let them know that if they want to play with fire the burns are going to be severe. I think they see waiting as a sign of weakness."

"Dino, the fox always gets the goose because the goose thinks it must act. I think the Cabreras are like the goose, over-anxious to strike, something that always takes them down. If we strike now, we will be forced to fight them on their turf. If we wait, they will come to us and we will snap the snare. Once they have invaded our territory, all is fair game. Then it is time to go for the jugular, to rip their throats and hearts out. Time for us to take over Atlanta and serve notice to their friends up the East Coast that when you mess with the Carbones you inherit big trouble, more trouble than you can fight against."

With that the old man sat back, breathing hard.

Dino frowned. "I told you to take it easy, Dad. Getting worked up is not good for you and it is not good for the family. We must have our don strong and healthy when trouble surfaces. Now let's have a quiet ride. When we get home, you must rest."

They left the old man in the care of his wife, and Dino, Pete, and Sam settled down in Angelo's study to talk. Soon Chandler joined them and talk swung to the new war with the Cabreras.

"Juan, like dad, is getting older," Dino explained. "His son Alejandro aspired to succeed him. Like me, Alejandro was the youngest Cabrera - and the most ambitious. He wanted desperately to control the south, and the only way that could happen was for him to defeat us and take control of New Orleans while doing it. Then I killed Alejandro and calm prevailed as Juan Cabrera began to think about his options.

"Nico has two sons older than Alejandro, Antonio and Benito.

With his father's decline, Antonio is determined to restore the family to its former status. He has launched a new crusade against our family. Before we go any further in our business dealings with you, you need to know this. We are not safe, no matter where we go. And neither is anyone who works with us."

30

inner that evening was dominated by talk of the Cabreras, and with Angelo absent from his position at the head of the table, the hawks in the family had a field day. With the exception of the women, Vonell and their mother, Rosalyn, the others favored revenge—swift, definitive revenge.

Afterwards, they adjourned to Angelo's study for dessert. Sam didn't participate in the discussion because she was deep in thought, beginning to hatch a plot to free up the Carbones.

Eventually Rosalyn rose to her feet. "My family," she said, looking at Sam and Pete, "believes we must fight fire with fire. I think Angelo believes that, too, but he is hesitant, afraid to lose any of his family members in the fight for superiority. He is not the man you once knew, Sam. He is old. The fight has nearly gone out of him. But he resists giving up his control for fear of open warfare."

"But Mama," Dino stood as well, and paced in front of the fireplace, "there will never be peace until one of the families has completely dominated the other. That has to be us!"

"Yes, my son, what you say is true. Those are words your father would have once used. At that time, he was fearless, afraid of no man. But age has sapped his strength. His most cherished possessions are his sons and his daughters, and Samantha, he includes you in that group. His greatest fear is losing any one of you."

Dino smacked the fireplace mantel. "That does not mean we can allow the fight to go out of the rest of us. Any sign of weakness would be an invitation to the Cabreras to come after us. I believe that, as Angelo's children, we must talk about how to keep the Carbone reputation intact."

Sam held up her hand and Dino nodded at her. "I have been thinking that, since the Cabreras saw me last, when Dino and I fled Augusta, I am a totally new person. I look nothing like the woman who was driving the motorcycle that night."

Pete started to get up, likely knowing where she was going with this, but she motioned for him to sit. "I think I can be the key to putting the Carbones back on top. Antonio has never seen me. That means I could get close enough to take him out with one of my poisons. And if I do it right, there will be little, if any, danger to me."

All of a sudden, everyone was talking. And no one was listening. Finally, Rosalyn rapped a spoon against her brandy snifter, quieting the group.

"Please," she implored, "do me the pleasure of minding the manners you were taught. I want to hear what Samantha has to say. The rest of you be quiet until she has finished."

None of the Carbones would dare refute Rosalyn's request, and when Sam continued, there wasn't another sound in the room.

"I have never seen a member of the Cabrera family, with the exception of Alejandro, and none of them has seen me. I'm confident that, with the new appearance Angelo gave me, I could gain access to Antonio. What do you think, Dino?"

"I think the Carbones have asked quite enough of you, Samantha. Your appearance is spectacular, no question about that. I'm sure that any red-blooded male would invite you into his company, but I think it's asking too much. This is our fight, not yours."

"I disagree." Sam stood up and went over to him. "You have taken me in and made me feel welcome. You provided a makeover, a new home, a new identity, everything that I asked. And you have agreed to help Pete and me with our new venture. It's pretty clear to me: I owe the Carbone family everything."

Vonell slid to the front of her seat. "I have listened to this carefully. I appreciate each of the points made. But I must tell you that I believe Samantha makes a compelling case to take down

Antonio. Based on everything I know, Antonio is your typical red-blooded male, a man whose brain is below his belt. That was likely the main reason Juan had planned to turn the family businesses over to Alejandro. I think you need to listen to what Samantha suggests."

Sam smiled at her. "Thank you, Vonell. I think it is the best and safest way to cripple the Cabreras."

Dino exhaled loudly. "Not that I'm agreeing to this, and I'm quite sure Pete isn't on board either ..." He glanced over that Pete.

Pete, dark eyes glowering, shook his head. "I certainly am not."

Dino nodded. "Still, for the sake of argument, if you were to do this, what would your plan be?"

Sam rested an arm on the mantel. "Amber Johansen runs a high-level escort business in Atlanta. I'm guessing the Cabreras are regular customers. I did Amber several huge favors while I lived in Alabama. I believe she might be willing to erase the debt with a favor to me. Why don't I call her? If I'm right, the issue of how to do it will be solved."

Dino hesitated before inclining his head. "Call her and see what she says. Don't commit to anything though. It may be that we can come up with another idea so you don't have to do this crazy thing."

Sam went back to her seat. Her eyes met Pete's but she glanced away quickly. Fire burned in his eyes and both hands had closed into fists on his thighs. Clearly, he would be letting her know as soon as they were alone just how he felt about her putting herself in such a position.

"We'll cross that bridge when we come to it," suggested Sam. "But right now, I'm dead tired. I think it's bedtime for me."

With that the party broke up. Rosalyn was the first out the door, anxious to check on Angelo. The rest were close behind.

Sam and Pete's bedroom was much more than a room. It was a three-room suite: bedroom, bathroom, and sitting room complete with a fully stocked wet bar.

When they entered the suite, Sam went to the bathroom to remove her makeup. Through the partly open door she could see Pete pacing, his demeanor that of a tiger. When she was ready for bed, she took a deep breath and walked out into the bedroom. He pounced immediately.

"What the hell was that? I know you feel indebted to this family, but you can't be serious about taking on an underworld family all by yourself. Do you have a death wish?"

Sam sat calmly on the loveseat and let him finish. When he quieted, she raised her gaze to his.

"Pete, I love you. Love you with all of my heart. Do you really think I would risk my life with you waiting for me?"

"Hell, yes, you would," he thundered. "You just said you would."

He was all European and he was wound up tight ... so tight he was ready to snap. "You decide to take on this Atlanta family all by yourself? That's beyond belief. I am dead set against this, Sam, and if you insist on going through with it, I'm out of here. It's your choice."

Saliva flew from his mouth. Sam swallowed hard. She'd never seen him like this. She was tempted to fight fire with fire, then thought better of it.

"Pete, honey, just calm down for one minute. One minute, that's all I ask. Sit down here and listen to me." She patted the loveseat, smiling.

He continued to pace, his face growing redder. "One minute? You couldn't convince me in an hour, a month, a year!"

Sam rose to her feet. She walked over to him, took his hand, and led him back to the love seat. "Pete Pernaska, you sit down right now. I'm going to mix you a drink. And then you are going to listen to me for sixty seconds."

"Well, I sure as hell need a drink. Single-malt over two ice cubes."

She dropped two ice cubes into a glass and splashed a liberal measure of Scotch over them. She also poured a glass of white wine and carried both glasses over to Pete. She handed the liquor to him and placed her glass on an end table before sitting down close to him. "Now, will you listen?"

"For one minute, and I'm counting." He pushed up his sleeve, exposing his watch.

"Pete," she began softly. "Think about what I do for a living. Think of all the things you have heard about me. Think about the things you have seen and have even said yourself about my ability to take care of myself. Based on what you know of me, of my skills, do you think that I can't maneuver a man into position for a lethal dose of poison?"

He stared at her for a long moment then said, "But Sam, these are nasty men. And they'd have to believe that you were a ..." He drove his fingers through his hair. "How could you even think about putting yourself in that kind of position?"

"If Molly were desperately in need of help, I mean real danger from some women who were threatening her, and she came to you, would you turn her away?"

"That's different," he said flatly.

"How?"

"That would be me against a few women."

"Do you really think that you would be more lethal than I could be?"

"I'd be stronger."

"Yes, you would. But would you rather strangle them or give them a shot?"

He chewed on his bottom lip. The scowl gradually softened and he drew in a long breath. "What would your plan be?"

"I believe, from what I have been told, and largely due to the skill of Angelo's surgeons, I could pass for one of Amber's women, don't you think?"

"You're beautiful and sexy enough, if that's what you're asking."

"Do you not think I could lure someone into bed?"

He exhaled loudly. "Of course you could; that's a given."

"And do you think that I might be able to distract him sufficiently to slip in a quick injection?"

"I'm sure you could, but there's always ..."

"Yes, there's always a chance that something could go wrong. But the lab we're putting together tomorrow could blow up and we could all be killed. Should we forget it and just go home?"

His shoulders sagged. She had him.

"So you'll give him a shot right away, before ...?"

"Absolutely, first thing. I promise you I will plan everything very carefully so the chances of anything going wrong will be very slim." She rested a hand on his arm. "And yes, I do owe the Carbones a great debt. Angelo is the father I never knew. Vonell is a sister. I love her and Dino, Chandler, Benton, and Elliott. They are my family. They have put themselves on the line for me many times. It's my turn to repay the favor. Please try to understand that, okay?"

"I do understand that. Still …"

She watched him for some sign of emotion, but his face was a blank canvas. He stood and carefully set his glass on the bar. Without turning around to look at her, he said, "I will sleep on it."

Sam stood too and followed him to bed. When she reached for him, he turned his back to her.

With a sigh, Sam turned too, and faced the opposite wall. Would Pete come around? For a few minutes he'd seemed to, partway at least. She hoped he would come the rest of the way, because this was something she had to do.

But she'd be praying every moment that she didn't lose him in the process.

31

Before dawn the next morning, Pete was woken by a knock on their bedroom door. He tossed back the covers and stumbled across the room to open it. Dino stood in the hallway, fully clothed and smiling at him. "Time to rise," his host told him. "There is much to do today. I think Vonell has plans for Samantha, so you can let her sleep, if you'd like."

"Be right with you." Pete closed the door and rummaged through his bag for jeans and a work shirt. He hadn't slept well, tormented by Sam's plan, and he didn't feel ready for the day.

He joined Dino in the kitchen and together they ate bacon and eggs prepared by the kitchen staff. "I got Chandler up, too, but his motor runs quietly early in the morning. To be honest, he's likely more capable of running the family than I am, but Dad had lots of trouble with his wanting to sleep in every morning."

"Seems to me," said Pete, buttering a slice of toast, "that there are no dummies in this family. I think Vonell is sharp as a tack."

"You're right about that. Maybe if she'd been born a few years later, Dad would have chosen her to be head of the family."

"Would he have done that?"

"Maybe; she's tougher than any of us." Dino reached for a crystal dish filled with jam. "When the chips are down, she's got ice in her veins. She always offers the best advice in a crisis. Her only problem is she's a woman. No family, here or abroad, has ever been governed by a woman. The old country ways die hard."

"I suppose they do." Pete reached for his mug of coffee. "Where

I come from—Albania—the man is the head of the house. It's just the way it is. There are no arguments."

"None here, either," said Dino, "but I'm damn glad Vonell is on my side. She's smart as can be, and shrewd, too. Same as Sam."

Pete studied him. *Have I been hasty in my judgment? Can Sam do it?* He sighed. *I guess she probably can.*

Chandler staggered into the kitchen, looking as if he had just gotten out of bed. One of his shirt-tails hung outside his pants, and his hair was disheveled.

"Dammit, Chandler." Dino's knife clattered onto his plate. "You've got to start paying attention. That means getting up early and getting ready to go. If Dad finds out about this, you'll be in trouble again."

"I'm always in trouble." Chandler ran his fingers through his hair, which only made it stand more on end. He shot Pete a sheepish look. "Does life in your part of the world begin in the middle of the night, too?"

"I'm afraid so." Pete poured a cup of coffee from the carafe on the table and handed it to Chandler. "Sam and I have pretty full days, running our new business."

Chandler took the mug and dipped his head in Pete's direction. "Thank you." He sank onto a chair beside Dino. "With the new work I'm taking on, I guess I'm going to have to change my ways." Chandler sipped from his mug and slumped against the back of his chair. "I going to try to do better, Dino, honest. I want to make you and Mom and Dad proud of me. Right now, they think I'm a playboy who wants to party all night and sleep 'til noon."

Dino shrugged. "You know what they say: if the shoe fits ..."

Pete laughed as he and Dino carried their dishes over to the sink. As much as he hated Sam's method of dealing with the Cabreras, he could understand why she wanted to help this family so much. In spite of her history with Dino, Pete was drawn to him, and to the rest of the family as well. That didn't mean he wanted Sam jumping into bed with one of their enemies, but it did mean that, if it turned out to be the only way to save the Carbones, he'd have to at least consider the possibility.

Thirty minutes later they were on their way to bayou country, as Dino called it, to begin work at the warehouse owned by the Carbone family.

Built just off a canal that Dino said had been all but abandoned, the warehouse showed signs of aging too.

"But she's got a great roof," said Dino, "and the mechanicals are in great shape. Doesn't hurt for it to look a little seedy on the outside. It helps to mask what's going on inside."

Pete nodded. "I can see that."

As the two men walked up to the building, they found a group of burly workmen standing outside the *Staff Only* door. There were five of them and Dino introduced them to Pete one by one. Louis was an electrician, Ramone a carpenter, Frederick a plumber, and Georg and McCoy were handymen ready to assist with any task that needed doing.

Having already studied the blueprints, Pete had a to-scale drawing of the equipment, each piece carefully marked by its number, size, and purpose. In addition, he had detailed any additional services that needed to be put in place, such as drains or electrical outlets. Some of the equipment required special grounding. The plumber, electrician, and carpenter studied his notes while the handymen began to move the boxes into place.

Pete's plan was to have the equipment in place by noon, if possible, with any work on electrical or plumbing to continue throughout the afternoon. That way he could help Sam unpack the drugs and supplies and put them away in the cabinets that had been ordered for them. In addition to the four storage cabinets, there were two commercial refrigerators to handle those items that required cold storage.

The workmen were very businesslike and soon boxes had been opened and the equipment removed. The carpenter was busy building platforms for anything that needed to be kept off the concrete. Frederick was breaking into the floor to put drains into place. Louis studied the electrical service to the building and set to work installing separate circuits for the machines that required more power.

By noon, all the equipment had been placed and work continued on the drains and electrical service. Georg and McCoy worked with the other three to finish the unpacking and setting up.

It was shortly after one when Sam and Vonell walked in. "Dino, you left the door open." Vonell waggled a finger at him. "Anyone could have come in here. Better keep the doors locked at all times. This building must be kept secure."

"You're right." Dino rested a hand on her shoulder. "We'll lock it from now on."

The two women moved to the boxes that contained drugs and supplies and Sam began to sort them, telling Vonell where to place everything. When the sorting was done, Vonell took a box cutter and began to open the cartons. Soon Sam was busy at work, putting the cans and bottles into place and labeling everything, including the containers going into cold storage.

As dinnertime rolled around, Pete surveyed the work, declared that it was good, and noted that production could be underway the next day, if needed.

Sam closed a cupboard door. "There will still be a few things to finish up over the next few days," she waved a hand at the men, still hard at work, "but nothing that would prevent production from going forward. Dino, do you know what arrangements have been made for orders that have been sent from overseas?"

"Dad and Vonell set that up." He held out a hand to his sister. "How will that work, Vonell?"

"The orders will come to our plumbing business," his sister told them. "Since I am there every day, I will pick them up. There are several orders already in that we can look at when we get home."

Sam nodded. "Good. That means Pete will be able to start training Chandler tomorrow. It would be good to have someone else learn the processes as well. Someone to help Chandler when Pete returns to Montana."

"We have several great candidates," said Vonell. "Do you want more than one?"

Sam shook her head. "Not right away. We'll want to get things up and running smoothly before we train too many people."

Pete came up beside her and slid an arm around her waist. "I agree. It's wise to limit the employees at first." He contemplated the warehouse. "That's a good day's work everyone; I think we should head home now and get some rest."

"Great idea." Sam grabbed her bag off the counter. "I need to call Amber and see if she is willing to help us out."

The muscles across Pete's shoulders tightened, but he didn't speak. He would wait to see what Amber and Sam agreed upon before he discussed the matter further with Sam. And before he talked to Sam, he had some serious thinking to do.

32

Al piloted an unmarked police car back to the office from North La Crosse where he had investigated the break-in and burglary of a liquor store. The thieves had made off with more than two thousand dollars in cash and sixteen cases of liquor—a sizable theft. *They might have taken plenty of loot, but they weren't very smart.* Al had found a business card the owner of the liquor store had never seen before lodged behind cases of beer that had been moved to get at the hard stuff. He had given the card to an old friend of his, a sergeant approaching retirement and looking for a last hurrah. He'd felt good about handing the case over to his pal, but his good feelings dissipated as he drove as he realized he hadn't heard from Tad Munson in more than a week.

I'm gonna call him the minute I'm back. They must have something by now.

Al wheeled the Dodge Charger into the police headquarters garage, tossed the keys to the vehicle maintenance man, and headed up the steps to his office. Once there he brewed a cup of coffee, sat down behind the desk, and dialed Tad's mobile number.

The phone was in the middle of its second ring when Tad picked it up. "Hi Al. You must have ESP. Twenty minutes ago and I wouldn't have had anything for you. I just walked out of the Missoula FBI office after stopping by to check on the labels we dropped off a week ago. I think you're gonna like what we found."

Al gripped the receiver tightly. "So tell me."

"It's your girl. The DNA is a 90 percent match to one Genevieve Wangen. That's probably what you wanted to hear, right?"

"Well, I surely would have been disappointed if it wasn't her." A grin spread across Al's face. "A 90 percent match. That's as good as it gets, Tad."

"Yessir, that's right. Now all we have to do is arrest her."

"Which will be a helluva lot harder than you think. I've told you over and over, she's a slippery one. At least now we have a good idea where she is, or the general area, anyway. Don't do anything yet. I'll talk to my chief. We may end up coming down there ourselves with a team, but I'll let you know. Good work, Tad. Be sure and tell Willie how grateful I am to the two of you."

"Will do. We'll continue to keep our eyes open, but if we see your girl we'll stay out of eyesight. We'll just try to pin down her whereabouts, if we can."

"That's a great idea." Al resisted the urge to stand up and do a little jig. "Can't thank you enough for all your help."

"Don't mention it. Just have a good day."

After he hung up the phone, Al slammed his fist down on the desk. "Yes!" He leapt from his chair and headed for the chief's office. He barged in without knocking then froze when he realized Chief Whigg wasn't alone. "Oh, sorry, Chief, Sheriff. I didn't mean to interrupt your meeting. Too excited, I guess."

The chief gestured for him to come in. "Now that you're here, you might as well tell us what has you so worked up. Or is this for my ears only?"

"No, in fact I'm glad Sheriff Hooper is here. He should hear this too."

The sheriff shifted in his chair to look at him. "What is it, Al?"

"We got her!"

"Who, Genevieve?" The chief jumped to his feet, and the sheriff followed suit.

"Yessir." Al closed the door and walked over to the desk. "I just talked to Tad ..." Looking at the sheriff, he added, "Tad Munson, Sheriff, our contact out in western Montana."

"Yup, got it. Charlie told me all about Munson and his sidekick Willie."

Al chuckled. "That's right."

The chief clapped his hands together. "So the DNA nailed her?"

"Tad just told me it's a 90 percent match to her sample here. I can't tell you how excited I am." He shifted his weight from one foot to the other. "Sheriff, do you suppose you'd let me tell Charlie? I'd hate to think he'd feel as if I'm holding out on him."

"Sure, Al, no problem. I'm sure he would have known before me if I hadn't been here when you came in."

"That's probably true." Al leaned a hip against the desk.

"So what do we do now?" The sheriff punched him lightly in the arm. "Send you guys out there to make the collar?"

The chief cleared his throat. "We've talked about that, Dwight, and Al and I agree that waiting makes more sense than sending them now. Al said he'd like Tad and company out there to have a more accurate fix on her location before he and Charlie go west. That way they can avoid wasting their time with a lengthy search, just help with the round up. Make sense to you?"

"Sure does, and best for the budget, too."

"Well, that's my news. I'll leave you to your meeting. Sorry to have barged in." Al pushed away from the chief's desk and headed for the door.

"Charlie should be in the office, Al, give him a ring."

"Will do, Sheriff."

When he reached his office, Al dialed his friend. After three rings, the familiar voice came over the line. "Berzinski."

"Charlie, it's me. I heard from Tad a few minutes ago. The DNA samples they turned in to the FBI prove it's our gal. Genevieve Wangen is alive and well and living in Montana."

"Hot damn." The comment was thunderous and Al smiled as he moved the phone away from his ear. "Whadda ya think, time to go out there?"

Al pressed the phone to his ear again. "I think we have to wait until Tad and Willie can pinpoint her location. Once we have that information, activating a plan for the takedown will be easier. I just spoke with the chief and the sheriff and they both agree."

"I know, I know, but we're so close. I'm hungry as can be to put the bite on her."

"I am too, but it's just not the right time." Al propped both elbows on the desk, trying to convince himself as much as his friend. Everything in him longed to jumped into his car and head west, but they'd made mistakes with this case before; he wasn't about to do it again.

"I hate this damn waiting. Seems like we're always waiting. What the hell kind of strategy is that?"

"A smart one. C'mon, Charlie, we've rushed in to try and grab this woman before and lost her, twice. Let's do it right this time. Besides, we need to listen to our bosses. They've been pretty damn good about all this."

"Yup, place the big card on me, that always works. And you're right, they have been good. Keeping them on our side makes perfect sense. So I'll twiddle my thumbs some more and try to be as patient as you are."

Al grimaced. "I'm every bit as impatient to nail this woman as you are, believe me. You're just a little more vocal about it. Both of us want to get this over with once and for all. And we will. It's just a matter of when and how. So we wait. And fidget."

"If you say so. Let me know if you hear any more."

"I will." Al hit the disconnect button and set the phone on the desk. Clasping his hands behind his head, he leaned back in his chair. They *were* close, he could feel it. It really was just a matter of time before they finally took the old lady down.

And this time, keep 'er down for good.

33

Not sure whether the number she had was still in service, it was with great pensiveness that Sam dialed the number. Before it rang a second time, the familiar voice of Amber came through the line.

"You mean after all this time, I finally get a call?" There was a heavy tinge of sarcasm in her voice. Before Sam could respond, her friend said, "And let me guess, you need a favor."

"Um, well, I—"

"Sorry, honey, you'll have to get in line."

"How long's the line?"

"Just the two of us," Amber conceded, "but I was first in line."

"Okay," said Sam. Was she going to be able to do Amber a favor in exchange for the one she wanted? "What's up?"

"The damn Cabreras, that's what's up!" shot back Amber. "I am so sick of them throwing their weight around; I'm ready to close the doors here."

Sam's eyes widened. Was it really going to be that easy? "What are they doing, Amber?"

Her friend launched into a long rant that left Sam happier than she had been in a long time. The new leaders of the group, Antonio and Benito Cabrera, were proving to be demanding and arrogant, to the point that Amber was sick of the sight of them and anxious to have something done about it.

"Both of them want free service whenever they walk in here," she told Sam. "To be honest, it's a pain, because either I save the best girls I have on the off chance they might arrive, or I book them and hope the Cabreras won't show. It's been a nightmare. Juan was a gentleman, but these two sons are bastards."

When she paused to take a breath, Sam broke in. "I know how we can both win here, Amber. How about I teach them a lesson them for you and, while doing that, also do a favor for my friends the Carbones?"

"Whatever it is, I'm in."

"Good. Here's the plan. I'd like you to set up a date for me with both men. I look nothing like I did when I lived near you, thanks to surgery paid for by Angelo Carbone. I don't think I ever saw Antonio or Benito, but even if I did, I doubt they would recognize me now. The doctors took away every blemish and made me beautiful."

"You were beautiful." Amber sounded skeptical. "You mean you look even better now?"

"Much, much better. So if you set me up with Antonio, I'll take care of him first, and then figure out a way to get rid of Benito, too."

"That may be a problem; they travel together, like wolves. They come in several nights a week, demanding my best girls, and if they don't get them, I pay for it. Of course, my girls never see any money, and neither do I."

This is going to work. Blood pounded in Sam's ears and she clutched the phone tighter. "Tell you what. I'm in New Orleans now. I have work to do here for the next several days. If I finish up here and drive over to Atlanta, would you put me up while we wait for the Cabreras to come in? When they do, I'll end your problem."

"Sounds too good to be true. Of course I'll have a room ready for you. Do you need a gun or a knife or ... something else?"

"Nothing at all. I will have what I need with me."

Sam hung up the phone and stared at it for a moment. *Unbelievable.* She thought she'd have a hard time convincing Amber to let Sam use her place to carry out vengeance on the enemies of the Carbones. Sam had even assumed she'd have to talk herself into staring into the beady little eyes of Antonio and Benito as she performed the deed.

The Cabreras had just made both incredibly easy.

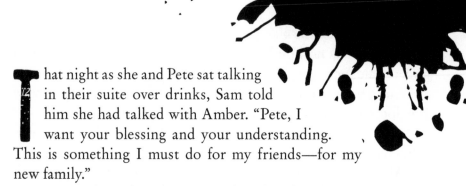

34

That night as she and Pete sat talking in their suite over drinks, Sam told him she had talked with Amber. "Pete, I want your blessing and your understanding. This is something I must do for my friends—for my new family."

Pete set down his glass. "I've thought a lot about this. I know you feel you are obligated to take care of the problem. I understand that, but I think I had better go with you. I don't want you with those hoods without a bodyguard present."

"Trust me, I know how to take care of myself. I was alive many years before I met you and I took care of a lot of problems like these without your help. I'm grateful for the offer, but your presence would be a problem. They would know right away that something was up."

"Maybe I could just be close by?"

"No." Sam kept her voice neutral but shook her head. As much as she appreciated his concern, she couldn't have him there, distracting her and possibly getting in the way. "You are needed here to instruct Chandler and the others how to fill the orders that come in."

"I don't like it."

"I know." Sam rested a hand on his knee and leaned close to press her lips to his. "But I'm grateful you are supporting me anyway. I need you on my side, Pete, or all of this is for nothing."

He wrapped his arms around her and pulled her close. "I'll always be on your side."

It was a fun night. When they tumbled into bed, Pete was in a playful mood. She was feeling randy, too, and they made love like two young kids. Once, when she squealed loudly, he clapped his hand over her mouth and said, "Sssh. You'll wake everyone up. No need to let everyone know what we're doing, is there?"

"I guess not." She pressed her lips together. "But judging from how Angelo looks at Rosalyn, I'm pretty sure this house has heard those sounds before."

"I'm sure it has, but not from us, or at least not from me." The last comment was punctuated with a poke to the ribs. She laughed, poked him back, and soon they were off on another round that produced groans and grunts and, finally, loud moans of fulfillment.

"Oh, m'god," he whispered. "That was incredible."

"No need to whisper." Her laughter shook the bed. "I think our other sounds were far louder than our voices in normal conversation. After all, we are at the end of the hall."

"Yes, but I think we're right above the dining room, and I'd be surprised if we didn't dislodge some plaster."

●——— •

The next morning, Sam was surprised to see both Dino and Chandler at breakfast when she and Pete walked into the kitchen. The two brothers must have been as anxious as she and Pete to see what the workmen had been able to finish up after they left the day before.

"We're having omelets," said Dino, glancing up. "They're delicious. Just order what you want and the staff will make it for you."

Sam requested ham and cheese while Pete asked for the works, with extra peppers.

"All I can say, Chandler," Sam slung an arm around the shoulders of Dino's brother, "is that I'm damn glad you're the one working with Pete. I know how he loves his peppers, and I also know what peppers do to him. Take my advice and stay upwind."

Both Dino and Chandler laughed. Sam chuckled. They thought she was kidding. Just wait until the real Pete showed up for work.

By eight thirty they were at the warehouse. The five workmen had gotten an incredible number of tasks completed. The drains and electrical outlets were in, tested, and working. All that remained to be constructed were a few platforms and two shelving units.

"Amazing." Pete tapped the wall above one of the outlets. "These guys are terrific."

"We aim to please." Dino waved an arm around the warehouse. "If you see anything that needs to be done or changed, just let them know."

Pete collected Chandler and went to the assembly line area, while Sam began to take out the things they needed to mix and compound. By ten thirty, the first set of orders was completed and awaiting packaging and shipping. Chandler, however, was looking peaked.

"What's the matter?" Dino cocked his head. "You're pale as a ghost."

Sam shook her head. "Pete got you, right?" Chandler nodded and excused himself to head outside.

When Chandler returned, Sam told him to relax. "We'll let Pete work by himself this afternoon. I have a few things to do and then we can head home. Dino's already gone back to go over some numbers with your dad."

"Sounds good."

Pete, a wry grin on his face, turned and went back to his work station. "Sorry, Chandler," he called over his shoulder. "I should have known better. From now on, peppers only when I'm not going to be around other people."

Soon Sam had finished up her work and she and Chandler and Pete returned to the big house. Rosalyn met them at the door. "Dino and Angelo are working in the study." She inclined her head in the direction of Angelo's sanctuary. "They said you should join them when you got back."

"All of us?" asked Chandler.

"Yes, I think that's what they intended." His mother smiled.

When they entered the study, Angelo looked much heartier than he had on Saturday. Sam exhaled in relief.

"Dino tells me great progress has been made," the old man said, gesturing for them to come in and sit down.

"He's right." Sam took the brown leather armchair across from his desk. "All the equipment is set up and operating and the first prepared orders are going out this afternoon. Tomorrow the real work starts."

Angelo's bushy eyebrows rose. "The real work?"

"Yes, we have an order for a thousand spray canisters from Abdi in Sweden, some for him and some for his allies. An order of that size will be a great test for us."

Dino perched on the arm of the couch set up against the far wall. "Do we have all the supplies we need?"

"I believe so, but I will put in another order tonight."

The old man propped his elbows on the arms of his chair and pressed his fingertips together. "Sam, Dino also mentioned that you have a plan to deal with the Cabreras. Is that right?"

"It is, Angelo. And before you say anything, let me say that it is only right that I repay all of the favors you have done for me. This will be one tiny down payment on what you are owed."

"You owe me nothing, *dolcezza*. Not a thing. You have already repaid every kindness we have extended with full interest. But tell me, Dino did not provide me with many details. Will this action expose you to danger?"

Sam chose her words carefully, not wanting to worry the old man. "You know how men are when in the throes of passion, Angelo. It is then that I will strike. They will never know what hit them."

"Aah, a passion-based extermination. I see. Hmmm, a tough lesson for Juan to suffer, but a situation that he should not have let get to this point. You see, Samantha, I found out long ago, from my father, that when turning the reins over to another, you must be sure to still keep your eye on the road. Do you hear what I say?"

"I do. It is a good lesson, too."

Angelo pushed back his chair and stood, pressing a palm to the desk for a few minutes as though to steady himself. Dino started to rise, but his father waved him off. Angelo rounded the desk and came over to rest a hand on Sam's head. "You are a godsend to this family of ours. You are as much one of us now as Vonell, Dino, Benton,

Chandler, or Elliott. You have become a wonderful daughter and a worthy sister for my children. You honor all of us by your presence."

With that, the don walked to the bar and poured snifters of brandy for each of them. When they had their glasses, he raised his. "To Samantha. May she live long and prosper greatly as a member of the Carbone family."

"Here, here," chorused the children. Sam scanned their faces, but there was no hint of jealousy there. One by one, the siblings greeted her with a kiss on both cheeks and best wishes for a long life.

"This is more than I could have dreamed of." Her voice quivered. "I am overwhelmed by your kindness and determined to make the Carbone family proud and prosperous." She raised her glass to all of them, too overcome to say any more.

●——•

The next day, Pete showed Chandler how the canisters were assembled while Sam sorted out all of the supplies needed.

As noon approached, Vonell, Benton, and Elliott joined the group, saying they would like to learn how to fill the orders, too. Between them, they soon had created a seven-step process and were busily turning out completed containers. When four o'clock arrived, they had 387 canisters completed.

"A great day's work," pronounced Sam. "Vonell, can we talk about how best to ship this order? Back home, Pete and I would package them ten or twenty containers to a box and mail them at a number of locations. Is that necessary here?"

"I don't think so. This is a regional headquarters for UPS; that's who you use, right? We should be able to package them any way you'd like. If they pick up the cartons by 5:00 p.m., they'll ship out that evening and be on their way to Europe for delivery the following day."

Sam nodded. "Great. Let's package them fifty canisters to a carton then. We can get seven of them ready now for pickup today. What time will UPS come by?"

"Whenever we want," said Vonell. "I think we should establish a regular pickup time, say, at four thirty or four forty-five. That will allow overnight shipment to Europe."

With all of them working together, the seven cartons were ready for pickup five minutes before UPS stopped by at four forty-five.

Sam watched the truck drive away before returning to the lab and wiping her hands on her apron. "That is one phenomenal afternoon's work, everyone. With service like this, I suspect we will see orders grow exponentially."

She surveyed the nearly completed warehouse. *I just hope we'll be able to handle them all to everyone's satisfaction. Our customers are not the type you want to disappoint.*

⁃

The evening again was festive, although Sam suggested to Angelo that having the family cut back on the alcohol would be a good idea in light of the work that needed to be done.

"I should also be hearing from my friend in Atlanta soon," she told the family gathered around the table. "I'll be heading there toward the end of the week. Hopefully things will go smoothly and I will be back in a few days. Then I'll need to get back home to take care of any domestic orders that have come in while we've been here."

Dino studied her. "We'll keep a plane on standby for your trip to Atlanta. When you're finished, we'll come back to get you. And when you're ready to fly home, we'll take care of that, too."

"Dino, that is very gracious, but perhaps it's asking too much."

"Not at all, this business is now a significant new component of the Carbone operation. If it goes like we think it will, it may well be the most significant component. It is only right that you have a plane at your disposal. In fact, I've been thinking that perhaps we should plan to make regular stops to pick up the packages that you get ready at home. We can bring them here for shipping."

"That's a wonderful idea." Sam reached for Pete's hand under the table and squeezed it.

He nodded. "It would likely be best to land at Missoula or maybe

Kalispell. You should be able to go in and out of the Fixed Base Operation without attracting too much attention."

"Speaking of orders, there are a stack of them at the office." Vonell reached for her father's empty plate and piled it on hers. "Why don't you drive with me in the morning, Sam? We can pick them up and drive over to the warehouse together."

"Sounds good." Her hand still clutching Pete's, Sam leaned back in her chair and watched the others talking and laughing. Her heart was full, and for the first time, she let go of her doubts about their new enterprise. With all of them working together, there was no way they could fail.

●——— •

Seven orders waited for them at Vonell's office, including two for canisters, both from Romania. Sam pursed her lips. Had the conflict spread that far south?

When she arrived back at the warehouse, Pete was watching Chandler work. Sam walked over to stand beside Pete. "How's he doing?"

"Great. He's picking up everything fast. So fast that I've been thinking I might actually be able to come with you when you go home next week."

Sam held up the stack of orders. "Better see how many more orders have come in by then." She glanced at Chandler and lowered her voice. "We don't want him getting overwhelmed."

Her phone rang and she pulled it from her pocket and glanced at the screen. "Amber," she told Pete, then walked outside where there was more privacy.

Amber told her that Antonio, in a rare display of thoughtfulness, had called to say he was coming in on Friday and wondered if she could have a woman waiting for him. "He asked for someone new, so I told him I had just the person. I tried hard to find out if Benito was coming with him, but he didn't have a direct answer. Best I could get out of him was that he didn't know, but Benito almost always wanted to end the week with a 'workout.'"

"Excellent. I'll plan to come Friday morning."

"That would be perfect. If I talk to Antonio again, I'll offer some incentive to Benito for coming along."

"If all goes well, I could take care of both of them."

"I'll see what I can do. You just come ready to deal with them."

"Don't worry, I always travel prepared. I'll have plenty of what I need to take care of the Cabrera problem once and for all."

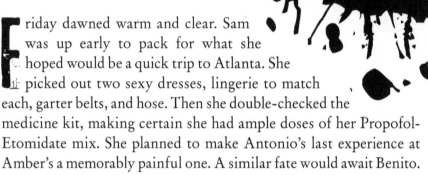

35

Friday dawned warm and clear. Sam was up early to pack for what she hoped would be a quick trip to Atlanta. She picked out two sexy dresses, lingerie to match each, garter belts, and hose. Then she double-checked the medicine kit, making certain she had ample doses of her Propofol-Etomidate mix. She planned to make Antonio's last experience at Amber's a memorably painful one. A similar fate would await Benito.

Dino came to the kitchen to say good-bye to her as she finished her breakfast. "Given the sensitivity of the mission, I'm going to tell the pilots to just wait there for you, so you can get away in a hurry. No matter what happens at Amber's, I want you out of Atlanta and on your way back to Montana as soon as you are finished there." He glanced at Pete, sitting across the table, before planting a chaste kiss on her cheek. "Good luck."

Pete delivered her to Lakefront before heading to the warehouse. The pilots were ready for the short hop to Atlanta. When they landed an hour and a half later, a car and driver were waiting for her. As they drove into the city, the driver, Rudy, informed her that he worked for Amber, who had told him he was picking up a "mighty important guest."

"I was sure it would be a man. I was certainly not expecting a beautiful young lady."

"Why, thank you, Rudy. Do you work full-time for Amber?"

"Yes, ma'am. I guess you could say that I'm her jack of all trades. She keeps me plenty busy, but this is one of the most pleasant assignments I've been given. She has a regular driver, but he's off doing something else today." He approached Amber's house, but drove by the imposing building. "I'm to take you in the back way, ma'am. Just hang tight; we're going around the block and into the alley."

Rudy deftly steered the town car through the alley and into a spacious garage that contained another town car, identical to the one in which she was riding.

"Two town cars?" Sam stared out the window at the gleaming vehicle. "Amber does take care of her clientele, doesn't she?"

"Oh, yes, ma'am. There are actually four town cars, all of them just like this one - and new, too. They are kept pretty busy, but usually we are driving gentlemen." He parked and climbed out of the vehicle to open her door.

"I'm very glad I got you, Rudy," she told him as he helped her out of the car. "Maybe I will see you later?"

"Not sure, ma'am. Will you be staying with us long?"

He thinks I'm a new employee. Her cheeks warmed. "No. In fact, I might be leaving later today. Amber and I have been friends for years and I just flew in to see her."

"Well, if you do leave later, I might be your driver. I sure hope so; I enjoyed driving you, ma'am." These last words were accompanied by a slight bow and a smile, the latter action reciprocated.

The reunion with Amber was heartwarming. While her hostess would have served generous amounts of wine, Sam accepted a glass of a fine pinot grigio, but covered her glass when Amber went to refill it.

"I want all my faculties about me when I meet Antonio. I need to show him a time he'll never forget."

"What do you have planned, if you don't mind my asking?"

"Not at all. I have with me liberal dosages of a special concoction that will guarantee him a most memorable departure from this life."

"Really?" Amber's eyes widened.

"Yes. Normally I use a mixture of drugs called Propofol and Etomidate. I usually go pretty lightly on the Propofol. It creates a fair amount of pain, but it is a great knockout solution. In this case,

I loaded up on the Propofol. Antonio will be very much aware of what is happening."

"Good, he deserves whatever pain you can administer." Amber rose gracefully. "Come, I'll show you the room you will be using."

Sam followed her down the hallway to the suite where she would be entertaining Antonio. It was large and lavishly appointed.

"Wow! Maybe I'm in the wrong business."

"Don't get any ideas. There's already plenty of competition."

"But you must be doing well." Sam's eyes swept the room.

"Just so you know, this is my own business suite. Since Antonio has never been here—I wouldn't let any part of that man touch me—I thought the surroundings might provide additional cover for you."

"It's perfect."

"So what is Antonio like?"

Amber's face darkened. "He's a brute of a man, extremely abusive. Two of my girls have been badly beaten by him. I'd have turned the son of a bitch in, but he paid all their medical bills and handed out generous tips to everyone. I hated to let him off the hook, but you know how it is." She stepped back into the hallway. "I'll leave you to become familiar with the room. Please ring if there is anything you need." She pointed to a buzzer on the wall above the night stand and Sam nodded.

After Amber had gone, Sam napped for an hour, then showered and changed into one of the dresses she had brought. It fit her like a glove and flattered her figure. Beneath it she wore vivid purple undergarments of the sheerest fabric made, a violet garter belt, and black stockings with patterns on them. As much as the thought of being with a man like Antonio disgusted her, she needed to look the part for this to work.

Those things done, she poured herself a vodka-tonic and sat on the sofa to wait. She was on her second drink when the phone rang and the receptionist announced that Antonio was being escorted to her room. Sam hung up and smoothed out her skirts with both palms. A few seconds later, a knock sounded on the door.

She opened it. A tall, handsome man with dark curly hair stood in the hall. Everything about him spoke of wealth, power, and arrogance. She repressed the shudder that threatened to betray her true feelings for the man.

"I'm Antonio. Amber says you're something special. We'll find out, won't we?" He grabbed her roughly by the arm, as if to shove her backwards into the room. Sam jerked her arm from his grasp and stepped forward to hiss into his face, "Don't ever do that to me again. Just because you're a paying customer gives you no special privileges with my body that I do not allow. Behave yourself and you will have a memorable time."

His ebony eyes narrowed to glittering slits. He pushed past her and turned around to look her up and down. "So you're beautiful. But I've seen and had many others just as beautiful. Amber says you have special talents. All I can say is, given what I'm paying, they better be very special. And for your information, I like it rough. I was told you knew that."

He stalked into the bedroom, pausing at the side of the bed as though examining the area where they would be.

"Amber mentioned it," she said quietly, then strode up behind him and knocked him forward on to the bed. Sam grabbed a rope she'd left lying on the mattress and trussed him up like a steer in a roping contest. Apparently thinking this was part of the game, he allowed her to tie him as she wanted.

When she was finished, he lay across the bed, his ankles and wrists tied together, making him look like a teeter-totter.

"Now, Mr. Cabrera, I'm going to teach you some manners." She walked around to the other side of the bed before unzipping her dress and stepping out of it. She moved close enough to the bed that his tongue came within an eyelash of her groin. "Hmm, you'd like a little of that, eh? Let's see how good you can be."

Apparently starting to wonder about her intentions, Antonio began to struggle against his bindings. "Untie me now!"

"Was that an order, Mr. Cabrera? If it was, you should know that I don't respond well to orders. Perhaps a *please* would get you closer to what you want."

"Never." He ground the word out between clenched teeth. "When I'm loose, we'll see who is going to beg whom here."

She waited until he was looking at her before opening the drawer on the nightstand and removing a hypodermic needle. "See this? I have a syringe filled with a drug that will remove all feeling from the area it penetrates. Think your penis would like a dose of that?"

All the color drained from Antonio's face. His struggles knocked him onto his side. In spite of his obvious rage, his arousal was plainly visible.

"Should we free him?" she asked coyly, reaching for the waistband of his pants. He snarled at her so fiercely that drool dribbled from his mouth. Sam frowned. "Now is that nice?"

Antonio continued to threaten her with the filthiest words, but she ignored him and concentrated on his trousers, first unsnapping them, and then pulling down the zipper. She then tugged his pants and shorts down as far as the rope permitted. "Does that feel better?"

"Don't touch me, you bitch!"

"Now, now, that's not very mannerly. Of course, I was warned you had no manners. Let me see if I can teach you some."

She reached down, grabbed his penis, and stuck it with the needle. Even as he struggled, the drug began to work its magic and he deflated like a punctured balloon.

He stopped fighting his bonds and stared at the affected area. When he twisted to look up at her, his face had contorted in fear.

Sam reached into the drawer and he began to wrestle with the ropes again.

She held up a longer needle. "Perhaps this can teach you some manners, but first we'd better do something about that smutty mouth of yours."

He opened it as though about to holler for help, but Sam was too quick for him. She took the longer needle, stuck it into his bottom lip, and depressed the plunger. Instantly his lip swelled. He appeared to be trying to speak, but his words were muffled and unintelligible.

"I can't understand you. But that really doesn't matter, now does it? I'm going to send you on a trip, Mr. Cabrera. My only chagrin is that the thousands of people who would enjoy seeing you suffer are not here to experience it."

She took the smaller needle and held it up to test it, spraying a bit of the solution into his face.

"Know what this is? It's a drug of my own making - a nasty, powerful drug that will kill you. But you won't die immediately. No, I'm going to watch you die, slowly and in excruciating pain. And as you do, I'll offer regards from all of those you mistreated in your miserable lifetime."

His eyes watered and he attempted to speak. It was obvious that he was pleading for her mercy.

"Too late, Mr. Cabrera, your time on this planet is up. I'm not sure where you're going, but I have a pretty good idea that you won't be happy there."

She moved to straddle him. His eyes met hers and she froze. *Do it, Sam. Do it now.* She moved the needle closer to his ear then pulled it back. *I have to do this, for the Carbones, and for Amber and all the other people he has terrorized in his pathetic life.* Pushing back her shoulders, she bent and jabbed the needle into his ear before she could change her mind.

His noiseless cries seemed deafening to her. He lost control and an evil smell permeated the room.

"Now look what you've done. No matter, you'll soon be gone, with special farewell wishes from all of the Carbone family and the Black Widow of the Woods. Sleep well, Mr. Cabrera."

He struggled fruitlessly against his bonds, and she watched every twitch until at last he was quiet. Then she closed his eyes and dressed before going to the phone and calling Amber.

Her voice shook a little, but she managed to say, "You can come in, if you're up to it."

36

When Amber entered the room, Sam was huddled at the end of the sofa, head in her hands. She was trembling.

"What happened?" asked Amber. "Did he hurt you? Are you all right?"

"No, he didn't hurt me. Physically, I'm fine. Mentally, Amber, I'm a mess. This one really bothered me. I guess I never really had to look someone in the eyes while I was killing him."

Amber wrapped her arms around her and held her close. "Sam, I am so, so sorry. You were doing this for me; it's my fault. Perhaps we need to end this now?"

"Antonio is in there." Sam inclined her head toward the other room. "And I'm afraid he and the bed are a mess."

"I'll take care of that," Amber told her.

"Then," said Sam, her lower lip quivering, "we have to talk about Benito. I just don't know if I'm up for another killing."

Amber put a finger to her lips, then went to the door and opened it.

Four men entered the room, one pushing a refrigerator cart bearing a large barrel.

The man pushing the barrel looked at Sam and winked. "Ms. Johansen has ordered a concrete casket for this bastard. And everyone who works for her is cheering. There is no one here who will shed a tear for this one. He was one evil bastard."

As two of the men wrestled Antonio's body into the barrel, Sam fled to the bathroom, shut the door, and vomited into the toilet. When her stomach was empty, she stood and looked at herself in the mirror. Dark shadows were smudged beneath her eyes and deep lines creased her forehead. *This one took a lot out of me.* She splashed cool water on her face, applied fresh makeup, and returned to the sitting room. The men had gone and Antonio with them.

Amber mixed Sam a drink. When they sat down, Sam looked at Amber. "I can't do another. I just can't. But that will leave you with a huge problem."

"You know, Sam, Antonio was a horrible, despicable human being. I can't bring myself to be remotely sorry that he is gone. Benito is different, though."

"In what way?"

"He can be despicable too." Amber set her glass down on the night stand. "But I always got the sense that he was trying to impress his brother. Benito's not as arrogant as Antonio was, and not nearly as smart, either, although he thinks he is. He takes all his cues from his older brother. I've often wondered what he would be like if he wasn't under Antonio's influence."

Sam shifted on the couch. "Look, I know I have killed my share of men, but never without a reason. If you think Benito is just a little puppet, pretending to be someone he really isn't, I'm all for attempting to reason with him, see if he is willing to change. Do you think there's any chance of that?"

Amber bit her lip. "I actually think there could be. With Antonio out of the way, I believe Benito might be persuaded to choose a better path. There just might be a halfway decent guy under all his bluster. It's as though everything he does is to impress his brother."

"Still, we can't just let him walk away. We'll need to teach him a strong enough lesson to bring about a change in his demeanor."

"Do you think that's possible?" Amber wrung her hands together.

"I don't know, but it's worth a shot. Let's talk to him, and if he doesn't seem willing to change, I can use the other needle on him at that point."

Amber nodded. "That seems like a reasonable plan. Let's try it."

"Okay. Give me a few minutes to check out what I brought. Then you can bring him in and we'll see what we can do." Sam glanced into the mirror and fluffed her hair. "I'll need a bit of time to fix myself up too. We want this to be an experience Benito Cabrera will never forget."

37

Sam quickly changed into the second dress she had brought, this one the proverbial LBD that also showed off her figure. She swapped the purple bra and panties for bright crimson silk and lace, then added a black garter belt and patterned hose. She was not dressing to entice, but rather to rid herself of the memory of what had happened in the room with Antonio.

She studied her image in the mirror and took several deep breaths. Her shoulders loosened. *This strategy is much better. Maybe I can teach Benito a lesson. I hope I can—I'm sure going to try.*

Not long after, a gentle knock sounded. Amber waited at the door to lead her to another suite just down the hall. When they walked in, they found a younger version of Antonio resting on the sofa in a black silk robe, open at the front to reveal a chest and abdomen covered in hair.

He was ruggedly handsome, but had a swarthy look about him, too - something sinister. Her stomach twisted in revulsion but she pushed back the feeling.

"Where you been? I been here a half hour. At my wage, that's a lot of wasted money. All I can say is you better be damn good - really damn good."

"Why, Mr. Cabrera, I'm sure you have the wrong girl." Sam kept her face carefully neutral. "I'm not a hooker. I'm a murderer."

His dark eyes widened. Then he began to laugh. "A murderer,

huh? I doubt it, little girl. How could anyone like you be deadly? You're nothing but a waif."

"And you, Mr. Cabrera, are a big, strong man, aren't you? A real tough guy, I bet. I suppose you're right; what could a little waif like me do to a big burly guy like you?"

"Get your ass over here!" he snapped at her.

"Mr. Cabrera, before I come over there I have a story for you and I want you to listen carefully." She sat down on the chair opposite him, clasped her hands in her lap, and looked him in the eye.

"Mr. Cabrera, I have good news and bad, and I'm going to give you the bad first. I met with your brother a few minutes ago, and when he left me he was encased in a barrel of concrete. All the life had gone out of him."

"What?" Benito jumped to his feet and approached her, a wild look in his eye. "Listen you little bitch, I'm not here for dark jokes. Any more of that, and you're gonna pay."

Sam nodded at Amber and the next moment Rudy and two of his henchmen were in the room. They surrounded Benito, daring him to try something.

"Mr. Tough Guy, you're gonna take a little trip with us," Rudy told him, "and you better pray you return."

The men grabbed Benito and hustled him out of the room. Sam looked questioningly at Amber.

"I thought seeing his brother might adjust his attitude," Amber said.

Sam pursed her lips. "Or maybe it will make him worse?"

Five minutes later Rudy and his friends brought a very beaten Benito back into the room, but it was apparent that not all of the fight had gone out of him.

"You bastards are gonna pay," he promised. "There'll come a time when your tough guys here aren't around. When that happens, I promise you're gonna pay—and it will be even worse for you than it was for him."

Rudy pushed Benito back onto the sofa he had left a few minutes earlier. The younger Cabrera sat staring at them for a few moments, then buried his head in his hands and wept, his body shaking.

Shaken herself, Sam drew in a quivering breath. "Benito," she began, haltingly, "you and your brother have done some very bad things. You have hurt a lot of people. Many people have a hard time understanding what has happened to your family. I've been told your father, although a Mafioso, was a gentleman. Do you agree with that?"

Benito lowered his hands. "You killed my brother. Why are you talking to me like this? You're going to kill me too, aren't you?"

"I'd rather not," she said gently. "I took no satisfaction in killing your brother, but he was a bad man, Benito."

"After Alejandro died, he felt he had to be tough," he said between gasps. "He felt he had to show how tough the Cabreras could be."

"And you did too, didn't you?"

"I had to, Antonio insisted."

"And what about your father?"

"He is old and ill. He never wanted us to be that way. It bothered him greatly. He predicted it would end like this."

"Like what?"

"He said Antonio and me would die. He talked about it constantly."

"And now you have come face-to-face with pay-up time."

"Yes ... yes ... I know."

Sam rose and walked to him. "Do you want to die, Benito?" She rested a hand on his shoulder.

He looked up at her, his cheeks streaked by tears. "No." He shook his head.

"Good. Then we can work together to make sure nothing bad happens to you. How does that sound?"

He swallowed hard. "Sounds good. I want to live. Please let me live. Just tell me what I have to do."

"This is a great start." Sam squeezed his shoulder. "I don't believe you are past redemption, or you would have met the same fate as your brother."

Amber, sitting near him on the couch, nodded. "I bet your father will be happy if you change your ways, too."

"What do I have to do?"

"Your continued life will require a complete attitude adjustment," Sam told him as she sat down next to him.

"And I will help," said Amber.

He straightened up. "Tell me what you expect."

"There can be no more tough-guy behavior," Sam told him. "Nor can you continue to treat people with such an appalling lack of respect, is that understood?"

He nodded. Amber touched his elbow. "And you must pay your way. No free dinners, no free tickets, or parking, and no free dates with my girls, is that understood?"

Again he was quick to nod.

"We will be watching and listening." Sam met his gaze evenly. "We may not see if you step over the line, but you can be sure we will hear about it. Amber is going to put out the word so you had better be on your best behavior."

"Do you know why we are offering you this chance?" asked Amber.

"No."

"Because your father has raised you to be better than you have been. We blame Antonio for what you have become. You need to prove to us that's the case," said Amber. "We all like your father. He's tough, yes, but he treats people with respect. From now on, Benito, you will too. Understood?"

"Yes … yes. I want to live."

"Words are easy to say." Sam stood and gripped the back of the couch. "Now you have to show us that we can trust you."

Amber got to her feet and the two of them stood looking down at Benito, who remained on the couch, his robe gathered around him.

"Oh, yes," said Sam, "there will be no love session here tonight, nor will there be any until you have learned how to treat the women here well. So Benito, go and get dressed, then we may have some final words."

He left the sitting room for the bathroom where he had left his clothes. He was gone about five minutes before he returned, fully clothed. He faced them, waiting for their final words.

Amber pointed a finger at him. "Turn over a new leaf, Mr. Cabrera, become a better man, apologize to those you have wronged, and promise that your way of life will become a force for good, for making up for the sins you have committed."

Benito closed his eyes for a few seconds. Then he sighed and opened them. "You do hold all the cards. It seems I have no choice."

Amber shook her head. "There is always a choice. You can embrace life and constantly try to do better. That's what we're asking, for you to try and do better. If you do that, you will live a long, happy life and make your father proud. Or you can go back to your old ways and join your brother in the depths. That's your choice."

"How am I supposed to embrace goodness?"

Sam motioned toward the door. "Your first job is to go home and tell your father what has happened today. You must tell him about Antonio's demise, the fact that you have been spared on your promise that you will do better, and that your life will continue to hang in the balance as the days unfold. Then you must apologize to all of the people here that you have wronged. As of this moment, you have no standing. The Cabrera Family's hold on Atlanta has ended. A new family is now in control. There may be a place in the new structure, but only if you prove yourself over the months to come."

Amber took a step forward. "In addition, each month you will come to see me to give me a report on your activities. These reports will be passed back to the new family in charge. You have a chance here, but it will require work—perhaps the first real work you have done in your life. Can you agree to these terms?"

"What option do I have? You have made things pretty clear." His eyes narrowed. "You mentioned new bosses?"

"Yes, Benito, the Carbone family is now in charge of Atlanta. They will be watching you closely. I don't think you want to cross them. Two weeks from today, Angelo Carbone will visit your father. He will have many things to tell him, about the new ways and about you."

"About me?"

"Absolutely, the Carbones will be watching you and they will permit no lapses," said Sam. "But if you can stay in line and do as we ask, you just might be happily surprised by the results. Now go, Benito, take the news to your father."

He nodded slowly. "All right, yes. I will do as you ask. But telling my father Antonio is dead will be terrible."

"I agree." Sam moved back so he could make his way to the door. "It will be terrible. Just remember, though, things could have been worse. How bad they get, or how good, rests on you. Do you understand that?"

He nodded. "Yes, I understand."

"Good, then go. And do not waste this chance you have been given."

He hurried from the room. Her knees weak, Sam sank down onto the couch. "Do you think we convinced him?"

"I think so." Amber sat down on the corner of the bed. "He's no dummy. He may not be as smart as he thinks he is, or as smart as he thought he was when he came in tonight, but I think he got the message."

"Good, then I have time for a glass of wine before Rudy takes me back to the airport."

Amber poured two glasses of Pinot Noir, handed one to Sam, and they clinked glasses, before sipping their drinks.

When they were done, Rudy, who had hung back as the others departed, took Sam gently by the arm and led her to the garage. Several workmen stood near a barrel they had recently capped. As Sam walked past the workmen and the barrel, she kept her eyes on the floor and shuddered. Rudy walked her to the car and opened the door for her. Sam hugged Amber before climbing inside.

They drove slowly from the garage, turned onto the street, and headed for the airport.

As he drove, Rudy peered at her several times in the mirror, bouncing in his seat a little as though barely able to contain his excitement. Sam waited. Finally he could hold it in no longer. "Although there will never be a public word, ma'am, you have made us all very happy today. If there is ever anything you need, just call Amber and we will be with you in a flash."

"Thank you, Rudy. All I ask is that you keep watch over Amber, make sure she is safe." Sam rested her head against the back of the seat, overcome suddenly with exhaustion.

38

Rudy expertly guided the big town car into the airport, through the fence and onto the tarmac, stopping at the foot of the steps of the Gulfstream waiting there for Sam. As she stepped out of the car, Dino, Vonell, and Elliott walked down the steps of the plane to greet her.

"We hear it went even smoother than planned." Vonell pressed both palms to Sam's flushed cheeks. "Great job, Sam. Once again you have done this family a true service."

Sam introduced them to Rudy. The driver greeted the trio warmly and promised to take good care of them while they were in Atlanta. "Sam, here, has earned the best for you. What a wonderful help she has been to us."

The good-byes were heart-felt. Both Sam and Vonell shed tears, and even Dino and Elliot blinked rapidly as Sam prepared to board the plane.

She saved her last good-bye for Rudy. "Rudy, thank you for all the help and encouragement you have given me. You have seen me at my absolute worst. I am hoping that the next time we meet it will be under more pleasant circumstances."

"Dear lady, I don't see today as having been unpleasant. We love Amber and those Cabrera boys were giving her a terrible time. I'm thrilled they have been dealt with."

"But perhaps only in part." Sam twisted a strand of hair around one finger as the right engine began to whine. She touched Rudy's shoulder. "Benito is a gamble, Rudy. You know that. Please be watchful. Don't let him get away with anything."

She stepped onto the stairs leading to the plane then stopped and turned back to the Carbones. "There may still be work to do here. I left the youngest son alive, but only after he promised to change his ways. Be vigilant. Rudy will help. Whatever you do, don't let any sign of Benito's old habits go unpunished."

She barely heard the promises to monitor him closely as she climbed the rest of the stairs and entered the plane, turning in the doorway to wave once more before the door closed.

When she was seated, the engines began to roar. In minutes they were taxiing down the runway. Sam slumped against the back of her seat. A large, dark figure moved out of the back of the plane and she bolted upright, heart pounding. What was happening? Had the Cabreras sent someone to exact revenge? She fumbled for her bag, but before she could open it, Pete materialized in front of her eyes and her muscles relaxed. He took her in his arms.

For several minutes he just held her then he brushed her hair back and whispered in her ear. "I'm coming home with you."

Sam sagged against his chest. *Home.* The word had never sounded more beautiful.

Pete held her out and studied her face. "You're shaking. Was it that awful?"

She couldn't talk about it, not yet. She nodded slightly and he pulled her to his again. "I can stay a week, as long as I drive each day to a place where I can make phone contact with Chandler."

Although Sam had told him she didn't need him with her, she was incredibly grateful now that he would be.

They lunched in Kalispell with Molly and caught up on news of the area—including another sighting of the Flathead Lake Monster, often described in similar terms as the more-famous Loch Ness monster in Scotland.

"We should try and catch it," Pete told the women. "We could mount it and put it on display here and make a lot of money."

It was a joyous lunch, and when Pete and Sam started south from Kalispell, they visited and laughed together, enjoying the beauty of the scenery. Atop the mountains there was snow now, although the shoreline and area around it wore the dull coat of early winter.

Sam didn't care. For the next week, while it was just the two of them alone together, she wasn't even going to think about what was going on in the world around them.

On the third day, Pete made his morning drive to the lake to visit with Chandler. He wasn't gone long. When he walked back into the house, he was energized. "I gotta go back," he told Sam. "There's a lot happening in Europe."

"So they want lots of canisters?"

"Apparently. The good guys have decided they are going to make a major offensive and try and put the rebels out of business. The canisters will be the primary tool. They want two thousand now and one thousand a week for four weeks following."

"Pete, that's great … and terrible. That's going to strain production to the limit and beyond. Will you need me there?"

"It will, but it will be the only order we get from Europe. They have all gotten together to take on these guys. As for your coming along, the only way we can do that is to switch domestic production there, too."

She shook her head. "I still think it will be better to handle that here."

"Much as I'd love for you to come with me, I agree. If the boys and Vonell continue to help, we'll fill the order. And if they can find a few additional people to train, Chandler will be able to handle everything without me."

Pete threw his belongings into a bag while Sam packaged up the orders they had filled. She would take him to Kalispell where Dino had promised to send the plane the next day.

The following day, Pete reluctantly tore himself away from Sam. Aboard the Gulfstream, he found a notebook waiting for his attention. In it were all the orders received from abroad, along with production reports from Chandler and financial updates from Vonell. His eyebrows rose. All the equipment they had installed had been fully paid for. The business had become profitable before the end of its first month.

Vonell had included a note, punctuated by her version of a smiley face. *I like this new business,* she'd scrawled across the small piece of paper. *Without taxes, you just can't miss. Anxious to see you.* It was signed, *Vonell.*

He liked the Carbone sister. She was sharp, attractive - a real business asset. Her intelligence stimulated him. Although Sam was his lady, he enjoyed working with Vonell.

He thought about all of the Carbones as the Gulfstream whisked him toward New Orleans and what promised to be a busy month. He already missed Sam and hoped he would be able to slip away for at least a quick trip to Montana before a month had passed.

Nostalgia had overtaken him when he was jogged back to the present by an announcement from the pilot that they were beginning their descent into New Orleans. Exactly as predicted, the wheels of the Gulfstream touched the Lakefront tarmac at 1:12 p.m. Soon he was seated in the Lincoln Town Car and headed for downtown and work.

Sam snuggled down in bed and lifted the copy of *USA Today* that she'd picked up on her rounds that afternoon.

Ten minutes later, a headline caught her attention. Her eyes widened and she straightened up, pulling the paper closer to read the fine print. "Body Found in Water off Florida."

Divers exploring a treasure site off north Florida had found a drum in the water. Believing it might hold valuable materials, they had hoisted it to the surface, opened it, and been startled to find a body well preserved by the concrete in which it was packed.

The report was simply too coincidental to be just that. Sam suspected that unkind fate had revealed the resting place of Antonio.

Oh well, no way anyone is going to turn that one back on me.

ccording to Pete's nightly report, work in New Orleans was continuing at a feverish pace. He told Sam he had fixed up a corner of the warehouse as a bedroom and spent his nights there to save travel time. Most of his meals were consumed there, too, as the small crew labored long hours to put together the canisters ordered by the Europeans. Sam felt terrible. When he called at bedtime, he sounded so tired she wasn't sure he'd remember anything she'd told him.

She was busy, too, but her work was manageable. The orders continued to come in, but at a much slower pace and lower volume. She was able to keep up, generally by working only half days. The rest of the day was spent relaxing, reading, and generally enjoying the peace and quiet.

Winter had arrived the second week Pete was gone, and she was grateful that he had taught her how to operate the plow. The first snowfall dumped thirteen inches, effectively snowing her in. The snow demanded all her attention. It was too heavy to just push aside, so she found herself going forward a hundred feet, then backing up to come at it at an angle to move it off the road. It took five hours to get the road clear enough for her to come and go.

The rest was short-lived. Two days later, a Chinook wind swept the area, bringing earlyfall temperatures and turning the road into mud. Now the plow was needed to smooth the huge ruts. And when she was done, winter made a reappearance, eight inches of light snow turning the forest into a postcard.

Sam had taken to leaving the pickup at the head of the road while she drove the Jeep on her rounds, nervous that she might not get in the laneway if it snowed while she was gone. In the middle of Pete's second week away, she left for her mail run early in the morning, turning south to Polson for her first stop, then proceeding up the west side of Flathead Lake to Kalispell and back down the east.

During lunch with Molly at the Golden Lion, she picked up a copy of a newspaper and couldn't help notice the headline that spanned the front page: Gang Leader Found; Warfare Threatened? So interested that she squirmed all the way home, she nonetheless resisted the temptation to read the article until she was inside her cabin.

Then, without opening the handful of orders she had collected, she sat in the rocker and began to read the report.

A body found in the Atlantic off the Georgia-Florida line had been identified as Antonio Cabrera, leader of the Atlanta-based Cabrera crime family. The report speculated that his death may touch off a war for control of the Atlanta mob.

The family had until recently been led by the dead man's father, Juan Cabrera, who was in failing health and was reported to have turned the reins of the family's operations over to his sons, principally to the oldest son, Antonio.

The rest of the report centered on what was known of the Cabreras, the family's operations and the sons' reputations that were anything but stellar. The reporter said Antonio was known for his meanness and bullying tactics. Benito, his younger brother, had a mean streak that that had rendered many associates and enemies maimed, but that was blamed largely on the influence of his older brother.

"Benito," the reporter wrote, "has not been seen since before the discovery of his older brother's body and speculation is that he likely has met the same fate. That potential was explored, however, by divers from the Georgia Bureau of Criminal Apprehension, who searched the area where Antonio's body was found. Although the search was maintained to be extremely thorough, Benito's body was not found.

"Given the presumption that Benito is dead," wrote the reporter, "whatever comes next is likely to be better than the situation under the Cabrera brothers."

Sam was pleasantly surprised to find no mention of the Carbones or speculation about what sort of organization, if any, would follow the Cabreras.

She put down the paper with a sigh. Nothing in the article that should cause her any harm. She and Pete discussed it that night, and he told her that Elliott Carbone was now living in Atlanta and working hard to consolidate operations under his leadership, apparently with the approval of the Cabrera patriarch. "And Benito Cabrera is proving to be a good soldier, from what I hear," Pete told her. "You did a great job with him, Sam."

Elliott Carbone had met with Juan Cabrera and received his blessing to pick up the pieces of the Cabrera empire and move it under Carbone control. The Carbones had promised the elder Cabrera and his son, Benito, a share of the action in Georgia, which would enable Juan and his wife to live the rest of their lives in comfort. Dino offered Benito a position in the Carbone machine. "He's assigned to keeping order at Amber's," said Pete, "and from what I hear he's doing it well and behaving himself. Dino believes he's destined for bigger things."

Sam was smiling when she got off the phone. Everything was going smoothly. Pete would be able to leave New Orleans soon and come home. Then the two of them could settle into a peaceful life. Now that so much time had passed, her friends in La Crosse had to have given up on ever finding her. They were safe.

●━━ •

Back in La Crosse, Al had just finished reading *The Atlanta Constitution*. Of particular interest that morning was the news about the demise of the Cabrera family.

After he finished reading the report, he picked up the phone and dialed Rusty Cunningham, his detective friend on the Atlanta Police Department.

"Damn, Al, I was just getting ready to call you," said Rusty when he answered. "I take it you've read about what has happened to the Cabrera family down here?"

"Yeah, just finished the article. What do you think happened to Antonio?"

"That's why I wanted to talk to you. Get this, he had a puncture mark in his ear. I just got the report from pathology this morning. The coroner estimated Antonio hadn't been in the water that long, given the condition of the body. He was sealed in a barrel of fresh concrete very soon after he died. Stroke of luck that treasure hunting firm was out there and came across the barrel or we might never have known what happened to Antonio."

"Funny how that happens, isn't it?" Al drummed his fingers on the desk, attempting to tamp down his rising excitement. Antonio had a pinprick in his ear? That could only mean one thing, Genevieve Wangen was involved. "This thing just doesn't want to go away, it seems."

"Guess not. Anyway, that's all I know at this point. I'll scan the coroner's report and send it to you. And I'll let you know if anything else turns up. Because of who the victim is, we'll be taking a close look at the case."

"Where are you going to start?"

"I'd like to go talk to Amber Johansen. Remember her?"

"Sure do, the beautiful madam. She's still doing business, huh?"

"Absolutely. Place is as busy and popular as ever," said Rusty. "One of her guys, a driver, is retired law and he stays close to us. We'll be talking to him too."

"All right, thanks Rusty. Appreciate you keeping me posted."

The conversation ended and Al called Charlie to fill him in on what was going on.

"Puncture in the ear? I'll be damned!" exclaimed Charlie. "Do ya think Genevieve is at it again?"

"Could be," said Al. "It just could be." He didn't want to get his hopes up, but with such an unusual method of killing, chances were their girl had been at it again.

●——— •

Several days later, Al was typing an investigation report when his phone rang. He kept typing with one hand as he snatched up the receiver and tucked it between his shoulder and chin. "Rouse."

"Al? It's Rusty."

Al stopped typing and bolted upright in his seat. He nearly dropped the phone but snatched it up and pressed it to his ear. "Rusty. What have you got?"

"I'm not sure. That is, I have some interesting news, just don't know how helpful it will be."

"Tell me anyway, you never know."

"That's what I thought. So I've been talking to Rudy Emmons, the former lawman and driver for Amber Johansen I told you about."

"Right. He have anything for you?"

"He mentioned that a couple weeks ago Amber asked him to pick up a beautiful woman at DeKalb-Peachtree Airport north of Atlanta and drive her to Amber's. That evening, around six, he returned her to the airport, where the jet that had brought her to Atlanta was waiting for her."

"Hmm." Al picked up a pen and tapped it on his mouse pad. "Timing would have been about right."

"Timing is exactly right. Rudy told us that on the same night, Juan Cabrera's oldest son was packed in a concrete coffin and taken from Amber's to be buried at sea. The other brother, Benito, left a much-changed man, or so it seemed.

"We've decided to let those facts go," Rusty told him. "The opinion at the top here is that the area is better off without Antonio. And middle management enjoys the relationship we have with Amber. I know it's unusual, but I agree with the strategy."

"Very interesting." Al tapped the pen harder. "Anything else?"

"Yea, one thing," replied Rusty. "We looked into the airplane the woman arrived and left on. It's owned by Carbone Industries, New

Orleans. There was no passenger manifest, of course, but it sounds like it definitely might have been your gal."

Al tapped the pen so hard it slipped out of his hand and skittered across the desk. "It certainly could be. Tell you what, let me talk to my boss. I'm thinking a trip to Atlanta sounds pretty good right now."

"You know you're always welcome. And bring that crazy Charlie with you; I've discovered a couple of new restaurants here that I think he'd be interested in."

"Will do. I'll take him out to lunch now to let him know what's going on, and I'll let him know you invited him to come along too. Thanks Rusty." Al hung up the phone and stared at the receiver. It shook in his trembling fingers. Could they really be closing in on Genevieve? It sure sounded like it, but after having her in his grasp twice before and letting her slip through his fingers, he was almost afraid to hope.

40

When the two lawmen met at the club a few minutes after noon, Charlie was "so hungry I can't even talk to you until we've placed our order."

Al smiled grimly. Food first with Charlie, always. "Fair enough."

"I'll have the French dip, ma'am, with lots of au jus," Charlie told the waitress when she arrived. "I'd like that with some coleslaw—not the creamy kind—a side of fries, and a slice of banana cream pie. Oh, and do you still have American fries? You do? Great, I'll have a side of those, too."

The waitress, a veteran at serving Charlie, shook her head and smiled at Al from behind her order pad.

"The French dip sounds good," agreed Al. "But I don't need the fries or American fries, the chips'll do nicely, thanks. And it'll be on my tab."

"Why don't you shame this big guy into buying a membership?" The waitress pointed at Charlie with her pen. "As much as he comes in here and leeches off you, he should have a membership."

"Ma'am, I'm a simple deputy. He's a detective with a capital D. He can afford a membership. I'm barely gettin' by."

The waitress looked at him over the top of her glasses, shook her head, and turned to Al. "Tell yer buddy I'm not buyin' it," she said and headed for the kitchen.

"See?" Al punched Charlie lightly in the upper arm. "Lots of people notice that you take advantage of me."

"Oh, m'god." Charlie threw his hands in the air. "That's a bunch of bullshit! Do you know how many bills I got? Do you? Charlene took me to the cleaners, man. If it weren't for Kelly workin', we wouldn't eat."

"Well, the way you eat, you *need* two incomes."

Charlie crossed his arms and stuck out his lower lip.

Al left him alone to sulk for a few minutes while he checked his messages. Nothing new from Rusty, not that he thought there would be already. He listened to a couple of other messages, neither important, before setting down his phone.

Charlie uncrossed his arms and opened his mouth, but before he could speak, the waitress reappeared with their orders, plates perched all the way up her arm. Seeing Charlie with his mouth open, she said, "Practicin', I see."

"Everybody's a smartass." Charlie spoke into his napkin, but loud enough for everyone in the club dining area to hear. Laughter echoed through the room.

When order was restored, Charlie had three large plates in front of him, plus a gravy tureen of au jus.

In an obvious attempt to get even, the waitress gestured to Charlie's plates. "I'd a brought the pie, but there wouldn't have been room on the table." She spun on her heel and disappeared into the kitchen.

Everyone was laughing again. But Charlie, clearly not the least bit embarrassed, settled down to eat. He tucked his napkin into the vee of his collar, pulled his chair a bit closer to the table, and daintily speared an American fry with his fork before popping it into his mouth.

He swallowed and smacked his lips together. "Yum!"

Al sat back and watched as his friend put away everything in front of him. His plates were nearly empty before Al had finished two bites of his sandwich. Even after years of watching his friend eat, it still astounded him how much the big guy could put away and not have an ounce of fat on him.

Charlie poured the remainder of the au jus onto his plate,

mopped up the sauce with the last of the buns in the basket, and ate those, too.

Al set down his sandwich. "Enough to eat?"

Charlie looked up. "My wife and I thank you sincerely for feeding me this noon. You have assisted us greatly with our meager incomes."

"Whaddya know, you were right for once. Everyone really *is* a smartass." Charlie made a face at him that Al ignored as the server set a serving of pie in front of each of them. She looked at Al, her hands on her hips. "You didn't order it, but you sure as heck deserve it. Your pie is on me."

As soon as Charlie stuffed the first bite in his mouth, Al waved his fork through the air. "Looks like we've got a new lead on our girl Genevieve."

Charlie choked on his pie, sending a spray of pastry crumbs across the table. Al pounded him on the back until his friend held up a hand. "Don't spring something like that on me when I have my mouth full of food."

"Then when would I ever be able to spring something like that on you?"

Charlie gave him a dark look before wiping his mouth with his napkin. "So whaddya got?"

"Did you read the story in the paper about those divers finding Antonio Cabrera's body down in Florida?"

"Yeah, why?"

"Rusty called me this morning. When the coroner examined the body, he found a pinprick in his ear."

Charlie's eyes bulged. "Shut up."

"Sounds like our girl, right?"

"It certainly does. So what are we gonna do about it?"

"I'd like to go down there, but I'm hesitant to ask the chief."

"Yeah, I'm sure the sheriff'll be reluctant to send us too early too, after all the time and money we've already spent chasing the old lady."

"That's what I figured. Guess we'll sit tight for now then, let

Atlanta and New Orleans pursue it. If the leads get a little hotter, we can approach our bosses then."

"Agreed." Charlie cut another slice of pie with the side of his fork.

"Sure would like to get my hands on her again though." Al pulled his plate closer. "She's gotten away from us twice now, and that's on me."

"Goddamit, Al, get over it!" shouted Charlie, hammering the table with his fist so hard the plates and silverware jumped and clattered. "Oops, sorry," whispered Charlie, looking around. "Guess I'm creatin' a spectacle. But I want you to forget that *poor me* shit. It could've happened to any of us. You just happened to be with her."

"Both times." Al winced. Sure, the first time Genevieve had drugged him and there wasn't much he could do to stop her from slipping away after that, and the second time she'd fooled the entire New Orleans police force, not just him, but still ... "Look, I appreciate you trying to make me feel better, but no matter how you spin it, the old lady hornswaggled me. I look for her every day, in thirty papers from around the country. Not a sign. Not one single sign, for three years now."

"Until now."

Al straightened in his chair. "Right. Until now."

"And this is huge. Finding another body with the same pinprick as the other fourteen who drowned is huge. We've got her this time, Al. I can feel it in my bones." Charlie stuffed another bite of pie into his mouth.

"I hope you're right. I'll keep in touch with Rusty and let you know if they come up with anything more." Al paid the bill and slapped his friend on the back again before heading to the office.

He was itching to get to Atlanta and look into the murder himself. All he needed was one more hot tip from Rusty and he'd be on his way.

41

Each day Al hoped for a call, but the South was silent. On the fourth day, as he was out doing rounds near the La Crosse Club, he decided he couldn't wait any longer. He dialed Charlie. "Lunch at the La Crosse Club, twenty minutes." He didn't give his buddy a chance to respond, terminating the call as soon as the words were out of his mouth.

Fifteen minutes later he walked into the restaurant and his mouth dropped open. Charlie sat at a table in the center of the dining room, his napkin already stuffed into his shirt.

"Damn, do you just wait for me to call—or do you intercept your calls on the way over here? I just phoned you, for cripes sake."

"Yea, well every time I suggest this place, you give me shit about your having to pay, so I wanted to get here before you changed your mind. Besides, you didn't even give me a chance to respond."

"But …"

"But nothin'. When you offer, I'm on. I've been here for five minutes. Where the hell you been?"

"I said twenty, didn't I? That actually makes me early." Al pulled out the chair across from his friend and sat down.

"Well, I figured you had to have talked to Rusty. Musta told ya somethin' good, right? Give it to me."

Al carefully rolled up his sleeves, one at a time, before positioning his napkin in his lap, and picking up the menu. Charlie's face grew so red Al set down the menu quickly and lifted a hand, worried his friend might have a stroke.

"There's nothing to report, unfortunately. I've been staring at the phone for days, waiting for it to ring, and I'm going crazy. I thought we might as well commiserate together."

"Com ... cominsurate ...what?"

"I said commiserate. That means sharing our sorrows."

"Well ..." Charlie peered at Al over his menu. "Best way I know to share sorrows is to eat together. What the hell, let's have a great lunch!"

"That's my boy. Cheer me up, big guy."

Charlie was clearly in the mood to drown his sorrows completely. He decided on a double order of steak frites, a garden salad with blue cheese dressing, and two pieces of pie, one coconut cream and the other lemon meringue.

Al listened to Charlie order, shook his head, and shrugged at the waitress. "And I invited him. Am I crazy or what?"

"Detective Rouse, you're just a heckuva nice guy." The waitress blushed, fussed with her order pad, and disappeared.

●——•

The next morning Al walked into the office and found a message on his desk asking him to call Aaron Wingate in New Orleans. His heart-rate picked up. Did Aaron have something for him?

He called the number on the notepad. Aaron answered after the first ring. "How are our boys in the North?" the detective asked in his lazy drawl. "We miss y'all down here. Life's interestin' when y'all are aroun.'"

"We're good, except itching to hear any news on Genevieve Wangen you might have for us."

"Well, I might be able to help ya there. Ah think you all may want to schedule another visit. There's a guy down here ya need ta talk to."

Al picked up a pen and tapped it on his mouse pad. "Really? What have you got?"

"While investigating the killing of Antonio Cabrera and the disappearance of his brother, we've picked up some information about a new business being run under the umbrella of Carbone Industries."

"What kind of business?"

"'Pears to be some kind of chemical weapons manufacturing."

Al's eyes widened as he tapped the pen harder on the pad. "Really. Sounds like something our girl could be involved in."

"That's what I thought. They're masking the product as drugs for international veterinarians, but I'm not so sure. Ah think you should consider coming down to talk to the guy they have in charge."

"And who would that be?"

"Guy named Pete Pernaska, a U.S. citizen but originally from Albania. Good-looking dude, cut from the same cloth as the Carbone boys. He's working with Chandler Carbone in the operation, but the way we hear it, Dino Carbone is the driver."

"You think this Pernaska might be dirty?"

"Well, he's working with the mob, and he surfaced about the same time that the Cabrera killing went down, coincidentally around the same time that the gang warfare began in earnest in Europe."

"So you think the business might be supplying families in Europe with the tools to fight the upstarts over there?"

"Could be Al, could be. We can't prove that yet, but the timing matches up. Soon as we have a solid lead, we'll get a warrant and search the place."

Al sighed. Of course they had to follow the proper procedures, but what he wouldn't give to bust into that place in the night and have a good look around. "Got anything else?"

"The report is that Pernaska and a female companion flew into New Orleans on one of the Carbone planes to supervise setup. One of our guys said she was a spittin' image for Savannah Harlowe. I told him he was crazy. In any event, our guy thought enough about it to go back, hoping to arrest her. She was gone. She'd never return here, would she?"

The drumming had now reached a crescendo pitch. *Sounds just like her. She's got bigger balls than a gorilla.* "I wouldn't put anything past her. Do they know where she and Pernaska came from?"

"I asked that, but our guy didn't know. And he had no idea where she went."

I'm pretty sure I know where she went. I'm pretty damn sure she went to Atlanta and stuck a needle in Antonio Cabrera's ear. Wonder if it's worth asking Rusty to shake down the Johansen woman. Might be worth a shot.

"Well, that's about it, ah guess. Anything new develops, I'll let you know. And if you decide to c'mon down, let us know and we'll set you up with things you need, like transportation and office space."

"Thanks Aaron, I appreciate that." Al disconnected the call. He decided to visit with his boss before calling Charlie, because he knew his friend would want to take the next plane to Atlanta or New Orleans—or maybe both.

42

A l knew his boss. Chief Brent Whigg was a pragmatist. He had a great record as La Crosse Chief and he earned it by being deliberate in his approach to investigations. After listening to Al fill him in on the discussion with Aaron, he sat back, folded his hands behind his head, and sat in silence for a full minute, clearly thinking the situation through carefully.

Finally he straightened in his chair and clasped his hands on the desk. "Seems to me you ought to ask your friend in Atlanta to visit Ms. Johansen and turn up the heat. I don't think there's enough to warrant a trip down there - at least not yet. From what Aaron told you, he's right, it doesn't sound as though there's enough evidence for a search. See what you can arrange in Atlanta. Then let's give it some time. You stay in touch with Cunningham and Wingate at least once a week. If we get anything more substantive, you can make a trip."

Al was disappointed, but he didn't disagree. He knew that the information was speculative and he considered the chief's decision fair. He would stay in touch with Cunningham and Wingate and wait to see if anything developed. Having made that decision, he typed an email to his friends in Atlanta and New Orleans, sent them on their way, and called Charlie.

"Why don't we grab a beer at Schmidty's after work?" he suggested. "I have some things to tell you about."

When the two met at the bar-restaurant on the southeast side of

La Crosse, the place was filled with workers on their way home, and the dinner crowd was beginning to show up, too.

To combat the noise, he and Charlie grabbed beers from the bar and settled into a booth in a far corner.

Al filled in his friend, careful to make it clear that they had little to go on at this point, because he knew Charlie would want to charge.

"Damn, Al, we oughta be down there lookin' into this stuff. I don't like this wait and see crap. Nothin' gets done that way!" Charlie's face had gone red, as it always did when he was excited.

"I don't disagree, Charlie, but Brent and Dwight have to make those kinds of decisions. They have budgets to meet and they can't have people running all over like loose cannons."

"Loose cannons? What the hell are you talkin' about? We aren't loose cannons. We produce results."

Charlie's face had turned burgundy now and he was leaning across the booth, his nose a foot from Al's.

"Well, Charlie, perhaps you've forgotten ..."

Charlie's threw his hand in the air, knocking over his bottle of beer in the process. The frothy liquid dripped over his side of the table. "Shit. Now lookit what's happened. Like hell I have forgotten! If you say one goddamn word about the old lady escaping, I'm gonna strangle you. We tracked down the killer didn't we? And we got her to confess, didn't we? And we had her in custody, didn't we? And how the hell were we supposed to know that the old bitch had a trick up 'er sleeve or, in this case, on her finger? I don't wanna hear any more crap about her getting' away. It coulda happened to anyone. Christ, lookit my pants."

Charlie stood up, displaying the growing wet patch on the crotch of his trousers.

Stifling a laugh, Al managed to gasp, "They do have bathrooms here, you know."

"Okay, okay, smart ass. Ma'am?" He signaled to their waitress. "Could I get some napkins please? A lot of 'em, if you don't mind."

The waitress rushed over with a stack of napkins and a bar rag to mop up the table. Al waited patiently while the two of them cleaned Charlie's side of the booth and Charlie worked at his trousers.

When he sat down, he continued to mop at his pants. "Not one word, not one goddamn word, hear?" He shook his finger at Al.

"Okay, but I'm not sure I can stay long enough for your pants to dry. I will buy you another beer, though, since it was kind of my fault you spilled that one."

Al walked to the bar and ordered Charlie another drink before returning to the booth and picking up where he had left off. "I don't think we can blame our bosses for wanting more than just a hunch to approve expenditures on, can we?"

"S'pose not." Charlie's massive shoulders slumped. "But I am damn hungry for one of them benny-yet things. I was kinda hopin' to get in a trip to the Big Easy one of these days."

"Listen to you: The 'Big Easy.' Yer talkin' like a southern boy now, Charlie."

"Well, those little donuts are great, and you know it. Bet you'd like one, too." Charlie stopped mopping his pants and tossed the pile of napkins onto the table.

"Sure would, but what I really want is Genevieve back in custody. I'd take that over a million beignets."

"I know the fact that she escaped bugs you." He fiddled with the glass the waitress had just set in front of him.

Al winced. "Just don't spill another drink. You do and they'll kick us outa here."

Charlie continued to play with his glass for a few seconds before taking a long draw and setting it back on the table with a thud. "Al, I know we're gonna catch her. It's just a matter of time. We both know she's gonna screw up, and when she does we're gonna be Johnny on the spot to grab 'er."

"I'd like to think that's true, but it's been what, three, four years now that she's been missin'?"

"Something like that," said Charlie. "She's a slippery old goose, that's fer sure. But we're gonna get her. I can feel it in my bones."

Al snorted. "Knowing you, what you're feeling is probably gas."

"Goddamnit, Al, I know the difference between gas and a good, damn feelin'. What I got is a feelin'. You just wait and see."

"Hope you're right."

"I am. I know this new thing, with the murders in Atlanta and the business in New Orleans, is gonna turn up something." Charlie lifted his glass. "How about another beer?"

"One more," agreed Al, "but then I gotta run. JoAnne plays cards tonight and she'll want to eat by six."

"Oh, crap, that's right, tonight is cards," acknowledged Charlie. "Kelly plays, too. Yup, one more and then I gotta get out of here as well."

They finished their beers and parted company in the parking lot of Schmidty's, Al heading south to his house, and Charlie driving east to his. As always, Al left his friend with a smile on his face, feeling slightly better about their chances of nabbing Genevieve Wangen sometime in the not-too-distant future.

●——•

When Al got home, JoAnne greeted him at the doorway with a smile. "Just in time, big guy," she said. "Dinner's ready, liver-and-onions. Thought you might like that after a long day."

"My favorite meal." Al rubbed his hands together. "Hope you made plenty of onions and bacon. I'll tear into that stuff like I would a filet mignon."

"Yuck." JoAnne shivered. "Definitely not my favorite meal, but I made it for you. I'm heading out to play cards. You didn't forget that, did you?"

"Of course not." Al followed her into the kitchen, where the tantalizing odor of frying bacon hung in the air. "That's okay, the Packers play the Bears tonight. It's a good time for cards, because I know you don't really enjoy watching the game with me."

"How can you say that?" JoAnne pressed a hand to her chest, her eyes widening. "I love to watch football with you."

"Yah, right. The only thing you love about football is getting me alone on the couch."

"Allan Rouse, you are incorrigible! I am a classy lady. You're in quite a mood."

"I'm in a good mood. It's been kind of a trying day, but I always feel better when I get home, with you."

She smiled. "I'm glad to hear it. Run up and change while I get supper on the table, then you can fall asleep on the couch and pretend you're watching the game."

Grinning, Al did as he was told. JoAnne knew him too well. Upstairs, he kicked off his loafers and work clothes and stuck them in the closet. In blue jeans and a sweatshirt, he headed back downstairs. He walked into the kitchen, pinched JoAnne gently on the bottom, and headed for the table.

"Much better," she said. "I like playful Al. Everything is ready. When you're finished, maybe even I'll be ready."

He shook his head. "If we play before you leave, I'll miss the football game. May I please have a rain check?"

She looked at him and smiled slyly. "Sure, but we both know that you won't be awake to collect it. When's the last time you were both awake and ready when I got home from a night out?"

Al thought earnestly but gave up and shook his head. "Not recently."

"Damn right, not recently. If it makes you happy, though, I'll pretend it might happen. But my guess is you'll be sleeping."

"I might surprise you." Al sat down at the table. JoAnne set a plate filled with liver, onions, bacon, and American fries in front of him. She pressed a kiss to the top of his head and headed for the door. "I'm going to get ready. Eat that up and help yourself to more." She stopped in the doorway and wrinkled her nose. "I hate that stuff, and I sure don't want any of it left. Even the dog won't eat it."

Al frowned. "That's unfair. The dog's old, and he's always had a sensitive stomach. Besides, he's never had the opportunity to taste liver. Don't I always eat it all?"

"That you do. It's the only reason I keep on making it." She laughed and disappeared into the hallway.

Al shoveled in the food, speared the last piece of liver from the frying pan, covered it with the remainder of the bacon and onions, simmering in another pan, and scooped the last of the potatoes out of the pan. When he finished, he rinsed his dishes and the cookware and stowed all of them neatly in the dishwasher. He added soap and hit the start button, then walked into the living room, tuned the TV to ESPN, and settled down to wait for the game to begin.

JoAnne came down the stairs, dressed in new jeans, a short jean jacket, and a heavy scarf. She looked sensational.

Al's mouth dropped open. "Look at you. You're beautiful in those new jeans. Really makes your ass look like a teenager's. If you weren't late, I'd jump your bones - right here, right now."

Pink tinged her cheeks. "Hold that thought, big fella; I'll be home by ten. Dessert then, okay?"

"Damn right." He jumped up from his chair and kissed her on the lips before opening the door for her.

When JoAnne drove off, he waved, closed the door, and returned to the living room sofa. Images of Genevieve Wangen continued to fly through his head, and even though the Packers-Bears game was a barnburner, he just couldn't get the case off his mind.

Tormented, he finally gave in and called Julie Sonoma in Arlington Heights. Julie was Genevieve's niece, and his former mistress. Their affair had ended several years ago, when JoAnne found out and put a stop to it, but they had remained friends.

"And to what do I owe a call from my favorite policeman?"

"JoAnne is playing cards with Peggy and Kelly, and I just can't seem to get Genevieve out of my mind tonight. I can't shake the feeling that I have overlooked something. I often feel that way, but tonight more than usual."

Silence stretched out between them. Al frowned. "Are you still there?"

"I am. I feel so badly for you. I wish there were something I could do to make you feel better."

"Your voice helps."

"I'm glad you called me."

"Look, I know it's unfair for me to call you when I'm frustrated over this case, but I didn't know where else to turn. If I call Charlie, he'll tell me I'm nuts and I should just let it go. Rick would suggest it's a guilt thing and urge me to see a psychologist or try medication or something. So that leaves you."

"I want you to call me whenever you are feeling down and you think talking to me will help. Even though we're not together anymore, I value our friendship and feel like being there for each other is the least we can do."

"But it's not fair. Genevieve is your aunt. I shouldn't be calling you in the hope that you can point me in a direction that you wouldn't necessarily want me to go, even if you did know something."

Another long silence followed his speech. Al gripped the receiver. What did that mean? A sick feeling struck him. Julie didn't know something she wasn't telling him, did she? Surely she wouldn't let him suffer for years, kicking himself for losing the old lady—twice—and failing to bring her in when she knew all along where her aunt was. Al shook his head. Of course not. Julie cared about him. Even if he had hurt her when he ended things with her, there was no way she could be that cruel.

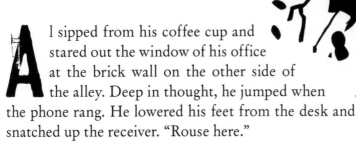

43

Al sipped from his coffee cup and stared out the window of his office at the brick wall on the other side of the alley. Deep in thought, he jumped when the phone rang. He lowered his feet from the desk and snatched up the receiver. "Rouse here."

"Hey, Al, it's Rusty."

Al set down his coffee cup. He hadn't heard from his buddy in Atlanta for a couple of weeks and had almost given up hope he would any time soon. "Rusty. Good to hear your voice. What have you got for me?"

"I had a little visit with Amber Johansen last night and I thought you'd be interested in what she had to say."

"Gimme a sec, will you Rusty? I want to close the door." Al set the receiver on the desk, strode to the door, and closed it tight before returning to his seat. "That's better; more privacy," he told his friend. "I'm all ears, tell me about the visit."

"I dropped into Amber's unannounced. She must have been pretty surprised to see me 'cause it's the first time I've seen her nervous. Normally she's as calm as a clam, but she sure as heck wasn't last night, and I think it had everything to do with my presence."

"How so?" Al propped an elbow on the desk.

"She was off her game, know what I mean? Just wasn't herself. She tried to act calm and gracious, like she always does, but she was just plain antsy—no other word for it."

"Did she answer your questions?"

"Kind of. I mean, yeah, she answered, but not like normal."

Al frowned. "What does that mean?"

"She took a lot longer to answer my questions than she has in the past. Usually when I talk to her, she's able to answer right away, and her responses seem quite rehearsed, as though someone might have told her what to say. Last night her answers were nothing like that."

"What'd she tell you?"

"I let her know we had a solid report that the murder of Antonio Cabrera had occurred at her establishment, something she quickly denied. She stuck to her story until I revealed every little detail I had for her. When I told her about Antonio being stuffed into a barrel, moved to her garage, and encased in the cement her men had mixed there, she broke."

Al's eyebrows rose. Broke was good. "What'd she do?"

"She began to cry, told me he was a bad guy who had done bad things to her employees every time he visited. She said a new girl she was trying had been given to Antonio the night of the murder. The woman wasn't even an employee, apparently. As usual, Antonio got rough with the woman. Slapped her around. According to Amber, the woman tied him up, alleging play, and wound up killing him. Then the woman walked out, calm as a cucumber, asked for a ride to DeKalb-Peachtree Airport and, as she got ready to leave, warned Amber that she had left a mess in the bedroom. When she was gone, Amber walked in and found Antonio dead. She said she panicked, called some of her workers in to help, and they came up with the idea of the barrel, the concrete, and the deep sea burial. I hammered at her for an hour, but she never once moved from the story."

"The pinprick in the ear is pretty much a dead giveaway, Rusty. It has to be Genevieve Wangen."

"But Al, Amber said she was younger. Said she looked about fifty; that's not Genevieve, right?"

"Remember, Rusty, she got a full-body makeover in New Orleans, courtesy of Angelo Carbone. So the answer is, yes, that is our girl—I'm betting on it. So where do you go from here? Have you arrested Amber?"

"No, we haven't, and we're not going to, either."

"What!" Al's chair snapped into place as he straightened up. "You're not going to arrest her? She's an accessory, for Christ's sake. She had the body disposed of, and covered it all up."

"Yeah, I know all that."

"And you're gonna let her go?"

"That's what the D.A. has decided."

"Rusty, how in the hell can that be? Just how in the hell can you look the other way on this one? Are you nuts?"

"Al, here's the deal. Amber is a really good person. She runs a first-rate establishment. We almost never have trouble with her—never, in fact. Apparently this was a simple transaction and she was trying out a new girl, who wasn't even her employee. Antonio got rough—real rough, she said. So the D.A. says there is a perfect self-defense alibi here. We don't know where the woman is, so we're just gonna forget it. You wanna talk to the chief?"

"No, no, I don't think so. Maybe my boss will, or maybe he'll contact the D.A."

"If you're gonna do that, Al, would ya let me know? I might have said too much here, and I could be in trouble. I'd at least like to give 'em a little warning."

"I understand, Rusty. And I appreciate you letting me know all this. I'm just a little stunned, that's all."

"All I can tell ya, is that's how things are. If we can find the perpetrator, then things will change. At that point Amber may be charged as an accessory, but I can also tell you any search for the killer is on the back burner."

"I got it, Rusty. Thanks again."

Al replaced the receiver and slumped in his chair. He thumped the desk twice with his fist. *I need to talk to the chief.*

Brent Whigg was working at his desk when Al knocked. He looked up and smiled, then waved Al in.

"Got a minute, Chief? I need an ear."

"Course, for you, for sure. C'mon in."

Al sat down across from the large oak desk. "I just talked to Rusty down in Atlanta. And I'm really confused."

The chief leaned back in his chair and folded his hands over his stomach. "Let me have it."

Al relayed the conversation with Rusty, concluding with, "And they aren't going to charge the madam with anything—unless they find the killer. Rusty said the D.A. doesn't think there's much of a case, since it sounds like clear self-defense and the killer has vanished. Apparently they are also close to Amber, which plays into this, too."

When Al finished, the chief hiked his chair closer to the desk, leaned across, smiled and said, "Al, it's the South. I know you haven't had a lot of experience with the folks down there, but trust me, that's how it is. You know, the D.A. might be right. There's not much chance of Amber talking. Even if they bring her in, how is that going to help them in the end?"

Al slumped back in his chair and shook his head. "Guess you're right, Chief. I can't make 'em arrest the madam and maybe there isn't much of a case. Just seems a crappy end to what might have been a great chance for us to get the old gal again."

"I know how you must feel, Al. Why don't you get out of here for the rest of the day? Go take JoAnne somewhere and have some fun. Clear your head."

Al blew out a breath. "All right, if you insist." He stood up and moved toward the door then paused and looked back. "What about Charlie? Do I tell him?"

The chief laughed. "I think I'd pass, if I were you. You know him better'n I do, but he'd blow his stack, wouldn't he?"

If Al hadn't been wound up so tightly, he might have laughed too. The chief was right though. If Al was upset about what was going on, Charlie would be completely apoplectic.

And nobody wanted to see that.

44

Sam awakened in her mountain valley retreat in Montana, thankful for the peace and quiet she had in this special place. She looked forward to the day. She had talked with Pete the previous afternoon and found that he and Chandler were buried in orders and floundering to keep up with the demand from their customers in Europe, where gang warfare continued to rage.

The outbreak of violence against Abdi Nur in Stockholm had grown. Pete had flown to Rome to meet with Abdi, Winston Kray of London, and Arthur McGraw of Glasgow, and now Kray and McGraw were under siege in Scotland and England.

The orders had grown exponentially, and the European mobsters were clamoring for new weapons. The opponents, for the most part street gangs across Europe's major cities, had banded together in an attempt to win turf from the more established mob bosses.

Instead of continuing the mass onslaughts, the upstarts had adopted a new form of attack, focusing on tracking down members of organized crime one by one. That meant that Europe's crime organizations had to equip each of their members with spray canisters, resulting in orders for six thousand canisters capable of directing spray up to fifty feet. In addition, the crime bosses were asking for canisters with adjustable spray nozzles that could reduce the distance to five feet from their target. Finally, they were appealing for new weapons that could be used in crowds to take down, but not necessarily kill, groups of people.

When Sam had talked to Pete, he had asked her if she could develop a spray system that would render large numbers of people unconscious without killing them.

That afternoon she drove to Kalispell and used Molly's computer to research sedatives capable of temporarily putting down large groups of people. As she searched, she found an incapacitating agent used in 2002 by Chechen terrorists.

Employing a fentanyl derivative called Kolkol-1, the Chechens used the agent on a number of hostages. While the agent proved effective, many of the hostages died.

Sam found the report intriguing and made a note to have Pete appeal to his friend Semion Moglevich, their USSR customer, to see what he might know about the drug.

She continued the hunt, but was disappointed to find little other information that appeared useful. She abandoned her search so she could be home before dark.

When she had just about reached the turnoff into her road, she pulled off at a wayside viewing area overlooking Flathead Lake and called Pete. She told him about the drug used by the Chechens and asked him to call Semion.

Pete told her he would do it that night. "They're desperate. I'm sure Semion will tap all of his sources immediately to find out what he can."

"Good. Let me know what you find out." Sam leaned back against the Jeep. "How is production going otherwise?"

"We're experiencing a supply problem with canisters," he admitted. "We just can't produce them fast enough to keep up with the demand."

"Why don't you have Chandler talk to his father and Dino? Tell him to ask Angelo if he has any connections in China. If he does, have him use them. We need those canister they supplied us with before."

"Good idea; I'll do that right away." Pete exhaled loudly. "Do you ever wonder if we're doing the right thing?"

Sam's chest tightened. "What do you mean?"

"I'm not sorry I joined forces with you, believe me. The work is exciting and I feel as though we're truly making a difference. Still, if we were a normal couple with normal jobs, I'd be home with you right now, snuggled up on the couch watching a movie and sipping wine."

Sam sighed. "That does sound incredible. Just hold on a little longer. As soon as things die down in Europe, which has to happen before too long, and Chandler has everything running smoothly in New Orleans, you can be home with me every night."

"I can't wait. I miss you, Sam."

"I miss you too. Talk to you tomorrow." Swiping away a tear that had started to slide down her cheek, she disconnected the call and climbed back into the Jeep. When she drove into the yard and into the garage, she breathed a sigh of relief. Her little home in the forest was snugly ensconced in a blanket of fresh snow. The only thing that would make it better would be smoke curling from the chimney. *A fire would feel great tonight, and so would a hot drink.*

As she moved from the car into the warmth of her home, the tightness she'd felt in her chest since speaking to Pete on the phone intensified. *I miss him so much.* It would have been so nice to have him here, a fresh snowfall blanketing their homestead. They could have made sweet love in front of a roaring fire. She loved the peace of the forest, but she loved it better when her man was with her.

She went to the bedroom, stripped down, padded naked to the bathroom, and filled the huge tub with hot water, adding a generous amount of bubble bath.

By the time she finished, she felt almost too tired to eat. The feeling of lonesomeness for Pete was overpowering. She mixed herself a Bailey's, decided she needed to eat something, and popped a TV dinner into the oven.

Drink in hand, she stood at the window and looked out over the yard. The moon cast its light through the branches of the trees and onto the snow below. The scene looked so serene, she immediately felt better. She got into bed, hoping that a few pages of her new book—*The Whistler* by John Grisham—would put her to sleep. Even the scintillating writing of Grisham wasn't enough to do it and she read until after midnight before turning out the lights.

Sam awoke sluggish and tired. *I need to get to work.* She had printed some information on Kolkol-1, and she studied it over coffee. "The agent was surmised to be some sort of surgical anesthetic or chemical weapon. Immediately after the siege, Western media speculated widely as to the identity of the substance that was used to end the siege, and chemicals such as the tranquilizer diazepam (Valium), the anticholinergic BZ, the highly potent oripavine-derived, Bentley-series opioid etorphine, another highly potent opioid, such as a fentanyl or an analogue thereof, such as 3-methylfentanil, and the anesthetic halothane were proposed."

Foreign embassies in Moscow, the report said, "issued official requests for more information on the gas to aid in treatment, but were publicly ignored. While still refusing to identify the gas, on October 28, 2002, the Russian government informed the U.S. Embassy of some of the gas's effects. Based on this information and examinations of victims, doctors concluded the gas was a morphine derivative. The Russian media reported the drug was Kolokol-1, either mefentanyl or a methylfentanil dissolved in a halothane base."

Sam tapped her fingers on the top of the wooden table. *Those are sufficient clues to allow me to mix up some things, but what the heck am I going to test the mix on? It will have to be something pretty big, and something I can bury if the subject dies.*

She'd begin by dissolving fentanyl, typically used to control severe pain, in Fluothane, an anesthetic that was inhaled. But how much should she use of each? The only way to figure that out would be to start small and work her way up, using a test she would also have to concoct.

After draining the last of the coffee in her mug, Sam set aside the report and headed to the bedroom to get dressed. She pulled on jeans and a sweatshirt and paused at her bedroom window. Her eyes widened at the sight of a large male moose at one of the bird feeders. Sam gripped the bottom of the window, about to lift it to yell and shoo the massive animal away, when she froze. *I might have just found my test subject.*

She strode to the lab, took the chemicals from the cold storage area, mixed what she thought was a sufficient amount of each drug together, and put them in a spray canister. Now, how could she get close enough to administer the drug? The minute she showed herself, the moose would likely run or, worse yet, charge.

Armed with the canister, she returned to the main living area and found that the moose had moved to a feeder just outside her garage. That was helpful, but not the total answer.

She went to the garage and found the sack of oats Pete had stored there to feed larger animals. Pursing her lips, she retrieved two dishpans from the mudroom. One she filled with water, carried to the garage, and set just inside the large automated door. The second she filled with oats and placed next to the water.

Sam donned a coat, took the canister she had filled, and grabbed the garage door opener. After activating the door, she waited until it opened and then leaned out and looked for the moose. He stood at the edge of the path to the lake, looking toward the house.

As she watched, the big animal pawed the ground, then took a few halting steps back toward the garage. It came closer then stopped again, pawed the ground, and lifted its nose into the air.

Apparently smelling the oats, it moved cautiously toward the garage. Her muscles tense, Sam waited, almost afraid to breathe. As the moose moved closer, a thought struck her. Setting the oats where she had was a stroke of unintended genius. The range from there to where she stood was roughly the distance an effective agent would have to travel to take down targets.

The moose drew closer, pausing every couple of steps. *Can he smell me?* If he did, it was unlikely he would come any closer. The smell of the oats must have been strong enough to overpower any other, for the moose trotted the last few steps then lowered its head to the pan and began to eat. *What a majestic beast.*

Sam carefully opened the spray nozzle on the canister, pointed it in the general direction of the big animal, and hit the button, counting one thousand one, one thousand two before stopping the spray.

The big animal reared its head, shook it vigorously, then turned, took two leaps, and fell to the ground.

A hand flew to her throat. *Oh my god, have I killed it?* She waited for five minutes, then five more before tentatively approaching the big animal. Fog formed in the air in front of the giant nostrils and Sam's shoulders relaxed. Although the animal was unconscious, it was still breathing. She moved close enough to lift one of its eyelids with her finger. The eye was clear but unseeing.

Sam went inside and sat at the window, glancing periodically at her watch. Five minutes and fourteen seconds later, the animal raised its head tentatively and immediately lowered it to the ground. Two more minutes and it raised its head again, shook it, and clambered to its feet. It weaved back and forth a little before stumbling back down the path.

Sam clasped her hands in front of her. The solution was almost perfect. Of course, a moose's body mass and circulation system were larger than a human's; a person might be out for eight minutes or so. She bit her lip. *That's not enough.* She would strengthen the mixture and hope the moose returned for another meal and a second test.

After increasing the strength of the drug, Sam loaded a new canister and focused on household chores for the remainder of the day. With dusk coming, she returned to the garage and her hiding place. Once secluded, she opened the door and waited. After two hours, she gave up her vigil.

When she awoke the next morning and looked out the window, the big animal was back at the bird feeders. She dressed hurriedly and went out to the garage, canister in hand. Careful to stay out of sight, she opened the door.

This time the moose made directly for the oats and water, stopping first to drink nearly all the water before starting on the oats. Sam depressed the button on the canister, counted to two, and watched to see what would happen. The big animal shook its head again, turned, and walked toward the path. After a few steps, it began to stagger before gently lowering itself to the ground.

The moose remained sedated for nearly forty-five minutes. When it awoke, it managed to get to its feet, stand on the path swaying for several minutes, then turn back to the garage and the oats, finishing the food before disappearing down the path.

Sam applauded enthusiastically. *It works!* She spent the day filling canisters. Early the next morning she called Pete to tell him she had fifty ready for the people in Europe to test.

"That's amazing, Sam. Dino's here working; I'll ask him to send a plane to Montana this afternoon to pick up the test canisters and return them here in time to ship tonight. Actually, he's coming over here now; I'll let you talk to him."

Dino came onto the line and Sam explained what she had done. He sounded thrilled as he congratulated her. "Sam, why don't I send the plane and you can bring the canisters here yourself? That way, if we get a positive report from our customers abroad tomorrow, you can help Pete and Chandler with the first mixing of the drugs here. How about it?"

And I can see Pete. Warmth flooded her chest. "I'd love to come." She clutched the receiver tightly. "I miss … all of you so much."

Dino barked a laugh. "Don't worry darlin', I'm under no illusions about who it is you miss. I hope you will find a little time to spend with the rest of us though. We miss you too."

"Of course I will. I'm anxious to see everyone."

"Great, then it's set. I'll send the plane to Missoula for two this afternoon. Can you make that?"

Sam readily agreed. That would give her enough time to pack a few clothes and drive down to the bigger city. Just after two, she boarded the now-familiar Gulfstream in Missoula and minutes later was in the air, bound for New Orleans. A huge smile on her face, she settled back in her seat.

I'm going home.

45

The night was another joyous occasion in the home of Don Carbone. The entire family was present to greet Sam, and the party atmosphere lasted until nearly eleven o'clock. Finally, Sam pushed back her chair. "I hate to end the evening, but I really need to get some rest."

"Aah, dolcezza," said the don gently, "we are poor hosts here. Yes, you need sleep. And perhaps something more." He winked at Pete.

Sam wasn't about to argue, especially when Pete took her hand and led her from the room, It was an exciting reunion. Finally spent around 3:00 a.m., she drifted off to sleep in Pete's strong arms.

After putting in a full day filling orders at the warehouse, Sam and Pete gathered in Angelo's study with the rest of the family. Dino mixed drinks and conversation was lighthearted as they talked about the day, their hopes, and how anxious they were to receive a report from Europe.

Every few minutes, Dino pulled out his phone and studied the screen intently.

Finally Angelo, smoking the one cigar a day that Rosalyn allowed, exhaled a cloud of smoke and said gently, "Dino, put that damn phone away. You looking at it every thirty seconds is not going to make it produce the message you're waiting for. We're having a nice family time, the kind we always used to have. It's been a long while since we've just sat down at the end of the day and talked about nothing important. I for one am trying to enjoy it. But you looking at your phone every few minutes bothers me!"

"Yes, Papa," said Dino, slipping the device into the back pocket of his jeans. "I am just anxious to hear from Europe."

"I understand, but why don't we enjoy our drinks and time together. When we get up for dinner, you can look. Okay?"

"Absolutely."

For the next forty-five minutes, laughter and conversation flowed. When Greta Bianchi, the cook, summoned them to dinner, Dino hung back to check his phone. After they were seated, wine was poured, and the staff prepared to serve the soup course.

"Excuse me," said Dino, walking into the room, one hand raised. "Before we begin I have a toast. Please raise your glasses to Sam, who has delivered to our European comrades a product they regard as superior and, to quote, 'Exactly what is needed to put down the insurgents and guarantee victory to our side.' Here, here!"

"Here, here," echoed across the room as they each saluted Sam before drinking deeply.

Rosalyn, seated at one end of the table opposite her husband, looked at Sam and said, "Pray tell, Sam, just what kind of a mixture did you send those folks and what did it do?"

Before responding, Sam looked at Don Angelo, who nodded assent.

She took a deep breath. Would Rosalyn approve? "Rosalyn, our European friends requested a chemical that would knock people out but not kill them. I experimented with a mixture of drugs, on a moose, actually, until I came up with one I thought would do the job. I am relieved to hear that it is working."

Pete stared at her, wide-eyed. "You tried it out on a moose?"

"Yes. I saw one at our bird feeders one morning and realized I had the perfect test subject right in our own yard."

He frowned. "That sounds dangerous."

Sam covered the fist he had clenched on his knee with her hand. "I was careful, I promise."

His fingers unfurled and he grasped her hand. "I hope so."

Dino held up his soup spoon. "Whatever you tested it on, it's definitely working. In fact, Semion said they want five thousand large canisters."

Sam's forehead wrinkled. "Large canisters?"

Pete looked a bit sheepish. "I forgot to tell you, sorry. Semion called me a week or two ago and wondered if we could expand the size of the canisters. Since I had handled discussions with the manufacturer the last time, I called and ordered fourteen-ounce canisters. We have a number of cases of the new canisters in stock, so we can start to fill them immediately."

A smile spread across Sam's face as she leaned back in her chair. "That's great news. I'm glad you went ahead and did that."

Pete squeezed her hand. "Vonell figured out the rates. She came up with a great pricing scheme. While the per-ounce price went down, the margin increased on the larger canisters. Vonell has been a godsend."

Sam tipped her glass in the direction of Dino's sister. "Thanks so much, Vonell. Partnering with this family is the best idea I ever had. We have access to expertise that is incredibly helpful. It's so much better if all we have to do is concentrate on the product we're making."

Over ice cream and cake, Sam talked to Dino about the test. He suggested she call Semion directly. "He started to tell me about everything you are asking, but I stopped him. Best that you talk to him yourself. That way you get the exact answers you need."

"All right. If everyone will excuse me, I'll go call him now." She left the table and went upstairs to their room.

Semion sounded as enthused as Dino had reported. "The intelligence we have from the sixty-some people we took captive last night is amazing. We already know where the next strikes will be and we have people armed with canisters—what's left from what you sent—waiting for them. I suspect tomorrow we will have more intelligence."

"That's excellent news, Semion. I'm so pleased the new product is helping you."

"It certainly is. However, what I really need now is something that will loosen their tongues. It may not always be as easy as it was last night to get our captives to talk. So if you have anything that can make the birds sing sweeter, we'd love it."

"I'll see what I can do and get back to you."

"Thank you. And bless you. You have done a great favor for us and we will not forget it."

Sam disconnected the call and stood in front of the window, looking out over the vast estate. Sodium pentothal was also called the "truth serum." Beyond that, though, she had no experience with psychoactive medications. Perhaps there was something even better out there, something more effective. If so, she needed to find out what it was.

Since Sam was in New Orleans and had access to high-speed Internet service, she used it the next day to do some basic research. If she came up with anything interesting, she could mix up something and send it abroad to be tested. If successful, it might mean another source of income.

Sam spent the next few hours reading everything she could find about truth serums. She was extremely intrigued by SP-117, a drug allegedly used by the Soviets to obtain secrets from people they captured during the Cold War. The problem was, she could find nothing that indicated what drugs this concoction consisted of.

It made sense that sodium thiopental and amobarbital might have been used. Still, there had to be another agent. But what? Sam pursed her lips. Was it possible Semion might have a contact in the former Soviet Union who would know something? She called him back to ask him and he promised to probe his sources immediately.

As she read, she found many possible options, but nothing that appeared to be a sure thing. She had a leisurely lunch, found Don Carbone in his study, and the two had a long talk about the state of the world and the don's empire. He told her how he had built the New Orleans machine, why he'd felt it necessary to take a more law-abiding path, and how he made his decisions about when to deviate from that.

"The European intervention is a reasonable step for two reasons. First, it will stabilize the continent under more reasonable crime lords; and, second, it will, if successful, protect our operations at home because of the new flow of money."

"You surprise me," she told him after they had talked for nearly three hours.

"Why, dolcezza?"

"You are so very calm. You deal with very heavy topics matter of factly and without apparent emotion. I don't understand how that's possible."

"I learned a long time ago that emotion clouds the clearest of pictures and causes you to do things that are irrational. Staying calm, it has always seemed to me, allows for the best decision-making."

"That makes sense, I suppose, but I don't think I could stay as cool as you. It just isn't part of my makeup to listen without wanting to act."

"Do you think I do not want to act? Do you think I am not sometimes seething inside?" He laughed. "Experience has shown me, however, that acting without thinking is rarely a good idea, and more often than not gives the upper hand to the one you are acting against. I know calmness is unsettling to those who would act without thought. It is confusing to see someone apparently unaffected by whatever is being discussed. My children are a perfect case. Dino is getting better, but he always wants to go, go, go. I try to teach him that thinking first is best."

"I have seen both sides of Dino, but, you're right, he's getting much better, much harder to read."

"Yes, Dino is going to take the family to new levels of effectiveness. He is wise beyond his years and anxious to learn. I credit you for much of that."

When she began to protest, the don held up his hand. "Samantha, let me assure you that is not an idle compliment. When Dino first met you, he was a brash, fire-ready-aim boy. Now he is a studious, thoughtful, contemplative man. Yes, I take credit for some of that. But I think that your touch as a mature woman helped, too. Whatever you have to say on the matter will not change my thoughts."

He smiled at her. "Now, dolcezza, an old man must sleep. I find that a nap about this time of the day makes me alert enough to keep up with the conversation at dinner. This is important, because I am not quite ready to turn over the reins of my empire yet."

Sam pressed his gnarled hand between both of hers. "And why would you? From what I've seen, no one else can keep this family, and all its various enterprises, on track as well as you can. May you live many more happy and healthy years, teaching all of us from your vast store of knowledge and wisdom."

He chuckled. "Well, if Rosalyn has anything to say about it, I just might."

46

For the next two days, Sam, Pete, Vonell, Benton, and Chandler labored at the warehouse, working on their current orders, as well as an additional order for one thousand canisters of Sam's version of "truth serum." Semione had told her about the missing ingredient he'd found out about from a source, and after she'd added and adjusted the amounts of each drug and sent off the new serum, he called to say that it worked like a charm. They'd tried it out on two captives and learned far more information than they had ever been able to procure before. The only problem, according to Semione, was that it took the two longer to come out of the trance than he would have liked, so Sam had tinkered a little with the formula until she felt she had it right.

"So you mean to say that you now have created a drug that will cause the person it is sprayed on to tell all his secrets?" the don asked her that night at dinner, his brow furrowed.

Sam nodded. "Essentially yes. First it creates unconsciousness, and then, when the victim is waking, they respond to questions with what we believe and hope is the truth. The basic ingredient is Sodium Pentothal. You know what that is, right?"

"Aah, the proverbial truth serum. Yes, I surely have heard of it. And it really works?"

"Semion seems to think so. He did tell me that the test mix was a little too long-lasting, so I toned it down a bit today and we packaged one hundred canisters and sent them. We'll see what he has to say tomorrow."

"If it does what you say, it will sell well." The don smacked an open palm on the table. "In fact, you may have trouble keeping it in stock. I think we will need some, won't we, Dino?"

"Yes, Dad. It will be helpful to have a nonlethal agent available. If we carefully control the supply, we can control the country, or at the very least keep a tight rein on anyone who might want to attack us."

The don leaned back in his chair, a small smile on his face.

"You're definitely thinking something, Dad. Are you going to fill me in?"

"All in good time, my son. All in good time." The don reached for his glass of cognac and took a sip. When he had drained the glass, he raised a hand and rose from the chair. "Time for an old man to retire. Come, my dear. The children can party if they wish, but it's time for people like us to be sleeping."

When Angelo and Rosalyn left them, Sam turned to Dino. "What do you think your father might be contemplating?"

"I really don't have a clue. I learned long ago that my father is very brilliant and very unpredictable. Whenever I try to outguess him, I'm always 180 degrees off. Now I just wait until he is ready to fill me in. When he does, we'll argue, I suspect."

"You fight?" asked Pete.

Dino laughed heartily, with his siblings joining in. Vonell shook her head. "Like cats and dogs. The worst part is that I think they love it. It's how they best relate to each other. I think it was the arguments that convinced Papa that Dino was the one to rule the roost. Benton, Chandler, and Elliott were a bit reluctant to engage, but Dino was like a banty rooster in a cock fight. It was obvious that Dad enjoyed it."

Dino wiped his mouth with his napkin and set it on the table. "One thing I do know is that the old man has something percolating in his mind, and that something is likely going to mean work for me. And I'll do it too, because, you know what, once I got over my ego, I realized that the old man is one crafty son of a bitch. He hasn't lost an ounce of brainpower, even though he's grooming me to take over."

His brothers and sisters nodded solemnly, although they didn't need to. From everything Sam had seen and heard from the don, she knew Dino was absolutely right.

A quiet knock on the door woke Sam early the next morning. After slipping out from under the covers so she wouldn't disturb Pete, who had been putting in sixteen-hour days at the warehouse, she padded to the door and opened it carefully. The maid stood in the hallway. When Sam held a finger to her lips, the young woman nodded and handed her a folded piece of paper. With a slight curtsy, she turned and went back down the stairs.

Sam closed the door behind her and crept into the washroom to read the note. It was an invitation from Angelo to join him in his study as soon as she was ready for the day. Sam folded the paper back up and tapped it against her chin. Hmm. *What could he want to see me about?* She lifted her shoulders. *Only one way to find out.*

Quickly and quietly she showered, dressed, and made her way down to the study. When she reached it, the door was closed and she tapped lightly on the heavy, paneled wood.

"Who is it?"

The old man's voice sounded strong and steady and Sam grinned, relieved, as she turned the knob and pushed the door open slightly so he could see her. "It's me, Angelo."

Seated behind his massive cherry wood desk, he waved for her to enter. "Come in, my dear." He smiled as she closed the door behind her and crossed the room toward him. "Just a minute of your time, please, to humor an old man."

When she had seated herself in front of his desk, he leaned forward and looked her squarely in the eyes. "This new drug of yours, Samantha, how much trust do you have in its efficacy?"

"I'd hesitate to claim that it is infallible at this point. We only have one report, from Semion, so far. We will know more today, I think. But we probably will continue to learn new things for a while and to work on perfecting it."

Angelo chewed on his bottom lip as he studied her. After a moment, he straightened in his chair and clasped his hands on the desk, as though he'd made an important decision. "I have something I want you to do for me."

Without hesitation, Sam said, "Of course. How could I refuse? Think of all you've done for me."

"Okay, here it is: I'd like you to eat lunch with Rosalyn and me then I want you to try the spray on me."

Sam's eyes widened. She opened her mouth to protest, but the don held up his hand and she closed it.

"After lunch, I will hand you a slip of paper. On it will be three questions. After you have sprayed me and I have begun to wake up, you will ask me the three questions, being very careful to record my responses. I want to see how good this new drug is, Samantha, and these three questions involve my greatest secrets. Because you will know the answers—if they are truthful—you will have great power. You must assure me that you will never use that power to harm any of the Carbones."

She frowned. "How could you even ask that? I would never knowingly do anything to harm a member of your family. I hope you know that."

"Yes, dolcezza, yes, but information is power and power is corrupting. Knowledge can create great temptation, especially when the prize is large. And it would be, of course, as it would mean control of the Carbone empire."

Sam contemplated him for several seconds before replying. "You know how much I owe you; I owe you my life. You can absolutely be sure that I would never, ever use anything you said to me against you. But please, I have not yet said yes to this idea of yours. Before I do, I must be certain that there will be no ill effects."

"I respect that, and if I see you for lunch, I will know that you have considered the issue and decided to proceed."

A lump rose in Sam's throat and she slid to the front of her seat and covered his hands with hers. "Thank you, my dear friend, for the trust you have in me. If I don't do as you ask, it will be only because I consider the risk too great."

Sam's morning passed slowly. She worked at the warehouse with the others, but her mind was on the conversation she'd had with the don. Should she do it? What if something happened to Angelo? The family would never forgive her. A shudder ran through her. *I would never forgive myself.*

Unable to concentrate, she slipped outside and sat down on an old bench in the shade along the side of the building. She had just gotten comfortable when her cell phone jangled softly and she tugged it from her pocket and pressed it to her ear. Before she could say hello, Semion shouted in her ear, "Now it is perfect!"

Sam pressed a hand to her chest. "Are you sure?"

"Yes. We used ten of the new canisters and the results were exactly what I had hoped. The time of unconsciousness has been shortened to the point that, once the subjects were in the interrogation rooms, they were ready to talk."

She exhaled. It sounded like Semion might be right; the product was now perfect. But was she ready to try it out on someone she cared about? Her fingers tightened around the phone. "So they gave you valuable information?"

"They told us everything we wanted to know. In great detail. You are a genius, Sam. Your creation will save many lives. Please don't change a thing, and send us the rest of the order as soon as possible."

After assuring him she would, Sam disconnected the call and sat for several minutes, staring off into the distance. Finally, she nodded. She would do it. When she went back into the warehouse, the others were about to order lunch. Pete slid an arm around her waist. "What would you like to eat, my love?"

She kissed him on the cheek and moved out of his embrace. "Actually, I think I will return to the house. I have some things to discuss with Angelo. If I don't get back here this afternoon, I will see you all at dinner."

Dino's eyes met hers. Sam swallowed, hoping he wouldn't interrogate her, but he didn't speak. She nodded at them all and excused herself.

Back at the don's house, Sam walked on trembling legs to the study. She stopped outside the door and drew in a deep breath before knocking.

Rosalyn opened the door. Sam searched her face, but if the don's wife had any qualms about what was about to happen, she didn't show it. She met Sam's gaze evenly as she stepped out of the way and ushered her in.

Angelo stood as she entered the room. "I knew you would come. Please, sit. First we will eat." He held out a hand toward the leather chair she had sat in that morning and Sam sat down, setting her bag, the canister of serum tucked inside, carefully down on the floor beside the chair.

The three of them made small talk as they enjoyed deli style sandwiches, devilled eggs, and assorted raw vegetables. Roslyn sat beside Angelo, and when the maid had taken their plates, Angelo rested his hand on his wife's arm.

"Rosalyn and I have no secrets," the don told her. "She knows the questions you must ask me, as well as the answers I will provide. No one but the two of us knows the things I am about to tell you, and the information must stay in this room until such time as I decide to share it with Dino. Do you understand?"

"I do."

After they had enjoyed a serving of Crème Brûlée each, the best Sam had ever tasted, the young woman who had handed her the note that morning removed the dishes, curtsied again, and disappeared, closing the door behind her. The don looked at Sam. "Are you ready, my dear? Why don't we get on with it?" He patted Roslyn's hand before standing and moving over to the couch on the far side of the room. He stretched out on it as Samantha took the canister from her purse, shook it, sat next to the don, and hit the spray button twice. The old man immediately closed his eyes and appeared to go into a deep sleep. Samantha turned her head to meet Roslyn's gaze. Regal matriarch of the family that she was, the don's wife displayed no emotion, only folded her hands on top of the desk and, like Sam, settled in to wait.

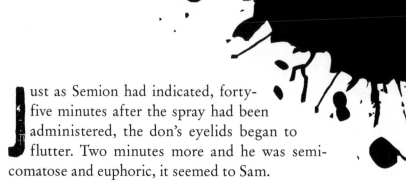

47

J ust as Semion had indicated, forty-
five minutes after the spray had been
administered, the don's eyelids began to
flutter. Two minutes more and he was semi-
comatose and euphoric, it seemed to Sam.

She picked up the sheet of paper he had set on the desk before
moving to the couch then took his hand. "Don Angelo, do you
hear me?"

"I do." The old man spoke with more clarity than she had
expected.

"I am going to ask you a few questions, and it is important that
you answer truthfully. Do you understand?"

"Yes."

"Here is the first question: What is the greatest disappointment
you have suffered since taking over the Carbone empire?"

"I deplore bloodshed, abhor it. My desire was to bring progress
and civility to our activities. The effort by the Cabreras to take over
our businesses was distressing. The fact that Juan Cabrera's sons
were killed was a waste of both brain and brawn." His words were
carefully articulated.

"Very good. Here is the second: you have one great secret that
only you and Rosalyn know. What is it?"

"I fathered a baby girl with another woman during the only
time I was unfaithful to Rosalyn. While none of my children know
about this, I have provided for this baby, who has grown into a fine
businesswoman with great talent. Her name is Amber Johansen."

Sam's head jerked. Amber? Her friend from Atlanta was the don's illegitimate daughter? The paper in her hand shook, but she pushed back her shoulders. One more question. *What more can he have to tell me?*

"Thank you, Don Angelo. And here is the last question: how does this factor into your long term plans for the businesses you control?"

As her mind flashed with images of Amber, Dino, Vonell, and their brothers—siblings, she realized with another jolt—the don stirred slightly. "Some of this has already begun. With the help of Amber, we now control Atlanta. She continues to operate her business independently. Dino and Elliott are already working to assimilate the Cabrera businesses with ours. When that is done, we will look south to Florida. Eventually, Dino has plans to control everything from New Jersey to the Gulf."

Sam's shoulders relaxed. Except for Amber's part in his plans, she knew, or had guessed, most of the rest. As the old man finished, Sam took his hand and said gently, "That's it, Don Angelo. I have no more questions for you. Rest comfortably. I will be with you until you awaken."

The old man seemed to settle into a deeper slumber, but an hour later his eyelids fluttered and opened.

Sam slid an arm behind his shoulders and helped him sit up. Roslyn came over and sank down on the couch beside him. She touched his knee. "How do you feel, Angelo?"

He covered her hand with his. "Fine, fine, never better. That was a great nap. I feel wonderful, like a young man again."

Sam removed some equipment from her bag and checked his blood pressure, blood sugar, and pulse. All of the readings fell squarely in the middle of the normal range. The last of the tension left her as she loosened the Velcro strap from his upper arm. "These results confirm that you are in good health. I recorded your answers on my phone. As soon as you listen to them, I will delete them."

She hit the button and set the phone on the arm of the couch as her voice, and then his, filled the room. The don listened quietly until the end of the recording. When it ended, he nodded at Sam and she erased the entire conversation.

She watched him carefully as she dropped the phone into her bag. Would he regret sharing that information with her? The don smiled and she let out the breath she'd been holding.

"Just as I hoped." He reached for Roslyn's hand and held it tightly. "Your new drug worked perfectly. I have no recollection of our discussion, but what I heard on the tape is exactly right." He held up their clasped hands in a victory salute. "This is great. It expands our thinking. Now we all have work to do."

Rosalyn tugged her hand from his and frowned. "Angelo, you're not getting any younger, you know. Why don't you turn off your mind and leave the business to the kids. You have told me they are ready. Let them go."

He smiled at her warmly and wrapped an arm around her shoulder. "I am not going to stop thinking, my dear, not ever. When I stop thinking, I will be dead. But yes, absolutely yes, it is time for the kids to step up. Let's ask the staff to fix something special for dinner. I think we will have an entertaining discussion." He turned back to Sam and grasped her arm lightly. "Sam, I'm so happy that you will be here for it."

"I will let the staff know." Rosalyn hurried from the room.

Angelo reached for Sam's hand. "This is a great tool. But it also brings with it huge responsibility. We must guard against it falling into the wrong hands. I worry about our shipping practices and how easy it might be to steal shipments. I worry about our opponents getting hold of it. Or anyone who would use it for evil." His face flushed. "Listen to me. I doubt anyone would suggest we run the most legitimate businesses in the land. But I also think we have a conscience. A conscience is important."

Sam squeezed his hand. "I couldn't agree more."

Later that evening, after the staff had poured coffee and served dessert, the don gently clicked his knife against his coffee cup.

When everyone was silent, he cleared his throat. "This family is a great joy to me. Mother and I have been blessed beyond our fondest expectations. For the past few years, I have been preparing for this day. You have all been marvelous students. Dino has proven himself a great leader. Vonell has demonstrated tremendous aptitude for financial matters. Benton, Chandler, and Elliott have also found their places. Everyone is a contributor. You all have made this family greater than it has ever been.

"A few years ago, quite accidentally, we met the newest member of our family. Samantha, as we now know her, has been very helpful. She in turn has brought us Pete, and in just a few short weeks you all act more like brothers and sisters than friends. Nothing could make your mother and me happier.

"Now, another gift has come our way. Samantha's new creation, I am told by Dino and Pete, is enabling our comrades in Europe to put down the greatest challenge our brothers there have faced. Amid reports from the continent, I have spent much time thinking. This new drug offers opportunities that we could never have dreamed of. Its use may well allow us to dramatically expand."

When Dino shifted, as though preparing to speak, his father shot him a stern look. "Dino, please allow me to finish. There will be time for questions. I have dreamed about the ability to take over the West Coast - Albuquerque and Phoenix included. San Diego, Los Angeles, San Francisco, Portland, and Seattle, too. This new drug of Samantha's will make that possible, I believe. We can systematically move into Albuquerque, then Phoenix, and work our way northward from San Diego to Seattle."

Dino's forehead wrinkled. "But ..."

His father looked at him, lightning in his eyes and thunder in his voice. "Dino, you must be still! Please, let me finish." His face softened. "Or must I yet again banish you from the table?"

That comment drew peals of laughter from all family members at the table. Sam grinned. Obviously she and Pete had missed some interesting dinners in this home.

The old man rose to his feet, cup in hand. "Armed with these new drugs Samantha has developed, Dino can visit Albuquerque and talk with our old friend, Miguel Aguano. Miguel is retired now, but still has his pulse on the community. Albuquerque is a bad one, but a big prize. Crime is rampant there. Dino can find out from Miguel who is running the city. Once we know that, we use Samantha's disabling spray on him and his guards to find out all we can about the operation. We use that information to dismantle the machine and step into the vacuum. We then do the same, using Jose Alvarado in Phoenix, and Pedro Garza in San Diego. When finished, we should have everything from here to Seattle in our control."

Angelo set down the coffee cup. "Now all of this will take time, years, even. More time than I have, anyway. Thanks to Samantha, though, it will not require huge resources. If all goes the way I see it, we can take over these cities with virtually no bloodshed. We simply convince the don that it is better to be in our group than outside it and fighting us. If we do this right, we will be the most powerful family in America, if not the world."

When the don paused, Dino could wait no longer. "Father, who will lead all this?"

The don smiled at him from the end of the table, his eyes twinkling. "You will be the leader, Dino. This is the opportunity for which I have been grooming you." He swept an arm around the table. "But there will be plenty of responsibilities to go around. All of you will play key roles. And that includes the two of you," he said, nodding at Sam and Pete. "The eight of you will be all that is needed, I believe."

Sam's throat tightened. She and Pete were to be included in the don's plans? They were part of the future of this family? Pete reached for her fingers under the table and squeezed them.

Angelo rested a hand on his wife's arm. "As I said, all of this will take time. Ten years, if all goes well. And it won't. You must be prepared for unexpected challenges and difficulties, but if you work together, there is nothing you cannot handle."

Dino frowned. "And what about you? What will you do?"

"Your mama and I have led a great life. Now we are tired. Next month we will move from this house to a quiet bungalow on a bayou nearby. There we can rest. I have a great desire to fish. People tell me the fishing is wonderful there, only a fifty-foot walk to the edge of the water and another few out on the dock to a comfortable chair."

Dino shook his head. "But Father, we can't do this without you; you must be involved."

Angelo smiled. "No, my son, you are ready - more than ready. I have watched you for months now and you already bring more to the role than I ever did."

Dino opened his mouth, but closed it when his mother rose gracefully to her feet. "Listen to your papa, please. He has talked about this for months, years even. We were ready to retire long ago but we had to wait until the time was right. Now it is. Do not argue. We have begun to pack and now that you know the plan, that effort will get underway in earnest. As Papa said, we will be near. But we have decided that there will be no advice unless advice is sought out. So think carefully before asking. Your father used to go fishing often. I learned then that the very worst thing I could do was interrupt him with a foolish question. It would be good for you to heed that advice."

Angelo raised his wine glass. "And now, let us drink to celebrate the new generation of the Carbone Family!"

Everyone clinked their glasses together and drank deeply. Angelo sat, his cheeks flushed and his eyes bright. Sam studied him. He was right; it was time for him and Roslyn to rest. They had certainly earned it. She scanned the table, a warmth spreading through her that had nothing to do with the wine she had just consumed.

I believe he is right about this amazing group of people too. If we work together, there is nothing that we cannot do.

48

While Angelo may have envisioned merriment after he and Roslyn had excused themselves for the night, that was not the result. The seven people left behind gazed at the door as if they could somehow mandate the don's reappearance.

Sam studied Dino. How did he feel about his father's big announcement?

Finally, as though he heard her unspoken question, Dino set his fork down on his plate and looked around the table. "What do you make of that? I have never seen Papa like this. So determined and, at the same time, so at ease."

"I think he's serious." Vonell ran a finger around the rim of her wine glass. "I believe he and Mama are retiring—not just to bed, but from business. I think he's made it clear what he expects. And that, Dino, includes you as leader."

"But I am not ready to run it all; there is so much more to learn."

Chandler waved a hand dismissively through the air. "If Papa thinks you are ready, you are ready."

Vonell nodded. "Chandler is right. Papa has worked his entire life to build up this empire. He would never turn it over to you if he didn't believe you were fully equipped to take it over. He would never make such a mistake." She pushed back her chair and stood. "Now I am going to bed. Tomorrow will be an interesting day."

For a few moments after Vonell left the room, no one said anything. Then Sam slid to the edge of her seat. "I have learned that when Vonell speaks, people listen. That suggests to me that what she says is worth listening to. Dino, I think she's right. Angelo has put you in charge. Like it or not, it's up to you now." She turned to Pete. "I think it's time for us to go to bed, too."

Benton, Chandler, and Elliott excused themselves as well. As Sam went out the door, she threw a look back over her shoulder. Dino sat at the dining room table, alone, staring into his snifter of brandy and looking as though he carried the weight of the world on his shoulders.

Vonell was right. Tomorrow would be a very interesting day.

By 6:00 a.m. the next morning, Pete was already seated at the kitchen table with Dino, drinking coffee and eating bacon and eggs. Angelo came in just after six and his son smiled at him.

"Good morning, Papa. I hope you slept well?"

"Like a log, my son. The burden of business off my shoulders, I slept like a log—perhaps the best sleep I have had in six decades."

Dino frowned. "What makes you think I'm ready to take your place?"

"Because I know it in my heart. Know it in my head. When those two places agree, it is so, my son."

Dino blew out a breath. "After you left us last night, I was sure I was not ready. Vonell gave us all a piece of her mind. She said you wouldn't make a mistake, implying you never do."

The older man smiled as he nodded at the servant who brought him his coffee cup. He stirred in two lumps of sugar and set the spoon down on his plate. "And?"

"And then Sam told us much the same thing. But she added that, like it or not, the family business is now mine to run."

"And?"

Pete repressed a smile. Angelo was not going to give his son an inch. The old man might be letting go of the reins, but he would expect a full report regularly on how things were going.

"And so I spent the next two hours thinking. Papa, my vision may be even bigger than yours. But I am not ready to tell you yet. All I can say is that I need a favor."

Angelo met his gaze steadily. "What is it?"

"There are many plans to make. I want all of us involved, and that includes you and Mama, too."

Angelo inclined his head toward Pete. "Does all of us include Sam and Pete?"

"Of course. They are family, aren't they?"

"They are, and you are smart to know it. They make us stronger."

Warmth rushed through Pete's chest. How was it possible that in such a short time he had come to care so much about this family? And how could they make him feel as though he'd been a part of them forever?

Dino wrapped both hands around his coffee mug. "I want all of us to go to Dewey Wills together. We need an uninterrupted weekend of talks. There is much planning to do."

"And when will this happen?"

"This weekend. We'll leave Thursday afternoon and meet Friday, Saturday, and Sunday. We'll come back Monday."

"And when we return, Mama and I will be free to move to our bayou home?"

"Yes, you will be free to move—with the understanding that you will not cut yourself off from us, at least not completely."

"That is fair." Angelo stared wistfully out the window as if seeing that chair at the edge of the dock, waiting for him along with his fishing pole. "I agree. When will you announce this retreat?"

"I will tell the others when I see them this morning. But I hope you will tell Mama."

"I will take care of that. We will be ready to go. Car travel is tiresome for your mother, though, so we will fly up on Friday morning if that is all right."

"Fine. I will let the others know first thing today."

Pete shoved a fork into his scrambled eggs, biting his tongue to keep from commenting on the fact that, in spite of his protests that he wasn't ready, Dino had clearly just taken charge of the family.

The three of them dug into the breakfast set before them. Angelo waved his gluten-free English muffin in Dino's direction. "Eat well now, my son. When you find your wife, she will have you on this garbage." He shuddered. "Fake food! I hate it. This is why I go to Coulis a couple of times a week. Mama has not yet penetrated there."

Dino laughed. "I know Mama watches your diet like a hawk. She—like the rest of us—wants you alive for a long time."

Pete nodded. "And remember, she allows you a cigar and snifter of brandy before bed."

"Only because I put my foot down; I said, enough is enough!"

"Sure, uh-huh, I believe that." Dino's voice had a tinge of tomfoolery about it and Pete chuckled. "You aren't fooling me, Papa, Mama has you wound around her finger. You do exactly as she says."

"When she can see me. Only when she can see me." Angelo smiled and winked at Dino and Pete.

Pete chuckled. As much as he pretended it bothered him, Angelo clearly loved his wife and would do anything she asked of him. Pete understood that. If Sam wanted to take care of him, he'd go along with whatever she wanted him to do, as long as it made her happy. The three men ate the rest of their meal in silence. Angelo had just finished when Benton, Elliott, and Vonell walked in.

"Good morning," said Dino. "I hope none of you have plans for the weekend."

Benton grabbed the carafe from the coffee maker. "Why?"

"Because Papa, Pete, and I were just talking, and I think a family retreat is in order. We'll all go to Dewey Wills from Thursday afternoon until Monday morning, longer if necessary."

Angelo looked around the room. "Where the hell is Chandler?"

"Oh, Papa, you know he has a hard time getting up." Vonell raised a placating hand. "He's trying to do better, honest he is. But progress is slow. Go easy on him."

Angelo shook his head. "I have always insisted on punctuality. But this is Dino's team. If he's gonna let Chandler sleep 'til noon, who am I to argue?" He sank a little lower in his seat. "Still, it drives me crazy. The boy's smart as a whip and can't get out of bed. What a waste."

Pete shoved back his chair. "I'll go knock on his door. I want to make sure Sam is up anyway."

"Did I hear my name?" Sam walked into the kitchen and took a deep breath. "Mmmm, something smells really good."

"Not my breakfast," corrected the don. "Everything else smells great. My food both smells and tastes terrible. I'm gonna take a walk."

Vonell watched him walk out the door, his cane tapping as he proceeded down the walk. "Whoa, he's in mood, isn't he?"

Dino sighed. "You know how hard he has always tried to get Chandler to get out of bed in the morning. It still bugs him that all his efforts failed—probably the only thing he's failed at. And so it irritates him. If you think I'm gonna be easier on Chandler, it's not gonna happen. He needs to grow up, and that starts with getting up with the rest of us in the mornings."

When everyone had finished eating, they carried their dishes to the sink. Anxious to get to the warehouse and start work, Pete led the way across the room. At the door, he stopped and stepped aside to let Chandler enter, rubbing his eyes.

Dino stepped in front of him and gripped both his shoulders. "Chandler, I know you are trying, but you have to do better. I want you up at six like the rest of us. No arguments now. If you think Papa was tough, don't expect me to be easier. Now eat quickly and get ready to go."

Knowing Sam would appreciate another cup of coffee herself, Pete volunteered to stay behind and wait. "We'll be right behind you, don't worry."

He tried to hide his impatience, but couldn't keep from tapping his foot on the floor as he leaned on the wall by the door, waiting for the two of them to join him. It took ten minutes, but finally the three of them headed out the door. The smile Sam flashed him as they made their way to the car made the wait worthwhile. Almost.

●———•

By noon Thursday, Chandler had trained one of the women they'd hired to keep production going in their absence, and Sam had shown another one how to handle the packaging and shipping process. Sam felt confident enough in the abilities of both women to keep the operations going smoothly while they were at Dewey Wills.

The siblings decided to take three Town Cars, in case the don and his wife decided to ride back with them. Sam hadn't been to Dewey Wills since Angelo had sent her and Dino there to hide from the Cabrera family three years ago, and she looked forward to spending some time in the peaceful, secluded place again. When they arrived at the landing, Joe, whom she remembered from the last time waited for them with the airboat.

"Anyone else here, Joe?" asked Dino, who had accompanied Sam and Pete in their vehicle.

"You're the first, but the rest should be along soon."

Sam shook Joe's hand. "Joe, this is my fiancé Pete Parnaska. Pete, this is Joe …" She turned to the man who had worked for the Carbones for years. "I'm sorry, I don't even know your last name."

He glanced at Dino, who nodded, before holding out his hand to Pete. "It's Pahoule, ma'am, pronounced Pahoolie. Kinda like spittin.'"

Sam laughed as the two men shook hands. The other two cars pulled up and everyone boarded the airboat. The area was beautiful in the escaping daylight, and Joe pointed out various species of birds and wildlife, including gators, as they flew along the calm waters. Soon they were at the camp. Joe told them to just head on up. "I'll be bringin' yer stuff."

When they got there, Miranda was waiting on the porch of the first cabin. She greeted Dino warmly before throwing her arms around Sam. "Miss Savannah, so good to see you again."

Sam shot a look over her shoulder at Pete. "It's good to see you too, Miranda. But I go by Sam now."

Miranda stepped back and examined her, still holding both Sam's arms. "Miss Sam. As lovely as ever, I see. And who is this handsome gentleman?" She let go of Sam and turned to Pete. Sam introduced Pete as her fiancé, and Miranda hugged him too, before ushering them all inside.

Joe had dropped their luggage on the porch and disappeared. Soon the chugging of the airboat faded in the distance, and Dino carried the last of the bags inside and closed the door.

Within an hour, they had all unpacked and assembled in the dining room for dinner. "Chicken," Miranda announced, setting the platter of meat in the middle of the table with a flourish.

Dino's eyes twinkled. "Right, Miranda. Better tell the truth; Sam and Pete might not approve."

Sam tilted her head. "Why? What is it?"

Miranda slapped Dino lightly on the arm. "Mr. Dino, you're no fun at all." A mischievous grin on her face, she nodded at the plate. "All right, it's alligator. But it tastes like chicken, I promise."

Everyone, including Pete, raved about the dish. And even knowing what it was, Sam found herself quite enjoying it. "Miranda, I don't think you could make anything that wasn't delicious, but how on earth do you know how to prepare alligator?"

Miranda beamed as she wiped her hands on the front of her apron. "It is from old family recipe," she told Sam. "Lots of peppers, onions, avocado, and … a special sauce."

Pete set down his knife and fork and patted his stomach. "I don't think I want to know what was in the sauce, but that was one of the best meals I have eaten."

Miranda beamed and told him she had more she would warm up for him the next day. After serving chocolate cake with ice cream for dessert, Miranda left them to go and finish cleaning up in the kitchen.

Dino pushed back his chair and stood, waiting until everyone had stopped talking and given him their full attention before he began to speak. "We have lots of work to do in the next three days. Papa and Mama will be here tomorrow, and when they arrive, we will get at it. But I want you to be thinking about something before then. Papa talked to us about controlling the West Coast. After thinking about that, I have a bigger vision. I agree that starting in Albuquerque makes sense, because Miguel Aguano is there and he and Papa have been best friends for years. Phoenix and the West Coast make sense, too. But if we are going to do that, I think we need to take Houston, Dallas-Fort Worth, Austin, and San Antonio, too. There is also Florida. Not right away, but Elliott, don't you think Orlando and Miami are fertile areas? And maybe Tampa Bay and Jacksonville, too?"

"Eventually, yes," said Elliott. "Orlando won't be bad, but Miami will be tough. It's changed a lot. I like Tampa Bay better, and Jacksonville will be great, too."

"Good," said Dino, "so we'll talk about Florida and Texas, too. I'm also thinking about breaking out of the States."

When everyone looked at him as if he was crazy, Dino grinned. "No, no one would be crazy enough to go into Mexico. Even I'm not that nuts. You know that Father and El Chapo hate each other. But Canada is fertile territory. I like Vancouver for a first step."

Sam blinked. Two days ago Dino hadn't been sure he could take over the territory they already had, now he wanted to expand out of the country? Her skin tingled as she watched him. This was the man he'd shown hints of when the two of them were together. Her chest swelled with pride. Dino was transforming into the leader his father believed him to be right in front of their eyes.

49

Friday was gloomy. Low-hanging clouds skudded over the bayou, appearing determined to drop rain before the morning was over. In spite of the low ceiling, Angelo and Rosalyn had arrived by helicopter, looking happy and ready to work. Sam filled a mug with coffee and joined Chandler at the table. Rosalyn stood at the counter with Miranda and she watched them as they laughed and talked.

Chandler whispered to Sam, "Mama and Miranda have been close since birth, it seems. They used to see much more of each other when Miranda was in charge of the kitchen back home. But when the work got a bit too much for her, Mama had her moved here. Miranda has not forgotten the favor."

Promptly at 9:00 a.m., Dino stuck his head into the kitchen and asked everyone to please join him in the dining room. When Sam walked into the other room, she was impressed at how organized it was. A flip chart had been positioned at the back of the room where everyone along both sides of the table could see it, and notepads and pens had been set at every place. As everyone assumed their seats, Dino asked Vonell if she would keep notes.

"I am not looking for an elaborate record, just a general outline. Before we are done, I want it firmly decided what role each of us will play. And Sam and Pete, I'm only gonna say this once: you guys are family. Don't forget it. I want your full participation."

Sam held up her pad and pen, ready to join in fully.

Dino rested a hand on Angelo's shoulder. "Papa, we've added

Houston, Dallas-Fort Worth, and San Antonio, plus Orlando, Tampa Bay, and maybe Miami. Do you have any thoughts on that?"

"Dino, you're the don. I'm hoping only to comment if I think of something important or believe you're going off track. I think the expansion of my list is fine, although Miami is a pit. Too many small-time drug dealers. Be careful; be very careful."

"We know that, Papa, which is why it's a maybe, but we know that there are also good cities in Florida—Orlando and Tampa-St. Pete. If we want those, we have to deal with Miami. No way around it. But I have already told Elliott he will make the call on how and when, since the territory will ultimately be his."

"Good, good." The old man tapped a finger against his chin thoughtfully. "It's good you have it covered; I knew you would."

As the day progressed, Sam marveled at Dino's leadership. The discussions were sometimes heated, but also respectful, and Dino kept everyone on task. More than once her gaze met Angelo's across the table. How did he feel about his son taking over? Even if it had been his idea, it had to be difficult, handing over power like that. Only pride shone in Angelo's eyes and Sam's shoulders relaxed. Angelo had been ready, and, in spite of his initial protests, Dino was clearly ready as well.

They worked through the sandwiches and chips the staff brought them at lunchtime, and kept at it steadily until 5:00 p.m. Finally Dino raised both hands and everyone around the table fell silent. "I think that's enough for today. I'm proud of all of you. We've made some excellent progress. It's time for cocktails, then dinner. We'll start again tomorrow at seven, so you may not want to drink too much tonight. And Chandler, will you need to set a second alarm?"

His eldest brother blushed. "I'll be fine, Dino, really I will. I'd like a chance to prove that to you."

"Okay, but don't let us down."

The weather outside had brightened and Miranda and Joe had set up a bar on the porch of the kitchen cabin. There were several scotch drinkers in the group. Pete and Elliott wanted beer. Sam viewed the selection carefully. "I'll have a brandy old-fashioned sweet on the rocks, please."

"What?" Pete nudged her with his elbow. "I've never known you to order one of those before."

"Neither have I," said Dino.

Sam's cheeks warmed a little at the reminder that the two of them had once been together. She lifted her shoulders. "I only order them when I know the bartender can mix them properly. Joe and I had a long session when I was here before about how to properly mix a brandy old-fashioned. He's a pro. Don't forget, brandy is the drink of choice in Wisconsin. Annually Wisconsin consumes more brandy than any other state, and much of that goes into old-fashioneds. I'm a Wisconsin girl and I love 'em." She flipped her long hair back over one shoulder. "Besides, neither of you knows everything there is to know about me, and don't think you do."

Elliott snorted a laugh. Vonell punched the new don lightly in the arm. "Guess she told you."

Dino laughed too. Sam stole a glance at Pete, but he didn't seem at all fazed by the intimation that Dino had once known her very well. She wrapped an arm around Pete's waist and rested her head on his arm, more content than she had felt in a very long time.

Saturday was another productive day. By lunchtime on Sunday, the plan was coming together. As the family munched on cold ham, rolls, and salads, and drank the best lemonade Sam had ever tasted, Dino reviewed the next steps they all would take.

Pete and Vonell were assigned to train people to handle the New Orleans production and shipping. Dino would seek an appointment with Miguel Aguano for the coming week. Depending upon how Albuquerque went, the next step would be Phoenix. Meanwhile Benton would take over the work Elliott was finishing in Atlanta, allowing Elliott to concentrate on the Texas cities, starting with San Antonio. The state's second largest city was the legitimate starting spot. Once that was taken, Austin, Houston, and Dallas-Fort Worth should be easy.

Sam would return to Montana and continue to take care of

domestic production. Given the planned takeovers, her job would easiest. Still, another production center would be needed and she would have to determine where and when before supervising start-up production. By the time Sam crawled into bed beside Pete—who was already snoring—on Sunday night, her head was spinning. A smile crossed her face, though, as she pulled the soft duvet up to her chin. As much work as there was to do, she loved being part of this amazing group of people. If everyone did their part, it wouldn't be long before they were the most powerful family in the United States. And after that? Only time would tell.

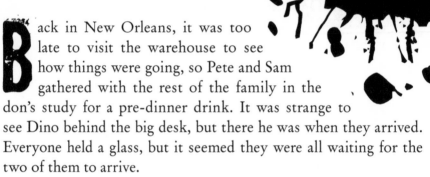

50

Back in New Orleans, it was too late to visit the warehouse to see how things were going, so Pete and Sam gathered with the rest of the family in the don's study for a pre-dinner drink. It was strange to see Dino behind the big desk, but there he was when they arrived. Everyone held a glass, but it seemed they were all waiting for the two of them to arrive.

Dino quickly reviewed what each of them would do the next day. When he'd finished, he held up his glass in the direction of his father, who had been sitting in a leather armchair in the corner, enjoying a cigar and a snifter of brandy. "Papa, you're awfully quiet. What do you think of all this?"

"I think you have a terrific plan. You did great work up at the camp. Mama and I were pleased to see you working so well together. We feel very comfortable leaving everything in your hands. I hope to be at the bayou fishing by the end of the week."

"Don't be in too a big a hurry. Are you absolutely sure you don't want to retain control a while longer?"

"No, my boy, not on your life," said the older man, his eyes twinkling. "I have earned my rest. Besides, the fish are waiting. The only battle I wish to engage in now is with them."

"It's true, Papa, you have earned your rest, and your new battles." Vonell sat down on the arm of his chair and slid her arm around his shoulders. "But we all want you to know that you are welcome here anytime—even if Dino is sitting behind the big desk."

Angelo smiled. "He looks good there, too, doesn't he? He belongs there, he's earned it."

Rosalyn came into the study and held out her hand to her husband. "Yes he has, and we have all earned a good dinner. Let's eat while it is hot." The family followed her into the dining room. Dino pulled out his usual chair along one side of the table, but Rosalyn took his arm. "Dino, your place is at the head of the table now." She led him to his father's former spot. "You sit here."

Sam shot a look at Angelo, but he was grinning as he sat down in Dino's old chair. "Ahh." He shifted around a little on the seat. "Feels pretty comfortable here."

Everyone laughed, and any tension that may have arisen from this tangible transfer of power evaporated into lively conversation and the clinking of dishes.

Sam sat back and watched them all as they ate and talked together. Pete covered her hand with his and smiled at her. Her chest tightened. As much as she loved being here with him, with all of them, it was time for her to return to their place in Montana. It would seem awfully empty and quiet, especially when Pete was in New Orleans, but they all had work to do, and it was time for her to get back to hers.

●——— •

Two days later, Sam boarded the Gulfstream for her trip home. The first stop would be at Albuquerque's Double Eagle airport. Dino, who was on his way to New Mexico, joined her for that leg. The two of them sat in silence for the first few minutes of their journey, until Dino turned abruptly in his seat to face her. "Sam, I'm seriously considering naming Pete my number two. What do you think?"

Sam blinked. "But he's not family. What will the others say?"

Dino shrugged. "You should know, he is Papa's choice, too, and if there is any bad reaction, he will help take care of it. But I don't think there will be. The family has come to not only love Pete, but to appreciate his range of skills and talents. He's got a great head, he's tough—tougher than any of the others—and I sense he's been through the wars and knows how to fight. That's something you can't teach, and having that experience makes him an obvious choice."

"Won't Vonell believe she deserves it?"

"I doubt it. She's a bean counter. She's not a people person. We must have that, too. Besides, Vonell is pretty happy where she is. She has as much to do with running the enterprises as I do."

Sam leaned back in her seat and contemplated the idea. When she'd met Pete, more than a year earlier, she'd had no idea how much the man would change her life. She'd gained so much more than a lover. She'd gotten a true partner in every sense of the word. The fact that the people she loved the most loved him too only confirmed the fact that she was one of the luckiest woman in the world.

She sighed. The only down side to being part of the Carbone Family empire was how much time they would have to spend apart. *Ah well.* A small smile crossed her face as she wrapped her arms around the pillow the attendant had handed her when she walked on board and hugged it to her chest. *When he is able to get away and come home, we'll just have to make the most of every moment.*

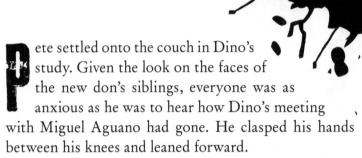

Pete settled onto the couch in Dino's study. Given the look on the faces of the new don's siblings, everyone was as anxious as he was to hear how Dino's meeting with Miguel Aguano had gone. He clasped his hands between his knees and leaned forward.

A huge grin crossed Dino's face as he sat behind the big mahogany desk, his eyes sweeping the room. "The meeting with Miguel was everything I could have hoped for and more. Miguel was delighted with our plan to move west from New Orleans. He immediately pledged his assistance, and then he did something quite unexpected but very pleasing."

He paused, for dramatic effect, no doubt. Vonell was having none of it. She circled her hand in the air impatiently and Dino's grin faded slightly.

Pete repressed a smile. Vonell was the perfect foil for her brother. While he was a visionary and a doer, he needed someone like his sister to keep him in line and on track. They made a great team.

Dino cleared his throat. "Miguel told me that the police in Albuquerque and the sheriff in Bernalillo County were fighting a losing battle with gangs. He said they would be delighted to have us in town. Then he called the two of them and invited them to lunch with us. They came. And they pledged their help to us in any and every way. Can you believe it?"

Pete's eyes widened. Could it really be that easy? Everyone started to speak at once, clearly unable to believe this incredible news. Dino raised a hand and the room fell quiet. "The chief and sheriff urged them to move swiftly.

Vonell frowned. "How swift is swiftly?"

"Immediately," said Dino.

"Hold on." Chandler set his coffee mug on the small table beside his chair. "All of this is happening a bit too fast, don't you think?"

Elliott nodded. "Chandler's right. Expanding our territory too quickly, without the proper planning, could end in disaster."

That's true. Pete didn't add his voice to the chorus of dissension, but when Dino's eyes met his, Pete didn't try to disguise the concern on his face either.

"Pete? What do you think?"

Pete unclasped his hands and straightened up. "I think your brothers have a point, and it can sometimes be a mistake to move forward too quickly. On the other hand, we do have a unique and powerful weapon at our disposal, and if the local authorities in a territory are willing to work with us, we could miss an opportunity if we delay. If you want my vote, I say we move forward into Albuquerque, while the door is open. We see how that goes and then plan our next steps from there."

The tension went out of Dino's shoulders as he flashed a smile at Pete. "I think that is sound advice. We should move quickly but with caution." He scanned the room again. This time no one disagreed. Vonell wasn't quite smiling, but the frown was gone from her face. Dino lifted both hands, palms up. "Here's the deal, the law enforcement guys told me the gangs are currently in disarray, but trying hard to get organized. There has been some progress, but not enough to make any real headway. Meanwhile, the Mexicans think they have a shot at taking over the Querk. The authorities are very afraid of that happening. They think we should move now, before either group gets any stronger. Which made perfect sense to me."

Vonell crossed her legs. "It makes sense to me, too. You and Pete are right, moving forward quickly but cautiously does seem like the best plan."

Dino took a deep breath. "Yes, Pete always has good advice. And he has a good head on his shoulders. Which is why, after a great deal of thought and consultation with Papa, I have decided to make him my consigliore."

Glad Sam had warned him this announcement was in the works, Pete held his breath, waiting for another round of protests, but none were forthcoming. Benton, Elliott, and Chandler nodded, which didn't surprise him. While all three had shown a willingness to follow orders and help out wherever needed, none had displayed any ambition to try and lead the family. His gaze shifted to Vonell, beside him on the couch. Hers was the reaction he was most leery of. Vonell had an incredible mind and admirable work ethic. She could easily have been named Dino's number two as well. Had she hoped to be? Would she resent him for pushing his way into the family and grabbing such a lofty position? He studied her face and found only relief. Pete let out his breath in a rush. *She's okay with Dino's decision.*

As though reading his mind, Vonell smiled at him before looking at Dino. "I think Pete is an excellent choice."

Dino exhaled, as though, like Pete, he'd been holding his breath, waiting for her response. "I'm glad you approve, Vonell."

Pete reached over and touched the back of her hand. "Me too. It means a lot to me." When she inclined her head to both of them, he pulled back his hand and leaned against the back of the couch. Being second in command of a powerful mafia family had never been something he had aspired to. In fact, the idea had never even crossed his mind. But it felt right, and if he had the support of the family, he was happy to take on the challenge. In fact, now that the unlikely scenario had played out, Pete's course was set. He would dedicate his life, even happily lay it on the line, on behalf of this family who had given so much to both him and the woman he loved.

●━━━ ●

Two weeks later, at nine thirty one evening, Sam's phone rang. When she saw it was Pete, she snatched it up and pressed it to her ear. "Hello?"

"It's me, love. How about being at the Kalispell Airport tomorrow morning at seven thirty? I'm flying in to help you. We're going to have a busy couple of days. We have to make one hundred sprayers."

Her heart leapt. *He's coming home.* Even if it was to work, she'd be able to see him, and touch him. It had been far too long. "Of course I'll be there. But I'm not sure I have that many canisters in stock."

"Don't worry, I'm bringing more with me."

"If you're making a surprise trip home, will there be any time for us?"

"Do you think I could keep my hands off you for forty-eight hours?"

"I hope not, but with this new high-level position of yours, I thought maybe you had gotten too good for me."

"Not a chance. Not one damn chance. But now, how about letting me sleep, so I can be at the airport here tomorrow by four. It's gonna be a short night, followed by a busy day." A yawn punctuated his message.

Realizing how tired he was, she ended the call quickly. *I'll see him tomorrow.* With that thought in mind, she headed for bed, hoping the hours between then and now would pass by quickly.

●——— •

The next day, when the Gulfstream landed in Kalispell, Sam was waiting. When Pete came down the stairs, she threw herself into his arms and kissed him, not caring that the crew was standing just behind him. When she let him go, they were all smiling. They helped load the sprayers into her truck and she and Pete jumped into the cab and headed for home.

He reached for her hand and held it tightly. "I'm anxious to get to the lab so we can start putting the sprayers together. If we finish quickly, we can have some alone time before I head back tomorrow night."

Sam squeezed his fingers. "I was thinking the same thing, so you aren't the only one who had a short night. I got up early this morning to get the drug mixed, so all we have to do is load the sprayers. Not that I had a choice. Ben, who's out of hibernation, came along at five, roaring for food. He must know you're on the way."

By seven that evening, the sprayers were loaded and boxed. Sam and Pete had made love once and now were sitting on the porch, waiting for Ben to appear. With the leaves getting ready to pop and the snow steadily melting, they expected the big bear would be around for his daily fix.

He showed up right on schedule and sat with them while consuming his customary two beers and a large plate of food. Then, with the sun sinking, he ambled back down the path and disappeared around the bend.

Pete leaned back in his rocking chair. "You know, Sam, I miss you terribly when I'm away, but I miss Ben, too."

"He seems friendlier when you're here. But he visits me every day now. It's almost like having a bodyguard."

"I hope he is that. I worry about you here alone."

"Pete, I haven't seen anyone since I moved here except you and the carpenters who built the lab. Our place isn't exactly on the beaten path, you know?"

"I know, but I worry."

Sam's chest squeezed. Although she was perfectly capable of taking care of herself, it felt pretty good having someone else worry about her. She stood up and reached for his hand. "I think we should call it an early night, don't you?"

He didn't protest, just followed her up the stairs. They played until after midnight, and slept late the next morning. Just before noon, Sam was awakened by a kiss on her bare shoulder, and opened her eyes to see Pete's cheerful face, something she could get used to doing every morning.

He kissed her again. "We should go. We just have time to grab breakfast if we want to ship those containers on the way to the airport."

A pang of sadness rippled through her at the reminder that he was leaving already, but Sam threw back the covers, dressed quickly, and joined him in the kitchen. Pete had cooked up piles of bacon and buckwheat pancakes with maple syrup. Although the weather was still cool, they carried their plates out to the porch in case Ben decided to join them again. Sure enough, they'd only been out for ten minutes when he came alone and polished off a plate of pancakes and bacon. He licked the last drop of maple syrup off the dish before shuffling off down the path, turning for one last roar, as if to say he would see them later.

Three hours later, Sam kissed Pete at the airport. A lump rose in her throat as she watched the Gulfstream lift off. It was getting harder and harder to say goodbye to that man. Hopefully the rest of the family would soon be able to handle the operations in New Orleans and elsewhere around the country, and Pete could return to her for good.

52

With work at the warehouse in New Orleans proceeding smoothly, Pete turned his attention to Albuquerque. A week after his visit to Sam, he was in New Mexico, training their supporters there to use the sprayers on recalcitrant gang members and anyone else who stood in their way. As soon as he was confident they were all proficient in the use of the weapon, he headed for a dinner at the home of Miguel Aguano. When he arrived at the stereotypical one-story adobe dwelling in the foothills outside the city, the older man was waiting for him.

The two enjoyed a leisurely dinner. Pete held up his hand when Miguel offered him a glass of wine, and the older man nodded, a look of approval on his face. Pete carefully unfolded the plans for the offensive that would begin the next afternoon. His host didn't say much, but he murmured assent whenever Pete described how things would go. When the large clock above the mantel struck ten, Pete wiped his mouth with his cloth napkin and set it down on the table. "I should get going. Tomorrow will be a big day."

Miguel led him down the hallway. At the front door, he paused and turned back to face Pete. "I must say I am impressed at the work you have put into this plan. You seem to have thought of every possible outcome and prepared yourself accordingly." He held out his hand. "I believe you and I will work very well together."

Pete grasped Miguel's hand and shook it firmly. "Me too. In fact, I look forward to a long and mutually beneficial relationship."

"As do I." Miguel let go of him and pulled open the door. "I wish you every success tomorrow."

"Thank you." Pete went out the door and made his way to his rental car, his head spinning. A year ago he would never have imagined himself sitting down to dinner with a mob boss, but he had not only done so this evening, he had enjoyed every minute of it. Meeting Sam had not only enriched his life, it had changed it completely. And he couldn't be happier about that.

Back at his hotel, Pete paced the room. Dino was scheduled to fly out the next morning to join him in Albuquerque, and Pete needed to talk to him before he boarded the family plane. He swiped his hand across his forehead. Dino wouldn't like what he had to say. Was Pete ready to take on the new don? He nodded and stabbed Dino's number into his phone with one finger.

"Pete. What's up?"

Pete swallowed. Dino sounded excited to hear from him. No doubt he was eagerly anticipating being part of the offensive tomorrow night. "Yeah, it's me. I've finished the training. Everyone is ready for tomorrow."

"Excellent. I am too."

"That's why I'm calling, actually." Pete stopped pacing and propped an elbow on the fireplace mantel. "I don't think you should come here after all."

"What?" Dino sounded more surprised than upset, which loosened the knots in Pete's shoulders slightly. "Why not?"

"Because everything is under control here, and it would be better for you to be in New Orleans, where you're safe."

"Pete, I didn't take this job to be safe."

Pete massaged his temples with his free hand. He could hear the frown in Dino's voice. "I know. And there will be lots of times where you will need to face danger, but tomorrow night isn't one of them. As I said, everything is under control. We have the support of the authorities and Miguel, and we have the canisters. There's no need for you to show up and take any unnecessary risks. The family needs you too much."

He bit his lip through the long silence that followed. Finally Dino blew out a breath. "All right, I see your point. I don't like it, but you may be right. I'll sit this one out. But I'll expect a full report the second it's over."

Pete lowered his hand. "Of course. I'll call you first thing." He disconnected the call with slightly trembling fingers.

As it turned out, there wasn't much action to report. Efforts that night concentrated on the four most active and popular gangs in the Querk, and the sprayers quickly rendered the kingpins helpless and talking. As they did, Pete directed efforts, using the new information they had gathered. Whatever resistance that had been expected was surprisingly mild. By midnight, Albuquerque's gang force was controlled by the Carbones and Pete was busy assigning new duties to members of the posse. When he boarded the Gulfstream a week later, things were running smoothly. The newly installed captains were competently discharging their duties, and whatever resistance they encountered was swiftly put down with the sprayers.

Albuquerque was theirs.

●━━ •

Pete returned to New Orleans and enjoyed a sumptuous dinner with the Carbones his first night back. After dessert, Dino stood and lifted his wine glass. "Join me in welcoming back Pete, who has been keeping me updated on events in Albuquerque. He is going to fill the rest of you in now on everything that has been happening." He tilted his glass in Pete's direction and his siblings followed suit. When he sat, Pete rose to his feet.

"I'm happy to report that we have taken over Albuquerque with no casualties. The operation went even more smoothly than we hoped. Miguel is delighted and the police and sheriff's forces are totally supportive of what we've done. Although the area is big, we believe we have managed to neutralize every gang in the city, and everyone is in the fold."

Every member of the family present applauded as Pete sat down.

I only wish Angelo, Rosalyn, and Sam were here to share the moment with us. He pushed back a wave of sadness and managed a smile when Dino told the group, "I talked to Papa today to report on Pete's efforts in New Mexico. He listened well for about a minute, said he had hoped for that result, then moved right on to tell me about the fish he had been catching."

Vonell laughed. "I guess he wasn't kidding when he said he was looking forward to his retirement."

Dino shook his head. "He wasn't. Mama is delighted because he has smoked only one cigar since the move, and his alcohol use is down, too. She has high hopes his doctors will be very pleased by those changes."

Elliott wiped his fingers on his napkin. "Sounds like his retirement is off to a great start. No doubt he will outlive us all now."

Dino grinned. "Well, if we're not going to live long, let's live well. I suggest we retire to my study for a drink."

The rest of the family followed him down the hallway. Dino poured each of them a glass of cognac before assuming his seat behind the desk. Chandler raised his glass. "To Pete and his work in New Mexico. Well done."

"Here, here." Benton clinked his glass to his brother's.

Dino raised his glass too and took a sip before setting it down. "The iron is very hot, which means the time to strike is now. We have already established that we will move cautiously, but also quickly on to new territory, so we should fix our sights on Phoenix soon, don't you think, Pete?"

"I do." Pete set his own glass down on the coffee table in front of him. "Give me another month in Albuquerque and we should be ready for Phoenix. I think you should make your exploratory visit this coming week."

"I will call Javier Ramirez first thing in the morning," agreed Dino. "Hopefully he will be willing to see me in the next few days. If things go right with him, we could go after Phoenix and Arizona by the first of April." He grinned. "Or maybe the second. No sense tempting fate by moving ahead on April Fool's Day."

Pete laughed along with the rest, but his mind had moved into full gear. All joking aside, they would have their work cut out for them heading into Phoenix and Arizona. And they would be fools themselves if they took their next moves lightly.

53

Deep into preparing a report for the chief on a break and enter he had investigated the night before, Al jumped when his phone rang. He grabbed it and scanned the screen. Tad Munson. His heart-rate jumped. He hadn't heard from anyone in Montana for weeks. He pressed the phone to his ear and leaned back in his chair, crossing one foot over the other on his desk. "Tad, talk to me. What have you got?"

"Hey Al. I actually might have something big this time. I'm pretty sure I know where the old lady is holed up."

Al dropped both feet to the floor with a thud. "Seriously?"

"Yep. We've been keeping a close eye on her, trying to follow her without her noticing. She's led us all over the countryside, but we were finally able to stick with her long enough to follow her to what we believe is her current home."

Al's heart thudded so loudly he could barely hear the state trooper on the other end of the line. "Where is it?"

"About seven miles from Highway 35, dropped into a hollow in the Bitterroots. Nothing but a rutted path leading to it. Good place to hide, actually, which is why she's been able to stay off the radar so long. When you turn off 35, blacktop runs for about two miles then turns north and the muddy path winds back into the mountains from there for about five miles. Near as I can tell, there's only one cabin on the road. How she found the site, I'll never know."

Al drove shaking fingers through his hair. "Who do you buy property like that from in Montana?"

"I'm guessing the state, but as far as I know, the state hasn't sold any land for a long time—years, maybe."

"Maybe that's how long she's been holding on to the property, waiting for the right time to use it. Can you check and see how she might have gotten her hands on it?"

"Absolutely. I'll head over to Helena tomorrow and look at the records. I could do it electronically, but I don't want to raise any alarms just yet."

"Good idea. Let me know what you find out."

Al sat at his desk toying with his pencil and planning out his next steps. *One, talk to the chief and appeal for a trip to Montana. Two, get Charlie to start working on Sheriff Dwight Hooper to also approve the trip. Three, wait to hear again from Tad and see what he finds out before getting too far ahead of myself.*

He sat there twirling the pencil and gazing out the window, barely registering the early buds on the trees or the tulips springing out of the ground in the municipal garden across the street. As he sat there, the options rolled through his head like a whirlwind and his good sense collided repeatedly with his impetuousness.

His good sense told him that the best solution was to wait and hear from Tad. If Genevieve Wangen had owned the property for a long time, she might be hesitant to simply abandon it. *Yes, that's best. But ...* He slammed an open palm down on the desk, snapping the pencil in two. *Damn, it's been too long ... too damn long since we had that woman in our hands.* Al had felt like an idiot ever since the woman had escaped his clutches the first time. *I want her back and now.*

Over and over, those thoughts rolled through his head. Finally, frustrated by his lack of clarity, he rose and walked out the door and down the hall to the chief's office. Brent Whigg was working amid a swarm of papers on his desk. When Al knocked, he looked up, smiled, and waved his chief detective in.

"Chief, I need the benefit of your thinking, if you have a minute."

"Darn right, I do. These time-slips are driving me crazy. Any excuse to take a break from them would be great. What's up?"

"I just talked to Tad Munson out in Montana and he told me they think they know where Genevieve is holed up."

"Really?" The chief set down the calculator he'd been holding and leaned back in his seat.

Al sat down on the hard plastic chair across from him. "As you know, Tad and his colleague, Willie Midthun, have been keeping tabs on the old lady. According to them, she makes a couple of runs a week up one side of Flathead Lake and down the other. They were finally able to tail her long enough to see her turn off onto a road they think leads to her cabin. It's up a dirt path about five miles off the blacktop and well hidden against a mountain. Tad said if he hadn't see her turn up it, he could have missed it. Do you think the time is right to take her down?"

Whigg scratched his head. He studied Al for a couple of minutes—which felt like an hour to Al—before he said, "We want to take her down as quick as we can. But we have to make sure she's there. How about you have those guys let you know the next time they actually witness her going right to the cabin? If it's later in the day, we can get you out there by jet in time to take her at first light, assuming you have things organized out there."

Al drummed his fingers on the chief's desk. "So when they call and tell me to come, I'll make sure they can meet me at the site with the manpower and the equipment to get the job done. And done right, this time."

"Sounds like a plan. Set it up with Tad, and make sure you bring Charlie and Dwight up to speed too. You and Charlie will need to be ready to go at a moment's notice."

"Got it." Al stood up so quickly he had to grab the chair to keep it from clattering onto the floor.

The chief snickered. "Keep me informed of what is going on."

"I will." Al offered him a quick salute and headed back to his office, practically at a run. After nearly dropping his phone when he picked it up, Al forced himself to sit a moment and take several deep breaths before calling Charlie.

His friend answered on the second ring. "Berzinski."

"Charlie, it's me. I know I've said this a few times before, but this time I'm 99 percent sure. We've got her."

He must have been on speaker, because the sharp sound of Charlie clapping his meaty hands together came over the line and Al moved the phone slightly away from his ear. "Yes! Let's go get 'er, Al. Just tell me when we're leaving and I'll be there."

Al grinned. That's what he loved about his friend. All impetuousness, with none of that pesky common sense to hold him back. "We can't go just yet Charlie, but hopefully soon. Tad and Willie think they've tagged the spot where she lives. They're going to let us know next time she arrives home late in the day and the chief says we can fly out and take her down first thing in the morning. So be ready for my call, okay?"

"You betcha. I'm heading home now to pack a bag then I'll be sitting on my phone, waiting to hear from you. I'll talk to Dwight, but I'm sure he'll agree to let me go. We're gonna get 'er this time, Al. I can feel it."

Charlie's confidence was contagious and a smile broke across Al's face. "I think you might be right, Charlie. This time I think we just might get her."

54

"The problem with you, Dino ..." Vonell jabbed her fork in the air, punctuating her words, "... is that you need a wife."

Pete choked back a laugh. The rest of the family did not do their brother the courtesy of holding back their amusement. Chandler wiped his mouth with a napkin and, still chuckling, pointed at his brother. "I agree. If you had a woman to give your attention to, maybe you wouldn't give the rest of us such a hard time."

Dino shot him a dark look. "I do not give you a hard time, no more than Papa did, anyway. I'm just trying to encourage you to be the best person you can be."

"Well thank you very much, but I'd actually be a much better person if you let me get a little more sleep."

Pete pressed his lips together to keep from laughing at that too. He was still a little too new to the family, and not quite cemented enough in his position as consigliore, to mock any of them at this point. Besides, Chandler probably had a point. He did get up earlier these days, but still dragged himself around all morning and never really woke up fully until sometime in the afternoon. It was unlikely he'd ever become the morning person Dino wanted him to be.

Dino rolled his eyes and turned back to his sister. "As for a wife, I love my fun, you know that. I have generally shied away from serious relationships. And my Number 2 took the only woman I ever loved. How's that for a clear act of piracy? So I frequent the ladies of the night here and elsewhere. It's safer—no promises, no debts."

"But Dino, you have great responsibilities now," insisted Vonell. "And one of those responsibilities is providing a continuation of our bloodline, is it not?"

He studied her for a moment before nodding. "I will give it some thought, I promise. I trust you will be satisfied with that?"

Vonell lifted her slender shoulders. "It is your satisfaction I am worried about, not mine."

Dino offered her a grim smile. "Good, then allow me to proceed in my own time and in my own way." Rosa came into the room to start clearing dishes, and he pushed back his chair and stood. "Pete, will you join me in my study for a few minutes?"

"Of course." Pete rose and touched Rosa lightly on the elbow. "Thank you for dinner, Rosa. It was delicious, as always."

She blushed and flashed him a smile as she picked up his plate and slid it onto the pile. "You're welcome, Mister Pete."

Pete followed Dino to his study and settled onto the leather armchair in front of the massive desk.

"Brandy?" Dino held up the bottle.

"Sure."

Dino poured them both a glass, handed one to Pete, then took his place behind the desk. He ran a finger around the rim of the glass, appearing deep in thought. Pete waited through the silence. Finally Dino picked up the glass and held it in his direction. "I wanted to fill you in on my meeting with Javiar Ramirez in Scottsdale."

Pete doubted that was the real reason for this tête-à-tête, but he'd play along. "Good. I've been wondering how it went."

"It went very well. He took me to his father, Mateo, and the three of us spoke about our families uniting under the Carbone umbrella. It took some negotiating, but Javiar has agreed to head up our operations in Arizona, and both he and his father seem quite content to join forces with us."

"Excellent."

Dino rubbed circles in the condensation on his glass. Pete waited patiently until he finally looked up. "What did you think of Vonell's suggestion?"

"That you get a wife? I completely concur. Being with a woman who works alongside you, someone you can share all your deepest thoughts and desires with, not to mention your bed, is one of the greatest joys in life. I highly recommend it." He lifted his own glass in response before taking a sip.

Dino set down his glass and leaned back in his chair, pressing his fingers together in front of his chest. "You might be right. I guess I haven't thought seriously about it since Sam …" He shot a look at Pete. "Since my last serious relationship didn't work out. It's been easier to just keep things light and fun, you know?"

Pete pursed his lips. "I do know. I thought the same way for a long time. Then I met the right woman and I realized the difference between just having fun and being in a committed relationship with the person you're meant to be with is night and day. Believe me, I'd never go back to living that way again." He leaned forward. "Have you met any women in your travels that you could see yourself settling down with?"

Dino face lit up. "Actually, I have. After Sam introduced me to Amber Johansen, I started going to her place whenever I was in the area. There are some amazing women there, but the last few times I've gone I've always asked for Daphne. I've been drawn to her since the first time I met her. She's beautiful, with long dark hair and dark eyes, but she also treats her customers with style and sophistication. Since the first time we were together, I've been impressed, not just with her skills in bed, but with her intelligence and her sense of humor."

Pete lifted both hands in the air. "She sounds perfect."

Dino settled back in his seat, nodding thoughtfully. "She is."

"So what are you going to do about it?"

"I believe I'll take a trip to Atlanta. Care to join me?"

"I certainly would." Pete picked up his glass and took another sip. Of course he'd like to join Dino on his quest for a wife. He wouldn't miss it for the world.

●━━ •

Pete and Dino flew to Atlanta the next day. As always, Amber welcomed them both graciously and led them to her office. Since he was merely there for support, Pete sat on the couch off to one side of the room where he could keep a close eye on Dino who sat directly across from Amber's desk. The don, one knee bouncing as though he could barely contain his excitement, got right to the point. "Amber, my sister recently reminded me that my new responsibilities extend outside the boardroom to the bedroom. She and my brothers told me that it is high time that I find myself a wife. I have been too busy to worry about that up to this point, but I guess I do need to do something about it. The most ideal woman I have met recently is Daphne, who works for you. If I were to court her, what might you say?"

A smile broke across Amber's face. "Of all the women who work for me, Daphne is the one I believe would make the best wife. She is very … how shall I put it … domestic, I guess is the word. She loves to work in the kitchen and often helps staff here on her free time. I know she worries about her future, too. She has talked to me about wanting a family and speculating that this is a poor business in which to meet a husband." Amber tapped a manicured finger against her bottom lip. "Yes, she's probably ideal. However, she is also my most requested employee and her loss would impact me greatly."

"I thought that might be the case." Dino's knee stopped shaking as he clasped both hands on the desk. Pete repressed a grin. Asking about a woman might make him nervous, but now that they were talking his language—dollars and cents—Dino was all business.

"In addition, you're a good customer. So this would be doubly bad for me." Amber laughed, but her smile didn't reach her eyes. Pete was pretty sure she was mentally totaling up the cost of Daphne and Dino both being out of commission.

Dino shook his head. "Well, I'm not going to buy a wife, but if I were to talk to her about coming to New Orleans with me and she agreed, then you and I would have to talk business. I don't plan to steal her away without fair compensation."

Amber rose and held out her hand. "Fair enough. I don't own my girls. Talk to Daphne and see what she says and you and I can discuss terms after that."

"Sounds good." Dino shook her hand and headed for the door.

Pete jumped to his feet and left the room after him. Things were about to get interesting.

—•——•

Pete, Dino, and Daphne had lunch together in a small café down the street from Amber's place. Pete had offered to eat at another restaurant, or at least another table, but Dino insisted he join them. As soon as Dino introduced them, Pete could see why his friend had been drawn to her. She was beautiful, nearly six feet tall with long dark hair and eyes, but it was more than that. Her smile was warm, and she answered all his questions with intelligence and a keen wit.

The three of them made small talk over sandwiches and salads, until Dino nudged his plate aside and reached for Daphne's hand. "Daphne, from the first time I met you, I felt you were a very special woman. I think of you often when we are not together, and I take every excuse to come to Atlanta to see you again."

Her porcelain cheeks tinged pink as she squeezed his hand. "And nothing makes me happier than to see you on my schedule and know that we will soon be together again."

Pete studied a painting on the wall closest to them, trying to appear as though he wasn't listening, although he was analyzing every word. After all, Dino's future wife would have a big impact on his life and their business; he had a right to know what she was like, and to judge for himself whether her feelings were sincere or if she was simply looking for a way out of her lifestyle and into a big fancy house.

Dino rubbed circles on the back of her hand with his thumb. "The thing is, I'm no longer just content to see you every few weeks, when I happen to be in town. I'd be honored if you would consider moving to New Orleans to be closer to me so we can see where this is headed. I will provide you with a home and introduce you to society, and you can decide if that is the kind of life you are interested in living."

"I suppose, Dino, that this is the point at which I should demure, pretending that I am less than interested," she said, smiling. "But that isn't what I want to do, so I won't. What I will do is tell you that I have feelings for you too. Much as we're cautioned in this business not to become attached to our clients, in your case, even though we have not had nearly as many opportunities to spend time together as I would have liked, I have. I don't really care what kind of life I am living, as long as I am with you. So yes, I am ready to move to New Orleans with you, today, if you want."

Dino's shoulders relaxed, as though he'd been afraid she would refuse.

Little chance of that. Dino was strong, handsome, rich, and the head of one of the most powerful families in the country. What woman would say no to all of that? Fortunately for Daphne, he was also a great guy with a good heart, and he'd make an excellent husband. *And I don't hate the fact that he'll be off the market now, and even less of a threat to me where Sam is concerned.* Pete frowned. He had no right to think like that; he trusted Sam implicitly.

Dino pulled Daphne's hand to his mouth and kissed the back of it. "Wonderful. You've made me very happy. Let's go back to the house so you can pack."

Her dark eyes shone. "I'm so excited! Should I start packing right away, or did you want to celebrate first in my bedroom?"

Dino glanced at Pete before smiling at Daphne. "I certainly do want to celebrate, but let's leave that for now. You gather your things while I meet with Amber. I'll come for you when I'm finished."

He and Pete walked Daphne to the door of her room. Pete stood back at a respectful distance as Dino kissed her tenderly and whispered something in her ear that sent a flush of color across her cheeks.

When Daphne had gone into her room and closed the door behind her, Dino and Pete started down the hallway towards Amber's chambers. Dino cleared his throat. "So what do you think?"

"Of Daphne or your, umm, unconventional methods for finding a wife?"

Dino shot him a look. "We both know my opportunities to meet women are extremely limited. And Vonell is right, it would be good for me to have a wife and a few children. They will keep me grounded and, if my instincts about Daphne are correct, she will be a tremendous help and support to me, as Mama has always been for Papa."

Pete elbowed him in the side. "I agree, and I'm just giving you a hard time about your methods. To be completely honest, Sam found me under similar circumstances."

It was Dino's turn to flush. "Me too. So maybe it's not as unconventional a way as we thought."

"Maybe not. As for Daphne, obviously I haven't known her long, but from what I've seen so far, and given Amber's endorsement and the chemistry I sense between the two of you, I think she may very well end up being just what you need. And want."

They reached the sitting area outside Amber's private quarters and Dino stopped and faced Pete. "So do I."

Pete clapped him on the shoulder. "Then let's work this out with Amber, shall we?"

Dino nodded and strode to the desk where Amber's personal assistant sat working on a laptop. She looked up as he approached, and flashed him a beautiful smile. "Hello, Mr. Carbone. Amber thought you might like to meet with her, so she canceled her afternoon appointments. You can go right on in." She held out a hand in the direction of Amber's suite.

"Thank you." Dino inclined his head before crossing the area to knock. Pete was prepared to wait outside the room, but Dino gestured for him to come along.

By 3:00 p.m., he and Amber had come to an agreement that was good for each of them. Dino agreed to provide Amber with a stipend that would cover the revenue Daphne could be expected to achieve over the next year, along with some other special provisions, including funds to be used by Amber to recruit someone to replace Daphne.

Pete led the two of them to the Town Car and held the door open for them both. When Daphne slid onto the back seat, her face was wreathed in smiles. By the time Pete climbed behind the wheel, she had slid over to rest her head on Dino's shoulder.

"Amber was a wonderful employer. I love her. But I didn't like the work as much as I liked the money it brought me. I am a rich woman, Dino. But earning money with my body was a job that gave me little comfort. I kept thinking about my parents, my God. Religion is very important to me, and it was hard to excuse what I was doing. I sometimes felt that even those to whom I confessed my sins had more interest in my body than my redemption. This new life makes me very happy. I shall go to confession next time with joy in my heart."

Pete watched in the rearview mirror as Dino smiled at her and held her hand. "Good, I am pleased you are happy. I am very happy. And I expect my family will be happy as well."

Sam will be too. Pete returned his gaze to the road and gripped the steering wheel with both hands. Although his fiancée had been the one to end the relationship with Dino, and as far as Pete knew she'd never had second thoughts about that, he knew she still cared for Dino a great deal. Seeing him with a good woman who made him happy would set her mind at ease. And it would free her and Pete up completely to move ahead with their life together, which, as far as Pete was concerned, made him the happiest one of them all.

As Pete knew they would, Dino's siblings welcomed Daphne into the family warmly. Vonell did fire a lot of questions at her, but Daphne handled them easily and comfortably, ending with, "Dino's visits were far too infrequent for me. I was surprised to see him this morning and bowled over when he asked me to return here with him. What a wonderful surprise it was for me. And meeting all of you is a pleasure. I look forward to getting to know each of you better."

Vonell leaned back in her chair and lifted her wine glass to her lips. Pete watched her carefully. *Good. She's accepted her.* Of course Dino's sister would be protective of him, and of the family, but Daphne appeared to have passed this most critical of tests.

By the time the group adjourned to Dino's study, Daphne was visiting with the others as if she had been among them for months.

As they enjoyed cognac or wine, Pete told them how pleased he was with Mateo and Javier's acquiescence to the Phoenix takeover.

"We think we can launch in a month, at the beginning of April. It won't go as quickly as Albuquerque, but we should have a pretty good foothold in about two months, if things go according to plan." He frowned. "Maybe I should talk to Sam about delaying our wedding."

Vonell shook her head. "No, don't do that. If things are so hectic here that we can't take a weekend off for a wedding, and you can't take a week or two off to celebrate, we're in bad shape. I'm pretty damn sure we aren't that desperate, are we?" She looked at Dino, her eyebrows raised.

He set down his drink with a decisive thud. "No, we definitely aren't. And we should never be so busy we can't celebrate important things, like a wedding. There will be no delay, Pete, understood?"

"Yes, boss." Pete responded quietly. "But …"

Dino threw up his hand. "No buts. And speaking of Sam, don't you think a week in Montana would do you and her some good? Things are running smoothly here, and it would be beneficial to get a report on how the domestic side of the business is coming along."

Pete grinned. "Well, if you need an update, I'm pretty sure I could clear my schedule for a few days. If it would help you out."

Everyone laughed, and Dino clapped him on the shoulder. "Always there for me. I can't tell you how much I appreciate it."

"It's my pleasure."

"I'm sure it will be." Dino, a glint in his eye, squeezed Pete's shoulder and let him go. Reaching for Daphne's hand, he drew her to his side. "Sam is an adopted sister to this family and Pete's fiancée. She used to live in New Orleans, but her house is sitting empty now."

"Oh, I know who Sam is." Daphne's voice was hushed, almost reverent. "She's been a legend around Amber's since she took care of the Cabrera brothers for us."

"Oh that's right, of course you've heard of her." Dino pressed Daphne's hands between both of his. "I think it would be best if you lived in her old house for a while. As tempted as I am to keep you here with me, I want to do this right, court you properly."

"Hear, hear." Vonell lifted her glass of wine in their direction.

"Sounds like my sister approves." Dino smiled at Daphne. "What do you think?"

Her cheeks were pink again, but she nodded. "That sounds perfect to me."

"Good." Dino kissed her on the cheek. "Then it's settled. You'll move into Sam's old place, and Pete will head back to Montana for a week or so."

"That works for me." Pete rubbed his hands together. "Ben's back now, and I'd love to see him, too."

Still holding Dino's hand, Daphne turned to him. "Who is Ben?"

"He's a big grizzly that lives on our property."

Her eyes widened. "Really? That sounds frightening."

"Actually, it's not at all. He's a good friend of ours. We had seen him from time to time, but never up close. Then one day he showed up at our door with a sore eye, as though he thought we could help. So we did. Using a book of ancient native cures, I created a compress that made the eye better. After that he started coming around pretty regularly. We found out he liked beer, and that sealed the deal. Now he shows up often for a meal, after which we enjoy a couple of beers together. I really like it because when I'm gone he's both company and protection for Sam."

Daphne, her eyes still wide, looked from him to Dino and back again, as if she wasn't sure if Pete was serious. Dino laughed. "He's not kidding; he and Sam really have a bear for a friend."

Daphne lifted her shoulders. "If you say so. Your life sounds very interesting, Pete. I'll look forward to meeting Sam ... and Ben, too."

"We all want to meet Ben," interjected Vonell.

"You will," said Pete. "In fact, I'm pretty proud to tell you that both Dino and Ben have agreed to be my best men."

Dino slapped him on the back. "Of course we have; neither of us would miss the big event for all the money—or beer—in the world."

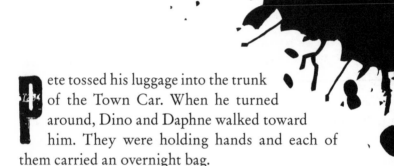

55

Pete tossed his luggage into the trunk of the Town Car. When he turned around, Dino and Daphne walked toward him. They were holding hands and each of them carried an overnight bag.

They stopped in front of him and Dino set his bag into the trunk. "Daphne and I thought we might come with you for a day or two. She'd like to meet Sam, so maybe the four of us could have dinner together tonight?"

Pete nodded and reached for Daphne's bag. "That would be great. If we fly into Kalispell, the Golden Lion has fabulous food. You and Daphne might want to stay over there, too. The innkeeper has some great rooms."

"Good idea," agreed Dino. "I'll call from the plane and make the reservations."

Pete slammed the trunk closed and climbed into the front seat beside the driver while Dino and Daphne slid into the back. Both the drive to the airport and the flight went smoothly, and before Pete knew it, he was bounding down the stairs and into Sam's waiting arms. Pressing his lips to hers, he kissed her until the sound of Dino clearing his throat discreetly behind him dragged Pete back to the present.

Reluctantly, he stepped back and held out his arm. "Sam, I'd like you to meet Daphne." He'd already filled her in on Dino's latest news, so Sam didn't look surprised to see the beautiful woman standing on the tarmac beside Dino, only pleased.

She held out her hand. "I'm so happy to meet you, Daphne."

Daphne took it and shook it. "And I'm happy to meet you. I've heard so much about you from Amber and Pete and Dino and the family. I hope you don't mind that we tagged along on this trip, but I just couldn't wait to meet the woman behind all the accolades and stories."

Sam let go of her and slipped her hand through Daphne's arm. "I don't mind a bit; I'm thrilled that you're here." She turned and guided the young woman toward the Sentinel. Looking back over her shoulder, she said in a mock whisper, "And speaking of stories, do I have some great ones about Dino to tell you."

She turned around and the two women headed off, heads together. Dino shot a helpless look at Pete. "Maybe this wasn't the best idea."

Pete grinned. "Don't worry, Sam will be kind. I'm sure the two of them will be best friends before dinner is over." He and Dino followed the women to the Sentinel and the four of them headed for The Golden Lion. Pete drove with one hand and held Sam's in his other. "Dino and Daphne are staying over at Molly's."

Sam straightened up. "We should stay over too. That way we could have breakfast with them tomorrow and show them around a little before we take them back to the airport."

He grinned at her enthusiasm. "I don't really care where we sleep darlin', as long as there's a bed there and you and I are in it together."

Dino cleared his throat again. "You know this isn't a limo, right? We can hear everything you're saying."

Pete laughed and turned into the parking lot of The Golden Lion. "Here we are."

The four of them enjoyed a fantastic prime rib dinner. Daphne and Sam talked non-stop and, as Pete had predicted, appeared to have formed a fast friendship before dessert had even been served. Following dinner, all four spent some time in the casino. Pete won several thousand dollars playing blackjack before they retired to the bar to have a nightcap. Sam offered the two men a few drops of a special concoction of hers that she promised would increase stamina. Both men held out their glasses, accepting without hesitation.

Finally Pete decided he couldn't wait any longer. Taking Sam's hand, he bid Dino and Daphne a good night and led her to their room. Sam took over when they got there, undressing Pete, massaging him, bathing with him, then drying him off before taking him to bed and making love to him until the sun threatened to invade their privacy.

After an hour and a half of sleep, Pete was up and wide awake. "It's amazing how good I feel. I'm not even tired."

"It's that elixir I offered you and Dino in the bar, remember?"

"I do remember. I didn't know it would make me feel this good, though. Gee, Sam, we could make a legitimate killing with that stuff. Maybe we should go straight and expand our fortune."

"You forget, I have a past." She frowned. "Besides, we have plenty of money, and more seems to be rolling in all the time. So let's just have breakfast with our guests, show them the area, drop them off at the airport, and get back home to our bed."

"An offer I can't refuse." He took her by the arm and guided her to the washroom and into the shower, following her into the large space fed by a myriad of water jets.

Dino and Daphne beat them to the dining room. By the time Sam and Pete arrived, they were sipping coffee at a table by the window.

"Sorry, we couldn't wait for you." Dino gestured to the scene outside the glass. "This Montana air agrees with me. We slept like the logs you cut out here."

"Slept?" Daphne winked at Sam. "Just when did we sleep?" She flashed both Sam and Pete a smile. "Dino was apparently determined to try every position in the Kama Sutra. I feel as though I've been through two or three spin cycles. Now I'm hungry as a bear." She clapped a hand over her mouth. "Oops, didn't mean to disparage your friend."

"You didn't." Sam was laughing as she and Pete took their seats. "Sounds like we were on the same train. Pete didn't want to sleep, either. It was that elixir I asked the men if they wanted me to add to their drinks last night."

"Which worked like magic." Pete motioned for the server to

bring more coffee. "I'm fresh as can be and I shouldn't be. It's been too long since I've seen Sam, and I barely let her sleep a wink."

Daphne shot a look at Dino. "I'm definitely going to need more of it, whatever it is."

He chuckled. "Yes, you are."

"Here." Sam unzipped her bag and pulled out a small bottle. "Take this for now. I have more at home and can make a fresh batch whenever we need it."

Daphne took it from her and stuck it in the side pocket of her bag.

Dino touched Sam's arm. "What the hell is in that stuff, Sam? It's worth a mint."

"That's what I said." Pete lifted his hands, palms up. "We need to make it and get it out there. It'll sell like hotcakes."

After a breakfast of sausages and eggs, Sam and Pete delivered their guests to the airport via the scenic route, and watched the Gulfstream depart for New Orleans. When it had disappeared from sight, they walked back to the Sentinel and took a leisurely drive down the west side of Flathead Lake and up the east before arriving back to the cabin. Ben was waiting for them on the porch.

"Look at that," said Sam. "I'll bet he spent the night."

"Hi, big fella!" Pete stopped the vehicle and jumped out. The bear raced across the yard, wrestled Pete to the ground, and slobbered his face with licks.

The two, man and bear, spent the afternoon together. They swam in the lake, sat on the porch "talking," and enjoyed their beers together. Sam joined them as the sun began to drift down to the lake.

"You know, Ben, we have to figure out how to get a flower pinned to you. You're gonna be in the wedding, you know?" Pete examined Ben's coat. "Maybe we can tie it on him somewhere." He shifted in his rocking chair to face Sam. "Speaking of weddings, we need to set a date. And where are we going to get married? We don't want anyone to find you, now do we?"

Sam stopped rocking. "If you really want Ben to be involved, it has to be here."

Pete pursed his lips. "That's not a bad idea. It's private, and no one will see what is going on. We just have to figure out how to get our guests here without attracting a lot of attention."

"We won't have a lot of guests, will we? Only the Carbones and Molly and Amber. What about your family, will they come?"

"I'll invite them and see what they say. I suppose the jets will create a little stir in Kalispell, but if they land on Friday and leave on Sunday it should be okay."

Sam bit her lip. "I hope so. I know we want the people we care about the most to be there for our big day, but we're definitely taking a risk."

Pete reached for her hand. "It's a risk I'm willing to take to make you my wife in front of our closest family and friends. And if anything does happen, we'll do what we have always done: we'll face it together."

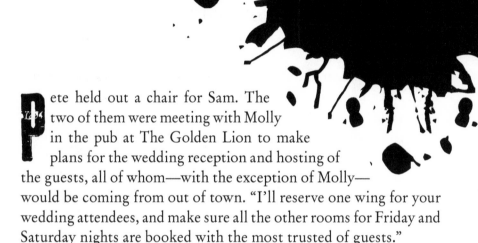

Pete held out a chair for Sam. The two of them were meeting with Molly in the pub at The Golden Lion to make plans for the wedding reception and hosting of the guests, all of whom—with the exception of Molly— would be coming from out of town. "I'll reserve one wing for your wedding attendees, and make sure all the other rooms for Friday and Saturday nights are booked with the most trusted of guests."

Sam sighed. "I hate to ask you to go to that much trouble, but you're right, we'll have to be very careful."

Molly patted her hand. "It's no trouble at all. Where will you hold the ceremony?"

"At the cabin." Sam scanned the catering menu Molly had given her. "Because we want Ben to be there."

"After all, he's one of my two best men." Pete leaned close to Sam, his shoulder pressed to hers, to read the menu.

"I think three hot hors d'oeuvres, plus meat and cheese, shrimp, and veggies should be enough." Sam pointed to the menu as she talked. "Yes, that should be good for food. Of course, we're going to need a full bar. Does all of that work for you?"

"Of course. We can use the same two staffers to tend the hors d'oeuvres table and the bar, if that's okay. It's better to keep the staff small and trusted, right?"

"Absolutely. I have one other question for you Molly." Sam set the menu down on the table. "Will you be my co-maid of honor?"

Molly leap to her feet and hugged her. "I'd be honored, very honored."

"Great. You will be attending me with Amber Johansen, a friend from Atlanta, and Vonell Carbone from New Orleans. Pete's thinking about a third, in addition to the bear and Dino Carbone."

Molly clapped her hands together. "Sounds wonderful. Now come with me and we can speak with Chef Grabau. Victor has been anxious to meet you and already has a few ideas for the evening dinner."

Two hours later, the plans all made, Pete slid an arm around Sam's waist and guided her to the door. "I think that was a productive day, don't you?"

His breath was warm against her cheek and Sam nodded, suddenly anxious to be home and have him to herself.

When they got to the cabin, they spent the afternoon relaxing, then decided to go to the lake for a swim. Ben joined them and they played until it was nearly dusk. The only annoyance was a light plane that twice passed overhead.

Sam ignored it, but Pete stood up in the waist-deep water and stared into the sky. "What do you suppose they're doing?"

Sam stood too, and rested her head against his arm, cool from the water. "It happens sometimes. I think it's the currents off the mountains. They create problems for small planes. They have to go around several times to get into position to land. It's no problem. Honest."

He smiled at her, but it didn't quite reach his eyes. She hadn't convinced him the presence of the plane didn't pose any threat to them. Not surprising. She pressed the side of her hand to her forehead to block the light of the setting sun and watched until the plane was a small dot in the distance.

After all, she was far from convinced herself.

●━━━ •

Al, Charlie, Tad, and Willie spent most of their weekend together on the phone. They too were planning.

"So Tad, you're certain there is only one way to enter and exit the property, right?" Al had asked the question before—more than once—but this time he was taking no chances.

"That's right. When we flew over the place on Saturday, we made sure of that. With the exception of the dirt path that enters the yard around the cabin, the place is very secluded, surrounded by mountains and trees and well hidden."

"And there were no boats on the lake?"

"None. The lake's only about twenty or thirty acres in size, not really big enough for boats. And no, before you ask again, there are no other cabins in the area."

Al didn't appreciate the hint of amusement in Willie's voice, but he let it slide. "So you don't anticipate any complications?"

"I don't think so, although we did see something interesting."

Al straightened up in his seat. Would they have to reevaluate their plans? "What? Anything that could be a problem?"

"I don't think so. When we flew over, there were two people swimming in the lake—the woman and a guy. The strange thing was that there was a grizzly in the lake with them. Looked like the people were playing with it."

Al frowned. Playing with a grizzly? That didn't seem like a good idea. "Really? Sounds odd. Better to plan for that, though, than dismiss it and have it foul us up. Is there a vet out there you trust?"

"Yes," Willie spoke up. "Rita Miller. She's practiced in the area for years. I'd trust her with my life."

"Good, can you get a gun and some darts from her that will immobilize a bear? We need something to make sure it's down and out." Al's stomach grumbled and he motioned for Charlie to push the box of doughnuts close enough for him to reach. When Charlie complied, Al stared at the box in disbelief. Only two doughnuts remained of what had been a baker's dozen.

"I'll talk to her tomorrow," Willie confirmed.

"Anything else you can think of?" Tad sounded eager, as if he couldn't wait to move on this.

Neither can I. Al cleared his throat. "According to the photos you sent, the plane that flew into Kalispell on Friday evening was carrying two men, a woman, and a crew of three—two pilots and an attendant. I recognized one of the guys, Dino Carbone. He might be the new don of the Carbone family."

Al glanced down at the photos he had spread across his desk.

"The tall, dark-haired guy, I'm pretty sure, is Pete Pernaska," Tad offered. "He arrived here several years ago and worked in the timber industry. I think he currently works for the Golden Lion, although we haven't seen much of him for a while."

Al studied one of the photos. "Any idea who the woman is?"

"None." Willie and Tad spoke at the same time.

"I've sent the photo to Detective Aaron Wingate in New Orleans. I haven't heard back from him yet, but I'll let you know if he is able to shed any insight on the photos." Al brushed powdered sugar from his doughnut off the desk and onto the floor. Charlie reached into the box and took the last doughnut.

"Charlie, for goodness sake, that's number eleven for you. How the hell can you eat so much and still be in shape?"

"Just good genes, Al—spelled g-e-n-e-s."

Al shook his head. "Anyway, I'm hoping Aaron will have something for me today. Tad, did you say you saw our suspect and this man you think is Pete Pernaska go into the Golden Lion on Saturday?"

"I did. They picked up Dino Carbone and the woman in the photo and delivered them to the airport." The enthusiasm was waning in Tad's voice.

Time to end the call before I lose them completely by going over old ground again and again. "All right gentlemen. Thanks so much. Let me know if you learn anything more, and I will do the same. Now all we have to do is wait for the right opportunity to move in. And this time we can't make any mistakes."

57

Al pushed his plate away and patted his stomach with both hands. "JoAnne, my love, that was delicious, as always."

"Glad you enjoyed it." She reached for his plate and carried both their dishes to the sink. "What do you want to do to—"

Al's cell phone buzzed and he tugged it out of his shirt pocket and scanned the screen. A New Orleans exchange. His heart rate picked up. Had to be Aaron Wingate. "Sorry, hon. I need to get this."

She waved a hand, dismissing his apology, before turning on the tap to run water in the sink. Al pressed the phone to his ear. "Al Rouse."

"Al, Aaron Wingate. Sorry to call you so late."

"No problem. Have you got something for me?"

"Ah believe ah do. I've been making nice with your friend Dino Carbone here. As you may know, he's been named the new don. His consigliore is a guy outside of the family, name of Pete Pernaska."

"I'd heard rumors about all that." Al wrapped the fingers of his free hand around his glass of water. "Glad to have it confirmed."

"There's more. I overheard Dino talking on his phone the other day, making plans with his number two. Seems Pete Pernaska and your girl Genevieve—although Dino referred to her as Sam—are going to be tyin' the knot a week from Saturday."

Al straightened up so abruptly he almost spilled the glass of water. He grabbed it before it could go flying, but water splashed across the table. "They're getting married? Where?"

"From what I could tell, it's going to be at Genevieve's place in Montana. You know where that is?"

"I do, actually." Al reached for a napkin from the holder in the center of the table and dabbed at the puddle of water. "I have a couple of deputies down there keeping an eye on her for us. We've just been waiting for the right moment to go in and grab her."

"Well, seems like a wedding might be a nice time to drop by, wish them well, then haul both of them off to jail. Whaddya think?"

Charlie's gonna love that idea. Al couldn't wait to give his friend the news. "I think you might be right, Aaron." Al let go of the napkin as JoAnne came over with the dishcloth and finished cleaning up the spill. He winked at her as a grin spread across his face. "You definitely might be right."

58

Sam was beside herself. There was so much to do before the wedding, which was just a week away. She felt good about the plans she and Pete had made and the work Pete had done, but now they needed to be executed and Pete was occupied with activities in Arizona.

This was an important weekend and Pete was nowhere near Montana. He had encountered an emergency in the efforts to take over Mesa in Arizona and was there working with Javier. She had just filled fifty sprayers and shipped them the day before. Now she had the cabin to clean, the three bars to set up—two in the yard and one down by the lake—and she had just gotten the forecast for the coming week, which wasn't promising.

Please, Lord, I know I'm the worst of sinners, but I'd like the weekend to be nice. Friday, too, if you have an extra measure of consideration for me.

When she finished the prayer, she got to work. By four thirty, when Ben ambled into the yard, she didn't feel she had accomplished nearly enough. Wherever she gazed, things were in place but also in need of finishing touches.

As she sat on the porch sipping a vodka and tonic and watching Ben with his beers, she was amazed to find she felt at ease. She glanced at her watch and set down her drink. She was supposed to be where she could receive a phone call from Pete in twenty-five minutes. Sam grabbed her keys and headed for the Jeep.

Pete's call came right at seven thirty, and she didn't like what he had to tell her.

"Sam, I really need you in Phoenix on Monday. I know how bad the timing is, but we're planning to bring in some guys I want you to interview. You know better than anyone how to take advantage of your truth serum. These guys are from Mesa and may be the key to taking over all of the gangs in the valley."

Sam pressed two fingers to her temple. There was so much to do ... She sighed. "It really is a bad time, but I know how much you want to get this Arizona plan wrapped up. If I can help, I'll be there, but I do have a condition."

"What is it?"

"Could you ask Dino to send Miranda Rodriguez and Joe Pahoule back with me to help with the cleaning and then the serving and bartending at the wedding? That would really help me out."

"Consider it done. I'll send the plane for you at 6:00 p.m. tomorrow."

"I'll be there."

Sam arrived at the Kalispell Airport at five thirty the next evening. The Gulfstream was already waiting for her. The flight was smooth, and a car waited for her when they landed. The driver whisked her to the Hilton Hotel and one of Pete's bodyguards escorted her to a suite.

A couple of hours later, noises in the hallway preceded the arrival of Pete, several members of his team, and four obviously reluctant "guests," all wearing hoods. Sam had no idea how Pete had managed to smuggle the men past the hotel staff and guests, but she knew better than anyone how resourceful he could be. When the hooded arrivals were guided into a bedroom of the suite, Pete told her they were leaders of the four most vicious gangs in the Mesa area. "We need to know everything they are involved in, where the attack points are, who they are affiliated with, and what the keys to their success are."

"Is that all?"

Pete ignored the sarcasm. "How do you want them?"

"In private rooms with one of your associates present."

The first subject was a swarthy man of Spanish descent. As soon as the hood was removed he spat at her, the blob falling short of her feet, and swore in his native language. Thankfully he'd been tied to his chair in such a fashion that only his mouth and head could move.

Sam opened her bag and extracted a needle and a bottle. After she plunged the needle into the bottle's rubber stopper and filled the cartridge, she turned to the man, moved closer, and plunged the needle into his arm.

Soon he was telling her all he knew about the gang he led, where it was headquartered, who its top members were, and what strategies were in place.

Systematically she moved her way through the four men, using her drugs to make certain that she obtained from them any information that would make it easier for Pete to acquire their territories.

She finished just after 2:00 a.m. A little after five the next afternoon, she had gotten a few hours of sleep and she and Pete were aboard the Gulfstream bound for New Orleans. Two hours later, they were enjoying a drink with Dino.

"Did you get what you wanted?" Dino swirled the ice around in his glass.

"Even more than I had hoped," Pete told him. "Sam got them to tell her every move they plan to use against us—both offensive and defensive. We have strategies in place to stop them all. By next Tuesday we should know if they worked. And if they did, the Phoenix valley will be ours."

Dino raised his glass. "To Sam, then. The Carbone Family will soon be the most powerful in the country, and we owe it all to you. With this new serum, nothing can stop us now."

Nothing except the wrong people finding me and bringing me in. The image of Al Rouse flashed through Sam's mind, but she pushed it away. No one knew where she lived, and no one was going to find out. She and Pete were less than a week away from starting their new life together, and nothing was going to stop them either.

59

Al went to work Monday with the theme of "take 'er down, take 'er down" running through his head. No matter how he tried to rid Genevieve from his mind, it just didn't happen. The paperwork on his desk was simply a blur, and if there were moonshiners supplying whiskey to La Crosse County, well, that was just too bad. Al had other things to tend to—and they were nowhere near La Crosse.

When he got to the office, he headed straight to the chief to tell him about Aaron's call. "You're not excited are you, Al?" The chief smiled widely, and a wink accompanied his question. "Not that I blame you; this is a big chance to get 'er. Imagine you'n Charlie will be heading west, right?"

"Absolutely, Chief. This time I think she's penned herself in. I'd like to get out there as soon as possible to make sure plans are in place with Tad, Willie, and their crew. You okay with that?"

"Of course, you gotta go. Make sure it's the way you want it, Al. Make sure you're runnin' the operation, okay? This is your bust and lord knows you've waited long enough for it. Need any help from me with the sheriff out there?"

"I'm not sure. I believe Tad has kept him informed, but after I round up Charlie and get him in here, we'll call out there to get more information. Once that's done, I think we can book."

"This is it, Al. This is our chance to get 'er back. You're the best there is. You gotta take the lead."

"I'm sure gonna try. This woman has taken up far too much

of my time and effort the last few years. Nothing would make me happier than to bring her down once and for all." He pushed to his feet. "Better get a call in to Charlie. Talk to you later."

Just as Al got back to his desk, his phone rang. *Aaron.* Al stabbed the button and pressed the phone to his ear. "Rouse."

Aaron skipped the small talk. "As we suspected, the wedding will be held this Saturday at Genevieve's place in Montana. We were able to hack into the airport computers and download the flight plans and it looks as if all of the Carbone planes will be used to take guests to the place on Friday morning."

Al smacked a palm down on his desk. "Excellent. Good work."

"Thanks. I assume you and Charlie will be joining us as uninvited guests to the shindig?"

"Are you kidding? I hear it's going to be the social event of the year—we wouldn't miss it. I'm just about to call Charlie to get him over here so we can talk to the guys in Montana and set it all up. That will be some shivaree."

"What the hell's a shiv-a-ree?"

"We have lots of 'em around here." Al smiled, thinking of some of the good shivarees he'd been to through the years. "It's a big blast following a wedding, often with fireworks, gunshots, tons of excitements. Only this one will be serious, the fireworks will be lethal, and so will the gunshots."

"Jeesus, sounds pretty horrible. Guess I'd better pack my Glock."

"God yes, come armed," urged Al. "Bring a rifle, too. The more firepower the better. Charlie and I will be flying out tonight or tomorrow."

"That early, huh? Not sure I can pull that off, Al."

"Probably better if we don't all get there at the same time anyway. Folks might start talking. That wouldn't be good."

"Guess not, but when the plan is set, please circle back, okay?"

"Will do. Thanks."

The conversation over, Al dialed Charlie and got his answering machine. He called his cell and got him on the second ring.

"Where are you?"

"Chasin' cattle rustlers. Goddammit, Al, you know how tough that is?"

"No, but the thought of you on horseback is a mental picture I'm hoping I can erase." Al twirled a pencil between his fingers at record pace.

"Now don't you be laughin'. I'm out here between Barre Mills and Middle Ridge. It's colder'n a witch's tit, 'n the wind is blowin' like a banshee."

"Well, why don't you get your butt back here and we can talk about a trip to warmer places?"

"Really? Yer kiddin' right?"

"Nope."

"I'm heading back to the ranch now. Can't tell you how glad I'll be to get out of this saddle."

"I'm sure the horse will be equally glad to get you off its back. How soon can you be here?"

"I'll try for an hour."

"Great. See you then." Al disconnected the call and stared at the phone for a minute, trying to get his heart to stop skipping around in his chest. Could they actually be getting close?

As anxious as he was to jump on a plane, he had to calm down and plan everything out in meticulous detail. No way on earth he wanted to let that old lady slip through his fingers again.

60

With everyone anxious to get going, Al and Charlie had huddled around the phone in Al's office, hammering out every detail of the plan with Tad and Willie until they were confident they had covered every possible contingency. When they'd finished, Al had called Aaron to fill him in, then made arrangements with the chief to be gone for a few days. At 6:00 a.m. the next morning, he and Charlie were on their way. The plane landed in Missoula just before 1:00 p.m. Mountain Time. Two men stood at the foot of the ramp as the Wisconsin officers entered the terminal.

"Al?" The taller man smiled as he asked the question, and when Al nodded, his hand came out instantly. "I'm Tad, and this is Willie. Good to put a face to the voice."

"Yes it is. And this is Charlie." Al slapped his friend on the back. The introductions made, the four made their way to luggage pickup to retrieve Al and Charlie's belongings. Charlie then went to the Delta office to sign for and get the firearms and ammunition.

A half hour later, they were on the road in Tad's squad—a new Crown Vic that purred like a kitten. When Charlie commented on the engine quietness, Tad looked back at him and grinned. "Want me to wind 'er up? She's like a wildcat when I let 'er go."

As they entered a straight stretch of freeway, Tad pushed on the accelerator, knocking Al and Charlie back in their seats. "Damn!" yelled Charlie, peering over the seat, "130 and she's not even laborin.'"

Tad throttled back and turned around, his wide grin in place.

"Once in a while ya gotta blow the carbon out. Seemed like a good idea to do it today."

Al couldn't focus on the vehicle. He tapped the back of the seat. "What have you heard, anything?"

"Yessir, Detective Rouse." Willie shifted in the passenger seat to face them. "We've heard some things. Carbone plane landed in Kalispell Sunday evenin', picked up Pernaska, and dropped off two people who went with Samantha, er, Genevieve. We think they're at the cabin helpin' her get ready for the weekend."

"Great." Al leaned forward to catch everything that was being said.

Charlie gazed out the window at the scenery. "So much different from Wisconsin. We got bluffs, ya know, but these are real mountains. Whadda ya call 'em—Bitterroots?"

"These are just the foothills. We'll show you some real mountains later, Charlie, not too far from here."

"Yeah, we're about two hours from the office," said Tad. "So we got some time to get acquainted."

After they'd been on the road for about an hour and a quarter, they passed through Bear Dance. Flathead Lake spread out to their left, but Willie pointed out a rural road that led off toward the mountains. "That's the road." Tad slowed the car so they could see. "The blacktop goes about four miles into the mountains before it makes a sharp turn to the north. There's a dirt road—path might be a better word—that creates a fork. The woman and Pernaska live up that path. All told, it's about seven miles up there, and the last four miles are a bitch."

Tad nodded. "I've surveyed the place from the air. The road Willie talks about is the only way for vehicles to get in—not even a timber road in the area. There is a ridge road on the top of the mountain above the house. We drove it the other day in a SWAT vehicle and it's just as bad as the road Willie was on. It's overgrown with brush, but we can get in there with the SWAT truck. I think the captain wants to put a few guys up there, just to stop anyone heading for the hills. We didn't walk down at all, but there is rumored to be a big cave about halfway down the mountain."

A few minutes later, Tad piloted the squad into the parking lot of what appeared to be a new building, set back about a half block from the highway. "Here we are," he said, "Kalispell District Headquarters for the Montana Highway Patrol. C'mon in and meet the crew."

Willie held open the door, and when Al and Charlie walked in, they found a group of people waiting for them, half of them dressed in the drab olive uniforms of the state and the other half in dark blue.

"Al Rouse, Charlie Berzinski, meet district patrol captain Joel Gilson, and this is Kalispell County Sheriff Sweeny Murphy. The rest of these folks you will meet shortly."

And so they did as Captain Gilson moved the group to a large conference room at the rear of the building. The blackout shades were pulled, a projector was suspended from the ceiling, and a generous luncheon was laid out on the table at the rear of the room.

"Heard Charlie likes to eat." Gilson was a big man himself, well over six feet tall and about 280. Murphy was even bigger—about two inches taller and twenty pounds heavier than Gilson.

"You grow 'em big out here." Al shook his head as he scanned the room. Most of the men in the room could easily be members of the University of Montana Grizzlies football team.

"Great segue." Murphy nodded at a tall, muscular woman dressed in blue. She reached underneath her chair and grabbed a couple of gray and burgundy hoodies, tossing one to Al and one to Charlie.

"Thought you better be in uniform for this trip," said Murphy, his eyes twinkling. "No sense having you marked as tourists your first day here."

For the next two hours the Montanans briefed their visitors on the area, the terrain, and what they knew of the event. Then Al and Charlie took over and gave everyone the story of the La Crosse murders, the arrest, confession, and escape of Genevieve Wangen, and what they had done to track her to Montana. As they did, they were generous in their praise for the roles Tad and Willie had played.

When the clock pushed past six, Gilson said, "I suspect that's enough for today. Tomorrow will be busy, too. Tad's going to take you two boys up for an airplane ride in the morning, and in the afternoon, Willie will show you the road in. Thursday we'll all be back together for a final briefing, we'll get some rest Friday, and half of us—the half that will be located above the place—will deploy that night. The rest of us will deploy after all the guests leave the Lion on Saturday morning and arrive at the cabin. Questions?"

Al raised his hand. "Captain, we haven't made any reservations for lodging yet, any suggestions?"

Gilson and Sweeny smiled and the patrolman said, "You're coming with us." Gilson told Al he'd be at his house and Charlie would be at Murphy's. Al wasn't sure about the split lodging, but in light of their hosts' hospitality, he just nodded.

Tad clapped a hand on his shoulder. "Your buddies Rusty and Aaron will fly in tomorrow, and we're hosting them, too."

So the gang will all be here. Al shoved both hands into the pocket of the hoodie to keep them from trembling. This was getting real, and there was no way he was going to let his emotions cause him to make any mistakes. Not this time.

61

The next morning, with Tad in the co-pilot's seat and Al and Charlie in the back, the State of Montana twin Beechcraft took off from Kalispell Airport at 10:00 a.m. Al clutched the armrests, trying to contain his excitement. The pilot made several circles over Flathead Lake as he gained altitude, then turned eastward over the Bitterroots.

Al stared at the ground; even though they were more than a mile high he had a good view of the trees and hills spread before them. Tad gestured to the window on the left side of the plane. "The cabin will be out that way," he yelled over the roar of the engine.

Not thirty seconds later, Al spotted a small opening in the trees, fronted by a tiny lake. And there it was—the cabin. He watched, swiveling his head as the plane sped across the lake and made a wide, circling turn before heading back across the area.

"Look," he cried, pointing downward to where three people seemed to be doing something in the opening. Two women and a man were in the yard. One of the women, hands on her hips, had tilted her head and was staring up at them. *Is that her?* If he'd had a parachute, Al would have been tempted to jump out and land right in her front yard and arrest her on the spot. Which likely would not have gone well.

"Sure hope she's not onto us." Al fidgeted in his seat as the opening slipped from his view.

Charlie gazed out the window. "Looks like the three of 'em are puttin' picnic tables in place. Don't look interested to me."

"Good." Al slumped back in his seat. "Could we take it down a little lower and fly by the ridge so I can try and spot the road you're talking about?"

"No problem," said the pilot, who until now had been silent. The circle widened as the plane began to lose altitude. The pilot steered the plane back across the ridge and Al could see a brief break in the foliage. "Looks pretty rough."

Tad glanced down too. "It is, trust me Al. It's rugged as hell." He tapped the pilot's arm. "Could you make a swing over the lake and up the road that leads to the cabin?"

"You got it." The pilot hunched over the controls and the small plane made a tight turn out across Flathead Lake, eventually leveling off at two thousand feet. "We've got a thirty-knot headwind; I think we can get inside two miles before turning. Doubt anyone in the clearing will hear us."

He expertly flew up the road that led into the hills from Highway 35. When the blacktop turned north, he followed the dirt path, eventually breaking off the route, climbing again, and bringing them in for a smooth landing in Kalispell.

"Thanks, Mack," said Tad, after the four of them had disembarked.

"No problem, happy to have had you aboard. If you need another look, just give a shout."

"Will do." Tad turned to Al and Charlie. "How about lunch?"

"Now yer talking." Charlie rubbed his stomach fondly.

"I'll take you to the Golden Lion. Be good for the two of ya to get a good luck at the place where a lot of the wedding guests will likely be staying. We can't dawdle, though. Gotta go pick up the boys from Atlanta and New Orleans. Need to be in Missoula by four thirty."

"No problem." Al fell into step beside him as they headed for the squad car. "I'm perfectly happy to keep things moving. I'm done sitting around waiting for something to happen with this case."

●──·

They walked into the Golden Lion just before noon. It was like stepping into an old movie set in the Old West. The lobby featured a large round wagon wheel suspended from the ceiling. The myriad of lanterns that hung down from it flickered realistically as they lit the area. The check-in desk featured crossed rifles on its face. The furniture had been carved out of heavy wooden logs. Off to one side, the saloon featured swinging doors, and sawdust covered the floor. They walked past the casino entrance. Al glanced in and caught a glimpse of the life-sized figures of a man with a star on his breast and a woman in a short dress and fishnet hose. The three of them passed through an authentic-looking chuck wagon, minus the wheels, as they entered the restaurant. All in all, the décor set the stage for what promised to be a fun time, right down to the wallpaper over the elevators covered with suspenders.

Charlie hooked his thumbs through the loops on the belt and announced in an exaggerated Texas drawl, "Ah like this place, y'all. Looks lak it was made for me."

Al nudged him in the ribs. "Maybe you'll find your cattle rustlers here."

"Could be, Al, could be."

"Where you cowboys from?" asked the pleasant-faced woman behind the desk.

"Points east, young lady." Al spoke up quickly, not wanting to give away the fact that they were from Wisconsin, in case there were listening ears around.

The woman led them to a table in the corner where they slid into a booth featuring barrel-backed seating.

Charlie tugged a menu from the holder in the center of the table. "You got any hot vittles in this place, little lady?" he asked the six-gun-bearing waitress.

"You bet your tush, cowboy. I'll give y'all a minute to study the menu." With a wink in Charlie's direction, she turned, skirts swirling, and strode toward the kitchen.

Twenty minutes later, they had ordered and been served well-smoked barbecue ribs, corn on the cob, corn bread, and sarsaparilla, which Charlie remarked tasted an awful lot like root beer.

Tad swallowed a bite of his steak and nodded toward the back of the restaurant. "There's a large banquet room behind that wall with its own entrance. We're guessing that's where the wedding dinner will be held."

Al made a mental note of the layout as Charlie plowed through four plates of food.

Tad contemplated him, his brow furrowed. "Didn't the sheriff feed you breakfast?"

"Hell, yes, but I got a big appetite."

"Mister, when you tie on the feedbag, you do it good, don't you?" The waitress, carrying two plates for another table, stopped beside them and stared at Charlie with wide eyes.

Charlie stopped eating long enough to offer her a salute with a hand that still clutched a bread knife. "When the food's this good, ma'am, then yes, I surely do."

She smiled. "I'll pass that along to the cook."

"Please do."

"Time to go." Tad pulled a wallet from his pocket and headed for the cashier. Al jumped up and stopped him with a hand on his shoulder. "Let me get it. No one in Montana should have to pay for Charlie's appetite."

Tad didn't argue. Al paid the bill, his fingers tingling. Time to go pick up the rest of the team and get this show on the road. The more time they had to prepare for the takedown of their slippery quarry, the better the chances they would do successfully. And that everyone would be alive when all of this was over.

62

Saturday dawned as forecast, dark and dreary. Rain seemed imminent as thirty law officers gathered in the Kalispell District Highway Patrol conference room. Along with Al, Charlie, Rusty, and Aaron, half a dozen FBI officers from the Northwest had joined the group. The federal agents were led by Lance Pearson. Everyone wore body armor, which made them look even more like a professional football team.

A woman, Ramona Olstad, led the crew that would make the frontal assault from the road into the cabin. Tall, dark-haired, and beautiful, she was all business. A petite blonde, Joey Mulholland, stood at her side. Although little, the woman had, according to Tad, proven herself tougher than most of the men in the room. Both were ranking officers with the State Patrol.

Dan Matejka, a tall, broad-shouldered man, fully outfitted in camo body armor, was in charge of the force that would protect the mountain area behind the cabin. Matejka's wife, Natalie, was in charge of communications for both groups from her spot in the SWAT vehicle that would head up the cottage path and block it to traffic. The Matejkas were members of the volunteer force that supported Montana officers. Captain Gilson would lead the entire operation.

A continental breakfast had been laid out in the conference room, but few people were taking advantage of the spread. The excitement was palpable as the captain shouldered his way to the front of the room and called for silence.

"As you know," he began, "we decided yesterday that deploying a group last night was unnecessary. The ridge top road is so hidden and dense that making our way up there this morning will give us plenty of time. The group under Lieutentant Matejka will depart shortly. They will start down the mountain on my call, spreading out to guard that potential exit point. We want your group, Dan, to move down only as far as the cave we've talked about, ensuring no one can enter or leave that area. We will give you plenty of time to make the trek. Although we think the brush and trees will shield any noise you make, please be as quiet as you can.

"Ramona, your group will travel to the main site with me and will begin to advance on the cabin after we are certain wedding activities are underway. Detective Al Rouse will accompany you. Mulholland, you'll take Deputy Charlie Berzinski with you. Detectives Rusty Cunningham from Atlanta and Aaron Wingate from New Orleans will stay with me.

"Mulholland, as you are aware, we believe our suspect has befriended a grizzly bear. If you spot the animal, you have permission to use your tranquilizer gun to put the bear down for the count. Charlie, you have a similar weapon also loaded with a dart. It's important that we neutralize the bear as soon as the raid starts."

Charlie nodded and patted the weapon in the holster strapped to his belt.

"Any questions?" Gilson gazed around the room. "Good. Now all of you get something to eat. We have no idea how long this exercise will take and we want everyone to have a full stomach when they head out. Matejka, your group will leave in twenty minutes, so get at it."

It was a businesslike group of regular law enforcement and volunteers that quietly went about breakfast. The volunteers had impressed Al and Charlie as being well-trained, confident, and very serious.

"They undergo the same training as our regular force," Gilson had told them. "Any one of them could be on the force."

Watching them confirmed that, and any pangs of worry that had troubled Al quickly dissipated as the group working with Dan Matejka finished breakfast, double-checked their packs, and prepared to deploy. Seven of them, plus Matejka, occupied one of the two SWAT vehicles.

After the first team departed, they sent radio updates every five minutes or so. They turned off Highway 35 about forty minutes later and made their way onto the fire road used to get to the ridge. As they ascended the rugged trail, things went slowly but smoothly and by nine fifteen they were in place on the ridge top.

About twenty minutes later, Matejka radioed to say that his group had found an ATV hidden in the brush and covered by a camo tarp. The leader reported the vehicle had been disabled and would not be useable.

At 11:00 a.m., just after Matejka had radioed to say all was quiet except for several million aggressive mosquitoes, the call came in from Tad that a caravan of limos—seven of them—had just left Kalispell and were headed south on Highway 35.

Tad clapped a hand on Al's shoulder. "Willie is hidden out along the cabin road to make sure Genevieve doesn't post any guards along the way into her place."

An hour and thirty minutes later, Willie called to say all the limos had passed his hiding place and proceeded up the road to the cabin. From his vantage point, he could see that no security had been deployed, although he suspected the clearing itself would be well guarded.

"Okay, time to go," said Olstad, her voice ringing with authority. "No laggards now. Snap smartly, we have work to do."

Part of the assault party clambered aboard the second SWAT truck and the rest into an open two-ton truck with huge tires. No one talked as the caravan roared south on Highway 35. They had been on the road for less than thirty minutes when Matejka radioed to say that his group was in place on the ridge and would stand ready to proceed down the mountain to the cave area on Gilson's order.

With the clock approaching 2:00 p.m., two fortified vehicles turned onto the blacktop side road and continued toward the mountains, gaining altitude as they went. When they reached the dirt path, the drivers shifted into a lower gear and proceeded slowly toward the cabin. Twenty minutes later they found Willie Midthun waiting for them.

The trucks stopped, the troops stepped from the vehicles, and Al joined the group as Willie conferred with Gilson and Olstad. They decided to leave their vehicles there and proceed on foot. They would start up the path in single file, led by Midthun with Gilson, Olstad, and Pearson. Al would follow, with Charlie coming after him. "The rest of you fall in behind Charlie," said Gilson as they prepared to depart the small clearing. The first act was for the drivers to make sure the trucks completely blocked the road. The two drivers remained behind to guard the vehicles and protect Natalie Matejka, who would coordinate communications between the group on the mountain and the group approaching the cottage.

Al watched as Gilson confirmed that everything was in place. As much as he would have loved to head up what he hoped would be a final rush to capture Genevieve Wangen, this wasn't his territory. He had to allow Gilson to take the lead. *Let's go, let's go, let's go.* Every minute that passed increased the possibility that they would be discovered. Shifting his weight from foot to foot, he attempted to tamp down his impatience.

Apparently satisfied, the commander finally nodded at Olstad and Mulholland and the order was given to move out on foot. The eight leaders donned flak jackets and armored up with high-powered rifles to augment the pistols they carried.

"Remember to save your strength," barked Olstad as they walked. "We've got two miles to cover and it's hotter and more humid than we had hoped."

Gilson led the way. Forty-five minutes later, after a hard uphill walk, he stopped. As the thudding of boots died away, Al caught the sounds of laughter and music drifting through the trees. His heart rate picked up. *That's got to be Genevieve's wedding.* He turned and caught Charlie's eye. *We've got her.* Charlie offered him a thumbs up. Gilson gave a command and the group moved off the road into the trees and picked their way carefully through the forest.

Al studied the ground carefully as he walked, careful to avoid branches that might snap beneath his feet. After a few minutes, the back of a spacious log cabin with a triple garage came into view. Al caught his breath. Was this where their quarry had been holed up? When they reached the building, Gilson held up his hand, signaling them to stop. He gestured for everyone to gather around. "Sounds as if the wedding's about to begin. Al, you move up and take a look around the corner, let us know what you see."

Al nodded, grateful the commander was acknowledging his special interest in this case. Pressing his back to the wooden side of the cabin, he crept forward until he reached the front corner. He peered cautiously around the corner of the house, assessing the situation. Although his view was limited, he could see guests walking about the lawn, talking. From his vantage point, he counted one bar, and a group gathered around what might be a second one.

As he watched, a tall, well-built man in a tux called out instructions and the guests moved down the hill toward the rows of chairs set out on the lawn. A stringed quartet began playing music. The tall man had disappeared, but he emerged now from the other side of the house, accompanied by a grizzly bear and another, swarthy man. *The tall one must be Pete Pernask*a. Al squinted. *And that's Dino Carbone.* He wiped his palms on the front of his pants. This had to be the right place, if the Carbones were involved.

The men and the bear walked up the aisle between the rows of chairs and stopped to the right of a man in a black suit and white collar. Three women walked up the aisle and arranged themselves on the other side of the priest. *So where is Genevieve?* As he watched, the woman he had been chasing for years started across the lawn, her gaze firmly on the tall, handsome man at the front of the gathering.

Al pressed his lips together to keep from letting out a shout of triumph. Finally, Genevieve Wangen was in his sights.

●━━·•

Al crept back to give his report to Gilson. The group retreated into the woods to plan their strategy. Olstad addressed the group in a loud whisper Al had to lean in to hear. "The snipers will take their places in the next five minutes. When we get the signal from them that they are set, the rest of us will move in. Detective Rouse will announce the arrest of Ms. Wangen, after which we will take everyone at the wedding into custody, including all guests. Our priority is the bride."

Olstad turned to Al. "Your mission, Detective."

Al stepped to the front of the pack, and with ten people following him and another five spread out in the woods, the move to the wedding site began.

Olstad touched Al's arm and he stopped. Leaning in close, Olstad said, "Snipers are reporting eight heavily armed guards around the perimeter of the property."

Al nodded. "Have them neutralize any they can, without injuring them, if possible."

Olstad spoke softly into the radio and nodded to Al.

This is it then. Drawing in a deep, steadying breath, Al stepped forward. The rest of the group followed him, but Al's attention zeroed in on one person, the woman at the front of the makeshift chapel who had made his life miserable for far too long.

63

The group inched forward through the trees, noiselessly. Everyone on the chairs on the lawn was focused at the front and no one glanced over at the woods. The armed personnel took up positions at the edge of the bush that surrounded the clearing.

Al stopped at the edge of the lawn and held up his hand. When the bride and groom had said their vows and the priest had pronounced them man and wife, Olstad, who had stopped beside Al, whispered into her shoulder microphone and a shot rang out across the clearing. A shattered revolver flew from the hand of the guard nearest the path to the lake.

As the guests looked around, puzzled looks on their faces, more shots rang out from the cover of the woods.

Al lifted the megaphone Gilson had handed him back in the woods to his mouth. "Hands up, everyone. The property is surrounded."

Focusing in on his quarry, he said, "Genevieve Wangen, you are under arrest for the murders of fourteen men in Wisconsin."

From the far side of the yard, another shot rang out. Agents pushed through the trees into the open space of the lawn.

As one of the Carbone guards raised his weapon, a sniper blew it out of his hand. A voice rang out from the wedding party. "Put your guns down, you idiots. Can't you see we're surrounded?"

Al led his group out of the trees and across the lawn to the back of the seating area.

Dino Carbone strode down the aisle and stopped in front of Al. "You folks are interrupting a wedding ceremony. I am sure whatever you want, you are badly mistaken. There is no one here by the name of Wangen."

"You know her as Samantha Walters. She's right up there, in the pale blue dress."

"Everyone stop where you are and raise your hands!" The shout came from Lance Pearson. "We're FBI and we're here to arrest the bride, who is wanted for crimes in Wisconsin!"

Al took one step up the aisle. A thunderous roar shook the area as a massive grizzly charged toward him. Mulholland stepped forward, a funny-looking gun at her shoulder. She aimed at the bear and fired. The animal hesitated, roared again, then began to stagger, eventually falling at her feet.

"Please don't hurt him." The voice was marked by a European accent. The groom strode toward them, both hands in the air. "Please, he is a friend, one of my best men. He was simply trying to protect us."

The man, Pete Pernaska, reached the bear, knelt, and wrapped his arms around the animal's neck.

"He'll be fine," Mulholland told the man. "I hit him with a knockout dart. He'll be down for a while but will feel no ill effects."

Genevieve. Tearing his gaze from the animal, Al looked around wildly, but the bride had disappeared. *No! Not again.*

"Everyone on your knees!" yelled Pearson, as the agents drew the circle of guests on the lawn into a tight circle.

An older gentlemen, so similar in appearance to Dino that he had to be his father, stalked over to Al. "Your presence here is surprising and unwelcome," he said, after clearing his throat. "I am Angelo Carbone. Just what in the hell brings you here today?"

"Angelo." Aaron moved to Al's side. "We simply want to take the bride into custody and question her about crimes in Wisconsin. We'll make this quick. Some of my men will accompany your drivers back to the limos. This party is officially over."

Al spun around, looking for Charlie. His friend stood just behind him. "Where is she?" Al shouted.

"I didn't see her; I was watching the bear." Charlie scanned the property. "Anyone see her leave?"

No one answered.

"Let's go!" Al motioned toward the house. "We have to find her."

Assuming she had entered the dwelling, Al sprinted across the lawn, up the steps, and into the cabin. Silence greeted him. Racing through all of the rooms, he searched each one frantically. They were empty. Charlie burst into the last bedroom. "Did you check the closets?"

"I did, but check them again." Al's stomach had twisted into knots. *This isn't happening.* "She's gotta be here. Where else could she be?"

After Charlie had plowed through the house and pronounced it empty, he grasped Al's arm. "Are there any hidden rooms? Remember, her lab was hidden in Illinois, and in Georgia, too."

Hope sparked in Al. "You're right." He ran back outside. Aaron had handcuffed Pete Pernaska, and Al signaled for him to bring the man over. When the two reached him, Al stepped up until he was inches from the man's face. "Are there any hidden rooms in the building? Tell us! If you don't, we'll level the place to find them."

Pernaska stared at him for a few seconds then his shoulders sagged. "Yeah, the lab is hidden. I'll show you. But I don't want her hurt."

"We aren't going to hurt her. We want her alive and uninjured. We're taking her back to Wisconsin."

Pernaska walked ahead of him into the house. "In here," he said, moving into the pantry off the kitchen. "There's a switch behind that picture." He gestured to a small framed painting on the wall. Al shoved it back, found the switch, pushed it, and a portion of the wall slid aside to reveal a sizable room filled with equipment that glistened when he turned on the lights.

Aaron pushed Pete into the room and stayed with him as Al and Charlie moved deliberately through the lab, looking in every corner, beneath every piece of furniture, and in the cabinets and refrigerators. No trace of the woman they were hunting.

Jaw clenched, Al headed back to Pernaska. "Any place else in the cabin she could be?" asked Al.

When the groom shook his head, Al and Charlie abandoned their search and moved back outside, looking through the garage as they went.

"Nothing?" called Pearson.

"Not a thing." Al shook his head. "She must be in the woods."

"She can't have gone far. Not in those shoes." Gilson waved an arm around the lawn. "Let's get these people out of here so we can start looking."

Gilson and Pearson sent seven of their troops to the cars with the seven drivers. They returned with the limos to collect the passengers. An FBI agent accompanied each car to make sure no one stopped to pick up the fugitive along the way.

Before the limos departed, Gilson tapped the arm of one of the agents. "When you're near town, call the Kalispell Police Department and ask for Lee Salisbury. I put him on alert this morning, figuring something like this could happen. He's got a pair of bloodhounds that he'll bring out here to help us search. Now go!"

The agents herded the guests toward the cars which, when loaded, turned in the yard and headed back down the road. An hour and a half later, one of the agents returned with Salisbury, a long, lanky, weather-beaten man, and two bloodhounds to aid in the chase.

While they waited, the lawmen helped themselves to food and nonalcoholic beverages. When their colleagues returned, they had them grab some food, then everyone grabbed bottles of water. Al paced beneath the tent that housed the tables of food abandoned by the wedding guests. Everything in him screamed to head into the woods and search for Genevieve himself, but he had to wait for the official order. He drove his fingers through his hair, unable to believe the woman had escaped his clutches once again. The dog handler, Salisbury, fed his two hounds, made sure they had taken drinks, then said he was ready.

Gilson, with Pearson, Olstad, Mulholland, Al, and Charlie around him, told the assembly, "Our fugitive has to be in the woods. When we realized that she was gone, we sent troops to cover the area from the lake up the mountain to meet with Dan Matejka and his force. We are reasonably confident she has to be in that area. Lee Salisbury here will lead us, moving with his bloodhounds. Remember, if you come across her, we want her alive, but understand she's likely armed and she's dangerous, especially if she took some of her potions with her. We'll move out on my signal. Remember to look under every rock and fallen tree. Take nothing for granted."

Al felt for his sidearm. Genevieve might be armed and dangerous, but if he was the one who found her, she would find out once and for all just how dangerous he could be.

64

Al grabbed a woman's shirt from the clothes hamper in the master bedroom and brought it out for the dogs to sniff. As soon as they had, their handler turned them loose. They wandered the yard, their long ears flapping as they moved. When the dogs reached the place where Genevieve had been standing with the bear, the yaps changed to brays and the hounds lunged into the woods. As they walked, the lawmen spread out behind them to cover a wider area of the forest.

The going in the woods was tough, the terrain rocky and uncertain. Trees clung to crags in the rocks and to the stony sides of small canyons that slipped off toward the lake to their right. But the dogs had the fugitive's scent in their nostrils and ranged ahead. When they got too far, they were whistled back by Salisbury. The group moved deliberately but steadily, constantly searching around them for signs of the woman.

At a speed that nearly drove Al out of his mind, the group moved through the forest, the elevation constantly rising as they moved up the mountain. The going now harder, the dogs ranged farther ahead, frequently called back by their handler lest they get too far ahead and fall prey to wolf or bear.

With shadows lengthening in the clearings, the dogs' howls changed pitch and cadence, the yips and yaps turning to brays and wails.

"They've got something!" Salisbury shouted to the searchers. "Better close in behind me."

The searchers drew in behind Salisbury, moving forward with caution as the trainer called steadily to his dogs, urging them to, "Hold … hold in place. Cannon. Nose. Steady now. Hold!"

The dogs continued to bray as the searchers moved closer to them, then closer still. Al caught sight of a hole in the rocks that appeared to be a large cave. As Salisbury approached, the dogs returned to him, jumping at him before returning to the entrance to the cave.

"Steady now!" he shouted. "Hold. Cannon, Nose, steady."

When they reached the dogs, now within a few feet of the mouth of the cave, Salisbury took a leash from the pouch at his side and clipped the two leads to the collars of the hounds.

Blood pounded in Al's ears. Was Genevieve in the cave? Did they have her cornered? If so, what would she do? His fingers tightened around the butt of this gun, but he didn't withdraw it from the holster.

"Mulholland, Al, Charlie, up here," he called. "I want those stun guns with me when we enter the cave. You have a taser, too, right?"

When the petite woman nodded, the three moved forward, following the dogs. Mulholland produced a high-powered flashlight that illuminated the mouth of the cave. It appeared sizeable, the light fading into the darkness of what could very well be a bear's den.

Olstad stationed two men at the cave's mouth and the rest of the group trudged forward. When they had gotten several hundred feet into the hollow, a thunderous roar sounded, its echo bouncing back and forth off the rock enclosure, sending chills up and down Al's spine.

Salisbury held up his hand, stopping the group. In the glow of the flashlight, Al could see a large bear, fangs bared and spittle dripping from its jowls. As the dogs continued to yelp, Mulholland shouldered the gun, aimed, and fired, the dart striking the bear in the chest. The bear yelped, leaped forward, then crashed to the ground, motionless.

Mulholland walked up to it. In the confines of the cave, the bear's strong smell assaulted Al's nostrils. Mulholland examined the animal. "Probably the other bear's girlfriend. This one's female. She'll sleep for at least two hours."

Salisbury released the dogs and they moved forward cautiously, smelled the bear thoroughly, and moved beyond the prone creature into the blackness. Once again they yipped and yapped, the sounds fading a bit as they plunged farther into the cave, out of reach of the light.

As the searchers followed them, the sounds grew louder until the group reached the dogs. The cave appeared to end just beyond the animals. Looking up, Al spotted an opening about ten feet in diameter. Dangling from the opening were a couple of rungs of what looked like a rope ladder.

"Damn!" exclaimed Al. "What next?"

Turning to Salisbury, Al asked, "Any idea where this opening might be? We're going to have to find it from the outside."

"I'm guessing it's farther up the mountain." Salisbury held the flashlight up to the hole. "We'll leave a trooper here. If someone keeps calling out, we'll find the opening quicker."

"I'll do it." Mulholland held up the dart gun. "If there are any other critters in this cave, I can take care of them." She pulled a flashlight from her belt, clicked it on, and held it in her free hand.

Al had to admire her. Staying here alone in a dark cave when it was impossible to tell what other predators—animal or human—could be lurking in the shadows was not an assignment he would relish. He offered her a quick salute as he brushed by her on his way out and she nodded.

The search team hurried from the cave and began to climb the mountain beyond the opening

The steepness of the incline increased as they climbed and the terrain grew even rockier. So arduous was the ascent that the searchers had to stop every few yards to recover their breath.

After about thirty minutes, Al heard a faint call that seemed to come from the mountain somewhere above him.

"I can hear her!" he gasped out to the group, resting a hand on one knee as he bent forward, and swiping his other hand across his forehead. "I hear her. This way." The other searchers joined him and Al held up a hand to quiet them.

In a few seconds, a voice, faint but distinguishable, drifted toward them. "Here; I'm here!"

"There." Olstad jerked a thumb to the left and up. They'd only climbed a few minutes when they were confronted by a rock outcropping that reached upward several hundred feet. When they stopped to reconnoiter, the voice guiding them became more prominent: "Here; over here!"

"She's above us." Al stared up at the sheer rock face. "I'd swear that voice is coming right out of the rocks."

"Me too," agreed Sheriff Murphy. "Somehow we have to figure out a way to get up on those rocks."

"How're we gonna do that? It's too goddamned steep." Charlie's face and neck were flushed bright red.

Alarmed, Al contemplated him. *Don't have a heart attack on me, big guy. Not here. Not now.*

The sheriff scowled. "We're gonna have to get someone to climb up there and drop a rope down. That way the next person can take their time walking up the cliff, searching for holes in the rock. It's gotta be up there somewhere. That's where the voice is coming from."

Matejka stepped forward. He slid his pack off his back and zipped it open. "No one has to climb up; I have a grappling gun."

Adrenaline surged through Al. "That might work. See how far up there you can get it."

Matejka extracted a small, cannon-like object from his pack, fastened the hook to the rope in the gun, then armed it, pointed it up at a steep angle, and fired. The rope played out, nearly eclipsing the rock, but the hook struck the sharp face and fell harmlessly back down, landing at Al's feet.

Al clenched his teeth. No way they were giving up, not when they were this close. He studied the terrain. "Let's try it over here."

Matejka re-set the gun, pointed it where Al had suggested, and fired. This time it topped the rocks and the hook lodged firmly. Two men put their weight on it and could not dislodge it.

Olstad looked around as if trying to decide whom she should send.

"I'm probably in the best shape, Ramona," said Tad. "I'll make the climb to get above the cliff."

When no one disagreed with him, Tad took the heavy coil of rope from Matejka, hitched it into place on his shoulder, and began to walk up the face of the cliff. Precariously he perched on a ledge about halfway up then disappeared.

Thirty seconds later, his head appeared over the precipice and he shouted, "This is the opening, but no one used it. The ladder is only two rungs long, like some kind of decoy. In addition, this ledge peters out in a foot and a half, and even a mountain goat couldn't use it. I'm coming down."

Tad finally dropped to the ground. He was breathing heavily and his face was flushed.

Olstad rested a hand on his back. "Are you okay?"

"Yeah, just have to catch my breath. No one's been up there. I don't know where she went, but it wasn't up that ladder, that's for sure. How long have we got before that bear wakes up?"

Olstad checked her watch. "About an hour. Lee, see if the dogs can pick up anything else."

Salisbury led the dogs back to the cave entrance, and though he tried to keep them outside, they kept braying and wanting to enter the opening. "They've got damn good noses. Although she isn't in there now, Wangen has to have been here recently."

Al gritted his teeth. They had searched every inch of the cave. *So where the hell is she?* With the sun sinking and time elapsing, the searchers decided to keep the Matejka crew on the mountain. Other troopers would guard the cabin and the roads.

Olstad stopped in front of Al and shrugged apologetically. "It's too dark to stay out in the woods. I say we head back and take another look around the cabin, in case she hiding in or around it. Can't do much else until morning. But I doubt that she can, either."

The group trudged back down the hill and gathered at the cabin. Olstad, Gilson, Al, and Charlie went back inside. Al and Charlie headed for the lab while the others spread out to search the rest of the house. Once again Al couldn't see any trace of Genevieve in the lab. Fuming, he stopped and smacked a palm down on the metal counter. "I can't believe she slipped through our fingers again! The woman is some kind of Houdini; just when you get your hands on her, she disappears into thin ..." Al's eyes narrowed. "What is it, Charlie?"

His friend had stopped in the middle of the room and was staring at the floor.

When he didn't respond, Al walked over and stood in front of him, hands on his hips. "What'a ya got?"

"This flooring looks different." Charlie got down on his knees and traced the area. "Lookit the grain. It breaks off in a rectangular pattern, doesn't it?"

Olstad and Gilson walked into the lab and Al waved them over. "Charlie might have found something." All three of them lowered themselves to the floor too.

After a moment, Olstad sat back on her haunches. "I think you're right, Charlie. Great eyes."

"That's for sure. Great eyes." Al smacked his friend on the back. "How about pounding on that area, hear what it sounds like?"

"Great idea." Charlie took his revolver from his belt, ejected the magazine, and used the handle to tap the floor. When he hit the area he had pointed out, the sound was different. "Hollow," he said. "We need to get in there."

Olstad stood up and left the room, then reappeared with a drill in her hand. "Let's try this. Maybe if we put a hole in it, we can open it up."

Al found an extension cord, connected the drill, and handed it to Charlie.

The bit made short work of the floor, and soon they had a hole punched in the area large enough to allow them to try and pull it up. It quickly became clear that the area was actually a trap door. Unfortunately, it was just as clear that the door was latched from below. Al opened and closed his fists, resisting the urge to grab hold of the piece of wood and rip the thing open.

"Gimme something to batter it with." Charlie set down the drill.

Al bolted from the room. He found a crow bar in the garage and hurried back to the lab to hand it to his colleague. Charlie inserted the hooked end into the hole and began to lever the opening, eventually using his foot to exert greater pressure. As he huffed and pushed, Al heard a cracking sound. Suddenly the door snapped apart, revealing a stairway.

Al tugged a flashlight from his belt and shone it down the hole. A set of stairs led to some kind of passage. "C'mon." He swung his legs into the opening and lowered himself onto the stairs. "Bring your lights; it's darker'n a coal mine."

The other three followed Al down, all carrying flashlights. As soon as he hit the bottom, Al dove into the six foot by four foot concrete passageway. They followed it for about five hundred feet before reaching a door. Without hesitation, he shoved a shoulder against it and pushed it open.

"Well, I'll be damned!" Al turned back to inspect the other side of the door as the other three came out. What was a heavy steel door on the inside had been covered with limbs, leaves, and twigs on the outside that blended perfectly with the hillside.

The knots in Al's stomach tightened. "Well, at least we know how she escaped." He slammed a fist against the door. "By now she could be miles away."

Charlie gripped his shoulder. "It's not likely. She wouldn't be able to get very far very fast in either the heels or bare feet. We just need to shore up the perimeter and keep her trapped inside. First thing in the morning we'll head out again with the dogs."

Al unclenched his fist. His friend was right. Trying to find the old lady on a moonless night on uncertain, unfamiliar terrain was a recipe for disaster. A few more hours of patience, though, and they would launch an all-out search. And this time they wouldn't stop until they had Genevieve Wangen in custody once and for all.

65

Al pushed open the front door of the cabin and stepped out onto the porch. When he saw what was out there, he stopped so abruptly that Charlie, who'd been following at his heels, slammed into the back of him. Al stumbled forward a couple of steps, but managed to grab the knob to regain his balance, turn around, and shoo Charlie back inside. He followed his big friend into the cabin and closed the door firmly behind them. "Look," he whispered, gesturing to the window in the door.

Charlie stepped up beside him and the two men peered outside.

A bear sat on the porch steps. It held a can of beer in both paws, tilted to pour into its massive mouth. Several empty cans were scattered around the bottom of the stairs. When the big animal finished the beer, it pointed its nose to the sky and swiveled its head, sniffing the air. Its head turned toward the house, and the animal let out a thunderous roar before lumbering to its feet.

Much as it was a dangerous situation, it was also comical. The bear, obviously somewhat under the influence of both the immobilizing drug and the alcohol, wobbled as it walked, staggering toward the lake. When it had closed within twenty feet of the path, it paused, snuffling and snorting.

The bear put its head down and slowly staggered down the path to the lake, eventually entering the water as if hoping the cool liquid would ease the effects of the shot and the beers. After frolicking for a few minutes, darkness continuing to close in, the bear stumbled from the water, looked up the path, gave another roar, and staggered north along the shore as if heading home.

Al and Charlie stayed in place for a while before summoning up the nerve to go out onto the porch. Al stared at the path where the bear had disappeared and shook his head. What a day. He'd seen things he had never seen before and still couldn't quite believe. A bear that drank beer? And that had become so comfortable with the humans who lived here that he would come right up to their …

A thought struck him and Al gripped his friend's arm. "I have an idea, Charlie. I know it's late, but do you feel like going on a little adventure?"

Charlie didn't hesitate. "I'm right behind you."

"Great." Al grinned. "It could be dangerous, but I have a feeling it will be worth it. In fact, if I'm right, this just might be a night the two of us will be telling our grandkids about for years to come."

●——•

Secreted behind a rock wall behind what had been build to look like the back of the cave, Sam continued to wait. The search party had departed hours ago, but she had no idea whether a sentry had been left at the mouth of the cave or not. She pressed a hand to the rock face of the opening to the small hideout at the back of the cave that she and Pete had discovered months earlier. Pete had installed the opening that could be opened and closed with switches that blended perfectly into the wall and that could not be detected from the outside. They had stored lanterns, dried food, and water in the small space, as well as a mattress and blankets. Still, the small, dark room felt a lot like a jail cell. *How long should I wait in here?*

Thank goodness Pete had urged her to plan ahead. They had followed Ben home, become familiar with his lair, and met him there on occasion with food and beer. They wanted him to see them there and to equate their presence with something good. They had also seen the bear's mate, but Sam had still held her breath when she encountered the female grizzly upon entering the cave. Thankfully, the bear had let her pass, then remained in the cave and provided impromptu confusion. The distraction had aided Sam, giving her enough time to slip into the hidden room and close the door behind her.

For now, she was content to wait in the dark. She wasn't very comfortable. Escaping from the cabin had required her to ditch her high heels, and she had arrived at the cave with her pantyhose shredded and her feet cut and bruised. She had also ripped the pale blue dress she had worn for the wedding, and she was anxious to get it off and to change into the spare clothes she had left there weeks before: jeans, T-shirt, socks, and hiking boots.

If she had heard nothing that indicated the presence of the searchers by midnight, she would turn on the light, change, and eat before venturing out of the cave and heading to the ATV, unless, of course, Pete showed up first.

The time passed with agonizing slowness, until she could hardly sit still. In fact, she wanted to scream, but couldn't risk alerting anyone to her presence.

Sam sank onto the mattress and rested her back against the cold stone wall. How had this happened? She thought they'd been so careful, so discreet. How had Al Rouse managed to find her all the way up here in the mountains? *Will he never stop tracking me down like an animal?* She pressed her eyes shut tightly. No, he wouldn't. He'd managed to find every one of her hideouts. Even a new name and a new face hadn't kept him from discovering who she was and continuing to chase her down. Did she want to live like this? Always on the run? Always looking back over her shoulder? *If I'm with Pete, yes.* Any kind of life with him, however vigilant they would have to be, was better than a life without him.

Exhausted, she stretched out on the mattress and tried to shut off the thoughts that continued to whirl through her mind, driving her crazy. Suddenly, something jogged her back to consciousness and Sam bolted upright. She must have fallen asleep. What time was it? What had awakened her? Had there been a noise ... was someone here?

She remained motionless in the dark for nearly ten minutes. Then, having heard nothing, she reached for the light, turned it on, and checked her watch. 11:40 p.m. *Close enough.* Sam got up and changed her clothes, carefully folding her wedding dress and placing it on the blanket. She tied up her boots then moved to the entrance, extinguished the light, and pressed the switch to open the makeshift door.

She listened but heard nothing. After several minutes of silence, she crawled from the hidden room, closed the door, and again activated her light. The cavern appeared empty. She moved cautiously toward the entrance.

The air was fresher now, but the bear scent stronger, too. *Almost there.*

As she moved forward, suddenly the cave was illuminated by a strong light that shone directly into her eyes, blinding her.

"Stop right there!" called the familiar voice. "Charlie, cuff her!"

Al Rouse. He'd found her again. Something inside Sam crumpled. She'd lost. She would never have that life with Pete that she had dreamed of. Everything she had hoped for and worked so hard to get was slipping through her fingers. Still unable to see because of the blinding light, Sam felt her arms pulled behind her and cold steel rings snapping around her wrists.

Her shoulders slumped. *It's over.*

◆━━ ·

"Shackle her, too." Al tossed the metal shackles toward Charlie. They landed on the floor of the cave, clanking loudly.

As Charlie forced Genevieve to the ground, a shot rang out, whining off the wall of the cave.

"What the …?" Al swore as he whirled around to find the shooter. One of the Matejka troopers left behind walked out of the darkness.

"What the hell were you thinking?" Al's voice boomed off the walls of the cave.

"I thought she was going for a gun," said the trooper.

"Well, she wasn't." Charlie started to attach the shackles around the prisoner's ankle and stopped. "Al, she's hit."

No! Al's stomach lurched. Genevieve was not going to get off that easily, not if there was anything he could do about it. Together the two lawmen knelt beside Sam and carefully raised her T-shirt to expose a bloody wound just above her left breast. It was spurting blood.

Al yelled for help from the troopers before tearing off his shirt to help Charlie try and staunch the flow of blood.

As they labored over her, Genevieve's eyelids flickered and she opened her eyes.

"Al ..." The word was barely a whisper. Al lowered his head to hear better. "Al, I want you to tell Julie I love her. Will you do that for me?"

"Genevieve, you can do that yourself." He pressed down harder on the shirt and she winced. "We'll have you out of here and to a hospital soon. Just conserve your strength."

"No, Al. I'm going ... to die. I want my niece to know that my ... last thoughts were of her."

Al pressed down on the wound with both hands as the woman who'd consumed his thoughts for so long closed her eyes. He clenched his jaw. *Don't you die on me, Genevieve. I want you to answer for your crimes. And I want to be there to see it.*

Troopers and FBI agents rushed into the cave, one with a first aid kit and two carrying a stretcher. "There's a chopper in-bound," said Matejka. "Should be here in a minute or two."

Al and Charlie kept pressure on the wound, even while Sam was loaded on the stretcher and carried from the cave. The two troopers carrying her moved swiftly but carefully as they carried her down the mountain to the clearing, the two lawmen jogging beside the stretcher.

The helicopter was touching down just as they reached the open lawn of Genevieve's property, and two medics jumped from the craft and made their way to the stretcher. Al and Charlie relinquished their spots to the paramedics, but as the stretcher was loaded onto the chopper and Sam was transferred from the stretcher to a gurney, the co-pilot yelled to Al and Charlie to ride along.

No sooner had they had leapt aboard than the chopper lifted off.

The helicopter landed at Kalispell just after midnight, and fifteen minutes later, Sam was in surgery.

"Think I should call the chief?" Al and Charlie had settled onto hard plastic seats in the emergency department waiting room. Al studied his friend. Charlie's clothes were caked with blood and his face and hands streaked with dirt. Al had to look the same. No wonder everyone else in the waiting room was staring at them from a wary distance.

"I wouldn't wake him." Charlie glanced down at his watch. "Nothing he can do about it. Might as well wait until we hear what the surgeon has to say."

"I guess you're right. What about Julie?"

"That's different; I think you should call her and probably JoAnne, too, while you're at it."

"Good advice." Al rummaged in his pocket for his cell phone.

He dialed Julie's number from memory and waited until the voice he knew so well, thick with sleep at the moment, spoke on the other end of the line. "Hello?"

"Julie, it's Al. I'm in Kalispell, Montana, and your aunt is in surgery."

"What?" Julie suddenly sounded wide awake. The bed creaked and he pictured her sitting up and throwing her legs over the side of the mattress. "What happened?"

"We tracked her down to a cabin in Montana where she was getting married earlier today. We busted up the wedding, but she managed to get away and hid in a cave. An hour ago we found here there. One of the troopers with us thought she was going for a weapon and fired a shot that ricocheted off the wall of the cave and struck Genevieve in the chest."

The sob on the other end of the line brought a lump to Al's throat. "Is she going to be okay?"

He paused. "I don't know. It's pretty bad. We're waiting to hear from the surgeon, but we likely won't for a few hours."

Julie didn't speak for a moment. When she did, her voice was firm and strong. "I'm coming out there. I'll catch the first flight and let you know when I've landed."

Al knew her well enough to not even try to talk her out of it. "Okay. See you soon then." He disconnected the call and walked back over to Charlie. Although he had no interest in making Genevieve feel better, he did hope, for Julie's sake, that she was able to have one more conversation with the aunt she loved. "She's catching the next flight here. I just hope she makes it in time."

66

ust after six thirty a.m., the doctor, still wearing scrubs and a blue cap, a mask hanging around his neck by the string, strode into the waiting room. "Are you with the gunshot victim?" he asked. Al nodded and both he and Charlie stood as the doctor moved closer to them. Looking around to make sure there were no other listening ears nearby, he gestured to their seats before slumping onto the one beside Al.

"She's alive." The statement was delivered by a professional who had expended all his effort in his life-saving mission. "But I surely can't guarantee that she will be that way in six to twelve hours. The damage was catastrophic. When the bullet entered the body, it splintered against the clavicle and several fragments punctured the subclavian artery on that side of the body. Her upper chest was a mess."

Al shifted. "Doctor …?"

"Mendenhall."

"Dr. Mendenhall, can you hazard a guess at whether she might survive? I'm Detective Al Rouse, by the way, and this is Deputy Charlie Berzinski."

"Al, Charlie, this is a very bad wound, complicated by the fact that the fragments that severed the artery might have contained rock fragments, too. Quite frankly, it's a miracle she's still breathing. How old is she, by the way? I'm guessing from her organs that she's a lot older than she looks."

"Yes, she's in her mid-eighties."

"I would have guessed that," said the doctor, with a sigh. "But in answer to your question, only God knows. I will say that the woman must have a constitution like a horse. Anyone else would have expired before she reached the hospital. To be honest, her vitals were about flat-lining when she came in, but she had a trace of a pulse, so I decided to give it a try. The artery repair went well, but she had lost a lot of blood before you got her here. It's fifty-fifty at best."

The doctor pushed himself from the chair, struggled into an upright position, shook each man's hand, and disappeared through the swinging doors.

"Nice guy," said Charlie.

"Very nice," agreed Al. "It's pretty obvious it took all he had to try and save her."

Two young troopers entered the room and approached them. The taller man said, "Sirs, Captain Gilson sent us over to guard the prisoner's room. He said you needed to get some rest."

He hadn't thought about it, but as soon as the trooper mentioned it, fatigue struck Al like a Mac truck. "From what I understand, she's in intensive care and likely to be unconscious for a number of hours. You probably know the layout here better than we do, so check with the supervisor and take up your posts outside her room." The two men nodded and turned to leave. Al straightened in his seat. "Gentlemen."

They both turned back and looked at him.

"This woman has escaped custody several times and likely has people willing to help her do it again. Stay alert and do not leave your post at the same time for any reason. Understood?"

The shorter man, a redhead with freckles sprinkled across his nose, nodded curtly. "Understood."

The two troopers left. Al and Charlie grabbed the backpacks they'd worn to the hospital and slung them back over their shoulders.

Charlie stopped in front of the revolving doors. "How the hell are we gonna go anywhere? I doubt the chopper waited for us."

Just then the red-headed trooper burst back into the room. "Sorry, sirs, the captain instructed us to give these to you." He handed a set of car keys to Al. "The car is in the first spot just outside the door. It's marked State Patrol, so you can't miss it. The captain said he will have beds ready for you when you get to his house."

Al took the keys from him and nodded. "Thank you." He and Charlie trudged from the building. It had been a long, long day, and there was still work to be done.

Al held out the keys. "Why don't you drive, Charlie? I've gotta call the chief. I'll ask him to call the sheriff for you too, if you'd like."

Charlie took the keys. "Sure. Thanks." He pulled open the driver's side door and pushed the seat back as far as it would go so he could climb behind the wheel.

By the time he had the car started and in gear, Al had the chief on the line.

"We got her, Chief," he began, "but based on what we just heard, whether we're able to bring her back to Wisconsin or not is very iffy."

"Why? What happened?"

"She was shot while being taken into custody. She's been in surgery for a coupla hours. We just spoke to the doc and he says it's fifty-fifty at best. Two patrolmen are guarding her room. Charlie and I are going to get a little shuteye. Genevieve's niece Julie will arrive sometime today. Maybe we'll know more by then."

The chief exhaled loudly. "Well, at least she's not out there free to hurt anyone else. Keep me posted, Al."

"I will." Al disconnected the call and immediately dialed Julie's cell.

"Hi, Julie. Your aunt's alive, but I'm afraid the prognosis isn't good. We just spoke with the doctor and he said there was massive damage. He gives her a fifty-fifty chance at best."

"Thanks for the update. I fly into Kalispell at one this afternoon."

"Okay, Charlie and I will be there to pick you up. See you this afternoon."

Al hung up and pressed the back of his hand to his mouth to stifle a yawn. "Julie gets in at one. I suggest we get some sleep so we can be up in time to meet her flight."

When they got to Gilson's house, his wife Greta was waiting, ready to fix breakfast for them. The captain was there, too.

Over platters of ham and eggs, Al and Charlie told Gilson what had transpired at the hospital.

"Mendenhall is the best we have." Gilson waved a forkful of eggs at them. "In fact, he's one of the best in the world. If anyone can save her, he can."

The food gone, Gilson showed Al and Charlie to their bedrooms. Barely able to tug off their outer clothing, each man fell onto his bed in his underwear, asleep nearly before their heads touched the pillows.

In what seemed to Al to be only seconds later, Gilson was shaking them awake. "Noon, guys. Time to get up if you're going to meet the plane."

The two rushed through showers and used the borrowed squad car to drive to the airport. They hadn't waited for five minutes when a blue and white CRJ commuter airliner pulled onto the tarmac.

Julie was the second passenger into the terminal. She ran to Al and threw her arms around him. "Is she still alive?" she gasped.

"We haven't heard anything since this morning." Al stepped back, reluctantly. Although he loved his wife too much to continue his relationship with Julie, he still missed her and thought of her often. "We'll take you there as soon as you have your belongings."

"This is it," she said, holding up a backpack. "Let's go."

Ten minutes later, Al parked the police car in the hospital lot and they hurried into the facility, stopping at the desk just long enough to confirm directions.

As they strode down the hallway to the ICU, floors glistened in the bright overhead lighting and a sign appealed for *Quiet, Please!* Entering the unit, they noticed one of the two patrolmen assigned to Genevieve seated outside the door, his chair tilted up on its back legs as he read a hunting and fishing magazine. The taller man was hunched over the counter, chatting with a pretty young nurse.

"Oh, hi, Al, Charlie ..." the trooper pushed himself up from the counter.

They greeted him, introduced Julie to him and to the nurse, and inquired about her aunt's condition.

"Grave," said the nurse, whose nametag identified her as *Nancy*.

"She hasn't regained consciousness. We're not sure that she will." She ducked her head in Julie's direction. "Sorry, ma'am."

"I understand. I've been advised of my aunt's condition. May I see her?"

"There's a no-visitor order posted, but in light of you being a relative, of course you may. Try and make your visit brief, though. I expect that Dr. Mendenhall will be in before four. He usually conducts rounds between three and four. You might want to talk to him."

"I will do that. Thank you, Nancy. May I go in then?"

"Of course."

Al touched her arm. "Would you like me to come with you?"

"Yes please, Al." Julie lifted her chin but her lower lip trembled slightly. She wasn't keeping it together as well as she would clearly like him to believe.

Al rested a hand on the small of her back and guided her to the room. The trooper lowered his magazine and inclined his head slightly to Al as they passed through the doorway.

The old woman looked tiny and pale. A myriad of tubes and lines led into and out of her body. She was unmoving and appeared lifeless.

A tear slid down Julie's cheek. "Oh, Al," she grasped the bed rail with both hands. "She's so little. She looks like a small child, even in that tiny bed."

"That's the hospital effect," Al told her, thinking about all the times he had heard the same thing from people visiting crime or accident victims. "C'mon, let's go wait for the doctor."

About thirty minutes later, a tall, dark, handsome man Al recognized from the wedding the day before came into the area. Al threw Charlie a look, but neither of them moved as he walked to the counter and said to the nurse, "I'm Pete Pernaska. I'm here to see my wife."

When the nurse pointed out Genevieve's room, Julie looked at Al, her eyebrows raised. "Did he say wife?"

"He did," Al told her. "That part of the ceremony was over by the time we raided the cabin yesterday."

Julie got up from her seat, walked over to the man, and introduced herself. They visited for a minute, then together they headed toward Genevieve's room. Al caught the eye of the trooper stationed outside the door and nodded, and the red-headed office allowed them to enter.

When they came out twenty minutes later, Julie was crying and Pete's eyes were red and slightly swollen. Julie took his arm and led him to the waiting area. Al and Charlie stood up as she introduced Genevieve's husband to them both.

Al cleared his throat. "Mr. Pernaska, I want you to know that, as much as we wanted to take your wife into custody, it was certainly not our intention for her to be harmed."

The big man nodded. "Captain Gilson explained that to me when he came to release me and the other members of the wedding party from the county jail a little while ago. I appreciate you calling her niece."

The man walked to a chair and sat down. Julie sat next to him and they began to talk. Soon, Dr. Mendenhall walked into the area. He nodded to Al and Charlie before making his way over to Julie and Pernaska and introducing himself.

"Let me check on the patient and then I will visit with you here." He turned and strode over to Genevieve's room, lifted the chart from the holder on the back of the door, and studied it a moment before going inside.

When he emerged, his face was clouded in concern. He went straight over to Julie and Pernaska and sat down on a plastic seat in front of them. "Ms. Walters is running a low-grade fever. That is very worrisome as it could signal the start of an infection. Gunshot wounds are problematic from that standpoint, and this one's even worse because of the bullet making contact with the cave wall before penetrating the body. She is on the maximum dose of antibiotics I can administer. I would say the next four hours will tell us a lot. If you leave here to eat or rest, I recommend letting the nurses know how you can be reached."

Pernaska swallowed. "Thank you, Doctor."

Dr. Mendenhall nodded. "I'll check on her in a couple of hours and keep you updated." He stood up and disappeared down the hallway past Genevieve's room.

Al took a deep breath and lowered himself onto the seat next to Julie. "Charlie and I need to head out for a little while. Will you be okay here by yourself for a few hours?"

"She won't be by herself; I'm not going anywhere." Pernaska leaned back in his seat and crossed his arms over his chest.

Why doesn't that make me feel better? Al studied him for a moment. They might not have enough on Pernaska to hold him, not yet anyway, but Al felt deep in his bones that the man in front of him was deeply involved in some kind of criminal activity that involved supplying weapons to mafia bosses. Once Genevieve was safely behind bars, he would direct his full attention to uncovering just what Pernaska and the Carbones had been up to. He turned back to Julie. "Call me if you need anything at all. I can be here in ten minutes."

She tugged a tissue from her purse and dabbed at her cheeks. "I will. Thanks, Al."

He hugged her and stood up. He and Charlie did have work to do, but he didn't feel right about leaving Julie either. He stood there, undecided, until Charlie shifted beside him. Right. Time to work. He touched Julie's shoulder. "I'll see you soon." Before he could change his mind, he left her and went straight to the exit.

Charlie followed him through the door. "I almost hope the old girl makes it, Al. Partly because no one deserves to die like that, and partly because I want nothing more than to see her face the consequences of what she has done."

"I guess I do too, more for Julie's sake than anything. Although it might be easier for her if her aunt does just die than if she has to sit through a trial and then see her sent to prison for life." He smacked the brick wall of the hospital as they walked toward the parking lot. "We were so close to taking her in alive. Damn. Can't blame the patrolman, though. He thought she was reaching for a gun. What say we go and get some dinner?"

The two officers went to the Golden Lion. Al choked down a burger while Charlie devoured a T-bone. As they were finishing dinner, the owner stopped by, introduced herself as Molly O'Leary, and asked about Genevieve. "I know you guys say she did some pretty terrible things in Wisconsin, but she is a dear friend of mine. I was at the wedding, you know."

"We do know, Ms. O'Leary, and we are also hoping your friend recovers. The gunshot wound was not something we expected or would have wanted to happen."

"I'm grateful to hear you say that." Molly rapped on the table with her knuckles. "Dinner is on me, gentlemen. If there's anything at all you can do to make my friend more comfortable, or to make sure she is treated fairly once she does recover, I would consider it a personal favor."

She was gone before Al could reply, which was just as well. No matter how good the food was here, he wasn't about to make any concessions because of it. Genevieve Wangen would be treated the same as any other criminal, no better and no worse.

After dinner Al and Charlie stopped by the State Patrol District Headquarters to fill Gilson in on Genevieve's condition and to get an update on the investigation. Gilson waved them to seats in front of his desk. "It hurt Al, I'm not gonna lie, but we had to let all the other guests go, including Pernaska and the Carbones."

"I know, we saw Pernaska at the hospital."

"We just don't have enough concrete evidence on this latest venture of theirs to hold any of them at this point. Don't worry though, we're not giving up. We'll assist Aaron Wingate and the New Orleans P.D. any way we can. We'll get them, hopefully sooner than later."

"I appreciate that. At least we have Genevieve Wangen off the streets. If she makes it, we'll arrest her and take her in immediately, and if she doesn't, well, either way her crime spree ends here."

"Exactly. And that's a huge victory—don't forget that."

"We won't. We're heading back to the hospital now. I'll keep you informed of any news, and I'd appreciate if you'd do the same for me."

"You know I will." Gilson clapped him on the shoulder and walked the two men to the door.

The doctor strode into the waiting area just as Al and Charlie came back into the hospital. They took seats close enough to hear what he had to say without being intrusive.

The doctor stopped in front of Julie and Pernaska and held up both hands. "I've done everything possible for her. Unfortunately, it doesn't look good."

Julie gasped and pressed a hand to her mouth. Pernaska slid an arm around her shoulder. Al stiffened. He should be the one comforting Julie, not some mafia supplier she didn't even know. As if he could read Al's thoughts, Charlie gripped his elbow. Al forced his muscles to relax.

"She continues to weaken," Dr. Mendenhall continued, his voice softening, "and there are additional signs of infection spreading throughout her body." He took a deep breath. "I think you should say your good-byes. I'm going in now for just a moment to make sure she's comfortable. I'll let you know when it's okay for you to come in."

When Pernaska nodded, the doctor went into Genevieve's room and closed the door.

Julie's eyes met Al's. Tears streamed down her cheeks. "Will you come with us?"

His chest squeezed. "Of course, if you want me to."

"I do." She stood up and came over to him. Al rose and wrapped his arms around her and she whispered in his ear, "I just found her again, Al. I don't know how to let her go."

He tightened his hold. "I know it's hard. But I'll be with you every minute."

When the doctor came back out, Julie stepped out of his arms. Dr. Mendenhall's expression was grave, and Julie reached for Al's hand. "I just gave her a pretty strong morphine shot. Whether or not she will hear you, I don't know, but I think you should have your last visit with her. I will be nearby, at least for a while."

Julie started for her aunt's room with Al at her heels. Pernaska's footsteps echoed on the tile floor behind them. Julie and Al stopped at one side of the bed and the tall Albanian took up his post on the other. Julie and Pernaska each took one of Genevieve's hands.

"Sam?" Pernaska's voice came out husky, as though he was fighting to keep himself together. The old lady's eyelids fluttered and her lips began to move.

All three of them bent closer, but as far as Al could tell, the old lady didn't say anything any of them could make out. For several minutes they all stood around the bed, not moving, watching as Genevieve's face slackened and grew pale. Sobs shook Julie's body and she turned and threw herself into Al's arms. Pernaska straightened and gently closed the old woman's eyes.

Dr. Mendenhall came into the room, placed his stethoscope on the woman's chest, then nodded and looked at his watch. He made a note on his chart before turning to the three of them. "I'm very sorry. She died at 9:14 p.m.."

67

The next morning, Al and Charlie drove to the Golden Lion to meet Julie for breakfast. When they walked in, they found her at a table near the window. Pete Pernaska was with her.

"Hi, Al, Charlie," Julie said, standing to hug each of the men. Al studied her carefully. Her eyes were red, as though she had been crying and hadn't slept much in the night, but her voice was steady and she stood straight and tall, as though sometime after her aunt's death she'd come to the conclusion that she was strong enough to get through this. Al's throat tightened. This was the woman he had fallen in love with. He'd have to watch himself. JoAnne's patience would only stretch so far, and he'd tested it past its limits already.

Pernaska got up, too, to shake their hands.

Julie sat down and laid her napkin across her lap. "I asked Pete to share breakfast with us. We have some planning to do, and I thought you might want to know what we decide. It seems funny, doesn't it? We're almost like family, brought together by a woman with a big heart but a psyche that none of us understands. Pete and I made some decisions last night that I want to share with you. After we eat, we're going to the cabin, where perhaps we can all find closure."

Charlie sat down across from Pernaska. He took the coffee pot, poured a cup for Al and then one for himself. "I'm real sorry, Julie. I know how much your aunt meant to you."

Al nodded. "In spite of the circumstances, neither of us wanted to see anything like this happen to her. We both owe her a debt of gratitude too; if it weren't for you, we wouldn't have met you, Julie, and Charlie wouldn't have found his wife Kelly. In a strange way, I guess we are kind of a family—a little dysfunctional, perhaps, but still family."

Charlie took a sip of his coffee and set down his mug. "So have you made any decisions yet about what happens next?"

"We talked about that last night," said Julie, her eyes brimming with tears. Al extricated his handkerchief from his pocket and handed it to her. She wiped her eyes. "I'm going to take her back to Wisconsin to be buried. She was born in Alma and I'll bury her there, next to my parents, as my mother was her sister. I talked to the Alma city clerk today and the lot next to my parents is available, since my parents had placed a hold on it for me years ago. I won't be buried there, though. I left Alma nineteen years ago and I won't go back. But for Genevieve, it's the right place. She was unsettled everywhere else. Now she can be at rest, with family."

"I'll make the trip with Julie and Sam." Pernaska had a full plate of food in front of him, but he hadn't touched any of it. "Sam was good for me, very good for me. I loved her with all of my heart. We were husband and wife for only a day, but in reality we had been for months. She befriended me, looked out for me, and taught me so much."

I'll bet. Al contemplated the man across from him. He did seem genuinely torn up, but Al couldn't bring himself to feel too much sympathy for him. He and Genevieve had chosen a life of crime, and that kind of life came with risks. And Al knew exactly what Genevieve had taught her protégé—how to make the weapons that had already likely ended a lot of lives. Until Al could get enough on the man to put him behind bars, his grief was the price Pete Pernaska would have to pay for that. Al forced himself to turn back to Julie. "How will you get her to Alma?"

"The Carbones have offered to send a plane, and Pete and I will accompany her as soon as the paperwork is finished and we have permission to take her. There will be a small graveside ceremony in Alma then the plane will take me to Chicago." She bit her lip. "Al, you and Charlie wouldn't want to come, would you? I ... have no other family, and I could really use the support."

Al glanced at Charlie, who shrugged his massive shoulders. *Chief'll love that.* Telling his boss he and Charlie had been invited to travel to the funeral of a serial killer on the private plane of one of the largest crime families in the world might be worth the time and effort it would take to go. Besides, it wouldn't hurt to keep an eye on Pernaska. And the Carbones, for that matter. He straightened in his seat. "We'll have to check with our bosses, but if they agree, then yes, we'd be happy to go with you."

When Pernaska and Julie finished moving food around their plates without actually taking any bites, the two of them excused themselves to go to Genevieve's cabin. Al and Pete returned to State Patrol District Headquarters. "We have some work to do, Charlie. I better call the chief and you need to get a hold of the sheriff. Tell him we plan to ride home on a plane owned and operated by one of the top crime families in the country."

Charlie grinned like the Cheshire Cat. "Any good ideas about how to break it to 'im gently?"

"None. He's your boss. I have my own to deal with."

Five minutes later Al was closeted in a spare office. Charlie was in another across the hall. The call to the chief went better than expected. Al told him about Genevieve's death and about Julie inviting them to the funeral. The chief agreed that it would be a good idea for him and Charlie to tag along.

"Keep your eyes open, Al. This might actually turn out to be a big break. We may have lost Genevieve, but if we can help bring down Pernaska and the Carbones, it'll almost make up for that."

Al grimaced. "Yeah, almost. I'll never quite feel as though I have closure on that one though."

"I know you won't, but you're gonna have to shake it off, Al. Find a way to move forward."

"Got it."

"Keep me informed, okay?"

"You know I will." Al hung up the phone and sat for a moment, staring at a framed certificate on the wall. *Move forward, eh?* He pushed himself off the chair and onto his feet with a heavy sigh. *Easier said than done, Chief.*

EPILOGUE

Two months later, the excitement surrounding the arrest and death of Genevieve Wangen had subsided. Julie was back in Arlington Heights, Illinois, in the home once owned by her aunt. Al and Charlie had resumed their ordinary routines. Life was as it had been before reports of a serial killer in the La Crosse area responsible for the drowning deaths of fifteen young men had surfaced and been confirmed.

On this late spring day, a howling north wind had invaded La Crosse, and Al stopped briefly at the mailbox before hurrying into the house and dumping several letters on his desk. A large, bulky envelope caught his eye and he slipped off his overcoat and hung it on the coat tree in the corner before sinking down on his desk chair and reaching for the envelope. The return address stole the breath from his lungs. *It's from Julie.*

Al grabbed the letter opener out of the top drawer and slid it under the flap of the envelope. Shaking its contents onto the desk, he was stunned when an array of driver's licenses spilled out.

For a moment he couldn't breathe. *Are these ...?* He picked up the top one and studied it for a moment before counting the rest of them. As he'd suspected, fourteen of them. A small square of paper had fluttered to the desk with the licenses and he picked it up and scanned it.

Dear Al,

I found these in Genevieve's bedside table. As you know, I have long wondered if I had anything to do with the murders and just couldn't remember. This proves I didn't, that my aunt really was the killer. I'm equally relieved and saddened to know she was the one to commit those terrible crimes. Thank you for everything you did to bring this to a close for me. I'll never forget it. Or you.

Julie

Al stared at the paper for a moment, his chest tight, before setting it down and opening up the bottom drawer of his desk. He withdrew a large file folder and opened it up. Lifting the licenses one at a time, he matched each to one of the individual sub-files he'd pulled out of the folder.

Tad Schwartz, a senior football player at University of Wisconsin-La Crosse, who was more than three-quarters of the way to his physical education degree. Died in November, three days after playing in the final football game of the 1998 season.

Jerry Przytarski, vanished from a bar in downtown La Crosse in November 1999. He was in the final semester of his freshman year at Viterbo University, a theater major.

Tedd Duncan drowned in October 2000. He had just started his sophomore year at UWL.

Jeremy Schultz vanished in May 2001, just one week before his graduation from Globe University with a job already lined up as a veterinary technician.

Trevor Justin, 2002, a junior at UWL.

Sam Dunlap, 2003, a sophomore at Viterbo.

Tom Hammermeister, 2004, a recent Viterbo graduate and the only victim who was married. He had two children.

Duane Rick, 2005, a recent graduate of Western Wisconsin Technical College.

Thomas Garth, 2006, a sophomore at UWL.

Philip Hintzle, 2007, a senior at Viterbo.

Abraham Shapiro, 2008, a sophomore at UWL.

Dustin Darst, 2009, a new student at Western Wisconsin Tech.

Jon Schneider, 2010, a senior at Viterbo.

One file did not have a matching license.

Shawn Sorensen. You started all this, young man … and what a tale it became. You were Julie Sonoma's first love. I can surely understand why you loved her. You must have been quite a guy to win her. She was a prize. You were a junior at La Crosse State … a bright, bright guy, working on dual degrees in chemistry and chemical engineering. Quite a combination. Wish I'd met you. You died all too soon.

Al leaned back in his seat. He'd already known, deep down, that Julie wasn't guilty, but confirmation never hurt.

Al carefully inserted each sub-file in its proper place. When each one had been returned to the file, he reached for the rubber stamp on his desk, inked it, and stamped the file.

Then he carefully put the file back in its place and closed the drawer with a decisive thud.

CPSIA information can be obtained
at www.ICGtesting.com
Printed in the USA
FFHW021930141118
49399664-53741FF